10/13

thinking
of you

Center Point
Large Print

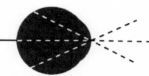

**This Large Print Book carries the
Seal of Approval of N.A.V.H.**

thinking
of you

JILL MANSELL

CENTER POINT LARGE PRINT
THORNDIKE, MAINE

This Center Point Large Print edition
is published in the year 2013 by arrangement with
Sourcebooks, Inc.

The text of this Large Print edition is unabridged.
In other aspects, this book may vary
from the original edition.
Printed in the United States of America
on permanent paper.
Set in 16-point Times New Roman type.

ISBN: 978-1-61173-919-0

Library of Congress Cataloging-in-Publication Data

Mansell, Jill.
Thinking of you / Jill Mansell. — Center Point Large Print edition.
pages ; cm
ISBN 978-1-61173-919-0 (library binding : alk. paper)
1. Single mothers—Fiction. 2. Empty nesters—Fiction.
    3. Large type books. I. Title.
PR6063.A395T57 2013b
813′.6—dc23
                                                    2013020274

To Charlotte Ash

And with many thanks to her husband Ian for generously supporting Bliss.

Chapter 1

IF IT WAS SYMPATHY she was after, Ginny Holland might have known she'd come to the wrong place. Then again, it was early on a bright but blustery Saturday morning in October and her options were limited.

And it was only over the road from her own house, which was handy.

"I can't describe how I feel." She clenched a fist, pressed it to her breastbone, and shook her head in frustration. "It's just so . . . so . . ."

"I know exactly what it is. Bird's-nest syndrome," said Carla.

Ginny pulled a face because it was so screamingly apparent that Carla didn't have children. "Bird's-nest syndrome would be the name for the state of my hair. I have *empty*-nest syndrome. My nest is empty, my baby has flown away, and I just feel all hollow inside like . . . like a cheap Easter egg."

"Well, I think you're mad." Carla was busy executing Olympic-level sit-ups, her bare feet tucked under the edge of the cream leather sofa, her hair swinging glossily to and fro. "Jem's gone off to university. You're free again. You should be out there celebrating. Plus," she added as an afterthought, "Cadbury's Creme Eggs aren't hollow; they're full of goo."

7

"Unlike you," Ginny pointed out. "You're heartless."

"And you're thirty-eight, not seventy." Having completed her five millionth sit-up, Carla raised her legs in the air and, without even pausing for breath, began bicycling furiously. "I'm a year older than you and look at me; I'm having a whale of a time! I'm in tip-top condition, men can't resist me, and sex has never been better. I'm a woman in my prime," she concluded. "And so are you."

Ginny knew her life wasn't really over, of course she did, but Jem's departure had nevertheless knocked her for six. She'd always been so happy and busy before now, so endlessly occupied, that this was a whole new experience for her. Nor did it help that it was happening as winter approached. Most of the jobs here in Portsilver were seasonal and she'd just spent the last six months being rushed off her feet working in a café down on the seafront. But the tourists had gone home now, Jem was in Bristol, and Ginny was finding herself faced with way more spare time than she was used to. To add insult to injury, two other female friends had separately moved in the last month, her favorite wine bar had been bought up and turned into a noisy haven for underage drinkers of alcopops, and the Latin American dance classes she'd so enjoyed attending had come to an abrupt halt when her dance teacher had slipped doing the samba and broken his hip. All in all, it hadn't been the best October on record. And as for Carla telling her she was a woman in her prime . . . well, she could end up being sued for false advertising.

Glancing at her reflection in Carla's glitzy over-the-top Venetian mirror, Ginny puffed away a section of overgrown bangs that were falling into her eyes. The aforementioned bird's-nest hair was long, blond, and wavy-with-a-definite-mind-of-its-own. Sometimes it behaved, sometimes it didn't, and she had no control over it either way. Face-wise, it wasn't as if she was a wrinkled old prune—if anything, Ginny knew she looked young for her age—but in glossy magazine world there was still plenty of room for improvement. It would be lovely to be as chic, groomed, and effortlessly femme-fatalish as Carla but, let's face it, she simply couldn't be doing with making all that effort.

"You need to get yourself together." Carla finished bicycling in the air, miraculously not even puce in the face. "Cheer yourself up; get out there and have an adventure."

"I'm just saying I miss Jem." Ginny hated feeling like this. She had never been needy in her life; the idea was as horrifying to her as suddenly developing a penchant for wearing puffball miniskirts.

"She'd want you to have an adventure," Carla said reasonably.

"I know." Ginny tugged at a loose thread on her sweater sleeve. "But I really want to *see* her."

"Fine. Go on then, if that's what you want to do. If you think Jem won't mind." Rising gracefully to her feet and automatically checking her sleek, serum-fed hair in the Venetian mirror—yep, still perfect—Carla said, "You've made a hole in that sleeve, by the way."

Ginny didn't care; it was a manky old sweater anyway. More importantly, she'd got what she'd come for. "Right, I will."

"Will what?"

"Drive up to Bristol to see Jem. It's a great idea!"

"Now? Shouldn't you give her a ring first? She's eighteen," said Carla. "She could be getting up to any number of naughty things."

To humor Carla, Ginny said, "OK, I'll call her. You have a lovely weekend and I'll see you tomorrow night when I get back."

"I always have a lovely weekend." Carla patted her flat brown stomach. "I'm a woman in my prime, remember?" Smugly she added, "Besides, Robbie's coming round."

Robbie was the latest in a series of inter-changeable pretty young boys Carla favored for their fit bodies, floppy hair, and . . . well, un-floppy other bits. The last thing she was looking for was commitment.

"Right, I'm off." Ginny gave her a hug.

"Give Jem my love. And drive carefully on the motorway."

"I will."

As Ginny let herself out of the house, Carla said, "And don't forget to phone first. She might not be pleased to see you."

God, best friends could be brutal. If Ginny hadn't been so excited, she might have taken offense.

But that was Carla for you; she wasn't a mother so how could she possibly understand?

"Mum! I don't believe it—how fantastic that you're here!" Jem's face lit up as she launched herself like a missile into her mother's arms, hugging her so tightly she could hardly breathe.

Oh yes, that was a good one.

Or: "Mummy, oh my God, this is the best surprise ever . . . you don't know how much I've *missed* you . . ."

Whoops, mustn't make herself cry. Deliberately banishing the happy scenarios her imagination had been busily conjuring up, Ginny blinked hard in order to concentrate on the road ahead. The journey from Portsilver in north Cornwall up to Bristol took three and a half hours and so far they were on schedule to arrive at one o'clock. Luckily, Bellamy enjoyed nothing more than a nice long ride in the car and was lolling contentedly across the backseat with his eyes shut and his tongue out.

11

Every time Ginny said in her excited voice, "Who are we going to see, Bellamy? Hey? We're going to see Jem!" he opened one eye and lazily wagged his tail.

If Ginny had owned one, she'd have been wagging hers too.

It was three weeks since Jem had left home. Ginny had braced herself for the worst but hadn't braced nearly hard enough; the aching void where Jem had once been was a million times worse than she'd envisaged. Her daughter was the most important person in her life; it was as simple as that.

As she drove toward Bristol, Ginny scrolled through some of her happiest memories. Marrying Gavin Holland on her eighteenth birthday . . . well, it may have been a mistake, but how could she possibly regret it when between them they had produced Jem?

Giving birth—gasping her way through ever more agonizing contractions and threatening to knock Gavin's teeth down his throat when he said plaintively, "Ouch, could you not squeeze my hand so hard? It hurts."

Holding Jem at long last and sobbing uncontrollably because the rush of love was so much more overwhelming than she'd imagined, particularly when you considered that the squalling creature you were cradling in your arms was covered in blood and gunk and slime.

Then later, tiny starfish fingers grasping the air
. . . the first magical smile . . . the first day at
school ("Mummy, don't leeeeave meeeee!") . . .
and that look of blind panic on Jem's face after
posting her letter to Father Christmas because
what if he got her muddled up with the other
Jemima, the one with sticky-out ears and glasses
in Miss Carter's class?

Oh yes, there were so many perfect moments.
Ginny's smile broadened as each one in turn
popped into her mind. She and Gavin had
separated when Jem was nine and that had been
sad, of course it was, but it truly hadn't been the
end of the world. Gavin had turned out not to
be the settling-down-and-staying-faithful kind.
Nevertheless, he'd always been a loving father
and had never once let Jem down. And Jem had
come through her parents' separation and
subsequent divorce wonderfully well, taking the
inevitable changes in her stride.

From that time on, Ginny and Jem had become
truly inseparable, as close as any mother and
daughter could be. Even the dreaded puberty
hadn't managed to spoil their relationship and
Ginny knew she'd got off lightly there; while
other teenagers grew rebellious and sulky and
slammed doors off their hinges, Jem had retained
the ability to laugh at herself and hadn't lost her
sparky, sunny nature. It had always been the two
of them against the world.

At that moment a wet nose touched Ginny's left arm, and Bellamy, his head poked between the front seats, licked her elbow.

"Oh, sorry, sweetheart, I wasn't thinking." Concentrating on the road ahead, Ginny gave his ears an apologetic rub. "How could I forget you, hmm? The *three* of us against the world."

The traffic on the motorway was light, and by ten to one, Ginny was on the outskirts of Bristol. Jem hadn't been keen on moving into the halls of residence. Instead, she'd got on the phone to local property agents, arranged a day of viewing back in September, and decided on a flat-share in Clifton with two other students. This was where Ginny had helped her to unload her belongings from the car three weeks earlier, prior to the arrival of the other flatmates.

Now she was crossing the Downs heading for Whiteladies Road, the location of Jem's flat on Pembroke Road indelibly printed in her mind and drawing her toward it like an invisible umbilical cord.

Actually, that conjured up a bit of a yucky image. Maybe not. Ooh, now that looked like an interesting Mexican restaurant over there on the left; maybe she and Jem could try it out this evening. And if Jem's flatmates wanted to join them, well, the more the merrier. As she indicated right and turned into Apsley Road, Ginny imagined them in the buzzy restaurant, all sitting and laughing together around a table bristling with plates and bottles of ice-cold beer, the others exclaiming, "You're so lucky, Jem. I wish my mum was as much fun as yours!"

Whoops, mind that bus.

Chapter 2

THE FLAT WAS SITUATED on the second floor of what had once been a four-story Georgian house. Ginny waited until Bellamy had discreetly relieved himself against a tree in the front garden before ringing the doorbell. This was it; they were here and Jem was about to get the surprise of her—

"Yes?"

"Oh, hi! You must be Rupert!" Ginny did her best not to gush in front of the flatmate Jem had told her about. "Um . . . is Jem here?"

"No." Rupert paused. "And you are?"

"Oh, I'm her mum! And this is Bellamy, Jem's dog. How silly of me not to realize she might be out. I did ring a few times but her phone was switched off, and I just thought she was sleeping in. Er, do you know where she is?"

Rupert, who was wearing a pair of white shorts and nothing else, was lean and tanned. He shivered as a blast of cold air hit him in the chest. "She's working a lunchtime shift in the pub. Eleven till two, something like that."

Lunchtime shift? Pub? Ginny checked her watch and said, "Which pub?"

"No idea." Rupert shrugged. "She did say, but I wasn't paying attention. Somewhere in Clifton, I think."

Since there were about a million pubs in Clifton, that was a big help. "Well, could I come in and wait?"

He looked less than enthusiastic but said, "Yeah, of course. It's a bit of a mess."

Rupert wasn't joking. Upstairs in the living room there were dirty plates and empty cups all over the pale green carpet. An exotic-looking girl with short dark hair was sprawled on the sofa eating a bowl of CocoPops and watching a black-and-white film on TV.

"Hello!" Ginny beamed at her. "You must be Lucy."

The girl blinked. "No, I'm Caro."

"Caro's my girlfriend." Rupert indicated Ginny as he headed into the kitchen. "This is Jem's mother, come to see her."

Ginny wondered if she was supposed to shake hands or if that would be the ultimate uncool thing to do. Caro, through a mouthful of CocoPops, mumbled, "Hi."

OK, probably uncool.

"And this is Bellamy." Thank heavens for dogs, the ultimate icebreakers.

"Right." Caro nodded and licked her spoon.

Oh.

"So! Are you at uni too?" Nobody had offered her a seat so Ginny stayed standing.

"Yes." Caro dumped her empty cereal bowl on the carpet, rose to her feet, and headed for the kitchen.

Ginny, overhearing giggles and a muffled shriek of laughter, felt increasingly ill at ease. Moments later, Rupert stuck his head round the door. "Would you like a cup of tea?"

"Oh, thank you, that would be lovely!" OK, stop it, stop speaking in exclamation marks. "White, please, one sugar."

"Ah. Don't think we've got any sugar."

Ginny said, "No problem, I'll just have a glass of water instead."

Rupert frowned and scratched his head. "I think we've run out of water too."

Was he serious? Or was this their way of getting rid of her?

"Unless you drink tap," said Rupert.

Gosh, he was posh.

"Tap's fine," said Ginny.

He grimaced. "Rather you than me."

"Just ignore him," said a voice behind Ginny. "Rupes only drinks gold-plated water. Hello, I'm Lucy. And I've seen the photos in Jem's room so I know you're her mum. Nice to meet you."

Oh, now *this* was more like it. Lucy was tall and slender, black and beautiful. Better still, she was actually smiling. Ginny was so overcome with gratitude she almost invited her out to dinner on the spot. Within minutes, Lucy had cleared away armfuls of plates, chucked a slew of magazines behind the back of the sofa, and installed Ginny in the best chair like the queen.

"Jem only got the job yesterday. It's her first shift today. Still, a bit of extra cash always comes in handy, doesn't it?" Lucy was chatty and friendly, the best kind of flatmate any mother could desire for her daughter. Having made a wonderful fuss of Bellamy, she brought him a bowl of water and gravely apologized in advance for the fact that it came from a tap.

Rupert and Caro stayed in the kitchen and played music, then Rupert emerged to iron a blue shirt rather badly in the corner of the living room where the ironing board was set up.

"I could do that for you," Ginny offered, eager to make him like her.

Rupert looked amused. "No thanks, I can manage."

"Jem's never been keen on ironing. I bet she's got a whole load that needs doing. Actually, while I'm here," said Ginny, "I could make a start on it."

"If I asked my mother to iron anything for me," Lucy said cheerfully, "she'd call me a lazy toad and tell me to do it myself."

Jem's room was untidy but clean. Ginny's heart expanded as she drank in every familiar detail, the happy family photos on the cork board up on the wall, the clothes, books and CDs littering every surface, the empty Coke cans and crisp packets spilling out of the wastepaper bin. Unable to help herself, she quickly made the bed and hung all the scattered clothes in the wardrobe. This must be the new top Jem had bought in Oasis. Oops, and there was an oily mark on the leg of her favorite jeans; they needed to be soaked if that was going to come out. And was that nail polish on—

The front door slammed and Ginny froze, realizing that she was clutching her daughter's jeans like a stalker. Hastily flinging them back onto the bed, she burst out of the bedroom just as Bellamy began to bark. A split second later she reached the living room in time to see Jem and Bellamy greeting each other in a frenzy of ecstasy.

"I don't believe this! Mum, what are you *doing* here?" Jem looked up as Bellamy joyfully licked her face.

"Your mother's come all this way to see you," Rupert drawled and Ginny intercepted the look he gave Jem, clearly indicating how he felt about mad mothers who drove hundreds of miles to see their daughters on a whim.

Shocked, Jem said, "Oh, *Mum.*"

"No, I haven't," Ginny blurted out. "Crikey, of course I haven't! We're on our way to Bath and I just thought it'd be fun to pop in and say hello."

"Really? Well, that's great!" Letting go of

Bellamy at last, Jem gave her mother a hug. Ginny in turn stroked her daughter's blond, pink-streaked hair. It wasn't quite the reunion she had envisaged what with Rupert, Caro, and Lucy looking on and her brain struggling to come up with an answer to the question Jem was about to ask, but at least she was here. It was better than nothing.

Oh, she'd missed her so much.

"Bath?" Jem stepped back, holding her at arm's length and looking baffled. "What are you doing going to Bath?"

Aaargh, I haven't the foggiest!

"Visiting a friend," said Ginny. *Quick, think.*

"But you don't know anyone in Bath."

I *know*, I *know!*

"Ah, that's where you're wrong," Ginny said gaily. "Ever heard me talking about Theresa Trott?"

Jem shook her head. "No. Who's she?"

"We were at school together, darling. I got onto that Friends Reunited website, left my email address, and in no time at all Theresa had emailed me. She's living in Bath now. When she invited me up to stay with her, I thought I couldn't drive past and not stop off here en route, that would be rude. So here we are!"

"I'm so glad." Jem gave her another hug. "It's lovely to see you again. Both of you."

"Your mother was about to start ironing your

clothes," said Rupert, his mouth twitching with amusement.

Jem laughed. "Oh, Mum."

Deciding she hated him and feeling relaxed enough to retaliate now, Ginny looked Rupert in the eye and said, "Hasn't your mum ever ironed anything for you?"

"No." He shrugged. "But that could be because she's dead."

Damn, *damn.*

Dddddrrrringgg went the doorbell.

"You may as well get that, Jem," Rupert drawled. "It's probably your father."

Jem grinned and pulled a face at Rupert, then skipped downstairs to answer the door. She returned with a thin, dark-eyed boy in tow.

"Lucy, it's Davy Stokes."

Lucy was in the process of pulling her gray sweater up over her head. Tugging down the green T-shirt beneath, she said, "Hi, Davy. All right? I was just about to jump in the shower."

Ginny heard Rupert whisper to Caro, "I expect he'd like to jump in with her."

"Sorry." Davy, who had long dark hair, was clutching a book. "It's just that I promised to lend you this so I thought I'd drop it round."

"What is it? Oh right, John Donne's poems. Great, thanks." Lucy took the book and flashed him a smile. "That's really kind of you."

Blushing, Davy said, "You'll enjoy them. Um . . .

I was wondering. There's a pub quiz on at the Bear this afternoon. I wondered if maybe you'd like to, um, come along with me."

Rupert was smirking openly now. Ginny longed to throw something heavy at him.

"Thanks for the offer, Davy, but I can't make it. Me and Jem are off to a party. In fact we need to get our skates on or we're going to be late. We're all meeting up at three."

Three o'clock? It was half-past two already. Ginny wondered if Lucy was lying in order to spare Davy's feelings.

"OK. Well, maybe another time. Bye." Davy glanced shyly around the room while simultaneously backing toward the door.

"Let me show you out," said Rupert.

He returned moments later, grinning broadly. "You've made a conquest there."

"Don't make fun of him," Lucy protested. "Davy's all right."

"Apart from the fact that he has no friends and still lives at home with his mum."

"So, what's this party you've been invited to?" Ginny put on her bright and cheerful voice and looked at Jem, whom she'd driven for three and a half hours to see.

"It's Zelda's birthday. She's on our course," Jem explained. "We're starting off at this new cocktail bar on Park Street. I'd better get ready. What time do you have to be in Bath?"

"Oh, not right this minute. I can drop you off at the cocktail bar if you like."

"Thanks, Mum, but there's no need. Lucy's driving and we're picking up a couple more friends on the way."

"Jem?" Lucy's disembodied voice drifted through from Jem's bedroom. "That black top you said I could borrow isn't here."

"It is! It's on the floor next to the CD player."

"The only thing on the floor is carpet." Popping her head round the door, Lucy said, "In fact all your clothes are missing."

"They're in the wardrobe," Ginny said apologetically. "I hung them up."

Rupert was highly entertained by this.

"Oh, Mum." Jem shook her head. "You'll be making my bed next."

Lucy grinned. "She's done that too."

"Checking the sheets," Rupert murmured audibly into Caro's ear.

"Well, I think we'd better leave you to it." Realizing that the girls had less than ten minutes in which to get ready and she was only in their way, Ginny clicked her fingers at Bellamy. She enveloped Jem in a hug and made sure it wasn't a needy one. "And you," she added, waggling her fingers in a friendly fashion at Rupert and Caro because, like it or not, they were a part of Jem's new life.

"What rotten timing," said Jem. "I've only seen

you for two minutes and now you're rushing off again."

Ginny managed a carefree smile. So much for her wonderful plan to spend the weekend with the person she loved more than anyone else in the world. "I'll give you a ring in a few days. Bye, darling. Come on, Bellamy, say good-bye to Jem."

Outside it was starting to rain. As she drove off, waving gaily at Jem on the doorstep, Ginny felt her throat begin to tighten. By the time she'd reached Whiteladies Road the sense of disappointment and desolation was all-encompassing and she no longer trusted herself to drive. Abruptly pulling over, willing the tears not to well up, Ginny took several deep breaths and gripped the steering wheel so hard it was a wonder it didn't snap in two. It's not *fair,* it's not *fair,* it's *just not*—

With a jolt she became aware that she was being watched. She turned and met the quizzical gaze of Davy Stokes. In the split second that followed, Ginny realized she'd pulled up at a bus stop, it was a bitterly cold, rainy afternoon and from the expression on Davy's face he thought she'd stopped to offer him a lift.

Oh, brilliant.

But it was too late to drive off. And at least she wasn't in floods of tears. Buzzing down the passenger window and reaching over, Ginny dredged *that* voice up again and said chirpily,

"Hello! You're getting terribly wet out there! Won't you let me give you a lift?"

He was a kind-of-friend of her daughter. She was the mother of a girl he was kind-of-friendly with. Just as she'd felt obliged to make the offer, Ginny realized, so Davy now felt compelled to accept it. Looking embarrassed, he said, "Is Henbury out of your way?"

Ginny had never heard of Henbury but after having driven two hundred miles up here and with the same again to look forward to on the return journey, what were a few more?

"No problem. You'll have to direct me, though. And don't worry if Bellamy licks your ear, he's just being friendly."

"I like dogs. Hello, boy." Having climbed into the car and fastened his seat belt, Davy flicked his long dark hair out of his eyes and said, "Can I ask you something?"

"Anything you like." *Yerk,* so long as it's nothing to do with contraception.

"Did they talk about me after I'd gone?"

Ginny paused. "No."

He smiled briefly. "Shouldn't pause. That means yes. Do they think I've got a crush on Lucy?"

"Um, possibly," Ginny conceded with reluctance. "Why? Don't you?"

"Of course I do. She's gorgeous. But I kind of realize nothing's ever going to come of it. I know I'm not her type." Wistfully, Davy said, "I had

25

hoped to win her over with my deadpan wit, kind of like Paul Merton, y'know? Trouble is, every time I see Lucy my wit goes out of the window. I turn into a gormless dork instead."

Bless him. Ginny was touched by his frankness. "Give yourself time," she said soothingly. "Everyone gets a bit tongue-tied at first."

"To be honest, she's out of my league anyway. You won't mention any of this, will you? Can it be just between us?" asked Davy. "I've made enough of a fool of myself as it is."

"I won't breathe a word."

"Promise?"

"Promise. Shall I tell you something in return? I wasn't that taken with Rupert."

Davy's upper lip curled with derision. "Rupert's a prat and a dickhead. Sorry, but he is. He looks down his nose at everyone. Carry straight on over this roundabout."

"And you're still living at home, did somebody mention?" Lucky parents, thought Ginny as she followed the sign to Henbury.

"With my mother. Dad took off years ago. Mum didn't want me to move out," said Davy, "so I only applied to Bristol. Just as well I got a place really; otherwise I'd have been stuck."

Lucky, lucky mother. She'd asked her son not to move out so he hadn't. So simple, thought Ginny. Now why didn't I think of that?

"She might change her mind. Maybe Rupert will

move out and you could take his place." Ginny was only joking but wouldn't it be great if that happened?

"Except Rupert's hardly likely to move out," said Davy, "seeing as it's his flat."

"Is it?" She hadn't realized that. "I thought they were all tenants."

Davy shook his head. "Rupert's father bought the place for him to live in while he's here at university."

"Oh. Well, that makes sense, I suppose. If you can afford it."

"From what I hear, Rupert's father can afford anything he wants."

"So the others are just there to help with the mortgage and keep Rupert company."

"Turn right here. And they just happen to be taking the same course." Davy's tone was dry. "He'll probably have them writing his essays for him before long. Now take the next left. That's it, and ours is the one there with the blue door. That's brilliant. Thanks so much; maybe we'll see each other again sometime." Twisting round in the passenger seat, he said, "Bye, Bellamy. Give me five."

He waited until Bellamy had raised a paw, then solemnly shook it.

"Good luck," said Ginny. "And you never know, things might work out better than you expect."

Davy climbed out of the car. "You mean tongue-tied good guy gets the girl in the end? Maybe if this was a Richard Curtis film I'd stand a chance." With a good-natured shrug, he added, "But I can't see it happening in real life. Oh well, at least it's character-forming. Everyone needs to have their heart broken some time."

Ginny watched him head into the house, the kind of modest, everyday, three-bed end terrace that Rupert would undoubtedly sneer at. Never mind other people having their hearts broken; hers was a bit cracked right now.

"Time to go home, boy." Patting Bellamy's rough head, Ginny said, "All the way back to Portsilver. So much for our weekend with Jem, eh? Sorry about that."

Bellamy licked her hand as if to let her know that he didn't mind and had already forgiven her. Ginny gazed lovingly at him. "Oh, sweetheart, thank goodness I've got you to keep me company. Whatever would I do without you?"

Bellamy died three weeks later. The cancer that had spread so rapidly throughout his body proved to be untreatable. He was unable to walk, unable to eat, clearly in pain. The vet assured Ginny that putting Bellamy to sleep, letting him go peacefully, was the kindest thing she could do.

So she did it and felt more grief and anguish than she'd ever known before. Bellamy had been with them ever since Gavin had moved out.

Someone had suggested getting a dog to cheer them up and that was it, a fortnight later Bellamy had arrived in their lives, so much better company than Gavin that Ginny wished she'd thought of it years ago. Gavin was unfaithful, a gifted liar, and emotionally untrustworthy in every way. Bellamy wasn't; he was gentle, affectionate, and utterly dependable. He never fibbed to her about where he'd been. His needs were simple and his adoration unconditional.

"You love that dog more than you ever loved me," Gavin had grumbled.

And when Ginny had replied, "Wouldn't anyone?" she had meant it.

Chapter 3

AND NOW BELLAMY WAS gone. Ginny still couldn't take it in, found it impossible to believe she'd never see his dear whiskery face again. This morning they had buried him in the back garden beneath the cherry tree. Jem had caught the train down last night and together they had sobbed their way through the emotional ceremony.

But Jem had lectures and tutorials back in Bristol that she couldn't afford to miss. Staying down in Portsilver wasn't an option. Red-eyed and blotchy, she had reluctantly caught the lunchtime train back to Bristol.

Ginny was pretty blotchy herself, not helped by having managed to jab herself in the eye with a mascara wand while she was doing her makeup. She felt bruised, emotionally drained, and wrung out but at the same time far too jittery to sit alone in an empty house gazing out at Bellamy's grave. Being miserable was alien to her character—she had always been the naturally cheerful type.

Set on distraction, Ginny drove down into the center of Portsilver and parked the car. At least in November it was physically possible to park your car in Portsilver. Right, now what little thing could she treat herself to? A gorgeous new lipstick perhaps? A sequined scarf? Ooh, or how about a new squeaky toy for—

No, Bellamy's dead. Don't think about it, don't think about it.

Don't look at any other dogs as you walk down the street.

And *don't cry*.

In a few weeks it would be Christmas, so how about making a start on some present buying instead?

Miraculously, Ginny began to feel better. Picking out stocking fillers for Jem, she chose a pale pink tooled leather belt and a notebook whose cover was inlaid with mother-of-pearl. In another shop she found a pair of blue-and-green tartan tights, acrylic hair bobbles that flashed on and off when you tapped them, and a ballpoint pen with lilac marabou feathers exploding from the top.

This was something she had always enjoyed, buying silly bits and pieces. Having paid for everything in her basket, Ginny left and made her way on down the street. A painting in the window of one of the shops further along caught her eye and she moved toward it. No, maybe not; up close it wasn't so great after all.

The next moment, glancing across the road, Ginny saw a woman she knew only as Vera and her heart began to thud in a panicky way. They weren't close friends but had got to know each other while taking their dogs for walks along Portsilver's main beach. Vera owned an elegant Afghan hound called Marcus who was at this moment sitting patiently while his owner retied her headscarf. She was the chatty type. If Vera spotted her, she would be bound to ask where Bellamy was.

Unable to face her today, Ginny ducked into the sanctuary of the shop. Inside, tables were decoratively strewn with china *objets d'art*, hand-crafted wooden animals, funky colored glass candelabra, and all manner of quirky gifts.

Quirky expensive gifts, Ginny discovered, picking up a small pewter-colored peacock with a jeweled tail and turning it over in the palm of her hand. The price on the label gave her a bit of a shock—blimey, you'd want real jewels for thirty-eight pounds. Then again, it wasn't her kind of thing but Jem might like it. Oh now, look at those cushions over there; she'd definitely love those.

Except Jem wasn't going to get the chance to love them because a surreptitious turning over of the price tags revealed the cushions to be seventy-five pounds each. Yeesh, this was a lovely shop but maybe not the place to come for cheap and cheerful stocking fillers.

Lurking by the table nearest the door, Ginny peered out to see if Vera was still there. Not that she disliked Vera; it wasn't that at all; she just knew that having to tell another dog lover that Bellamy was dead would be more than she could handle just now. And breaking down in public was the last thing she needed.

No, thankfully, the coast appeared to be clear. Glancing around the shop to double-check that there was nothing else she wanted to look at and might be able to afford—shouldn't think so for one second—Ginny became aware that she was the object of someone's attention. A black-haired man with piercing dark eyes, wearing jeans and a battered brown leather jacket with the collar turned up, was watching her. For a second their eyes locked and Ginny saw something unreadable in his gaze. Heavens, he was good-looking, almost smolderingly intense.

And then it was over. He turned away with an

infinitesimal shrug that indicated he'd lost interest. Brought back to earth with a thump, Ginny gave herself a mental telling off. As if someone who looked like a film star was likely to be bowled over by the sight of her, today of all days, with her puffy, post-funeral eyes and tangled hair.

Dream on, as Jem would say with typical teenage frankness. And quite right too. Oh well, at least she hadn't made an idiot of herself and tried smiling and batting her eyelashes at him in a come-hither fashion. Relieved on that score, Ginny turned away as the door was opened by another customer coming into the shop. She ducked past them and left, still keen not to bump into Vera, and began heading swiftly in the direction of the car park. That was enough for one day; time to go home now and—

"I saw you."

Like a big salmon, Ginny's heart almost leaped out of her body. A hand was on her arm and although she hadn't heard him speak before, she knew at once who it was.

Who else could a voice like that belong to?

Whirling round to face him, she felt color flood her cheeks. Crikey, up close he was even more staggeringly attractive. And clearly intelligent too, capable of seeing beyond her own currently less-than-alluring external appearance. Like those scouts from model agencies who could spot a pale lanky girl in the street and instinctively tell that she would scrub up well.

"I saw you," he repeated.

He even smelled fantastic. Whatever that aftershave was, it was her favorite. Breathlessly, Ginny whispered, "I saw you too."

His gaze didn't falter. His hand was still on her arm. "Shall we go?"

Go? Oh, good grief, was this really happening? It was like one of those arty black-and-white French films where two people meet and say very little to each other but do rather a lot.

"Go where?" Steady on now, he's still a complete stranger; you can't actually go back to his place, tear off his clothes, and leap into bed with a man you've only just—

"Back to the shop."

Ginny's imagination skidded to a halt in mid-fantasy. (He had a four-poster bed with cream silk drapes that stirred in the breeze drifting in through the open window—because in her fantasy it was a balmy afternoon in August.)

"Back to the shop?" Perhaps he owned it. Or lived above it. Oh God, he was reaching for her hand; this was *so romantic*. If only she could stop herself idiotically parroting everything he said.

"Come on, do yourself a favor and give up. You might be good," he drawled, "but you're not that good."

What was *that* supposed to mean? Puzzled, Ginny watched him take hold of her hand, then turn it face up and, one by one, unfurl her fingers.

Her blood ran cold. The next second she let out a shriek of horror followed by an involuntary high-pitched giggle. "Oh my God, I didn't even realize! How embarrassing! I can't believe I just walked out with it in my hand. Thank goodness you noticed! I'll take it straight back and explain . . ."

Ginny's voice trailed away as she realized that she was attempting to retrieve her hand and this man wasn't letting it go. Nor was he smiling at her absentmindedness, her careless but innocent mistake.

In fact he was gripping her wrist quite tightly, making sure she couldn't escape.

"Now look," said Ginny, flustered. "I didn't do it on purpose!"

"I despise shoplifters. I hope they prosecute you," the man said evenly.

"But I'm not a shoplifter! I've never stolen anything in my *life*. Oh God, I can't believe you even think that!" Hideously aware that people in the street were starting to take notice, some even slowing down to listen avidly to the exchange, Ginny turned and walked rapidly back to the shop still clutching the jeweled peacock and fighting back tears of shame. Because like a hammer blow it had struck her that while she had been mentally drooling over a man she ridiculously imagined might fancy her, she had completely forgotten about Bellamy.

That's how breathtakingly shallow and selfish she was.

Pushing open the door to the shop, she saw that there were a dozen or so customers wandering around, plus the woman who worked there. Hot on her heels—evidently ready to rugby-tackle her to the ground if she tried to escape—the man ushered her inside and up to the counter. Ginny pushed the jeweled peacock into the woman's hands and gabbled, mortified, "I'm so sorry; it was a complete accident. I didn't realize I was still holding it when I left."

"Sounds quite convincing, doesn't she?" The man raised an eyebrow. "But I was watching her. I saw the way she was acting before she made her getaway."

Was this like being innocent of murder but finding yourself on death row?

"Please don't say that." The tears were back, pricking her eyelids. Gulping for breath and aware that she was now truly the center of attention, Ginny clutched the edge of the counter. "I'm an honest person. I've never broken the law; I just wasn't *concentrating*."

"Obviously not," the man interjected. "Otherwise you wouldn't have got caught."

"Oh, will you SHUT UP? I didn't mean to take

it! As soon as I'd realized it was in my hand, I would have brought it back," Ginny shouted. "It was an *accident*." Gazing in desperation at the saleswoman, she pleaded, "You believe me, don't you? You don't think I was actually planning to steal it?"

The woman looked startled. "Well, I . . ."

"See that sign?" The man pointed to a sign next to the till announcing that shoplifters would be prosecuted. "It's there for a reason."

Ginny began to feel light-headed. "But I'm not a shoplifter."

Gesturing toward the phone on the counter, the man said to the saleswoman, "Go on, call the police."

"It was a mistake," sobbed Ginny. "My dog died yesterday. I only b-buried him this morning." As she said it, her knees buckled beneath her. The tears flowed freely down her face as the saleswoman hastily dragged a chair out from behind the counter. "I'm sorry, I'm so sorry . . . everything's just getting too much for me." Sinking onto the chair, Ginny buried her face in her hands and shook her head.

"She's in a bit of a state," the saleswoman murmured anxiously.

"That's because she's been caught red-handed. Now she's trying every trick in the book to get out of it."

"Ah, but what if her dog's really died? It's awful

when that happens. And she's looking a bit pale. Are you feeling all right, love?"

Ginny shook her head, nausea swirling through her body like ectoplasm. "Actually, I'm feeling a bit sick."

A large blue bowl with pink and gold daisies hand-painted on the inside was thrust into her hands. The attached price ticket announced that it was £280. Breathing deeply, terrified that she might actually be sick into it, Ginny felt beads of sweat breaking out on her forehead.

"She looks terrible."

"That's because she's guilty."

"Hello, love, can you hear me? You shouldn't be on your own. Is there anyone we can call?"

Pointedly, the man said, "Like the police?"

It was no good, even being thrown into a police cell and chained to a wall would be better than being gawped at by everyone here in the shop. Shaking her head, Ginny muttered, "No, no one you can call. My daughter's not here anymore. She's gone. Just get it over and done with and call the police. Go ahead, arrest me. I don't care anymore."

There was a long silence. It seemed that everyone was holding their breath.

Finally, the saleswoman said, "I can't do it to her. Poor thing, how could I have her arrested?"

"Don't look at me. It's your shop." The man sounded exasperated.

"Actually, it's not. The owner's gone to Penzance for the day and I'm just covering. But we've got this back." The clink of the jeweled peacock's feet against the glass-topped counter reached Ginny's ears. "So why don't we leave it at that?"

The man, clearly disappointed, breathed a sigh of resignation and said brusquely, "Fine. I was just trying to help."

The door clanged shut behind him. Ginny fumbled for a tissue and wiped her nose. Patting her on the arm, the saleswoman said kindly, "It's all right, love. Let's just forget it ever happened, shall we?"

"It was an accident," snuffled Ginny.

"I'm sure it was. You've had a rotten time. Are you OK to leave now? You need to take it easy, look after yourself."

"I'll be all right." Embarrassed and grateful, Ginny rose to her feet and prayed the Terminator wouldn't be waiting outside. "Thanks."

Chapter 4

"YOU'LL NEVER GUESS WHAT I did last week." Even as she said it, Ginny felt herself begin to blush.

"Hey, good for you." Carla, tanned from her fortnight in Sardinia, gave a nod of approval.

"Welcome back to the real world and about time too. So where did you meet him?"

Honestly.

"I wasn't doing *that,*" Ginny protested. "We're not all sex-crazed strumpets, you know."

"Just as well. All the more men for me." Amused, Carla said, "So tell me what you were doing instead that was so much better than sex."

"I didn't say it was better than sex." Entirely unbidden, the image of that cream four-poster bed with its hangings billowing in the breeze danced once more through Ginny's mind, accompanied by the shadowy outline of a tall, half-dressed figure. "It was horrible. I accidentally shoplifted something and got caught by this vile man who didn't believe I hadn't meant to do it. Don't laugh," she protested as Carla's mouth began to flicker. "It was one of the worst experiences of my whole life. I was almost arrested."

"I hate it when that happens. What were you trying to make off with anyway? Something good?"

Friends, who needed them? Aiming a fork at Carla's hand, Ginny said, "I wasn't trying to make off with anything. It was a miniature jeweled peacock. I didn't even like it."

"Never shoplift stuff you don't like. What were you thinking of?"

"That's just it, I *wasn't* thinking. It was after we'd buried Bellamy. And then I'd taken Jem to the station. I thought a spot of shopping might cheer me up." Ginny pulled a face. "Now I daren't even go into a shop in case it happens again. At this rate it's going to be tinned carrots and cornflakes at Christmas."

"You need to sort yourself out," said Carla. "Get your social life back on track, find yourself a new man. I mean it," she insisted. "Tinned carrots and a suspended sentence isn't the way forward."

"I know, I know." Ginny had heard all this fifty times before; her manless state was a continuing source of pain and bewilderment to Carla. "But not until after Christmas, OK? Jem'll be back soon."

"There, you see? You're doing it again. Putting your life on hold until Jem comes home." Swiveling around on her chair, Carla peered accusingly up at Ginny's kitchen calendar. "I bet you've been crossing off the days until the end of term."

"I can't imagine why I'm your friend. As if I'd do that," said Ginny.

As if she'd cross the days off on the kitchen calendar where Jem would see it when she got back; she wasn't that stupid. She was crossing them off on the other calendar, the secret one hidden under her bed.

"Anyway, enough about you. Let's talk some more about me," said Carla.

So far they were up to day eight of her eventful

holiday in Sardinia. No man had been safe. "Go on then, what happened after Russell went home?"

"*Thank you.*" Carla's eyes danced as she refilled their wine glasses. "I thought you'd never ask. Well . . ."

Ginny smiled. Only nineteen more days and Jem would be back. She'd definitely drink to that.

It was the week after Christmas and Ginny was in the kitchen loading the dishwasher when Jem bellowed from the living room, "Mum! GET IN HERE!"

Ginny straightened up. Had a spider just galloped across the carpet?

"Mum! *NOW!*"

In the living room she found Jem no longer draped across the sofa but catapulted bolt upright gazing at the TV screen. It was one of those daytime magazine-style programs and the presenter was talking chirpily about singles clubs. Ginny, her heart sinking, said, "Oh no, I'm not going to one of those, don't even try to persuade me—*oh!*"

The camera had swung round to reveal the person standing next to the presenter.

"I'm so embarrassed," groaned Jem. "Tell me you had an affair and he's not my real father."

Ginny, her hands covering her mouth, watched as the female presenter interviewed Gavin about the difference joining a singles club had made to his life. Gavin was beaming with pride and wearing one of his trademark multicolored striped shirts—some might call them jazzy; Ginny called them eye-wateringly loud. In his jolly way he chatted with enthusiasm about the fun they all had together and the great network of friends he'd made since joining the club. Never what you'd call shy, Gavin went on cheerfully, "I mean, I know I'm no Johnny Depp, but all I'm looking for is someone to share my life with, and I know the right woman has to be out there somewhere. That's not too much for a forty-year-old to ask, is it?"

"Forty!" Ginny let out a squeak of disbelief because Gavin—the cheek of the man—was forty-three.

"Uurrrgh, now he's flirting with the presenter!" Jem buried her face in a cushion. "I can't watch!"

Excruciatingly, the presenter and Gavin ended up dancing together before Gavin swept her into a jokey Hollywood embrace. Jem was making sick noises on the sofa. Then that segment of the TV program was over and singles clubs were replaced by a three-minute in-depth discussion on the subject of cystitis.

"I can't believe I'm related to him." Finally daring to uncover her eyes again, Jem wailed, "God, as if it isn't bad enough having a dad who *joins* a singles club. But oh no, mine has to go one better and appear on TV to boast about it. Without even having the decency to have his *face* blurred." Reaching for her mobile, she punched out her father's number. "Dad? No, this *isn't* Keira Knightley; it's *me*. And, yes, of course we've just seen it. I can't believe you didn't warn us first. What if all my friends were watching? Why do *I* have to be the one with the embarrassing dad?"

"It's his mission in life to make you cringe," said Ginny.

Jem, having listened to her father speak, rolled her eyes at Ginny. "He says he's feeling a bit peckish."

"He's always feeling a bit peckish. That's why he has to wear big stripy shirts to cover his big fat stomach. Go on then," Ginny sighed, "tell him to come over."

"Hear that?" said Jem into the phone. She broke into a grin. "Dad says you're a star."

"He doesn't know what we're eating yet." Ginny wiped her wet hands on her jeans. "Tell him it's salad."

Chapter 5

GAVIN ROARED UP THE drive an hour later in his filthy white mid-life crisis Porsche and they ate dinner together around the kitchen table. Jem's efforts to shame him, predictably enough, failed to have the desired effect.

"Where's the harm in it?" Breezily unrepentant, Gavin helped himself to another mountain of buttery mashed potato. "I'm expanding my social life, making new friends, having fun. I've met some smashing girls."

Girls being the operative word. Ginny found it hard to believe sometimes that she and Gavin had ever been married. These days he was forever announcing that yet again he had met the most gorgeous creature and that this time she was definitely The One. Needless to say, Gavin was an enthusiastic chatter-upper of the opposite sex but not necessarily a sensible one. The girls invariably turned out to be in their twenties with short skirts, high heels, and white-blond hair extensions. These relationships weren't what you'd call a meeting of minds. They usually only lasted a few weeks. When Gavin had come round over Christmas he had spent all his time extolling the virtues of his latest amour, Marina. And now, ten days later, here he was extolling the virtues of a singles club.

"What happened to Marina?" Ginny dipped a chunk of bread into the bowl of garlic mayonnaise.

"Who? Oh, right. Her ex-boyfriend got jealous and kicked up a bit of a fuss. They're back together now."

"And you're back to square one," said Ginny. "Aren't the women at this singles place a bit older than you're used to?"

"So? Not a problem. Some of them have cracking daughters." Gavin was unperturbed. "And don't give me that look. You should try it yourself."

"What? Chatting up fifty-something women, then running off with their daughters?"

"The club. It'd do you the world of good. Jem's back at uni next week," Gavin went on. "You want to be getting out more. Come along with me, and I'll introduce you to everyone. It'd be fun."

"Are you mad? I'm your ex-wife." Ginny couldn't believe he was serious. "It's not normal, you know, to take your ex-wife along to your singles club. Even if I did want to go to one, which I *don't*."

Gavin shrugged. "You've got to move with the times. And think of what you're going to do with the rest of your life."

"Dad, leave it. This is like when you keep trying to persuade me to eat olives just because you love them. Mum's fine; she's not desperate like you."

"I'm not desperate." Gavin was outraged at this slur on his character.

"No, you're just a bit of a tart." Reaching over, Jem gave his hand a reassuring pat. "And that's not a criticism; it's the truth. But Mum isn't like that. She's happy as she is." Turning to Ginny, she added, "You never get lonely, do you, Mum? You're not the type."

"Um . . . well . . ." Caught off guard by what

had clearly been a rhetorical question, Ginny wondered if this might perhaps be the moment to confess that sometimes, if she was honest, she did get a bit—

"Thank *God,*" Jem continued with feeling. "And let me tell you, I seriously appreciate it." She shook her head in disbelief. "I mean, you wouldn't believe what some parents are like. There are some completely hopeless cases out there. Like Lizzie, one of the girls on my course, her mum and dad ring her up almost every day; they have no idea how embarrassing they are. Everyone bursts out laughing whenever her phone rings—it's like her parents are living their whole lives through her. And Davy's another one—crikey, he's in an even worse situation. Poor Davy, his mother wouldn't even let him leave home. He's just, like, *stuck* there with her and everyone teases him. I mean, can't the woman get a grip? Doesn't she realize she's ruining his whole life?"

Poor Davy. Poor Davy's mother. Poor *her*. Feeling sick, Ginny drank some water. Part of her was relieved that Jem hadn't an inkling how utterly bereft she felt. The other part realized that, clearly, from now on, she was never ever going to be able to admit it.

"She doesn't mean to," Ginny protested on Davy's mother's behalf.

"Yes, but it's so . . . pathetic! I mean, it's not as

47

if we're babies anymore." Jem waved her fork around for emphasis. "We're *adults*."

"It's not very adult to tease a boy just because he's still living at home." Ginny recalled how Jem, as a toddler, had sat in her highchair imperiously waving her plastic fork in exactly that fashion. "I hope you haven't been mean to him."

"Oh, Mum, of course I haven't been mean. It's just a bit of a nerdy thing to do, isn't it? And it means he doesn't fit in. It's like if a crowd of us go out for a drink we always pile back to somebody's rooms or flat afterward for beer. But what can Davy do, invite everyone round to his mum's house? Imagine that! Sipping tea out of the best china, having to sit up straight and make polite conversation with somebody's *mother*."

Ginny winced inwardly. Why didn't Jem just stab her all over with the fork? It couldn't hurt any more than this.

"Don't bother with him. Just leave him to get on with it." Gavin, who was to political correctness what Mr. Bean was to juggling, said, "Concentrate on your other friends. That one sounds like a nancy boy, if you ask me."

Ginny was balanced on a stepladder singing along to the radio at the top of her voice when she heard the distant sound of the front doorbell. It took a while to wipe her hands on a cloth, clamber off the ladder, and gallop downstairs.

By the time she reached the hall, Carla was shouting through the letterbox, "I know you're in there; I can hear all the horrible noise. Are you crying again? Come on, answer the door. I've come to cheer you up, because that's the kind of lovely, thoughtful person I am."

Ginny opened the door, touched by her concern. "That's really kind of you."

"Plus I need to borrow your hairdryer because mine's blown up." Impressed, Carla said, "Hey, you're not crying."

"Well spotted."

"You're wearing truly revolting dungarees."

"Not much gets past you, Miss Marple."

"And there's bright yellow stuff all over your face and hands." Carla paused, considered the evidence, and narrowed her eyes shrewdly. "I conclude that you have been having a fight in a bath of custard."

"You see? That's why the police never take a blind bit of notice when you try and interfere with their investigations."

Carla grinned and followed her into the kitchen. "Any man having his 'investigations' interfered with by me is definitely going to take notice. So what's brought all this on? What are you painting?"

"Spare bedroom."

Carla, who was no DIYer, raised her eyebrows. "For any particular reason?"

"Oh yes."

"Am I allowed to ask why?"

Ginny made two mugs of tea and tore open a packet of caramel wafers. "Because I've had enough of feeling sorry for myself. It's time to sort myself out and make things happen."

"Well, good. But I don't quite see where decorating the house comes in."

"Jem rang last night. She and Lucy were on their way out to a party. She sounded so happy," said Ginny. "They're having such fun together. Lucy got chatting to one of the boys from the rugby team and he invited her and Jem along to the match on Saturday."

"Poor Jem, having to watch a game of rugby." Carla, who liked her creature comforts, shuddered and unwrapped a caramel wafer. "I can't imagine anything more horrible."

"But that's not the point. She's making more friends all the time. And before you know it, she'll be meeting *their* friends," Ginny explained. "Once you start, it just carries on growing."

Carla couldn't help herself. "As the bishop said to the actress."

"So last night I decided that's what I should do too. Here's this lovely house with only me in it and that's such a waste. So I'm going to advertise for—"

"A hunky rugby player of your very own! Gin, that's a fabulous idea! Or better still, a whole *team* of hunky rugby players."

"Sorry to be so boring," said Ginny, "but I was thinking of a female. And preferably not the rugby playing kind. Just someone nice and normal and single like me. Then we can go out and do stuff together like Jem and Lucy do. I'll meet her friends, she'll meet mine, and we can socialize as much as we want. And when we don't feel like going out, we can relax in front of the TV, just crack open a bottle of wine, and have a good gossip."

Carla pretended to be hurt. Inwardly, she *felt* a bit hurt. "You mean you're going to advertise for a new friend? But I thought I was your friend. I love cracking open bottles of wine! I'm great at gossip!"

"I know that. But you already have your life exactly the way you want it," Ginny patiently pointed out.

"You'll like her better than you like me!" Carla clutched her hand to her chest. "The two of you will talk about me behind my back. When I turn up on your doorstep, you'll say, 'Actually, Carla, it's not really convenient right now. Doris and I are just about to crack open a bottle of wine and have a good old girly gossip.'"

"Fine." Ginny held up her paint-smeared palms. "I give in. You can be my new lodger."

Now Carla was genuinely horrified. "You must be joking! I don't want to live with you! No thanks, I like my own space."

"Well, exactly. But I don't. I hate it," Ginny said simply. "I'm used to having someone else around the house. And as soon as I get this room redecorated, I can go ahead and advertise." Brightening, she added, "And now you're here, fancy giving me a hand with the painting?"

"Are we still friends?"

"Absolutely."

"In that case I'm sure you'll understand," said Carla, "when I say I'd rather eat raw frogs than give you a hand with the painting. Why don't you just lend me your hairdryer and I'll leave you to it? Too many cooks and all that."

Ginny grinned as Carla rose to her feet and brushed wafer crumbs from her perfect black trousers. "Except you've never cooked anything in your life."

"Ah, but I have other talents." Carla experienced a rush of affection and gave Ginny a hug. "And you're not allowed to replace me. If a lodger's what you want, then that's great. But I'm your best friend and don't you forget it."

Chapter 6

"YOU DON'T HAVE TO do this, you know." Jem smiled at Davy Stokes, who had taken to dropping into the Royal Oak before closing time and walking her home after her shift.

"I know, but it's practically on my way." Davy shrugged and said mildly, "Sorry, is it embarrassing? I won't do it if you'd rather I didn't."

"Don't be daft. It's nice having someone to talk to. And when my boots are pinching my toes," Jem added because her new boots were undoubtedly designed to be admired rather than worn to work in, "it means you can give me a piggyback."

"In your dreams." Grinning, Davy dodged out of the way before she could grab his shoulders and jump up. "Should've worn trainers like any normal barmaid."

"But look at them! How could I leave them at home? They're so beautiful!" Jem's pointy pink cowboy boots were the new love of her life. "You're just jealous because you don't have a pair."

Together they bickered their way along Guthrie Road, shivering as a cold drizzle began to fall. On impulse, Jem said, "Kerry and Dan are having a party tonight. D'you fancy coming along?"

Davy reluctantly shook his head. "Thanks, but I have to get home."

Every Saturday after walking her to her door, he caught the bus back to Henbury. Feeling sorry for him, Jem urged, "Just this once. Come on, it'll be fun. Everyone's going. And you're welcome to crash at our place afterward." What with Davy's continuing crush on Lucy, if this wasn't an incentive, she didn't know what was.

He stuffed his hands into his coat pockets. "I really can't. Mum'll be waiting up for me."

"Davy, you're eighteen!"

Davy looked away. "I know, but she doesn't like to be on her own. Please don't start all this again. My mum isn't like your mum, OK?"

Jem slipped her arm through his and gave it a conciliatory squeeze. "OK, sorry. I'll shut up."

He relaxed. "That'll be a first."

"Anyway, I haven't told you about my mother's latest plan. I phoned her yesterday to tell her about my new boots," said Jem. "And that's when she told me, she's getting a lodger!"

"Crikey. Who?"

"No idea, she hasn't found one yet. She's just finished redecorating the spare room. Next week she's going to put an ad in the local paper."

"Wow. So how do you feel about that?"

"I think it's great. She wouldn't get anyone I didn't like, would she? Good for her, that's what I say." Jem was proud of her mother. "She's getting on with her own life, doing something positive. Now that I'm not there anymore she could probably do with the company. You know, you should suggest it to your mum. Then you could move out without feeling guilty about leaving her on her own."

Davy rolled his eyes. "You're doing it again."

"Sorry, sorry, it just seems such a shame that—"

"And again!" They'd reached Jem's flat; Davy checked his watch. "I'd better make a move if I'm going to catch my bus. You enjoy your party."

"I will. And thanks for walking me home. See you on Monday." Jem waved as he headed off in the direction of Whiteladies Road, a lone figure in an oversized coat from Oxfam, on his way home to share cocoa and biscuits with his mother. No wonder other people made fun of him.

Poor Davy, what kind of life did he have?

Jem let herself into the flat expecting it to be empty. It was midnight and Rupert would be out at some trendy club somewhere. Lucy was already at Kerry and Dan's party. All she had to do was quickly change her clothes, slap on a bit more eye shadow, and re-spritz her hair, and she would be on her way. This time in footwear that didn't pinch like delinquent lobsters.

But when she pushed open the door to the living room, there was Rupert lying across the sofa watching TV and with an array of Chinese food in cartons spread out over the coffee table.

"Crikey, I thought you'd be out."

Amused, Rupert mimicked her expression of surprise. "Crikey, but I'm not. I'm here."

"Why? Are you ill? Where's Caro?" As she shrugged off her coat—the great thing about Rupert was he was never stingy with the central heating—it occurred to Jem that Caro hadn't been around for a few days now.

"Who knows? Who cares? We broke up." He shrugged and reached for a dish of chicken sui mai.

"Oh, I didn't realize. I'm sorry."

"Don't be sorry on my account. She was boring. Spectacular to look at," Rupert sighed, "but with about as much charisma as a soap on a rope."

This was true, but Jem diplomatically didn't say so. In her experience, this was a surefire method of ensuring they'd be back together within a week, plus they'd then both hate your guts.

"So here I am, all alone, with more Chinese food than one person could ever eat. But now you're here too." Patting the sofa, Rupert said, "So that's good. Come on, sit down and help yourself. I've got a stack of DVDs here. How was work this evening?"

Jem hesitated. He'd never asked her about work before. She suspected that Rupert was keen to have company and more upset about Caro than he was letting on.

"Um, actually I'm supposed to be meeting up with Lucy. At Kerry and Dan's party. Why don't you come along too?"

"Kerry the bossy hockey player? And carrot-top Dan the incredible hulk? I'd rather cut off my own feet. You don't really want to go there," Rupert drawled. "All those noisy rugby types downing their own vast bodyweight in cheap beer. It's cold outside, it's starting to rain so you'd be drenched by the time you got there, and what would be the point of it all?"

He *was* lonely; it was obvious. And speaking of cutting off your own feet, hers were certainly killing her. Jem hesitated, picturing the party she'd be missing. She was starving, and the most anyone could hope for at Kerry and Dan's would be dry French bread and a bucket of garlic dip. Whereas Rupert didn't buy ordinary run-of-the-mill takeaways; he ordered from the smartest Chinese restaurant in Clifton, and all the food on the table looked and smelled like heaven.

"Maybe you're right." Giving in to temptation, she sank down onto the sofa next to him.

Rupert grinned. "I'm always right. Want a hand with those?"

Jem tugged off her left boot and heaved a sigh of relief as her toes unscrunched themselves. Having helped her pull off the right one, Rupert held up the boot and sorrowfully shook his head. "You shouldn't wear these."

What was he, a chiropodist?

"They're leather," Jem told him. "They'll stretch."

"That's beside the point; they'll still be horrible."

"Excuse me!"

"But they are. How much did they cost?"

"They were a bargain. Twenty pounds in the sale."

"Exactly."

"Reduced from seventy-five!"

"*Exactly*. Who in their right mind would want them?"

"*I* would," Jem protested, looking at her boots and wondering if he was right.

Smiling at the expression on her face, Rupert chucked them across the carpet. "OK, that's enough boot talk. Have some wine. And help yourself to food. Are you warm enough?"

The king prawns in tempura were sublime. Greedily, Jem tried the scallops with chili sauce. The white wine too was a cut above the kind of special-offer plonk she was used to. Closing her eyes and wriggling her toes, she said, "You know what? I'd rather be here."

"Of course you would. Staying in is the new going out." Wielding chopsticks like a pro, Rupert fed her a mouthful of lemon chicken. "Listen to the rain outside. We're here with everything we need. Turning up at some ropy old party just for the sake of it is what people do when they're too insecure to stay at home. They're just desperate."

Swallowing the piece of chicken, Jem thought how much chattier Rupert was when it was just the two of them together. While he and Caro had been a couple, their attitude had always been . . . well, not stand-offish exactly, but distant. Now, taking a sip of wine, she realized he was showing definite signs of improvement. Wait until she told Lucy that super-posh Rupert might actually be human after all.

Actually, better text Lucy and tell her she was giving the party a miss.

By half-past one they'd finished two bottles of wine. *Gangs of New York* wouldn't have been Jem's DVD of choice, but the food more than compensated. When the film ended, Rupert said, "Want to watch *The Office* next?"

"Ooh yes." Relaxed and pleasantly fuzzy, she beamed up at him. "You know what? I'm really glad I stayed in."

"All the best people do it. Unlike that rabble," said Rupert of a group of noisy revelers making their way along the road outside. "Listen to them, bunch of tossers." Raising his voice, he repeated loudly, *"Tossers."*

Jem giggled. "I don't think they can hear you."

Rupert leaped up from the sofa and crossed the room. Flinging open the sash window, he bellowed, "TOSSERS!"

A chorus of shouting greeted this observation. Whistles and insults were flung up at him and a beer can made a tinny sound as it bounced off a wall.

"Close the window," Jem protested as cold air blasted through the room.

"Are you kidding? They tried to throw a beer

can at me." Casting around the living room, Rupert searched for something to throw in return.

"No bottles." Jem swiftly grabbed the empty wine bottle before he could reach it. Then she let out a shriek as he snatched up her boots and flung the first one out of the window. "Not my boots!"

Chapter 7

"WANKERS," YELLED RUPERT, HURLING the second boot before she could stop him, then slamming the window shut.

"Are you mad? Go and get them back! They're *my* boots."

"Correction. They're horrible boots." Amused, he reached out and grasped Jem's arms as she attempted to dart past him. "And it's too late now; they've run off with them."

"How dare you!"

"Hey, shhh, they've served their purpose. I'll buy you a new pair."

"That was the last pair in the shop!" Jem struggled to break free.

"And they were cheap and nasty. You deserve better than that. I'll buy you some decent boots." Rupert was laughing now. "Now there's an offer you can't turn down. OK, I'm sorry, maybe I shouldn't have just grabbed them like that, but

I've done you a big favor. We'll go out tomorrow and find you a fabulous pair. That's a promise."

Jem stared past him, lost for words. Her beautiful pointy pink cowboy boots, the bargain boots she'd been so proud of, gone, just like that.

Had they really been cheap and nasty? Davy had said they looked nice.

Then again, Davy wasn't exactly known for his unerring sense of style.

"Come on." Rupert tilted her face up to look at him. "You know it makes sense." His gaze softened as he stroked her cheek. "God, you're a pretty little thing."

Jem knew he was going to kiss her. This wasn't something she had ever imagined happening. But now that it was, it seemed entirely natural. As his mouth brushed against hers, she felt warmth spread through her body. Rupert's fingers slid through her hair, then he drew her closer to him and kissed her properly.

It was great. Then he pulled away and cradled her face in his hands, his hazel eyes searching hers.

"What?" whispered Jem.

"Sorry, shouldn't have done that." He smiled briefly. "I just couldn't help myself."

Jem hesitated. Would it be too forward to suggest that he could do it again if he liked?

But Rupert was shaking his head now, looking regretful. "Probably not the best idea."

This was his flat, she was his tenant. Maybe he

was right. Not hugely experienced sexually, one part of Jem was relieved that he wasn't launching himself at her, employing all his seduction skills and doing his level best to inveigle her into his bedroom for a night of torrid passion.

The other part of her wondered why not and felt, frankly, a bit miffed. Wasn't she attractive enough?

"Come on, let's watch *The Office*." Rupert affectionately ruffled her hair before turning away to sort through the pile of DVDs.

And that was what they did. For the next hour, Jem sat next to him on the sofa gazing blindly at the TV, completely unable to concentrate on what was happening on screen. Her mind was in a whirl; all she could think about was that kiss and the way Rupert had looked at her. Why had he stopped? And wasn't he feeling anything now? Her whole body was fired up, awash with adrenaline, and he was acting as if nothing had happened between them.

Had the kiss put him off? Had she done it wrong? Was Rupert regretting it now or did it genuinely not mean anything to him at all?

One thing was for sure, she wasn't going to be the one to ask.

Jem's heart broke into a gallop as Rupert moved, reaching forward for the remote control. He switched off the DVD and the TV, yawned widely, and said, "That's it. Time for bed."

Was that some kind of code? Hardly daring to breathe, she watched him stand up, yawn again, and stretch his shoulders. Turning briefly, he said, "Night then," before heading for the door.

OK, not some kind of code after all.

"Night," said Jem, confused and disappointed. All these months of sharing a flat with Rupert and she had honestly never thought of him in a romantic way, but that had been because he was so out of her league it had simply not occurred to her that anything could happen. Rupert's background, his gilded life and upper-class glamour, set him apart from the rest of them. He and Caro moved in elevated circles, whizzing up to London at weekends, staying with friends in country houses, and flying to Paris when the mood took them.

It was a different world. He'd kissed her.

And now he'd gone to bed.

Let's face it, nothing was going to happen. She'd been naive to even think it might.

Jem had been in bed for ten minutes when the knock came on her bedroom door. Before she had time to reply, the handle turned and the door opened.

Rupert stood framed in the doorway, wearing shorts and nothing else. "I can't stop thinking about you."

"What?" It came out as a quivery whisper. Her pulse was going for some kind of world record.

"I think you heard." It was dark but Rupert sounded as if he was smiling. "I can't sleep." He tapped his head. "You're in here. I've tried to get you out but you won't go."

Oh, that voice, that silky upper-class drawl.

Moving toward her in the darkness, he went on, "And I wondered if it was the same for you."

Jem's tongue was stuck fast to the roof of her mouth. She couldn't say no; she couldn't say yes; she couldn't say anything at all.

"Room for one more in there?" Rupert tilted his head to one side. "Or would you rather be on your own? If I've just made a horrible mistake here, I'll go back to my room."

Her fingers trembling, Jem reached for Barney Bear, the battered soft toy that had accompanied her to bed since she was five years old. Surreptitiously she dropped him down between the side of the bed and her chest of drawers, then lifted the duvet and pulled it back, moving over to make room for Rupert to join her.

"You're sure?" said Rupert as he slid into bed and took her into his arms.

"Yes," Jem whispered into his ear. She'd never been more sure in her life.

At four o'clock, Rupert climbed out of bed and located his shorts.

Jem pushed herself up on one elbow. "What are you doing?"

"Being discreet. Better if Lucy doesn't know about this." Combing his fingers through his hair, he said, "She might think three's a crowd, feel a bit of a third wheel. Easier all round if you don't tell her."

He had a point. This was Rupert's flat, she and Lucy were his tenants, and it could cause awkwardness.

That made sense.

Except . . . did it mean what they'd just done was a one-off, nothing more than a meaningless shag?

Was that *it?*

"Hey, don't look at me like that." Having pulled on his shorts, Rupert bent over and kissed her. "It'll be fun. Like having an affair without all the hassle of being married to other people. It's more exciting when no one else knows."

Relieved, Jem wrapped her arms around his neck. "You're right. It's easier if we don't tell Lucy. It'll feel a bit funny, though. We tell each other everything."

"Well, this time you're just going to have to stop yourself." Straightening up, Rupert grinned. "We don't want this to be spoiled, do we? Trust me, some secrets are better kept."

Chapter 8

THE ADVERT HAD GONE into the classified sections of today's *Western Morning News* and the *Cornish Guardian*. Ginny had spent ages composing it, finally settling on, "Cheerful divorcee, 38, has lovely room to let in spacious home in Portsilver. Would suit lady in similar circumstances. £60 pw inclusive."

There, that sounded OK, didn't it? Friendly and appropriately upbeat? If she were looking for somewhere to live, she'd be tempted herself. Gazing with pride at the adverts in the papers—all fresh and new and filled with promise—Ginny felt a squiggle of excitement at the thought of the fun she and her new lodger would have, going shopping together and—

Yeek, phone!

"Hello?" She put on her very best voice.

" 'Ello, love, you sound up for it. Fancy a shag?"

Oh God. Outraged, Ginny said in a high voice, "No I do *not*," and cut the connection. Her hands trembled. How completely *horrible*. Was this what was going to happen? Would she be harassed by perverts?

The phone rang again an hour later. This time Ginny braced herself and answered it with extreme caution.

"It's me. How's it going?"

Oh, the relief. Gavin. "Nothing so far. Except some vile pervert."

"What did you say to him?"

"I told him to get lost."

"Listen, let me know when anyone's coming around to look at the room. I should be there. It's not safe, inviting strangers into your home when you're on your own."

Ginny relented. Gavin had offered before but she'd told him there was no need, seeing as she'd only be meeting women anyway. Now, though, she realized he was right. It was silly to take the risk. Gavin might be disastrous in many ways, but he did have his good points.

"OK. If anyone *does* call." Reluctantly, she said, "Thanks."

"No problem. I'm free this evening. You didn't, by the way."

"Didn't what?"

"Tell me to get lost."

Ginny counted to ten. "That was you? Thanks a lot."

"Ah, but I got my point across. It might not be me next time."

Gavin was annoying enough when he was wrong. When he was right he was insufferable. Ginny, who hated it when that happened, said, "Fine then, but you can hide upstairs. I'm not having you sitting there like some minder while I'm talking to them."

"You spoil all my fun," Gavin protested. "Never pass up the opportunity to meet new women, that's what I say. Hey, what if a foxy young chick moves in and I start dating her? That'd be a laugh, wouldn't it? Would you be jealous?"

"No, just astounded by her bizarre taste in men." Ginny was patient. "And no, it wouldn't be a laugh either." Counting off on her fingers, she added, "And thirdly, I can promise you now, my new lodger isn't going to be a foxy young chick."

The doorbell rang at seven o'clock on the dot, heralding the arrival of the first of the three potential tenants who had phoned that afternoon. More nervous than she let on—heavens, was this what it was like to go on a blind date?—Ginny shooed Gavin upstairs and took a steadying breath before opening the front door.

"Hello, love, I'm Monica. I've just been having a look at your window sills; you know they'd benefit from a quick going over with a dab of bleach. Brighten them up lovely, bleach would. Ooh, and those skirting boards could do with a dust."

The trouble with blind dates was, it wasn't considered polite to take one look at the no-hoper in front of you and say, "Sorry, this is never going to work out, so why don't we just give up right now?"

But here she was, faced with the equivalent of a blind date with John McCririck, and Ginny knew she was going to have to be pleasant and chat politely to the woman because that was how these things were done. Even if this one had just criticized her window sills and she'd saw off her own head rather than allow her to move into this house.

Monica was short and squat, with permed gray hair and flicked-up spectacles. She looked like a short-sighted turtle. She also looked sixty-five years old. And she hadn't stopped talking yet.

". . . that's what I do, love. My little secret. Just dab a toothbrush in vinegar and scrub away like billy-o—those taps will come up like diamonds! Here, you take my coat. Oh dear, haven't you got a hanger? Now, why don't we have a nice cup of tea and a good old chat before I take a look at my room, hmm? Then we can start to get to know each other. Ooh, I say, Gold Blend, that's a bit extravagant, isn't it? And washing-up liquid from Marks and Spencer, well I never. Nice and weak, please, love, we can share the teabag. No sugar for me, I'm already sweet enough."

Oh help, oh help, get me out of here. Ginny said, "Sorry, how old did you say you were?"

"Forty-two, love. That's why I knew we'd have plenty in common, what with being the same age."

"Ri-ight." Ginny considered calling Gavin down

from upstairs to see if he might like to flirt with the woman.

"I'll tell you a bit about myself, shall I? Well, my hubby and I are getting a divorce so we're selling our bungalow, which is why I'm looking for a place to rent. And sharing's nice, isn't it? Cozy, like. Between you and me I'm not that bothered about losing him. My hubby's a bit of a misery, quiet as a church mouse, never been the sort to join in with conversations. Used to spend all his time in his blessed garden shed when he wasn't at work, so I can't see me missing him much at all. Mind you, could have knocked me down with a feather when he said he wanted a divorce! Didn't see that one coming! Men are funny creatures, aren't they? I'll never work out what makes them tick. Silly old fool, how he thinks he's going to manage without me I can't imagine. Did you know there's a mark on the outside of your window? Some bird's gone and done its nasty business on the glass. You want to get that cleaned off, it doesn't look very nice. I could do it for you now if you like."

"She sounds perfect. When's she moving in?" As soon as the front door closed, Gavin came downstairs.

"Shhh, my ears hurt."

"Want me to give them a polish with Brasso? That'll bring them up a treat."

"What a nightmare." Ginny shuddered. "That

was horrendous. I told her I had lots of other people interested in the room and that I'd let her know tomorrow."

"You've only got two more to see. What if they're worse than her?"

Dumping the coffee cups in the sink and thinking longingly of the bottle of white wine in the fridge, Ginny said, "There can't be anyone worse than Monica."

"Hi, come in, I'm Ginny."

"Zeee."

Ginny hesitated, wondering if the woman had a bumble bee trapped in her throat. "Excuse me?"

"Zeee. That's my name. With three *e*'s." There was a note of challenge in the woman's voice, as if daring her to query the wisdom of this. "Zeee Porter. You shouldn't have a table there, you know. Not in the hallway like that. Bad feng shui."

"Oh." In that case, Ginny longed to tell her, you shouldn't have grubby blond dreadlocks and earrings bigger than castanets emphasizing your scrawny chicken neck, and you definitely shouldn't be wearing purple dungarees and homemade leather sandals over woolly toe socks, because that's bad feng shui too.

Zeee Porter, she learned, was thirty-six and—incredibly for such a catch—still single. Currently the only man in her life was her spirit guide, Running Deer. During the summer months, Zeee

71

surfed, worked as a henna tattooist, and just, like, generally chilled out. The rest of the year she just, well, generally chilled out and waited for summer to come around again. Yes, she'd had a proper job once, in a vegan café in Aldershot, but being told what to do and having to get up in the morning had done her head in.

"It was a bad vibe, man." Zeee shook her head dismissively. "I just don't need that kind of hassle in my life."

She evidently didn't need the hassle of shampoo or deodorant either. Ginny wondered if Running Deer wore a peg on his nose or if spirit guides weren't bothered by those kinds of earthly matters.

Heaven knows what Monica would make of her. She'd probably march Zeee out into the garden and set about her with neat bleach and a scrubbing brush.

Ginny dutifully showed her the room she wouldn't be living in then said brightly, "Well, I've got *lots* of other people to see, but I'll give you a ring tomorrow and let you know either way."

"I haven't got a phone," said Zeee. "Phones are, like, destroying the planet."

"Oh." Except for when Zeee had rung earlier to make the appointment, presumably.

"To be honest," Zeee went on, "I think we'll just leave it. No offense, but I wouldn't want to live here anyway. It doesn't really do it for me, know what I mean?"

Flabbergasted, Ginny said, *"Oh."*

"Plus, Running Deer's telling me I shouldn't move in. He wouldn't be comfortable here."

"Right." Awash with relief, Ginny sent up a silent prayer of thanks to spirit guides everywhere. Hooray for Running Deer.

Zeee flicked back her moth-eaten dreadlocks. "Plus, he says you have a muddy aura."

"God, what a stink. Open the windows," Gavin complained. "Who's next?"

Ginny wasn't getting her hopes up. The third and final prospective lodger was male. "His name's Martin. I told him I was looking for a female to share the house with, but he said I couldn't specify like that because it was sexual discrimination and I could be sued if I refused to even interview men."

Gavin's lip curled. "Sounds like a nutter. Just as well I'm here."

"Actually, he didn't sound like a nutter. He was quite nice about it. He's split up from his wife," said Ginny, "and just needs somewhere pretty fast."

"Probably because he murdered her and the police are on his tail."

Ginny was fairly sure Martin wasn't a murderer. "He apologized for being a man but said he really wasn't difficult to live with, he didn't play loud music and he was fairly sure he didn't have any annoying habits. So what else could I do but agree to see him? You never know, he might be all right."

"Soft, that's what you are. I'll keep an ax upstairs with me," Gavin said cheerily. "Just in case."

Chapter 9

MARTIN MASON DIDN'T LOOK like a murderer. He politely introduced himself, appeared happy with the room Ginny showed him, and complimented her on her decorating skills. In the kitchen he accepted a cup of tea and said, "Well, I expect you've got plenty of other people to see, but just to let you know, I'd be very interested in the room." Drily he added, "Although I daresay you'll end up choosing a female."

"I don't know. I'll decide when I've met everyone." Was her nose getting longer? He seemed pleasant enough, but Ginny knew she wouldn't be inviting this man to be her housemate, although she didn't doubt that he'd pay his rent on time. Sharing her home with a gray-haired, suit-wearing, fifty-year-old assistant bank manager wasn't what she'd had in mind at all.

"I'd appreciate a quick decision," said Martin. "I'm sleeping in a work colleague's spare room at the moment, you see. I don't want to outstay my welcome."

Ginny nodded, remembering that his marriage had just broken up. Poor man, it couldn't be easy for him; it must have come as a terrible shock.

"So what happened? Is your wife still living in your house?" Was it impertinent to ask this? Oh well, she was curious.

Martin blinked behind his owlish spectacles. "For now, yes."

"And she just kicked you out, told you you had to leave?" Ginny was indignant on his behalf; that hardly seemed fair.

"Oh no. I was the one who left." His tone was mild. "It was absolutely my choice. I just couldn't stand being married to my wife a minute longer."

Good heavens, she hadn't been expecting that. Ginny said with bemusement, "Why? What was it like being married to her?"

Martin's mouth curled up at the corners. Behind his steel-rimmed spectacles his eyes glinted with amusement. "Believe me, if you'd ever met Monica, you wouldn't need to ask."

"Monica's husband. Poor man," Ginny said with feeling. "No wonder he was glad to be out."

"Did you tell him she'd been here?"

Ginny nodded as she sloshed wine into two

glasses up to the brim and handed one to Gavin. "He said, whatever you do, don't let her move in. She'd drive you demented."

"But you aren't going to be asking him to move in either. So that's it." Gavin shrugged. "You've seen all three and none of them fitted the bill. What happens now?"

"Re-advertise I suppose. Try again. Hope for better luck next time." Ginny made headway into her much-needed glass of wine, more disappointed than she cared to let on by the events of this evening. She had been so looking forward to meeting someone lovely, the two of them hitting it off from the word go. Now she knew how naive she'd been and the sense of disappointment was crushing. What if she kept on advertising and no one suitable ever turned up?

By eight o'clock they had finished the bottle and Gavin was preparing to leave when the phone rang.

"Hi," said a warm male voice, "I'm calling about the house-share. Is it still going, or have you found someone now?"

It was more than a warm voice; it was a gorgeous voice, the kind that made you think the owner had to be gorgeous too. Wondering if maybe all might not be lost after all, Ginny said, "No, it's still free."

"Fantastic. Now it says here in the ad that you'd prefer a female . . ."

"Either. Really, I don't mind."

"As long as it's someone you can get along with." He definitely sounded as if he were smiling. "I know, that's the important thing, isn't it? My name's Perry Kennedy by the way. And your house sounds great, just the kind of thing I'm after. How soon could I come around and take a look?"

Giddy with hope and three hastily downed glasses of wine, Ginny said recklessly, "Well, whereabouts are you? If you want to, you can come around now."

Having expected so much, Ginny was relieved to see when she opened the front door that he wasn't a troll. Perry Kennedy was six feet tall, with wavy reddish-gold hair, sparkling green eyes, and a dazzling smile. He was also athletically built and wearing a dark casual jacket over a white shirt and jeans.

"It's really good to meet you." As he shook Ginny's hand he said, "I've got a great feeling about this place already. Hey, I love the way you've done the hall."

Twenty minutes later they were sitting together in the kitchen chatting away as if they'd known each other for years. Perry's current flat was too small; it was driving him crazy. He was thirty-five, single but with a great crowd of friends in Portsilver and he loved socializing. A year ago he had moved down from London to Cornwall, selling his flat in Putney and plowing the equity into a T-shirt printing business. He enjoyed jet-skiing and scuba-diving in his spare time. His favorite food was Thai. He drove an old MG and his all-time favorite film was *The Color Purple*.

"But I don't normally admit that to people," said Perry. "I don't know why I told *you*. That film always makes me cry." He shook his head confidingly. "This could ruin my street cred."

"I can't tell you how many times I've sobbed my way through *The Color Purple*," said Ginny.

"Yes, but that's allowed. I'm not supposed to, though, am I? I'm a man."

Ginny laughed at the expression on his face. He was perfect.

"Anyway, I'm taking up too much of your time. The room's great," said Perry. "And so are you. What shall I do, then? Leave my number and wonder if I'll ever hear from you again?"

Could she ask for anyone better? Ginny raced through everything she knew about him in her mind, searching for flaws and finding none. Perry was charming and brilliant company. OK, he wasn't a woman and they probably wouldn't spend a lot of time discussing nail polish, but other than that, were there any drawbacks at all?

"Or," said Perry with a smile, "do you think there's a chance we might have a deal?"

Three glasses of wine didn't make the decision for her, but they certainly played their part. Seeing no reason to prevaricate, Ginny threw caution to the wind. Her mind was made up. She beamed at Perry and said, "We have a deal."

He looked at her in delight. "You don't know how much this means to me. It'll make all the difference in the world. How soon would the room be available?"

"Whenever you like." Ginny watched him take out his wallet and count his way through a sheaf of twenty-pound notes.

"Would Saturday be all right?"

"Saturday? No problem."

"Here, one month's deposit and the first month's rent in advance." Perry pressed the notes into her hand and said cheerfully, "Before you change your mind. And you'll be wanting references of course. I'll bring them along on Saturday. Thanks so much for this." He fixed Ginny with the kind of look that made her insides go wibbly. "I'm so glad I met you tonight."

"Me too." She watched as he rose to his feet and reached for his car keys.

"I'd better get back. Saturday morning, OK? Elevenish, or is that too hideously early?"

Ginny shook her head. This was the start of her new life and as far as she was concerned Saturday couldn't come soon enough. "No problem. Eleven o'clock's fine."

The trouble with ex-husbands was you could always rely on them to notice things you'd much rather they didn't.

And, naturally, to take huge delight in pointing it out.

"Ha!" Gavin pointed a triumphant finger at her as he came down the stairs.

Ginny was determined to bluff it out. "What?"

"You fancy him."

"I do *not*."

"Oh yes you do. You fancy the pants off him. *And* you're going red."

"Only because you *think* that," Ginny protested. "Not because it's true."

"I don't think it, I *know* it. I *heard* you." Smirking, he launched into a wickedly accurate imitation of her, repeating random overheard phrases punctuated with girlish giggles and slightly too loud laughter.

Why couldn't she have an ex-husband who lived five hundred miles away? Or in Australia? Australia would be good.

"You were eavesdropping." Ginny curled her lip accusingly to let him know how she felt about such low behavior.

"I was making sure you were safe. It was my job to listen to what was going on. Fine chaperone I'd be," Gavin remarked, "if I sat upstairs with my Walkman clamped over my ears. You could be screaming your head off and I wouldn't hear a thing. I'd come down to the kitchen just in time to see him stuffing the last bits of you down the waste disposal. Then you'd be sorry."

"Anyway, he's moving in on Saturday." Ginny was defiant. "And I don't fancy him, OK? He just seems really nice and we get on well together, that's all."

"Hmm." Gavin raised a playful eyebrow. "Very well indeed, by the sound of things. Good-looking, is he?"

"Average," said Ginny. "Better looking than the other three that came round here tonight. Four, actually." To get her own back she pointed at Gavin. "Including you."

He grinned. "This is going to be interesting."

Ginny felt a squiggle of excitement. *Interesting.* She hoped so too.

Chapter 10

BY ELEVEN O'CLOCK ON Saturday morning the house was all ready and, as if in celebration, the sun had come out. Perry Kennedy would be here soon. Ginny, working on not sounding as if she fancied him, had been practicing her laugh as she tidied around the kitchen, making sure it didn't get too loud or high-pitched. Of course, once Perry had settled in and they became more used to each other, things would hopefully settle down and she'd stop feeling so—

Oh God, that sounded like him now! Flinging the dishcloth into the sink, Ginny wiped her hands on her jeans and fluffed up her hair. The throaty roar of a sports car outside died as the engine was switched off. She went to the front door and opened it.

"Hi there." Perry was already out of the car and waving at her. Today he was wearing a dark blue sweater, cream jeans, and Timberlands.

"Hi!" Ginny watched as the passenger door opened to reveal a slender woman with a mass of long, red-gold curls and pale, freckled skin. She was staggeringly beautiful and wore a long black coat falling open to reveal a pale gray top and trousers beneath.

"This is Laurel." Perry ushered the slender woman toward Ginny. "My sister."

Oh, phew, of course she was. All that incredible red-gold hair—what a relief.

"Hi, Laurel, nice to meet you." Ginny shook her hand with enthusiasm.

Tonelessly, Laurel said, "Hello."

"Come on then, let's get this lot upstairs." Already busy unloading the MG's tiny boot, Perry said, "Laurel, you take these. I'll bring the rest of the bags."

"Give some to me." Keen to help, Ginny held out her arms. "I can carry those."

Perry looked across at Laurel and said, "See what I mean? Didn't I tell you how great she was?"

Ginny flushed with pleasure. She'd done the right thing.

Laurel nodded. "You did."

Once all the bags and cases had been taken up to the spare room, Ginny left them to it. In the kitchen she boiled the kettle and began making tea. After a couple of minutes, Perry rejoined her.

"Don't bother with tea."

"No? Would you prefer coffee?"

He shook his head and produced the bottle he'd been concealing behind his back.

"Woo, champagne. On a Saturday morning!" And Veuve Cliquot at that, none of your old rubbish.

"The very best time to drink it. Quick, glasses," said Perry as the cork rocketed out and bounced off the ceiling.

"Well, cheers." Ginny clinked her glass against his; he'd only filled two of the three she'd set out. "Isn't Laurel having any?"

"Laurel doesn't drink. Cheers. Here's to you."

If Gavin were here now, he would tell her that replying "here's to both of us" would be flirty beyond belief. So Ginny didn't; she just smiled instead and took a demure sip of the champagne. As they heard the sound of furniture being moved around in the bedroom overhead, she said,

"What's Laurel doing? Doesn't she want to join us?"

"She's fine, best to leave her to get on with it." Perry's eyes sparkled. "She's just rearranging the room, getting her things unpacked. You know how it is."

"Sorry?" Ginny thought she must have misheard. "What?"

Or it had been a slip of the tongue. Of course, that was it. Ginny smiled. "You just said she was getting *her* things unpacked."

Perry nodded. "Yes."

OK, hang on, had she fallen into some kind of parallel universe here? Her heart beginning to thump unpleasantly, Ginny said, "But . . . why would she be unpacking her things? She isn't the one moving in. I've rented the room to you."

Perry looked at her. "God, I'm sorry, is that what you thought? No, no, the room's not for me. It's for Laurel."

This couldn't be happening.

"But you were the one who came to see it! You said it was just what you were looking for!" Her voice rising—and not in an I-fancy-you way—Ginny said, "You said it was perfect!"

He blinked, nonplussed. "It *is* perfect. For Laurel."

Frantically, Ginny ran back through everything he'd told her. "No, *hang on,* you said your flat was too small . . ."

"It *is* too small. I mean, it's all right for me on my own," Perry explained, "but it's definitely a squash for two. Laurel moved in six weeks ago and, to be honest, it's been doing my head in."

Doing *your* head in! What do you suppose this is doing to *my* head? Still in a state of shock, Ginny repeated, "B-but I rented the room to *you*."

"I know you did. That's right. I paid the deposit and I'll be paying the rent," said Perry. "No need to worry about that. I'll set up a direct debit. Really, everything's going to be fine."

Fine? How *could* it be? Ginny's head was about to explode.

"You made me think it was you! You never once mentioned your sister. You *knew* I thought it was you."

Perry spread his arms. "Honestly, I didn't."

"But the whole point of interviewing people when they come to look at the room is so that you can decide whether you want to share your house with them!"

"Is it?" Perry looked genuinely bewildered. "I didn't realize." He paused, then said eagerly, "But it doesn't matter, because you won't have any problems with Laurel. As soon as I met you, I knew the two of you would get on brilliantly. You're just the kind of person Laurel needs."

What?

What?

Ginny wanted to yell, "This isn't about what

somebody else needs, you idiot; it's about what I need."

"Oh, and I've brought the references. You don't have anything to worry about with Laurel." Perry withdrew a couple of envelopes from his pocket. "She's honest, tidy, considerate—everything you could want in a housemate."

This was all going so desperately, horribly wrong that Ginny was struggling to think straight. She wished Gavin could be here to back her up because right now she appeared to be the only one who thought there was anything amiss. Except if Gavin were here, he'd be too busy laughing his socks off at the mess she'd managed to get herself into. Ha, that was what happened when you got carried away and were silly enough to think someone might actually find you attractive.

"Besides," Perry went on, "you did advertise for a female to share with. That was what you really wanted."

"So why didn't Laurel phone up the other night? Why didn't she come round to see the house herself?"

He sighed and refilled his glass with champagne. Offered the bottle to Ginny, who shook her head.

"Laurel was happy to carry on sleeping on my sofa. Finding somewhere else to live wasn't a priority as far as she was concerned. To be honest she's been a bit down lately. She broke up with her boyfriend last summer and things haven't been easy for her since then. She lost her job in London. Her ex-boyfriend met someone else and got engaged, which didn't help. Laurel was pretty fed up. I told her she should move out of the city and the next thing I knew, she'd turned up on my doorstep." Perry paused, shrugged. "Well, it was fine for a few days. It was great to see her again. Except she's decided she wants to stay in Portsilver now and my flat really isn't big enough for the two of us."

"So move to a bigger flat."

"Oh, Ginny, I'm sorry. I didn't mean to spring this on you. But I'm used to living on my own. I like my own space. And when I met you, I just thought how fantastic you were, so chatty and bubbly, and I knew you'd be perfect for Laurel. Sharing a house with you is just what she needs to perk her up again."

Ginny shook her head. This wasn't supposed to be happening; it wasn't what she wanted. And she was going to have to tell him.

"The thing is, I—"

"Look, you'll have a great time with Laurel." Perry gazed at her. "And much as I'd like to be the one moving in here, that could never happen."

"Why couldn't it?" Ginny rubbed her aching temples; she didn't understand why not.

His eyes crinkled at the corners. "Come on, you

must know the answer to that one. You're gorgeous. How could I live in this house when I fancy the landlady rotten? That would be . . . God, that would be impossible."

Oh. Ginny hadn't been expecting this. Talk about a bolt from the blue. So he *did* find her attractive.

"Sorry, was that a bit sudden?" Perry's smile was rueful. "Have I scared you witless?"

"No, no . . ."

"I'm usually a bit more subtle. But you did ask. If I'm honest, I've been sitting here wondering if you'd consider coming out to dinner with me next week. But who knows if I'll have the courage to ask you?" He pulled a wry face and said, "It's a scary thing, you know, being a man. We always have to run the risk of inviting someone out and being turned down flat. You women don't realize how fragile our egos are."

Ginny was lost for words. As she was floundering for a reply, they both heard footsteps on the stairs. The next moment the door had swung open and Laurel entered the kitchen.

"I've unpacked."

"Great." Perry beamed at her. "Well, that didn't take too long, did it? Good girl."

Oh hell. Ginny took another gulp of champagne and found herself unable to meet Laurel's eye. If she was going to say something it had to be now, this minute. But how could she say it? How could she tell Laurel that she wasn't moving in after all, that she should get back upstairs and start repacking all her things?

"Is something wrong?" said Laurel.

Her heart beginning to gallop, Ginny mentally rehearsed telling her that there had been a terrible mistake, that she couldn't stay here because . . . well, because . . . um, because . . .

"Perry? What's going on?"

Perry looked at Laurel and shrugged.

"Look, I'm sorry," Ginny blurted out, "but I didn't realize you were the one who'd be moving in. There's been a bit of a misunderstanding here. I thought your brother was the one looking for a room."

Laurel frowned. "No. He's already got his flat."

"Well, I know that *now*." Her knuckles white, Ginny exclaimed, "But he didn't mention it before."

Laurel gazed steadily at her. "So what are you saying?"

Oh God, what was she saying? In a complete flap now, Ginny felt the heat rushing back to her face. She was British, for heaven's sake. It wasn't in her nature to deliberately hurt another person's feelings. If she didn't have Laurel, she'd have to go through the whole advertising-and-interviewing rigmarole all over again and who was to say she'd get anyone better next time round? Plus, Perry fancied her anyway and was going to invite her out to dinner. Which was good news and almost better, in a way, than—

"Don't you want me here?" There were now tears glistening in Laurel's huge green eyes. "Do I have to go?"

That was it. How could she say yes and live with herself? Shaking her head, Ginny said, "No, no, of course you don't have to go. Everything's fine."

Laurel blinked back her tears and smiled a watery smile. "Thank you."

Perry beamed with relief. "Excellent."

Instantly, Ginny felt better, no longer twisted with guilt. There, she'd done it. And she had a first date with Perry to look forward to, so everything *was* going to be fine. Forgetting what he'd told her earlier, she seized the champagne bottle and said gaily to Laurel, "Let's celebrate!"

"I'm not allowed to drink." Laurel shook her head. "Because of my tablets."

Tablets. Everything was going to be fine, Ginny reminded herself. Aloud she said sympathetically, "Antibiotics?"

Laurel blinked. "Antidepressants."

Oh.

"Right, I'd better get back to the shop." Perry jumped up. "I'll leave you two girls to get to know each other. Bye."

Hastily, Ginny said, "I'll just show you out," and followed him to the front door.

"She's a lovely girl. You won't regret it." Perry

kept his voice low. "Listen, I'll be in touch. If I manage to pluck up the courage to ask you out to dinner sometime soon, do you think you might say yes?" His smile was playful.

Ginny replied flirtatiously, "I might."

"Great. I'll give you a call. Just do me a favor, don't mention it to Laurel."

"Why not?" Ginny was puzzled.

"Oh, it's just that she's been through a bit of a bad patch with men, you know? She's kind of anti-relationships right now. I told her you were divorced and she liked the idea of sharing a house with someone else in the same boat. If she knew we were meeting up with each other, she might feel a bit odd-one-out."

Ginny wondered if she really was doing the right thing here. Somehow, in the space of a morning, all her plans had been turned inside out. What had she let herself in for?

"Shhh, stop worrying." Evidently capable of reading her thoughts—or more likely the panicky God-what-have-I-done look in her eyes—Perry raised his right index finger to his lips then smiled and tenderly pressed that same finger against her own mouth. "You two'll have a great time. You're just what Laurel needs to get over her dip."

Brushing his finger like that against her lips had set off a deliciously zingy sensation in Ginny's knees. Crikey, if that was kissing by proxy, she couldn't wait for the real thing.

Anyway, of course she and Laurel would get on; hadn't she been through dips of her own in her time? Together they would bond and forge a real friendship.

"I really have to go." Perry was glancing at his watch.

Ginny opened the front door and said, "Bye then," her mouth still tingling from the proxy kiss.

Everything *was* going to be fine.

"I think Perry got fed up with hearing me talk about it," Laurel said tonelessly. "Men aren't into that kind of thing, are they? Especially brothers. Every time I mentioned Kevin he'd try to change the subject. But I *have* to talk about Kevin," she went on. "It's like a compulsion. I loved him so much, you see. *So* much. And I can't just wipe him out of my life because he's still here." She tapped the side of her head. "I think about him all the time. How can you forget someone who's broken your heart, smashed it into a million pieces?"

"Well," Ginny said uncertainly, "er . . ."

"Although he's probably forgotten me." Laurel wiped her eyes with a proper hanky. (Not even a tissue.) "Because I just don't matter to him anymore, do I? Kevin's moved on now; he met someone else in no time flat and loved her enough to ask her to marry him. I used to drive past his house, you know. One evening I saw them kissing on the front doorstep. I was so unhappy I thought I'd die. And you know what? She had fat ankles. Fat ankles, I swear! Really . . . *chubby*."

Ginny did her best to look suitably shocked and sympathetic, but a terrible urge to yawn was creeping up her rib cage, threatening to make a bid for freedom the millisecond she relaxed the muscles in her jaw. For ninety minutes now she had been listening to the Story of Kevin. Ninety minutes was the length of an entire film. She could have watched *Anna Karenina* and been less depressed.

"I suppose I'm boring you," Laurel said flatly.

"No, no." Hastily Ginny shook her head.

"It's just that I thought we'd get married and have babies and be happy together for the rest of our lives, but he changed his mind and now I'm just left without *anything*. He'll probably have babies with her now instead. I can't bear to think of it. Why does life have to be so unfair?"

Oh dear, yet another unanswerable question. Slightly desperate by now, Ginny said, "I don't know, but how about if you try to . . . um, stop thinking about him quite so much?"

Laurel gave her a pitying look, as if she'd just suggested switching off gravity. "But I loved him so much. He was my whole world. He still *is*."

Oh God.

Chapter 11

DESPITE HAVING PROMISED TO be in touch, Perry Kennedy hadn't called and Ginny was in need of some serious cheering up. Carla, who hadn't said as much yet but already wasn't sure she trusted Laurel's smooth-talking brother, made an executive decision and said, "Right, I'm taking you out to lunch."

Ginny looked up, surprised. "When?"

"Today. Now. Unless you don't want to."

"Are you kidding?" Ginny's eyes lit up. "Of course I want to."

"Sure?"

"Yesss!"

Carla shrugged. "Because if you'd rather stay at home and have a lovely girly chat with your new best friend Laurel, I'd quite understand."

"Noooo!"

"No, really, I mean who in their right mind would want to come out to lunch with me when they could sit in their kitchen talking about Kevin Kevin Kevin . . ."

"*I* would," Ginny pleaded.

"Kevin Kevin Kevin Kevin . . . ooh, and then a teeny bit more about Kevin."

"Shut up and take me out to lunch."

Carla loved her job and was good at it. When potential clients contacted Portsilver Conservatories, she made an appointment to visit them in their homes and employed her own special no-pressure sales technique to persuade them that if they wanted the perfect conservatory, then her company was the one for them.

And in almost every case Carla succeeded. She was great at charming the clients and enabling them to imagine the joy a sunny conservatory would bring into their lives. She traveled all over the southwest and often worked in the evenings and at weekends, but that was a bonus too because it meant she could take other days off whenever she liked.

Like today, which she was determined was going to be a memorable one because the last few months hadn't been easy for her friend Ginny. She deserved a break. Personally, Carla suspected that this sudden crush on Perry was largely down to the fact that it had been a long time since Ginny had been so comprehensively targeted by an attractive man. From what she could gather, Perry Kennedy had made quite a play for her and she had been flattered by the attention. For Ginny's sake, Carla hoped she didn't end up getting hurt.

Ginny was enjoying herself already. Here they were whizzing along in Carla's sporty black Golf, the sun was out, and she wasn't going to feel guilty about leaving Laurel at home cleaning the kitchen floor. She hadn't asked or expected her to, but Laurel had volunteered herself for the task, saying sadly, "I like doing housework; it makes me feel useful. I used to do the kitchen floor every day when I was with Kevin."

She had also, as Ginny was escaping the house, leaned back on her heels and said, "I do like living here. It's nice us sharing, isn't it?"

Ginny hadn't known how to respond to this. She could hardly announce that it was about as much fun as sharing a house with Sylvia Plath.

Anyway. Three blissful Kevin-free hours stretched ahead. Maybe this was the answer to all her problems; she would simply have to become one of those ladies who lunched, every day of the week.

Well, maybe if she won the lottery first.

"I wonder what he's doing now?" said Carla.

Instantly thinking of Perry, Ginny said, "Who?"

"Kevin."

"Don't. We mustn't make fun of her."

"I'm not making fun, I'm really wondering. I'd love to meet him," Carla said mischievously. "Drag him into bed. Find out what all the fuss is about, see if he's worth all the hoo-ha."

"Just as well he's living in London, then. So what's wrong with Jamie?"

"Nothing at all." Her boy toys didn't usually last four months, but Jamie had spent three of them away in Australia. "He's great, better than any keep-fit video," said Carla. "But you know me; I like to keep my options open. You just never know, do you, when you might meet someone that little bit more perfect. Ah, here we are." She indicated right and slowed down before turning into the driveway.

Ginny, reading the blue-and-gold sign, said, "Penhaligon's. It's supposed to be good here. We tried to book a table over Christmas but it was full."

"One of my clients recommended it. Lunch cost him two grand," said Carla, "and he still reckons it was worth it."

Two *grand?* Yikes. "I promise I'll just have the stale bread and tap water," said Ginny.

The restaurant was housed in a long, white-washed, and ivy-strewn sixteenth-century farm-house with a gray slate roof and a bright red front door. A series of smartly renovated interlinked outbuildings extended from one end of the farm-house, forming three sides of a rectangle around the central courtyard. As Carla parked the car between an old dusty blue Astra and a gleaming scarlet Porsche, a black cat darted out of one of the outbuildings ahead of a middle-aged man carrying a small wooden cabinet. The man proceeded to load the cabinet into the back of a van. The cat, tail flicking ominously slowly, looked as if it might be about to launch itself at the man's legs.

"It's a restaurant and antiques center," explained Carla, fairly pointlessly as there was a sign saying so above the door. "Quite a nifty idea. My client came here last week with his wife to celebrate their wedding anniversary. They got a bit tiddly over lunch, went to have a look around afterward, and ended up buying a Georgian chandelier for eighteen hundred pounds."

Ginny was out of the car gazing up at the buildings. Sunlight bounced off the windows, and the glossy tendrils of ivy swayed gently in the breeze. The smell of wonderfully garlicky cooking mingled with wood smoke hung in the air. Animated chatter spilled out of the restaurant, and from the antiques center came the sound of Robbie Williams singing "Angels." Well, it probably wasn't Robbie Williams in person. But wouldn't it be completely brilliant if it was?

The black cat took a swipe at the man who was now closing the van doors. Darting out of the way, he said, "Don't get pissy; it's mine now."

"Nnnaaarrh," sneered the cat, before turning and stalking off.

"Bloody animal," the man called after it.

"You've gone quiet." Having watched him jump into the van and drive off, Carla gave Ginny a playful nudge. "Cat got your tongue?"

And in a way it had. Well, maybe not the cat, but the sights and sounds and smells of Penhaligon's Restaurant and Antiques Center. Captivated by the unexpected charm of it all, Ginny felt as if she was falling a little bit in love at first sight.

"One more drink," Ginny urged, waggling the bottle of Fleurie at Carla. "Go on, you can have another."

"I mustn't, I'm driving."

"Leave the car. We'll come and pick it up tomorrow morning. God, I *love* it here. Why can't all restaurants be like this?"

For a Tuesday lunchtime in February, Penhaligon's was impressively busy. The restaurant, with its deep red walls covered in prints and original paintings, was eclectically furnished with an assortment of antique furniture. The atmosphere was unstuffily friendly and the food divine. Having guzzled her starter of scallops in lemon sauce, Ginny was now finishing her smoked beef main course. Not to mention the best part of a bottle of wine.

"Go on then, you've twisted my arm," said Carla. "Just don't let me buy anything next door."

One bottle became two. They talked nonstop for the next hour and watched through the window as the black cat stalked and intimidated visitors crossing the courtyard. A selection of music ranging from Frank Sinatra to Black Sabbath drifted across from the antiques center and every so often they could hear the kitchen staff joining in and singing along.

"Coffee and a brandy, please," Carla told the waitress when she came to take their order. "Gin?"

Ginny nodded in agreement. "Lovely."

The waitress looked startled. "Coffee and a gin? Crikey, are you sure?"

"Two coffees and brandies." Carla was grinning. "Her name's Gin."

"Oh phew! I thought it sounded a bit weird! Just as well I checked." The girl shook her head by way of apology. "Sorry, my brain's had enough today. Busy busy."

"Hey, Martha," one of the men at the next table called over. "On your own today, sweetheart? What happened to Simmy?"

"Simmy shimmied off to Thailand with her boyfriend. Well, three hours' notice—what more could we ask? So now we have to find a new waitress before my feet drop off. If you fancy the job, Ted, just say the word."

Ted, who was in his sixties, said, "I'd make a rubbish waitress, love. Don't have the legs for it. Table six are asking for their bill, by the way."

"Thanks, Ted. Right, two coffees and two brandies. I'll bring them as soon as I can."

Martha hurried off and Carla shared out the last of the second bottle of wine. She looked over at Ginny.

Ginny gazed back at her.

"What are you thinking?" Carla said finally.

"You know what I'm thinking." A little spiral of

excitement was corkscrewing its way up through Ginny's solar plexus. "I could work here. I'd love to work here."

"Are you sure? It's only February."

"I don't care." Working seasonally meant she was usually employed from April to October, but what the heck? Penhaligon's was calling her name. Last year she had worked in a tea shop down on the front, which had been busy but not what you'd call riveting. Currant buns and cucumber sandwiches lost their appeal after a while and practically their entire clientele— evidently attracted by the ruched cream lace curtains and the sign above the door saying Olde Tea Shoppe—had been over eighty. Ginny's toes had been run over by more recklessly driven wheelchairs than you could shake a walking stick at.

Her toes flinching at the memory, Ginny said, "It's got to be better than the Olde Tea Shoppe."

Nodding in agreement, Carla shuddered and said, "Not to mention Kid Hell."

It hadn't really been called that, but it should have been. Kid Heaven!—complete with jaunty exclamation mark—was the children's activity center where Ginny had worked as a face painter two summers ago, struggling to paint animal faces on screaming, wriggling children who either had ice cream already smeared around their mouths, lollipops they refused to stop licking, or summer colds accompanied by extravagantly runny noses and cheeks awash with . . . well, let's just say it played havoc with the face paints.

Not that Carla had ever witnessed this debacle firsthand—she was no fool and children were in her view quite pointless—but she'd heard enough about it from Ginny to know that this was a job on a par with sifting sewage with your bare teeth.

"I want to work *here,*" Ginny repeated. "I've just got a feeling about this place." Counting off the reasons on her fingers she burbled excitedly, "It's only . . . what, three miles from home? And no problems parking, *that's* a bonus. And the only reason I've never done proper waitressing before is because I didn't want to work evening shifts while Jem was at home, but now she's gone it doesn't matter!"

"And you'd be getting away from Laurel," Carla drily pointed out.

"Oh God, that sounds terrible!"

"Terrible but true. You've gone and landed yourself with the world's most boring lodger and any sane person would get rid of her. But you're too soft to do that, so you're going to take a job to keep you out of your own house because anything's better than having to stay in it and listen to loopy Laurel droning on about Kevin."

This was only semitrue. OK, maybe she was soft—a *bit*—but there was also Perry to be factored into the equation. Ginny sensed that turfing his sister out into the street might not win her too many Brownie points in his eyes.

Knocking back her wine with a flourish, she said, "Laurel or no Laurel, it makes no difference. If I want to be a waitress, I *can* be a waitress. I think this place is great, and I'd love to work here."

"*Would* you?"

"Oh!" Ginny hadn't realized Martha was standing behind her with their drinks, patiently waiting for her to stop waving her arms around before putting the tray down on the table. Filled with resolve, she exclaimed, "Well, yes, I would. Definitely!"

"Hey, excellent." Martha's freckled face lit up. "I'll tell Evie, shall I? She manages the restaurant. She'll be thrilled."

"They're desperate; they're going to sign you up before you can say slave labor," Carla murmured as Martha hurried away. "This must be a hellhole of a place to work. Now don't go rushing into anything."

"I want to rush into it! Oh listen, now they're playing Queen." Ginny clapped her hands as the drumbeats of "We Will Rock You" rang out across the courtyard. "How can it be a hellhole when they play Queen?"

"Better stop talking about hellholes. And don't sing," Carla ordered. "Save the Freddie Mercury impression for later—the big boss is on her way over."

The manageress click-clacked across the floor in double-quick time. She was in her midfifties, tall, and as elegant as a racehorse, with tawny blond hair fastened up in a chignon and beautifully applied makeup including Bardot-style eyeliner and glossy red lipstick. Smiling broadly she held out her hand. "Hi, I'm Evie Sutton. Lovely to meet you. When you've finished your lunch, would you like to come and have a chat with me in my office, or . . . ?"

"We're just drinking our coffee." Indicating the spare chair at their table and feeling deliciously proactive, Ginny said, "If you like we can talk about it now."

Twenty minutes later she had the job. Three lunchtime and four evening shifts a week, starting as soon as she liked.

"Tomorrow, if you want," said Evie as she handed her an application form. "Just fill this in and bring it with you, and we'll sort you out with a uniform then."

"Perfect." Ginny could hardly wait. "Thank you so much, I know I'm going to love it here."

"Oh you will, I can tell. We'll soon have you charming those customers. And you've certainly made my day." Evie's blue eyes danced. "There's nothing more depressing than having to interview a bunch of no-hopers."

Liking her more and more, Ginny said with feeling, "Tell me about it."

Chapter 12

"WE AREN'T GOING HOME yet. I want to see the antiques center." Buzzing with excitement and with her inhibitions loosened by alcohol, Ginny practically skipped across the sunny courtyard.

Inside the converted outbuildings, the stone walls were painted emerald green and an Aladdin's cave of well-lit paintings, mirrors, polished furniture, and *objets d'art* greeted them. In the center of the main room stood a magnificent jukebox currently playing Stevie Wonder's "Superstition." Further along, in one of the interlinked rooms to the right, they could see someone showing a couple of potential customers a walnut bureau. On the sales desk by the window stood a mug of coffee, a half-eaten KitKat, and an open copy of *Miller's Guide to Antiques*. Just poking out from beneath it was the latest edition of *Heat*.

"Look at this." Ginny longingly ran her fingers over a bronze velvet chaise longue. Turning over the price tag, she blanched and abruptly stopped envisaging it in her living room.

"Never mind that, look at *these*." Twenty feet away, Carla held up a pair of heavy silver Georgian candlesticks. "I love them!"

"Stop it." Ginny's eyes danced as Carla

attempted to stuff them into her cream leather handbag. "*Bad* girl. Put them back."

"Damn bag's not big enough. No forward planning, that's my trouble. Ooh, now this is smaller." Picking up an enameled box, Carla playfully waggled it.

"Antlers!" Ginny let out a shriek of delight and rushed over to take a closer look. "I've always wanted a pair of real antlers."

"They wouldn't suit you. And you definitely couldn't slip those into your handbag." As she said this, Carla's gaze slid past Ginny.

"And I'd rather you didn't try it."

The moment she heard the voice behind her, Ginny knew. So did her skin, which came out in a shower of goose bumps, and her stomach, which reacted with a nauseous lurch of recognition.

"You can put that down too," the voice continued, this time addressing Carla.

Taken aback by his tone, Carla put down the decorative enameled box and said chippily, "I wasn't going to steal it, you know. We were just having a bit of fun. It was a *joke*."

"Good job you're not a stand-up comedian then. People might ask for their money back."

"Well, you're full of charm, aren't you?" Her eyes flashing, Carla demanded, "Is this how you treat all your customers?"

"Not at all." His reply was cool. "But you don't appear to be customers, do you? Call me old-fashioned but I'd class a customer as someone who pays for what she takes from a shop."

Ginny closed her eyes. This was awful, just *awful,* and Carla was practically incandescent with—

"How dare you!" Carla shouted, marching toward the door. "As if anyone in their right mind would even *want* to buy anything from your crappy shop. Come on, Gin, we're out of here. And don't worry; I won't ever be coming to this dump again."

But *I* will, Ginny thought in a panic.

"Excellent." Moving to one side, the man allowed Carla to stalk past him. "Mission accomplished."

"No, it isn't," Ginny blurted out. "Stop! Carla, come back, we're going to sort this out."

"*Ha.* The only way we could sort this out is if I gored him to death with his own antlers." Jabbing furiously at her phone, Carla said, "Hello? Hello? Yes, I want a taxi this minute . . ."

"We came here for lunch." Ginny turned in desperation to face the man. "We had a lovely meal."

"Did you pay for it?"

"Yes!"

His eyes glittered. "With your own credit card or with somebody else's?"

"Oh, for crying out loud, will you stop accusing me? We haven't—"

"Oh great, you're still here!" Evie appeared in the shop doorway, a bright smile on her face. "I just came over to tell Finn all about you, but I see you've already met. Finn, did Ginny tell you the good news?"

"No, I didn't," Ginny said hurriedly. "You see, there's been a bit of a—"

"We don't have to advertise for a new waitress!" Evie turned to Finn. "This is Ginny Holland, and she's coming to work for us; isn't that—"

"No, she's not," Finn said flatly. *Very* flatly.

"I'm coming to work for *you,*" said Ginny, looking at Evie and praying she'd believe her when the whole sorry story came tumbling out.

"Maybe you thought you were," Finn countered, "but Evie only runs the restaurant. My name's Finn Penhaligon and I own it, which means you *won't* be working here because I say so."

Evie's expression changed. "Finn, could I have a private word with you outside?"

He actually looked amused. "Probably not the wisest idea. I'd prefer it if we were in here and these two stayed outside."

Ginny felt as if her head was about to burst with the unfairness of it all. She'd *so* wanted to work here, and it clearly wasn't going to happen now.

"It's him, isn't it?" Having worked out what was happening, Carla's lip curled with disgust. "He's the one from that shop who made you cry."

"I'd love to know what's going on here," said Evie, bewildered.

"I'm sure he'll tell you. Sorry about the job." Ginny swallowed hard. "I'd have loved to work for you." Following Carla to the door she checked she wasn't inadvertently holding some antique *objet* then opened her bag wide to demonstrate to Finn Penhaligon that there was nothing that belonged to him inside. Determined to retain at least a shred of dignity, she then met his gaze and said steadily, "I know you think you're right, but you're wrong."

"I know what I saw." Unmoved by her declaration, Finn shrugged. "You know what really gave you away? The way you looked at me when I stopped you outside that shop."

The way she'd looked at him. In any other circumstances, Ginny might have laughed. He would never know it, but that hadn't been guilt flickering in her eyes.

It had been lust.

It was midnight, clouds were scudding past the moon, and Ginny and Carla were on a mission under cover of darkness to retrieve Carla's car from the courtyard of Penhaligon's without being seen.

"What a *jerk*." Carla was still seething about the treatment they had received earlier at the hands of Finn Penhaligon.

Ginny concentrated on the road ahead. "I know."

"I mean, that man has a serious attitude problem!"

"I know." Nearly there now.

"You didn't tell me he was that good-looking."

Ginny knew that too. She hadn't told Carla that she'd fantasized about Finn Penhaligon. And since it was pretty irrelevant, she didn't see the point in telling her now. "Is this the turn, up here? God, what if he's there? We should have worn balaclavas."

"Balaclavas aren't my style. Besides, then he'd probably threaten us with a shotgun and I'd have to kill him with my bare hands. OK, here we go." Carla leaned forward as they entered the courtyard and saw her green Golf parked on its own by the far wall. "Just swing round, pull up next to my car, and I'll jump out. We'll be gone in—what's that on the windscreen? If that sad git's given me a parking ticket . . ."

She was out of the car in a flash. As she wrenched the envelope out from under the windscreen wiper, a dark shadow darted across the yard, meowing loudly. For a couple of seconds the cat was caught in the beam of Ginny's headlights before it leaped forward again and disappeared from view. Oh brilliant, now it was probably under the car and if she tried to drive off she'd kill it.

Hurriedly buzzing down her window, Ginny hissed, "Where's the cat?"

"Don't know, but this is for you." Carla handed her the envelope. "Probably a restraining order warning you not to go within five miles of him."

"My pleasure." Ripping open the envelope, Ginny said, "Just see if that cat's under the car, will you?"

She was forced to switch on the interior light to read the note, which was from Evie. It was brief and to the point.

Dear Ginny,
We need you! Sorry about today—Finn can be a grumpy bugger sometimes, but he's all right really. I've spoken to him now and sorted everything out. I really hope you'll come and work here. Please give me a ring.

"What is it?" Carla was peering through the open window. "What does it say? God, what's that?" As a door suddenly slammed across the yard, she jumped and whacked her head on the window frame. "Ow, that hurts."

"It's him." Reading Evie's words was all very well, but Ginny still had an overwhelming urge to stick her foot down and, tires squealing, make a high-speed Steve McQueen–style getaway.

Except it wouldn't only be the tires squealing if she ran over the damn cat. Stuck where she was, Ginny watched warily as Finn Penhaligon made his way across the courtyard. He was wearing a white shirt and dark trousers, and she didn't trust him an inch.

"On the bright side," said Carla, "he isn't carrying a gun."

"Unless there's one in his pocket." Ginny gave a nervous hiccup of laughter. "Although I can't say he looks pleased to see us."

"Damn, he's good-looking though."

Carla hadn't said it loudly but noise evidently traveled across an otherwise empty courtyard.

"Thank you." Gravely, Finn nodded at her, then turned his attention to Ginny. "Have you read Evie's note?"

"Yes."

"And?"

"And she's right." With a surge of reckless bravery Ginny said, "You are a grumpy bugger."

The look in his eyes told her he hadn't read the note himself, hadn't realized that this was what Evie had said about him. The next moment, to his credit, he smiled briefly.

"Well, maybe that's true. But I wouldn't necessarily call that a bad thing. What else did she say?"

"That she'd spoken to you and everything was sorted out." Ginny still couldn't quite believe this was happening, that she was here, in the early hours of the morning, sitting in her car, having this conversation. "And she still wants me to come and work in the restaurant. Well, officially, I'd be working in the restaurant. Unofficially, of course, I'd be fiddling the bills, pocketing all the tips, and cloning people's credit cards."

"I may have overreacted," said Finn. "When you're in this line of business, believe me, shoplifters are the bane of your life."

Furiously, Carla hissed, "Excuse me, she's *not* a—"

"OK, OK." Finn held up his hands. "Let's not get into all that again." Addressing Ginny, he said evenly, "Look, if you want the job, it's yours."

Ginny could hear her pulse thud-thudding in her ears. On the one hand it would be gloriously satisfying to be able to tell him to stick his magnanimous offer *and* his lousy rotten restaurant up his bum.

On the other hand it wasn't a lousy rotten restaurant, was it? And despite everything that had happened, she did still want the job.

Finally, Ginny said, "What did Evie say to make you change your mind?"

His eyes glittered. "Truthfully?"

"Truthfully."

"I told her about the first time we met in that shop in Portsilver." Finn paused. "And Evie told me that she'd once walked out of a department store holding a Christian Dior mascara. She didn't realize until she'd reached her car; she took it back to the store, and the saleswoman said not to worry, that she'd once left a shop carrying two bath mats and a toilet brush."

Ginny looked at him. "Is your cat under my car?"

He shook his head. "No, she shot past me into the flat when I came out. So how about this job then? What shall I tell Evie?"

Revving the car's engine, Ginny said cheerily, "Tell her I'll think it over." Then, because it wasn't often she felt quite this in control, she flashed Finn Penhaligon a dazzling, up-yours smile. "Bye!"

Chapter 13

GINNY'S HEART LIFTED WHEN she heard Jem's voice; a phone call from her daughter always cheered her up.

"Hi, Mum, how's it all going? Are you and Laurel having a blast?"

If only. What was the opposite of a blast? A tired phfft, perhaps. Expecting Perry and getting Laurel instead had been like setting out on holiday to Disneyland then having your plane hijacked and diverted to Siberia.

"We're fine!" Ginny was determined not to admit her catastrophic mistake to Jem. "Laurel's settling in. How about you? Everything OK?"

"Better than OK." Jem sounded on top form. "I'm having such a great time, Mum."

"Oh, darling, I'm so glad." Impulsively, Ginny said, "Listen, you haven't been home since Christmas. Why don't you and Lucy come down this weekend? It'd do you good to have a break, and Dad would love to see—"

"Mum, I can't. My shifts at the pub, remember? I'm doing Saturday evening and Sunday lunchtime."

Bloody pub.

"Well, I hope you're not wearing yourself out," said Ginny. "I could send a bit more money if you want. Then you wouldn't have to work so hard."

"I like working in the pub. Don't worry about me. And it's not long now until Easter, is it? I'll pop down then."

Pop? Ginny didn't like the sound of pop one bit. Her composure momentarily slipping, she said, "Pop? I thought you'd be back for the whole of the Easter break."

"Well, that was the plan, obviously. But the landlord's already asked me to work through Easter. If I tell him I'll be away for a couple of weeks I might lose my job. Oh God, is it half nine already? I've got a tutorial at ten. Mum, I'll ring you again next week; you look after yourself and give my love to Dad. Have fun! Bye!"

Ginny had always been a great one for singing in the shower but this morning she wasn't in the mood. She missed Jem so much it hurt. She missed Bellamy dreadfully too. Instead of a life-enhancing new lodger-cum-friend, she had Laurel. And instead of some form—*any* form—of love life, she had a big empty void. Perry Kennedy, needless to say, had reneged on his promise to call and arrange a date for dinner, which made her feel not only unattractive, but also a complete fool to boot, because she'd been gullible enough to believe he might.

Well, enough was enough. This was her life and it was up to her to be in charge of it. Ginny switched off the shower and wrapped herself in a blue towel, then wiped condensation from the bathroom mirror and gazed steadily at her reflection. She wasn't a doormat and the time had come, yet again, to prove it. This morning while she'd been in the kitchen making a cup of tea, she had seen squirrels chasing each other across the lawn and said aloud, "I bet they can't believe their luck, having the garden to themselves after all these years. Bellamy used to chase them nonstop."

Laurel, scraping margarine very thinly indeed over her slice of whole meal toast, had replied, "You won't get another dog, will you." It had been a statement rather than a question. "I don't like dogs."

"Why not?"

"They're dirty. They smell."

As offended as if she'd said, "*You're* dirty, *you*

smell," Ginny had vehemently shaken her head. "Maybe some dogs. Not Bellamy."

But Laurel had simply shrugged and said, "Anyway, I still don't like them," before wandering out of the kitchen with her plate of toast.

Now, recalling this exchange, Ginny vigorously towel-dried her hair. It was too soon to replace Bellamy—she would feel as if she were betraying his memory—but if she told Laurel that she was getting another dog, would Laurel decide she could no longer live here? Could this be the answer to her prayers? OK, so it would be a lie, but infinitely easier than announcing to Laurel that due to the fact that she was boring and miserable and droned on endlessly about Kevin, she would have to move out.

Ginny brightened. Oh yes, this was an excellent idea, a fictitious dog.

And a smelly one at that.

"There you are." Radio Two was playing in the background and Laurel was in the kitchen making bread when Ginny headed downstairs, dressed and ready to go out. "You look great. I really like your dress."

"Thanks." Laurel had a disconcerting habit of being nice when you were least expecting it.

"Look, I'm sorry if I seemed a bit rude earlier. I didn't mean to imply that your dog wasn't clean. And I'm sure he was lovely."

"He was." Terrified that Laurel was about to announce that she adored dogs, Ginny said hastily, "Although he wasn't always clean, of course. Dogs will be dogs! Bellamy loved nothing more than splashing through muddy puddles or rolling in foxes' poo."

"Anyway, I'm sorry. And as soon as this bread's done, I'm going to make a cherry and almond cake. Your favorite."

"Right. Well, thanks." Guiltily, Ginny said, "You don't have to do that."

"I want to. You deserve it. Perry rang while you were in the shower, by the way. I told him how happy I was here."

Perry had rung! Ginny's cheeks heated up at the mention of him. Or should he be addressed by his full name of Perry Bloody Lying Jerk?

Kneading away at the dough on the table, Laurel went on, "He said could you give him a call when you've got a moment. Something to do with setting up the direct debit."

"Right, thanks." Did that mean he really wanted to talk to her about the direct debit? Casually, Ginny said, "Well, I'd better be off. See you later."

"Bye." Laurel's clear green eyes abruptly filled with tears and her chin began to tremble.

Oh God, what now? Bewildered, Ginny hesitated in the doorway.

"Are you . . . will you be OK?"

"Yes, yes." Floury hands flapping, Laurel wiped

her eyes with her thin upper arms and nodded at the radio, now playing the Osmonds' "Crazy Horses." "Sorry, it's this song. It just reminds me so much of Kevin."

Climbing into the car, Ginny told herself she'd phone Perry in her own good time. No need to appear overeager. She had lots to do today, *lots* to do, not least paying a visit to Penhaligon's to see Evie and discuss—

Oh sod it.

The moment Ginny was round the corner and out of sight of the house she pulled up at the curb and dug her mobile out of her bag.

"Hi there! How are you?" Perry sounded delighted to hear from her. "How's everything going with Laurel?"

"Um, well . . ." Clutching the phone, Ginny cursed her inability to tell him the truth; it was all her parents' fault for drumming into her as a child the importance of being polite. "Fine."

"You see? Didn't I tell you it would be? And Laurel's so much happier now. You've done wonders with her."

Ginny's mouth was dry with anticipation. "Laurel said something about the direct debit?" Here was Perry's cue to laugh and reply, "Hey, that was just an excuse to speak to you about our dinner date."

Instead, he said, "Actually, that was just an

excuse to speak to you about Laurel's tablets. The thing is, she'd hate it if she thought I was checking up on her but it's important that she keeps taking them. I thought maybe you could subtly remind her next week about dropping the repeat prescription into the pharmacy; otherwise, she'll run out."

And become even more depressed. It didn't bear thinking about.

"Right." Ginny bit her lip.

"Great."

Disappointment flooded through her. "Is that all?"

"Yes, I think so. Well, I'll leave you to get on . . ."

Buggering hell, that *was* all! Sick to the back teeth of being polite—walked all over, more like—Ginny blurted out, "To be honest, I don't think this is going to work. Maybe you should start looking for somewhere else for Laurel to live. I did say that if things didn't work out I'd give you four weeks'—"

"Whoa, *whoa*." Perry sounded alarmed. "I can't believe you're saying this."

Ginny couldn't quite believe it either, but she just had. The words had come tumbling out in a rush like baked beans from a can.

"Ginny, where are you now? We need to talk about this. Look, I know you don't want to go out to dinner with me but could we at least meet up for a quick drink? Are you busy today?"

Flummoxed, Ginny heard herself stammer, "W-well no, I suppose not."

"How about the Smugglers' Rest? Around one-ish, would that suit you?"

One-ish. That was two whole hours away. Trying not to sound too eager, Ginny said, "One o'clock, the Smugglers' Rest. Fine."

Perry was already there when she arrived, waiting at the bar. Hesitantly, he greeted her with a hand-shake—a *handshake!*—and said, "It's good to see you again, you're looking . . . no, sorry, mustn't say that. What can I get you to drink?"

Ginny waited until they were seated opposite each other at a table by the window before uttering the question that had been rampaging through her mind for the last two hours.

"On the phone, why did you say you knew I didn't want to go out to dinner with you?"

Perry shrugged, glanced out of the window, looked uncomfortable.

"Because I could tell. Sorry, I really liked you and got carried away. Made a bit of an idiot of myself, I suppose. Not for the first time. Like I said, it's scary having to make the first move and risk getting it wrong. And I realized I had, that's all. It was pretty obvious you weren't interested." Clearing his throat, he took a drink. "Look, this is embarrassing for me. Could we change the subject?"

"No." Far too curious to leave it now, Ginny said, "I don't know what I did to make you think that. I thought everything was fine. You asked me if I'd like to go out to dinner and I said yes."

Perry shook his head. "You said you might."

"I *meant* yes."

A glimmer of hope shone in his eyes. "I thought you were just being polite, sparing my feelings."

"Well, I wasn't," said Ginny. "I've been waiting for you to ring, like you said you would. I wondered why you hadn't called."

Perry looked as if he didn't believe her. "Seriously?"

"Seriously."

"I got it wrong?"

Ginny loved it that he was so vulnerable. "Completely wrong."

He clasped his head in his hands. "I'm such a prat. It's that fear-of-rejection thing. If I'm not five thousand percent convinced that someone's interested, I back off."

"Well, you shouldn't."

"Easier said than done." Perry's smile was crooked. "When you've been traumatized as a teenager, it kind of sticks with you. I plucked up the courage to invite a girl to the school disco when I was fifteen. She said OK and I was over the moon. Then I knocked on her front door to pick her up and her dad told me she'd gone out."

"You poor thing!" exclaimed Ginny.

"So I went to the disco on my own and there she was, with all her friends, and everyone knew. It turned out she'd only said yes for a bet. I was the laughingstock of the whole school."

Ginny's heart went out to him; she could picture the scene, imagine the agony he must have endured.

"Children are so cruel."

"Still, I should have grown out of it by now. Just goes to show what a coward I am." Pausing then taking a deep breath, Perry said, "So if I asked you out to dinner, you'd really say yes?"

"I would."

"*Really* really? And mean it? Five thousand percent sure about that?"

Who would have believed such a good-looking man—and one who appeared so confident on the surface—could be so unsure of himself? "Of course I mean it," said Ginny. "Five thousand percent sure. Maybe even six."

A broad smile spread across Perry's face. "OK, before I lose my nerve again, how about tomorrow night?"

"I'd love that." Ginny found herself nodding to emphasize just how much she'd love it.

"Great. We'll go to Penhaligon's."

Ah.

"Maybe not Penhaligon's. I'm seeing them this afternoon about a waitressing job."

"Hey, good for you! They do fantastic food. OK,

how about the Green Room on Tate Hill? I could meet you there at, say, eight o'clock?"

"Eight." Ginny was nodding again, happier than she'd imagined possible.

"Promise you won't stand me up?"

"I promise. So long as you don't stand me up either."

"No chance of that." Perry grinned and took her hand, gave it a quick squeeze. "You're incredible. No wonder Laurel's so happy living with you. She'd be distraught if she had to leave."

Oh God, that was true. Her conscience pricking, Ginny reached for her spritzer and took an icy gulp.

"So what's she done?" said Perry. "Is she untidy?"

"No."

"Doesn't do her share of the housework?"

"No, it's not that."

"Makes too much noise?"

Ginny squirmed. If anything, Laurel didn't make enough noise. She was quiet, thoughtful, considerate—technically, a model tenant with no annoying habits or antisocial tendencies.

"Does she break things? Use up all the hot water? Hog the TV remote?"

Laurel did none of these things. She just talked too much about Kevin, the man who had broken her heart.

"OK," Ginny conceded. "She can stay."

Perry's look of relief said it all. "Thank you. Really. God, I could . . . kiss you!" He glanced around the pub, which was filling up. "Well, maybe not in here."

"Chicken," Ginny said playfully.

"Is that a challenge?" He rose to his feet and pulled her up to meet him. The next moment he was kissing her—kissing her *properly*—right there in the middle of the pub with everyone watching.

Crikey, not so chicken after all.

"Bloody disgusting if you ask me." An ancient fisherman propping up the bar gave a snort of disgust.

"Wow. They're, like, really *old,*" giggled a skinny girl in a Day-Glo pink tube top.

A waitress, emerging from the kitchen with two plates piled high, shouted, "One vegetarian tart, one king-sized sausage."

Cue sniggers all round.

Hastily collecting herself, Ginny took a step back. "Let's get out of here."

Perry looked amused. "Your fault. You dared me to do it." Men, they really were the limit.

"Only because I didn't think you *would*."

Chapter 14

WHEN GINNY ARRIVED AT Penhaligon's, Evie Sutton greeted her like a long-lost sister. It was three o'clock and lunchtime service was over. They sat together over a pot of coffee in the empty restaurant discussing the job, hours, and wages, and Ginny filled in an application form.

"The shifts can be flexible, can't they? I mean, we're allowed to switch shifts if something crops up?" Apologetically, Ginny said, "It's just that my daughter's away at university. If she decides to come down and see me one weekend, I'd hate to be working nonstop." Not that Jem was showing much sign of coming down any time soon, but she lived in hope.

"No problem." Evie nodded to show she understood. "My three are all scattered around the country now; they've got their own lives. But when I can, I grab the chance to see them . . ."

"Oh I know. I miss Jem so much it's embarrassing!" Recognizing a kindred spirit, Ginny said eagerly, "In fact I've got a couple of photos in my purse."

"Me too!" Delightedly, Evie fetched her handbag from the office and brought out photographs of her own children. As they pored over them together, Ginny wondered why someone more like Evie—or better still Evie herself—couldn't have replied to her ad for a lodger.

The phone rang in the office and Evie, in the middle of an anecdote about her younger son, went to answer it. Moments later the door of the restaurant opened and Finn Penhaligon strode in, raising an eyebrow when he saw Ginny sitting there. "Oh. Hi."

"Hello." Ginny felt her mouth go dry; it was still hard to look at him without being reminded of a four-poster bed and ivory drapes billowing in the breeze. She really was going to have to knock that fantasy on the head, particularly seeing as she was the hussy who'd been kissed not two hours ago in front of a whole pub full of customers.

"Where's Evie?"

"In the office. I'm starting work here on Thursday, by the way. I'll be working three lunchtime and four evening shifts." Ginny indicated the filled-in form in front of her and watched him pick it up.

"Right. Fine." Scanning through it, he nodded then glanced at the photographs still on the table. "Who's that?"

"My daughter. Jem." With Evie she had felt free to glow with pride and extol her daughter's many virtues, but this time Ginny kept it low-key. Men were different.

Finn studied the photograph in silence. Finally, he said, "What happened to her?"

"What? Oh, the hair! It's blond, but she had the tips dyed pink."

"No, I mean . . ." He frowned. "Is this not the one who died?"

What?

"I don't know what you mean." Bemused, Ginny said, "Jem's my only daughter. She isn't dead!"

He shook his head. "You said she was. In the shop that day. That's why the woman couldn't bring herself to call the police."

"I swear to God I didn't say that! Why *would* I?"

"Who knows? To play on our sympathy and get yourself off a shoplifting charge?"

"You're making this up!" Her eyebrows knitted in disbelief, Ginny shouted, "That's a wicked thing to say!"

"You were hysterical. You told us you'd buried your dog that morning." He shrugged. "Maybe that wasn't true either."

"It *was* true. I loved my dog!"

"And then the woman asked who we could call and you said there was no one," Finn persisted. "You said your daughter wasn't here anymore, that she was gone."

The penny dropped. Mortified, Ginny realized that she had inadvertently misled them. "She was, but I didn't mean she was dead. Jem's alive and well and living in Bristol."

Finn surveyed her steadily. "And there we were, feeling sorry for you."

"You don't say. Well, excuse me if I didn't notice."

"Anyway, you weren't arrested. So it did the trick."

"Let me guess," Ginny said heatedly. "You don't have any children. *Do you?*"

He surveyed her for a moment, then shook his head. "No."

"Well, that's pretty obvious, because if you did, you'd know that no decent parent would *ever* tell such a terrible lie to get out of *anything*. I would *die* for my daughter."

"OK, OK. I'm sure you're right. Anyhow, can we put all that behind us?" Raising his hands, Finn said, "We got off to a shaky start. But now you're going to be working for me, so it'll be a lot easier all around if we can just get along together. Don't you think?"

Still outraged but realizing he was right, Ginny shook his outstretched hand and said, "Yes, I do."

"Good. Now if you'll excuse me, I need a word with Evie."

He disappeared through to the office. Ginny drank her lukewarm coffee and sat back, idly twirling the ends of her hair. This was where she would be working, in this sunny, eclectically furnished restaurant with its beamed ceilings and burnished oak floor. The paintings on the crimson walls were a beguiling mix of old and modern, the velvet curtains at the windows were held back with fat satin ropes and on every table stood an unmatched bowl or vase containing greenery and spring flowers.

Waiting for Evie to return and having nothing else to do other than study her surroundings meant that only a few minutes had elapsed before Ginny spotted the scrunched-up note on the floor.

Bending down and retrieving it from its position halfway under table six, she briefly considered tearing it into teeny tiny shreds.

That would teach him.

But twenty pounds was twenty pounds and she couldn't bring herself to do it. Instead, reaching into her handbag and taking out her purse—luckily she'd paid a visit to the ATM this morning—Ginny swapped the crumpled twenty-pound note for two crisp tens and replaced them under table six.

Minutes later, Evie burst back into the restaurant, followed by Finn.

"Sorry to leave you all on your own! Finn kept me talking."

I'll bet he did, thought Ginny, watching as Finn's dark eyes flickered in the direction of table six. When he saw the two ten-pound notes on the floor he almost—*almost*—smiled.

"Nice try," said Ginny as their eyes met.

"What?" Evie clearly hadn't been in on the impromptu test.

Finn shook his head. "Nothing. Right, I'll leave

you to it. Looks like my New York dealer's arrived."

A long black car had pulled up outside the antiques center. Ginny and Evie watched as Finn strode across the courtyard to greet the dealer.

"Yikes, it's a female. She won't stand a chance." Evie looked sideways at Ginny. "Did he just have another go at you?"

"He tried, but I'm getting used to him now. In fact, I had a bit of a go back." Proudly, Ginny said, "He made one comment about Jem, and I told him it was obvious he wasn't a father."

"Ah. And what did he have to say about that?"

"Nothing. Well, he admitted he didn't have children."

Evie sat back down opposite her. "OK, seeing as you're going to be working here, I'd better tell you. Finn was due to be married at Christmas. He and Tamsin had a baby last summer."

"Oh God!" Covering her mouth in horror, Ginny gasped, "Don't tell me the baby died!"

Evie shook her head. "No, nobody died. Mae was born in July, and she was the most beautiful thing you'd ever seen—well, with parents like that, what else would you expect? Finn was completely besotted, you can't imagine. He was just . . . lit up. You wouldn't credit the change in him. He'd just bought this place, and we were working night and day to finish the renovations and get the restaurant up and running. But he couldn't bear to tear himself away from Mae. She was always with him. You've never seen a happier man," Evie said sadly. "He was a born father."

Ginny was utterly mystified. "So what happened?"

"Oh God, it was awful. Finn was away one day at an auction in Wiltshire. I was here supervising the decorators in the restaurant when a taxi pulled up outside. This dark Italian-looking guy stepped out of the taxi, and I went over to see what he wanted. He said he'd come to collect Tamsin and Mae. The next thing I knew, Tamsin came running out of the flat above the antiques center—that's where she and Finn were living with Mae—carrying a load of bags. She told me they were leaving. I couldn't believe what was going on. She packed all her things and Mae's into the taxi and gave me a letter to give to Finn. Well, by this time I was *shaking*. I said, 'You can't take Mae away from Finn; he's her *father*.' And this Italian-looking guy, who *was* Italian by the way, just laughed at me and said, 'No, he isn't. I'm Mae's father.' Then he looked at his watch and told Tamsin to get a move on, the helicopter was waiting and he had to be back in London by three."

Ginny felt sick. What a terrible, terrible thing to happen. "And was it true? About him being the father?"

"Oh yes. Finn let me read the letter that night. Basically, Tamsin had met this Italian—Angelo

Balboa, his name was—in a nightclub one night while Finn was away on a buying trip. They had an affair that carried on for a few weeks then ended when Angelo had to go away to Australia on business. When Tamsin found out she was pregnant it was a toss-up which of them might turn out to be the father. And when Mae was born—well, Finn and Angelo both have dark hair and dark eyes, so she could have got away with it."

"So why didn't she?"

"For the first couple of months she did." Drily Evie made a whirly motion with her finger. "But maybe the mention of the helicopter gave you a clue? Angelo Balboa is seriously wealthy. His family made zillions in the olive oil industry. And Tamsin's always had a liking for the good things in life, especially good-looking zillionaires. I mean, Finn's done well for himself, but he's not in the same league as Angelo. And I imagine this swayed Tamsin's judgment. In the letter she told Finn that she'd had a DNA test done and that Mae wasn't his. Naturally, she'd then felt obliged to write to Angelo and let him know he had a daughter. And bingo, Angelo came up trumps! In the romantic modern way, he demanded more DNA tests to prove it. But as soon as they had, he did the honorable thing and announced that from now on, Tamsin and Mae were *his*."

"What a nightmare. Poor Finn." Now there was

a sentiment Ginny had never envisaged herself feeling. Raking her fingers through her hair, she said, "What did he do?"

Evie shrugged. "What could he do? Nothing at all. Well, apart from drink himself stupid for a while. And cancel the wedding. And come to terms with the realization that he wasn't a father after all."

"God. And he hasn't seen them since?"

"Nope. They're in London with Angelo."

"When did it happen?"

"October."

October. And Mae had been born in July. So that meant Finn had had three whole months in which to bond with this living, breathing baby, believing her to be his daughter and loving her more than life itself, before she'd been whisked away without even a chance to hold her in his arms one last time and say good-bye.

Imagining it, Ginny felt a lump form in her throat. She couldn't speak. How would she have felt if someone had tried to take Jem, as a baby, away from her?

"Maybe I shouldn't have told you." Evie looked worried.

"No, you should." Vigorously, Ginny shook her head. "God, I've already put my foot in it once. That's more than enough." Another thought struck her. "And it was only a few weeks after it happened that he saw me in the shop that first time. No wonder he wasn't in the sunniest of moods."

"Now you know why Finn's got such a thing about honesty and trust." Fiddling with the freesias in the vase in front of her, Evie said, "Can't blame him, I suppose. Up until Tamsin left, he'd always prided himself on being a great judge of character. It must come as a kick in the teeth when you realize you've got it so badly wrong about the woman you were planning to marry."

Well, quite. Lots of people later discovered they'd got it wrong when it came to choosing who to marry (mentioning no names . . . OK, *Gavin*).

But what Tamsin had done was beyond belief.

Chapter 15

WHEN SHE ARRIVED HOME at five o'clock, Ginny saw Gavin's white Porsche, muddier than ever, parked outside the house. She winced slightly, because this meant he'd introduced himself to Laurel without her being there to act as a buffer.

She winced even more when, upon letting herself in through the front door, the first thing she heard was Gavin saying, ". . . I mean look at your shoes, they're *ugly*. You're never going to get wolf-whistled at in the street wearing shoes like that."

Good old Gavin, as subtle and sympathetic as ever. Hastening into the living room, Ginny saw that Laurel was sitting bolt upright on a chair with a trapped-rabbit look in her eyes.

"Gavin, leave her alone."

"Me? I haven't laid a finger on her. We're just having a friendly chat." Gavin spread his hands. "I popped over to see you and you weren't here so Laurel and I have been getting to know each other. And let me tell you, I've learned a *lot*."

Ginny didn't doubt it. Asking impertinent questions was a specialty of Gavin's.

"He says I'm boring," said Laurel, her knuckles white as she clasped her knees.

Not to mention offering impertinent opinions, whether they were welcome or not.

"Gavin." Ginny shot him a fierce look. "You can't go around saying things like that."

"Yes, I can." Unperturbed, he turned back to address Laurel. "You *are* boring. It's not rocket science. You're never going to get over Kevin until you meet someone else to take your mind off him, and you're never going to find someone else because all you do is talk about Kevin."

"How long have you been here?" Ginny wondered if a good clip round the ear would do the trick.

"An hour. A whole hour, and believe me it's felt more like a week. I've been telling her, it's time to move on. Put the whole Kevin thing behind her."

Gavin made helpful, pushing-backward gestures with his arms. "And just move on. Which means getting out and socializing. And wearing shoes that won't send men screaming in the opposite direction."

Laurel was still looking shell-shocked. "Are you always this rude?"

"Yes," said Ginny apologetically.

"I prefer to call it honest. If you were wearing beautiful shoes, I'd tell you. And you're not a bad-looking girl," Gavin went on, sizing Laurel up like a racehorse. "Nice face, shiny hair, decent figure. I don't much go for redheads myself, but—"

"Good, because I don't go for men with double chins and receding hairlines."

"Fair point. Each to their own." Gavin wasn't offended. "But I'm serious about you needing to get over this ex of yours." He paused, looking thoughtful for a moment. "In fact, I bet I know someone you'd hit it off with."

Hurriedly, Laurel said, "No thanks!"

"See? Don't be so negative! I think the two of you would really get along."

"I'm not interested."

Despite her misgivings, Ginny said, "Who?"

"His name's Hamish. Lovely chap. Bit on the shy side, but a heart of gold. He's the sensitive type." Gavin was warming to his theme. "You know the kind. Writes poetry. Reads books."

Ginny stared at him. "How on earth do you know someone who writes poetry?"

"He's joined our club. It's a singles club," Gavin explained to Laurel. "Fabulous fun. We meet twice a week. What I could do is mention you to Hamish, put in a good word on your behalf, then when you turn up I'll introduce you to him, and Bob's your uncle."

Laurel's light green eyes widened in horror. "I'm not doing that."

"Oh, come on, live a little! You know, the more I think about it, the more sure I am that you two would be perfect for each other. He's tall and skinny, just like you. And quiet! Half the time he sits on his own in the corner and we hardly even notice he's—"

"No." Vehemently, Laurel shook her head. "No way. Me, go to a singles club? Not in a million years."

"So you'd rather be miserable for a million years."

"I'm not going to a singles club," Laurel repeated flatly.

"Leave her alone," Ginny protested, but weakly because while Gavin might not be subtle, what he was saying made a lot of sense. It would be heavenly if Laurel were to meet a kindred spirit.

"You don't want to go on your own? Fine. Gin, how about the two of you coming along together?" Gavin the perennial salesman raised his eyebrows at Ginny, making an offer she couldn't refuse.

Maybe it would be worth it. "Well . . ."

"Tomorrow night."

"Oh." Tomorrow was dinner-with-Perry night. "I can't," Ginny apologized. "I'm busy."

"Doing what?"

"Seeing a friend!"

"Well, how about next week?"

"Excuse me, am I invisible?" Shaking back her hair, Laurel stood up and said impatiently, "I told you I wasn't going and I meant it, so will you please stop trying to make me do something I don't want to do?"

"If you met Hamish, you'd like him," Gavin wheedled.

"That's your opinion." As she stalked out of the living room, Laurel said, "If you ask me, he sounds like a complete drip."

Ginny met Perry the following night at the Green Room, the clifftop restaurant on the outskirts of Portsilver. This time he didn't stand up and kiss her in front of everyone but the food was good, they talked nonstop, and she still felt that spark of attraction every time she looked at him.

"Your ex sounds like a character." Taking her free hand when she'd finished telling him about Laurel's run-in with Gavin, Perry idly stroked her fingers. "How long have you two been divorced?"

"Nine years." Ginny was finding it hard to concentrate; all of a sudden her hand had turned into an erogenous zone.

"Nine years. That's a long time. You must have had other relationships since then."

"Well, yes." Was he trying to find out whether she was a saucy trollop who bundled men into bed at every opportunity? "Not many. Just . . . you know, a few."

Perry raised a questioning eyebrow.

"OK, three," said Ginny.

He smiled. "That's good. Three's a nice ladylike number. I knew you were a lady."

It was a compliment, but Ginny wasn't sure she deserved it. If she had been free of responsibilities, her life, sex-wise, might have been far more eventful. But with Jem around, that kind of thing hadn't been a priority. Motherhood had come first and men had been a distraction she simply hadn't needed.

"You know, I appreciate that, I really do." Perry nodded and carried on stroking her hand. "It's more romantic when people take the time to get to know each other properly, isn't it? Too many people just go from one one-night stand to the next. And that just cheapens everything for me." He gazed into Ginny's eyes. "I'm so glad you're not like that."

Bugger, thought Ginny. Just because she'd been

like that in the past didn't mean she wanted to be like it now.

True to his word, when the meal was over, Perry kissed her in the car park then did the gentlemanly thing and helped her into her car—before Ginny could throw him over the bonnet and rip his shirt off, which was what she really wanted to do.

Oh well, it was flattering in its own way. If Perry thought she was a lady worthy of respect, that was . . . *nice*.

"You're gorgeous," Perry murmured. Cradling her face between his warm hands, he kissed her again, lingeringly, before pulling away.

See? That *was* nice. And a million times more romantic than being groped by some panting Neanderthal intent on getting inside your bra.

"I'll be in touch," said Perry. "Take care."

He really likes me, thought Ginny, happiness bubbling up inside her as she drove out of the car park.

Wasn't that *great?*

Chapter 16

GINNY STILL FOUND GOING for a walk without a dog a strange experience, like waking up on Christmas morning and finding your stocking empty. Even after all this time, she still found herself glancing around, expecting to see Bellamy either trotting along beside her or madly bounding around in circles in search of treasure.

Even more disconcertingly, at least for anyone who happened to be watching, she still sometimes picked up sticks and went to hurl them into the air before realizing Bellamy was no longer there to retrieve them.

That got you some funny looks from passersby.

The beach had always been their favorite place. Now, as she made her way along the shoreline, Ginny kept her hands stuffed firmly in the pockets of her black padded jacket. There, tangled in a skein of glossy wet seaweed, was a piece of driftwood ideal for throwing. (*Mustn't* pick it up, *mustn't* throw it.) A crab skittered across the sand heading for the shelter of a semi-submerged rock. One of Bellamy's favorite games had been snuffling after crabs, nudging them with his nose then leaping back like an outraged maiden aunt confronted by a male stripper when the crabs retaliated with their claws.

Oh God, she missed Bellamy so much. Strolling along the beach wasn't the same without him. Nor without Jem. For years it had been the three of them splashing through the waves, playing frenetic games, and collecting shells for Jem's bedroom windowsill.

Now it's just me, thought Ginny, gazing out to sea and watching a lone fishing boat chug along with seagulls swooping in its wake.

The phone rang in her pocket.

"Mum?"

"Hello, darling!" The sound of Jem's voice, just when she most needed to hear it, lifted Ginny's spirits in a flash. "How lovely to hear from you! What have you been up to?"

"Oh, you know, all the usual stuff. Buckets of work. Boring old essays, bossy lecturers . . . did you get my email yesterday?"

"I did." Jem had attached a photo to the email, of Lucy and herself on their way out to a party. "And I can't believe you weren't wearing your new boots." When Jem bought anything new, she had a habit of wearing it nonstop for the next three months.

Giggling, Jem said, "I was."

"I meant the pink ones. Oh, you naughty girl, don't tell me you've bought another pair."

"I didn't; Rupert did. He didn't like my pink boots so he threw them out of the window at some people who were annoying us." Still laughing, Jem said, "Then the next day he gave me the money to buy a new pair. Can you believe it? He gave me a hundred pounds!"

Ginny was incensed. "He just threw them out of the window? What kind of person does that? You *loved* those boots."

"And now I love these ones! Oh, Mum, it was *funny;* you should have been there. And mine were a bit cheap-looking. These are much nicer.

I'm wearing them now. Rupert thinks they're great; he says I don't look like a hooker anymore."

Rupert was a prat and an arrogant one at that; if he'd tried chucking anything of hers out of a window, Ginny would have thrown him out after it. Hearing Jem, normally so sensible, leaping to his defense sent a faint chill down her spine.

"And is he still with his girlfriend? What's her name . . . Caro?"

"Nope. They broke up." At this, Ginny's sense of foreboding increased. "Anyway," Jem went on, "I want to know how your new job's going. Is it good?"

Right. Change of subject. For the next few minutes, as the seagulls wheeled overhead, Ginny told Jem all about her first evening shift yesterday at Penhaligon's. Finn hadn't been there and she had enjoyed herself hugely; Evie and Martha were fun to work with, the kitchen staff was hardworking and cheerful, and she had enjoyed getting to know the regular customers.

Jem was delighted. "Hey, Mum, good for you. Maybe I should come down and meet them too."

"Except you're working." Ginny darted out of the way as a wave lapped against her trainers.

"Ah, but I'm not! That's why I'm ringing." Jem was triumphant. "The pub landlord called me this morning—a pipe burst in the roof last night and the place got flooded, so it's closed until next week. Which means I'm free," she went on gaily, "so I thought I'd shoot down for the weekend, if that's OK with you."

This time, Ginny was so overjoyed she didn't even notice the next wave breaking over both her feet. She wouldn't have noticed if a shark had reared up out of the water with a mermaid on its back.

"Of course it's OK with me. Oh, darling, that's *fantastic* news. I can't wait!"

"You can't do that." Rupert emerged from the kitchen as Jem came off the phone. "You mustn't go home. That's a complete waste of a weekend."

"How can it be a waste of a weekend? I'll be seeing my mum."

"I mean a waste for *us*." In the middle of the living room he slid his arms round her. "I'll be here all on my own. What'll I do with myself while you're gone?"

"You won't be on your own. Lucy's going to be here."

"She isn't. She's just told me she's off up to Manchester for some cousin's wedding."

"Damn." Lucy was in the shower; Jem gazed in dismay at the closed bathroom door. "I thought she'd be around so we wouldn't have the chance to . . . you know . . . *be* together."

"Well, she won't be. Which gives us all the time

in the world to . . . you know . . . *be* together." As he mimicked her choice of expression, Rupert grinned wickedly. "I mean, think how much *being together* we could do."

Jem was torn. It was an opportunity they weren't often likely to get. If only she'd known twenty minutes earlier that Lucy would be away.

"Mmm," Rupert murmured. "Being together, being together . . ."

"I've told Mum now. She's expecting me."

"You're starting to sound like Davy Stokes. Hey, come on, you only told her five minutes ago. Call her back and say you can't make it." As he nuzzled her ear, Rupert said with amusement, "Just tell her something's come up. That wouldn't be a lie now, would it?"

Weakening, Jem imagined telling her mother that she would be staying in Bristol after all. Maybe think up a less lascivious reason than the one Rupert was suggesting, for decency's sake. Would her mum be disappointed, though?

"She sounded so pleased when I said I'd be coming down."

"That's what mothers do." Rupert shrugged. "They have to sound pleased; it's part of the job description. You wouldn't like it if she said, 'Oh God, do you have to?' "

Was that true? Actually, it was, come to think of it; she might be in the way. Her mum had a new job now and a new housemate. She had a busy, happy life. The last thing she needed, probably, was a nosy daughter arriving back to take up more of her time.

"If you leave me here on my own"—Rupert gave her a mournful look—"I might have to go out and shag some ugly fat bird. And I'd really hate that."

Jem grinned and made up her mind. "You know what? I'd hate it too."

Ginny's phone rang again as she was standing in the queue at the delicatessen waiting to pay for her basket of luxuries.

"Mum? It's me again. Look, I'm not going to be able to make it after all—I've only just realized how behind I am with my essays. If I don't spend the weekend catching up, I'm going to be in big—*yeeek!*—trouble. So, that's all right, isn't it? I expect you're rushed off your feet anyway!"

Ginny's mouth was dry. Her heart sank. Jem was gabbling at warp speed, a sure sign that the excuse wasn't genuine. And she wasn't coming home. Disappointment flooded through her. And what had provoked that squeak?

"What just happened?"

"When?"

"The squeak. You were saying you'd be in big trouble, and you squeaked."

Jem giggled. "Oh, that was just Rupert mucking

around. It's nothing. So is that OK then? I won't be around to interrupt your hectic life!"

The basket was suddenly far too heavy. Moving out of the queue, Ginny said carefully, "Fine, darling. It would have been lovely to see you, but it's your decision. If you need to catch up on your essays . . . well, that's what you have to do."

"I knew you wouldn't mind. OK, Mum, better go now. Love you!"

Having tucked the phone back into her handbag, Ginny retraced her steps around the delicatessen, emptying the basket. Back onto the shelves went the jars of stuffed olives, the packets of cashews and macadamia nuts, the prosciutto slices and the marinated artichokes. All Jem's favorite things.

"Come out without your purse, love?" An older woman gave her a sympathetic look.

Ginny shook her head. "I thought my daughter was coming to stay for the weekend. She's just phoned to say she can't make it. Too busy."

"Tuh, heard that one before. Kids are selfish, aren't they? Mine used to do that to me." The woman clicked her tongue. "We had some arguments about it, I can tell you. Right humdingers."

Ginny didn't want to argue with Jem, but her disappointment was so great that she was willing to give almost anything a try. "Did it help?"

"I wouldn't recommend it, love." Heaving a

sigh of resignation as she picked up a jar of pesto, the woman said sadly, "She married a man I didn't like. We had a few rows about that too. Then fourteen years ago they upped and immigrated to Australia."

Chapter 17

IT WAS SATURDAY EVENING and the restaurant was busy. Finn was there, greeting new arrivals, working the tables like a pro, and attracting plenty of attention from the female diners. Watching him in action, Ginny saw the way they lit up and sparkled when he spoke to them, then chatted equally easily with the husbands of the married ones, ensuring they realized he wasn't a threat.

The single women loved that bit too. All the more chance for them. When a man as attractive as Finn Penhaligon moved into the area, it gave them all hope.

"Watching how it's done?" Evidently amused, Evie paused on her way to table six with two plates of mussels. "Can't you just *feel* all those flirty female hormones in the air?" With a wink, she added, "Good old Finn, he hasn't lost his touch."

"I can see that." As Finn crossed the room in order to answer the ringing phone, every female eye followed him.

"You'd better watch out. You could be next."

Ginny grinned because the idea was so ludicrous. "I don't think that's going to happen. He'd be too worried I might nick his wallet."

Finn beckoned her over to the desk a few minutes later.

"Relative of yours?"

"What?" Ginny peered down at the diary where he'd written the name Holland for nine thirty.

"Table for two. I've just taken the booking. She didn't say so, but I thought it might be your daughter."

Her heart leaping like a fish, Ginny wondered if it could be Jem. Had she come down after all, to surprise her? And a table for two . . . did that mean she'd brought someone with her?

If it was Rupert, Ginny vowed to be as nice to him as she knew how.

An hour later her foolish hopes were dashed as the door of the restaurant opened and Gavin walked in with a blond who looked as if her lifetime ambition might be to appear on page three of the *Sun*, adopting one of those "Good gracious, where *did* my clothes go?" pouts.

Clearly struggling to match this vision in four-inch sparkly stilettos with the photograph he'd seen of Jem, Finn said doubtfully, "Is that your daughter?"

"If it was, I'd tell her to get her roots done and

wear a bra." Awash with disappointment at having even thought it could be Jem, Ginny said, "It's my ex with one of his lovely young things. At a guess I'd say he's probably not with her for her mind."

"Now now." Finn's mouth twitched. "Never judge someone on first impressions. You of all people should know that."

He was having a dig, but Ginny's thoughts flew immediately to someone else whom she had met and disliked on sight. Maybe she'd got it wrong about Rupert and he wasn't obnoxious after all.

"Except men pointing guns at you." She picked up a couple of leather-bound menus. "If they're doing that, it's generally best to go along with your first impression. And run like hell."

"Thought we'd surprise you," Gavin said cheerfully when Ginny went over to hand them their menus. "This is Cleo, by the way. Cleo, this is Gin."

"Hiya!" Cleo actually had a sweet and friendly smile, but with her gauzy low-cut top and missing bra, it wasn't likely that many men would notice.

"You did surprise me. When Finn said a girl had booked the table, I thought it was Jem."

Cleo giggled. "That was me. Gavin asked me to make the call while he was in the shower." She gazed around eagerly. "I've never been to a restaurant like this before; I'm more of a burger girl myself. Are these . . . serviettes?" She was pointing to the dark blue linen napkins.

Politely, Ginny said, "Yes, they are."

"Wicked! Fancy having serviettes that aren't made of paper!"

After their main course, Cleo tottered off on four-inch heels to the loo and Gavin beckoned Ginny over.

"Well? What do you think of her?"

"Nice enough. Pretty. Young." Ginny shrugged helplessly; what did he expect her to say? "Just don't marry her, OK?"

Gavin beamed; he never took offense. "She's fun. We're enjoying ourselves. Speaking of fun, how's the lodger? Still the life and soul of the party?"

"OK, OK." Ginny acknowledged that if she was going to have a dig at his choice of girlfriend, it was only fair that he should be allowed to have a go in return about Laurel.

"So, Wednesday. Bring her along to our singles do."

"Not that again. She won't go."

"Ah, but it's up to you to persuade her." Gavin looked pleased with himself. "And you know it makes sense. Now listen, because I've had one of my ideas."

"Would that by any chance be similar to the idea you once had about pouring a can of petrol on the barbecue to liven it up a bit? The idea that left you without eyebrows for the next three months?"

He ignored this disparaging reminder. "You

have to tell Laurel that you want to go to the singles night, but that you're too shy to do it on your own. You beg her to go along with you for moral support. Brilliant or what?"

Transparent was the word that sprang to mind. Rather like Cleo's top. Ginny said, "And you'll be there?"

Gavin looked at her as if she'd just suggested the sea was pink. "Of course I'll be there!"

"But what about Cleo?"

"We're not joined at the hip, you know." His eyes twinkled. "Besides, Wednesday's her yoga night."

He was never going to change. When Gavin was eighty he'd be the scourge of the nursing homes; no still-sprightly widow would be safe.

"Everything OK?" Finn joined them.

"Wonderful, thanks. Great food." Patting his stomach, Gavin said cheerily, "I've just been persuading Ginny here to give the local singles club a try."

The temptation to grab hold of Gavin's chair, wrench it backward, and tip him to the ground was huge. Would a bruised coccyx be painful enough? Did her ex-husband seriously not realize that she might prefer it if he didn't blurt out this kind of thing in front of her new boss? The new boss who was struggling to keep a straight face.

"I'm not interested in singles clubs!" Ginny felt herself going very red.

"Sorry, of course you're not." Infuriatingly, Gavin winked and raised a finger to his lips, indicating that it was their little secret. "Wednesday, eight o'clock. You'll love it. OK, shhh, Cleo's coming back."

"Hiya!" Cleo trilled when Gavin had introduced her to Finn. "It's really nice here, isn't it?" Leaning closer and resting her hand on Finn's shirtsleeve, she whispered, "Only I hope you don't mind me telling you, but someone's made off with the towel in the ladies. I had to dry my hands on bits of toilet paper! I mean, you don't expect people to nick things in a posh place like this, do you?"

"I'll go and check," Ginny murmured hurriedly before either Finn or Gavin could come up with some oh-so-witty retort.

Twenty seconds later she was back. "They're all there." Then, because Cleo was looking baffled, "Dark green, in two piles on the shelf above the linen basket."

Cleo's expression cleared. "Oh *those*. But they're only little! I thought they were flannels in case you wanted to wash your face!"

Gavin roared with laughter and gave her shoulders a squeeze. "My little Eliza Dolittle. They're towels, darling. You dry your hands on them then throw them in the basket to be washed."

For a moment, Cleo looked flustered. "Oh! Well, that's very extravagant."

Poor Cleo. Feeling a stab of sympathy toward her, Ginny said, "I think it's extravagant too."

It was Wednesday night and they were actually here. Ginny still couldn't quite believe it. Yesterday, she had discovered, was the anniversary of the day Laurel and Kevin had first met. As a result, Laurel had been inconsolable, gazing helplessly at a battered photo of her former love and mournfully wondering aloud, over and over again, why she was bothering to carry on, because what was the point?

By the evening, Ginny couldn't have agreed more. If Laurel wanted to end it all by electrocuting herself in the bath, she'd have happily supplied the hairdryer and the extra-long flex.

"Sorry, I know how boring this must be for you." Laurel tugged the last tissue out of the box and wiped her eyes. "I just miss Kev so much, you know? It just feels like life isn't worth living. It's all right for you, you're completely over Gavin, you don't want him back. But I still want Kevin, more than *anything*."

"I don't want Gavin back," Ginny blurted out, "but I'd like a man in my life. In fact, I'd love to try that singles club Gavin was talking about. Except . . . I couldn't go on my own."

Laurel sniffed damply. "You could. Gavin would be there."

"Exactly! That's what makes it impossible. I

wouldn't know anyone apart from my ex-husband!" Out of sheer desperation, Ginny pleaded, "But if you'd come along with me, just once, you'd be doing me the biggest favor. Tomorrow night. Would you? Please?"

She didn't for a moment expect Laurel to say yes.

"All right then."

What?

Ginny gazed at her. "Really?"

"If it's what you want, I'll do it," Laurel said sadly. "I'll hate it, of course, but I suppose I owe you that much. If it makes up for me being a bit miserable sometimes."

A *bit?*

Stunned, Ginny said, "Well, thanks."

"Don't expect me to talk to any men though. Especially not that Hamish person Gavin was going on about."

"Absolutely not." Ginny crossed her fingers behind her back.

"And I'm only going the once."

"Absolutely." Bugger, now that meant she had to go too.

The singles club was held in the back room of the White Hart. Now, pausing in the doorway, Laurel said, "Are you sure you want to do this?"

"Of course!" Ginny flashed a bright smile. "This is exciting! Just think, I could be about to meet the man who'll change my life!"

Laurel looped a strand of long red hair behind her ear. "It must be nice to feel so hopeful. I hope he's in there."

Me too, thought Ginny. More to the point, I hope his name is Hamish.

Chapter 18

THE CLUB WAS BUSY, which was a relief. The music didn't stop nor did an eerie saloon-bar silence fall as they walked in. But heads turned, they had definitely been noticed. Aware of dozens of pairs of eyes upon her, Ginny realized she was being subjected to the lightning appraisal afforded each newcomer. The other women were sizing up the competition, their collective gaze flicking over her hair, her face, and her clothes. Gavin may have praised these people to the skies, assuring her that everyone was wonderfully friendly, but they weren't looking that thrilled to see her right now.

A quick glance around revealed that the women outnumbered the men in the club by about two to one, so their lack of enthusiasm was perhaps understandable. Ginny longed to run up to them and blurt out that it was OK, she wasn't here to snaffle their men.

But with Laurel at her side she could hardly do that.

Laurel said ruefully, "Well? Seen anyone you like?"

Poor Laurel. She couldn't wait to be out of here. If she had her way, Ginny would pick her man, twirl a lasso above her head, and bring him crashing to the ground. The sooner she'd captured him, the sooner they could go home.

"I think it might take more than twenty seconds." Ginny briefly scanned the males on display wondering if there were, in fact, any she did like the look of. There was a wide-ranging choice—fat men, tall men, ones with hair and some without, men in trendy clothes and others wearing the kind of outfits their mothers might have chosen for them. Some were blessed in the looks department, while some . . . well, you could only hope they had sparkling personalities on their side.

But none, at first glance, made her heart beat faster. None of them was Perry-shaped.

However, there was one who was Gavin-shaped. Having spotted them, he made his way over. Her eyes narrowing, Laurel muttered, "He'd better not be rude to me."

Which was a bit like hoping that a man-eating tiger wasn't going to take a bite out of your leg.

"Girls, girls, you made it! Excellent." Gavin clapped Laurel on the back, almost flooring her. "You're going to enjoy yourselves."

"I won't. I'm only here because Ginny begged

me to keep her company." Tetchily, Laurel said, "And don't call us girls. That's sexist."

"Oh God, are you starting already? Would you rather I called you a middle-aged misery?"

"Drinks," Ginny cut in hastily before Gavin *did* start calling her a middle-aged misery and Laurel stormed out. *Be nice,* she mouthed at her ex-husband.

"I am being nice," Gavin retorted. "She started it. I don't see what's so terrible about being called a girl. But anyway," he added as Ginny shot him another fierce look, "let's not bicker. We're all here to have fun, aren't we? Laurel, why don't I introduce you to a few of my friends . . ."

Wasting no time, he whisked Laurel off. Ginny approached the bar and ordered their drinks—an orange juice for Laurel and a vodka tonic for herself. In the mirror above the bar she could see Gavin introducing a clearly reluctant Laurel to a mixed group of people. Craning her neck, Ginny wondered if one of them was Hamish but since none of the men was wearing a kilt or brandishing a set of bagpipes, it wasn't possible to tell. Although he couldn't be that chubby one, surely, the one who looked like a Weeble, nor the guy in the orange cardigan who had to be sixty if he was a day.

"Are you Gavin's ex-wife?"

Turning, Ginny saw an attractive, interested-looking brunette of her own age, wearing a cream trouser suit.

"That's right. I'm Ginny. Hi." Shaking the proffered hand, Ginny said, "How did you know?"

"Gavin told us you'd be coming along tonight. He said you were very pretty, like a young Goldie Hawn. Which didn't go down too well with the female contingent, I can tell you." The woman smiled. "I'm Bev, by the way."

"Maybe I should have blacked out some of my teeth and stuck on a big wart." Ginny pulled a face. "Gavin did say everyone was friendly, but . . ."

"That's because everyone loves Gavin. He's our star performer. All the women want him and all the men want to be like him. But it doesn't work that way for us. And I know how it feels, believe me. The women aren't wild about me either."

"Because they want to keep all the men here to themselves?"

"Not *these* men. They just can't bear the thought that one night George Clooney might walk in and they won't get first go at him."

Entertained, Ginny said, "And is that who you're waiting for too?"

"Well, I wouldn't say no. But I've actually got a bit of a crush on one of the men here."

"Really?" Fascinated, Ginny scanned the room. Not that one, surely. Or him, or him. Definitely not him . . .

"It's Gavin," said Bev.

"Blimey."

"I know." Bev tilted her head in rueful acknowledgement. "It's hopeless. I'm forty! Maybe if I was ten years younger I'd stand a fighting chance, but I'm not. So I don't."

"He might come to his senses one day, sort himself out, and realize it's time to settle down with someone his own age. I wish he would," Ginny said with feeling.

"But you can't see it happening."

"To be honest, no. More chance of George Clooney walking in here."

"He'll just have to do, then. Poor old George, relegated to second prize. And you'll probably want him too." Bev's eyes danced. "I'd have to fight you for him."

If Ginny had her way, she'd never be coming here again after tonight. But she couldn't tell Bev she was only here because of Laurel.

"Speaking of George Clooney," Bev added in an undertone, "here comes someone who looks . . . absolutely nothing like him."

For the next ten minutes, Ginny chatted to Bev and an earnest bespectacled divorcé called Harold who was an accountant, forty-nine, and very keen on growing his own vegetables. He was even keener on explaining to her, step by step, how he grew them. After that they were joined by Timothy, a thirty-four-year-old butcher by day and would-be Elvis impersonator by night.

Elvis with a lisp.

"You might not think I look much like him now," Timothy said eagerly, "but jutht wait till you thee me in my wig and makeup!"

And—not for the first time, Ginny suspected— he proceeded to demonstrate his moves. Since Timothy had wispy blond hair and a round pink face like a fat baby, it was as surreal as Princess Anne pretending to be Freddie Mercury. His white Lycra Elvis jumpsuit, Timothy told her with pride, had been made to measure and he'd thewn on every thequin himthelf by hand.

Jim was next, a math teacher whose wife had died three years ago. His interests were rock-climbing and playing badminton. "But not at the same time!" With an ear-splitting guffaw, Jim clutched his sides. "That would be dangerous!"

After hilarious Jim came David the cattle farmer, who was quite handsome in a ruddy, outdoorsy way and seemed absolutely charming but had an unfortunate saliva-spraying thing going on whenever he spoke.

"God, I'm so sorry, I've done it again." Apologetically, David fished a large cotton handkerchief out of his pocket and dabbed at Ginny's cheek. "It's because I'm nervous. I'm always doing it here, but when it's just me and the cows on the farm I'm fine." It was a relief when Gavin came over and reclaimed her. He had his drawbacks, but at least he'd never sprayed spit in her face.

"How's Laurel getting on?"

"Great guns. Hopeless with the men," said Gavin. "I warned her not to talk about Kevin but she couldn't help herself. Not the world's greatest chat-up line, telling men the reason you're not drinking is because you're on antidepressants because your boyfriend chucked you and you know you'll never get over him because he's the only man you ever loved. To be honest, they couldn't get away fast enough. Happily, I had the bright idea of introducing her to the three witches. Their husbands chucked them too," he explained when Ginny looked blank. "Bitter doesn't begin to describe them. They spend all their time huddled together muttering about how all men should be drowned in a bucket at birth."

"I thought this club was supposed to be friendly," Ginny protested.

"Oh, come on, it's hilarious. And they're being friendly to Laurel. Look." Gavin pointed them out, gathered around a table in the corner. Laurel was crying and talking and the three witches were nodding vehemently, evidently in agreement that Kevin was a jerk of the first order.

"So no joy with Hamish. Which one is he, by the way?" Ginny peered around hopefully.

"Not here. Hasn't turned up tonight."

Typical. After all the effort she'd put into dragging Laurel along in the hope that she and Hamish might hit it off, he hadn't even had the decency to show his face. Oh well, it had been a ridiculous idea anyway, one of Gavin's mad notions. And since when had he shown an iota of talent for matchmaking?

Actually, speaking of matchmaking . . .

"Bev's nice, isn't she?"

"Bev's great." Gavin shrugged then caught the look in Ginny's eye. "Oh no, don't go getting any ideas. She's not my type."

Honestly, he drove her insane—was Gavin the most frustrating man in Cornwall?

"Because she doesn't wear skirts up to her knickers?"

He grinned. "That could have something to do with it."

Ginny looked at her watch. "Do you think Hamish might still turn up? He could just be late."

"He's always here by eight thirty."

That was that, then. "Brilliant. What a waste of an evening."

"Hey, don't get niggly. He'll be here next week."

"But we won't be. I'm not doing this again." Ginny couldn't face another evening here; people were starting to dance and some of them were people who should never be allowed to dance outside the privacy of their own bedrooms. This wasn't her kind of place. She could be out with Perry now, having a lovely time . . .

Except that wasn't quite true, sadly. She

couldn't be out with Perry because he hadn't phoned her all week. And out of practice with dating though she might be, even Ginny knew it wasn't cool to ring the man and demand to know why he hadn't rung you.

"You know, you might not have to come back." Gavin turned her in the direction of the corner table. "Look at Laurel."

Ginny looked. Laurel was no longer crying. All four women were in hysterics, clutching each other and giggling like eighteen-year-olds.

"I didn't know she could laugh," Ginny marveled.

"She's joined the coven. You mark my words; she'll be back every week from now on." Modestly, Gavin said, "God, I'm brilliant."

Was he? Could he actually have done something right? Deciding that he might have, Ginny gave him a grateful hug and was instantly aware of the waves of resentment being directed at her by all the single women in the room. Hastily she let go, stepping back and landing on somebody's foot.

"Ouch . . . thorry!" Wincing but putting on a brave face, Elvis Presley said, "I wondered if I could perthuade you to danthe?"

"Of course she will," Gavin said heartily before Ginny could open her mouth.

The coven beadily watched as Timothy led her onto the dance floor. Ginny's heart sank as the music changed. Over in the corner the witches were sniggering.

Timothy, his mouth millimeters from her left ear as he steered her around, crooned happily along to "Thuthpiciouth Mindth."

Thank goodness Jem wasn't here to see her now.

They drove home at eleven o'clock. Encouraged by the fact that the three witches appeared to have taken Laurel under their wing, Ginny said brightly, "Well? Not as terrible as you expected?"

Laurel looked shocked. "What makes you think that? It was *worse*."

"But you made friends with the wi—um, with those women, didn't you? I thought you were getting on really well with them."

Laurel said flatly, "They were awful."

"I saw you laughing," Ginny protested.

"It's called being polite. Sitting with them was awful, but marginally less awful than having to talk to the men. That's the only reason I stayed where I was."

"So you didn't enjoy yourself."

"Of course I didn't enjoy myself! Did *you?*"

"I thought it was . . . good." Ginny gripped the steering wheel in order to lie with more conviction. "I mean, it's always a bit scary going somewhere new for the first time, but maybe if you tried it again next week you might find yourself—"

"Oh no." Laurel shook her head with such

determination that her long hair almost slapped Ginny across the face. "No, don't even *try* to persuade me."

"But—"

"I've done it once and that was enough. To be honest, I didn't realize you were this desperate to meet a new man." In the orange glow of the streetlamps, Laurel looked at Ginny as if she were a particularly slutty teenager and a severe disappointment to boot. "I'm sorry, but if you really want to go to that place again, you'll just have to go by yourself."

Chapter 19

"HE STILL HASN'T RUNG," said Ginny.

Carla was on her living-room floor doing sit-ups, her flat stomach sheeny with perspiration but her ability to speak unimpeded. "Have you called him?"

"I can't."

"So you're just going to wait?"

"What other choice do I have?"

Carla shrugged in mid-sit-up. "Call him."

"No! The thing is, I don't understand it. He's so nice when I do see him. He really seems to like me. He said he'd be in touch and he said it as if he meant it. So I believed him." Ginny heaved a sigh and glanced over at the TV, where a guilty-looking bearded character in an Aussie soap was being confronted by both his wife and his mistress. ("Noelene, ya don't understind, I kin explain ivrything . . .")

Following the direction of her gaze, Carla said, "Maybe he's seeing someone else."

This had already crossed Ginny's mind. "If he is, I wish he'd just tell me."

Carla finished her two hundredth sit-up. Reaching for the phone on the coffee table, she said, "What's his number?"

"Why?"

"Because you're my best friend and he's treating you like dirt."

"He doesn't," Ginny protested. "That's the thing; when we're together, he treats me like a princess."

"Are you working on Friday night?"

"No. Why?"

"Just give me the number."

Ginny was torn between stuffing her fingers in her ears—her own ears, not Carla's—and listening to Carla giving Perry a hard time.

"Is that Perry? Hi, my name's Carla James, I'm a friend of Ginny's." Carla was in brisk, don't-mess-with-me mode, pacing the living room as she spoke into the phone. "You remember Ginny; she's the one you haven't rung for the last week and a half."

Ginny flinched and stuffed her fingers in her

ears. Sadly it didn't block out what Carla was now saying.

"So I was wondering, do you have another girlfriend taking up all your free time? Or a wife perhaps?" Pause. "Sure about that? OK, in that case, have you decided you don't want to see Ginny anymore?" Pause. "Well good, I'm glad to hear that, although I have to say I'm not sure you deserve her. If you were my boyfriend, I'd have chucked you by now." Pause. "Oh, don't give me that. We're all *busy*. If you want to see someone you just have to make time. So how about tomorrow night?"

By this time squirming for England, Ginny was amazed she hadn't disappeared down *inside* the sofa. Jumping to her feet she escaped through to the kitchen with the sound of an irate Aussie wife yelling, "Bruce, you're nothin' but a no-good lyin' *cheat*," echoing in her ears.

By the time she'd finished noisily unloading the dishwasher, Carla came through to the kitchen looking pleased with herself.

"All sorted."

"You bullied him into it," Ginny wailed. "That makes me feel so wanted and desirable."

"Hey, you gave me his number. You wanted to see him again and now you're seeing him. More to the point," Carla said crispily, "so will I."

"Why?"

"So I can check him out and give you my

verdict. If I think he's giving you the runaround, I'll tell you. If I don't like him, you'll be the first to know. If I don't think he's trustworthy, I'll give it to you straight. Because you deserve better than to be mucked about by some smooth-talker and I won't stand by and see you hurt."

This was Carla all over, in-control and no-nonsense. She had never had a dithery moment in her life.

"You'll like him. You couldn't not like him," said Ginny.

"Don't be so sure. So far he hasn't made the greatest impression. Anyway"—Carla took a bottle of Evian from the fridge and gulped half of it down in one go—"you're both coming along to the Carson Hotel tomorrow night."

The Carson was Portsilver's biggest hotel, reopening in grand style following a refurbishment that had taken eight months and cost many millions. It had been a coup for Carla, who had sold them the biggest conservatory her company had ever built. Ginny already knew no expense had been spared for tomorrow's bash. Hundreds of people had been invited. On the one hand, she didn't want Perry to be seeing her because Carla had forced him into it. Then again, it would be a spectacular night out.

Ginny had never been inside Perry's shop before. Every wall was covered with printed T-shirts.

Behind the counter sat a gum-chewing girl with surfer's hair and a lip ring, wearing a T-shirt that said I'M CLEVERER THAN I LOOK. To prove it, a copy of Tolstoy's *War and Peace* lay open next to the till.

"Hi, is Perry around?"

"He's in the back."

After waiting for a couple of seconds, Ginny said, "So could I see him?"

"I expect so." The gum-chewing didn't falter. "What's your name?"

"Ginny Holland."

There was no flicker of recognition; clearly, Perry hadn't mentioned her to his assistant. Oh well.

"Just go on through." The girl tilted her head in the general direction of the door and yawned widely.

Maybe the copy of *War and Peace* belonged to someone else.

Perry was in the back room unpacking boxes of T-shirts in every color. He jumped to his feet when he saw Ginny standing in the doorway.

"Sorry, I know you're busy." Having rehearsed what to say, Ginny blurted the words out. "I just wanted to apologize for Carla; she gets carried away. And forget about tomorrow night, that's off too. So don't worry about it. Right, I've got to get to work and—"

"Whoa, hey, stop." Perry reached out and

grabbed her arm as she turned to leave. "What's wrong?"

Only a man could ask that question.

"Nothing's wrong. I just don't need other people making arrangements for me. And neither do you," said Ginny. "So let's just leave it there, OK? I'm sorry Carla phoned you."

"Stop saying sorry. That's my job." Pausing, Perry studied her face. "I really have been busy, you know, getting ready for the start of the tourist season. But I should have phoned you. Your friend Carla was right to give me a hard time. And I would like us to go to the Carson tomorrow. Very much indeed."

Oh God, more confusion. When he was looking at her like this and sounding so genuinely regretful, Ginny no longer knew what to do or say. She'd come here to be strong and now she was weakening again, because she so badly wanted to believe him.

"Please?" prompted Perry, drawing her closer and smiling his twinkly irresistible smile. "Give me the chance to make it up to you. We'll have a fantastic evening, I promise. And I'll do my best to prove to Carla that I'm not as heartless as she thinks I am. Is she as scary as she sounds, by the way?"

"Scarier," said Ginny. It was no good; she couldn't hide her relief that he was saying all the things she'd hoped he'd say. "OK, I'll see you there tomorrow night."

"Hooray." He kissed her. "You're gorgeous."

Oh, the bliss of his mouth on hers. "And I want you to win Carla over."

"You're the important one. As long as I've won you over, I'm happy." Perry's eyes danced. "Besides, what can Carla do to me?"

"Put it this way," said Ginny. "You might want to wear a bulletproof vest."

It took Ginny, emerging from the restaurant kitchen, a couple of seconds to place the three women who had just arrived for lunch. Then it clicked. Eeurgh, the coven.

Worse still, Finn was greeting them and taking their coats because it was Evie's day off.

"I'm the duck, love. He's the crab."

"Oops, sorry." Ginny hastily switched the plates she'd just put down. Behind her, she could feel the witches turning their attention in her direction.

"Ginny, over here." Finn beckoned her over to the bar where they had congregated to order drinks. "These ladies are saying they recognize you from somewhere."

"It's Gavin's ex-wife, isn't it?" Up close, the head witch was heavily made up with lots of lime-green frosted eye shadow and an unpleasant gleam in her eye. "You came along to our club last night, dumped your friend on us. We didn't get a chance to speak to you, which was a shame." Turning to Finn, she explained, "It's a singles

173

club; we're very friendly. But some people don't like to waste time socializing with members of their own sex. Ginny here seemed far more interested in meeting the men. In fact I think you spent pretty much all evening talking to our men, didn't you? Nobody else got a look-in."

Ginny squirmed. On the other side of the bar, Finn's face was a picture. Of course it was; only last week she had been outraged by Gavin's suggestion that she might like to go along to the club.

Finn, the corners of his mouth twitching, said, "You didn't tell us you were going. What changed your mind?"

Blood pulsated through Ginny's face; she didn't need to look in the mirror behind the bar to know she was the color of Campari. "I wanted Laurel to meet someone. I only went along to keep her company."

The second witch smirked. "You didn't though, did you? You abandoned her. And she told us you were desperate to meet a new man, that's the only reason *she* agreed to go with *you*." She paused to light a cigarette, blew out a plume of smoke. "Well, you certainly met plenty, by the looks of things. Timothy seemed pretty smitten when you were smooching together on the dance floor."

Finn raised an eyebrow. "Sounds like you had a good night."

"He asked me to dance. It would have been rude

to say no. And I didn't only meet men," said Ginny. "I talked to Bev."

"Oh well, *her*. She thinks she's a cut above the rest of us." The third witch shook back her oversprayed, overstraightened hair. "She's man-mad too. Nothing but a slut. Nobody likes her."

"I did." Ginny reached for the leather-bound menus and handed one to each of the witches. "But I won't be going back to the club."

"Shame," Finn drawled. "Sounds like fun."

"He's single, you know." Ginny eyed the coven who immediately perked up. "If he thinks it's fun, why don't you persuade him to go along?"

Bingo. The first witch's eyes gleamed beneath layers of caked-on mascara. Clutching Finn's sleeve, she exclaimed, "Now that is an *excellent* idea."

"And you wouldn't have to worry about being on your own," Ginny told him breezily. "I'm sure these ladies would look after you."

"Thanks for that." Finn had waited until the restaurant was empty, the three witches having been the last to leave.

Revenge was sweet. Energetically clearing the tables, Ginny beamed at him. "My pleasure. You'll have a lovely time."

"I'd rather throw myself off a cliff. Not that there's anything wrong with singles clubs *per se*," Finn said quickly. "I just couldn't handle those three being there, following me around. But there's no shame in being on your own and wanting to change that."

Ginny contemplated explaining all over again then decided against it. The more she protested, the more of a desperate Doris she sounded. Instead she nodded and said, "I know."

"Now, this isn't a date," Finn announced when she returned from the kitchen to collect the tablecloths, "it's a straight offer. I've been invited to the reopening of the Carson Hotel tomorrow evening and I can bring a guest. If you want to come along with me, you can."

Talk about a turn-up for the books. Clutching the mound of tablecloths to her chest, Ginny said, "You want me to go with you to a hotel? Aren't you worried I might steal a few bathrobes?"

Finn smiled. "I'll just have to trust you to behave."

"I might not be able to. Will there be lots of single men there?"

"I'd say it's a possibility. That's why I thought you might enjoy it. And while you're talking to them, you can put in a good word for Penhaligon's."

Ginny considered this. "So I'd be allowed to plug your restaurant and chat up men at the same time?"

"Absolutely. As many as you like."

Maybe he meant to be helpful but she couldn't

help feeling slightly patronized. Beaming at him, Ginny said, "That's really kind of you. But no thanks."

"No?" Finn looked taken aback, rather like a do-gooder whose offer to have a lonely pensioner round for Christmas has been rejected.

"Actually, I'm already going along to the Carson do tomorrow night. With my boyfriend." Was it yucky to call someone your boyfriend when you were thirty-eight? Oh well. "So I'll see you there."

"Fine." He looked amused. "Good for you. I just thought I'd offer."

"See? I'm not as much of a charity case as you thought."

"I didn't think you were a charity case," said Finn. "Anyway, you can still plug the restaurant while you're there."

"Of course I will." As she swept past him with her armful of tablecloths, Ginny flashed him a jaunty smile. "If I'm not too busy having fun."

Chapter 20

"YOU LOOK NICE," SAID Laurel.

Ginny was immediately overcome with guilt. Laurel was sitting on the sofa in her droopy dressing gown, half reading a novel with a depressing cover and half watching a documentary about alopecia. The title of the book on her lap was *How Can I Live without You?* Ginny couldn't help feeling that if Laurel needed cheering up she'd be a lot better off with some nice breezy chick lit.

"Thanks." She smoothed her lime-green silk dress over her hips and showed off the lilac shoes that matched her bag. "These are a bit high, to be honest. I'll probably tip over and break an ankle. It's a shame you couldn't have come along too, but . . ."

"I know. Carla only had one spare ticket." Laurel didn't seem too distraught. "Don't worry, I'm fine staying in."

"And you've made that great curry," Ginny went on with too much enthusiasm. "So there's that to look forward to!"

Ergh, now she sounded like a hospital visitor.

"I know. Actually, I thought I might ring Perry and invite him round. He likes curry." Catching the flicker of alarm in Ginny's eyes, Laurel said, "That's all right, isn't it?"

Oh God, more deceit.

"Of course it is! Well, I'll just—"

The phone in her bag was ringing. Praying it wouldn't be Perry, Ginny fished it out.

It wasn't, thank goodness. "Jem! Hello, darling, how are you?" She waved, mouthed good-bye to Laurel, and headed out to the hall.

"Great, Mum. I'm just calling to say don't ring

me tomorrow morning because we're having a party tonight here at the flat and lots of people will probably end up staying over, so we'll all be asleep until midday."

Ginny smiled, picturing the scene the morning after. The flat would be in a revolting state. "OK, sweetheart, I'll let you have your lie-in. And don't forget to rope in all those overnighters to help with the clearing up. Don't let them slope off leaving you with all the work."

Jem laughed. "No need for that. Rupert's already booked a team of cleaners to come and blitz the place tomorrow afternoon. One of the advantages of being rich—we don't have to do a thing."

"That's good news then. So you're all still getting on well together?" Since Jem had never volunteered any information about her relation-ship with Rupert, Ginny hadn't asked. Jem might regard it as prying, Ginny knew she wouldn't be able to pretend to be overjoyed, and the last thing they needed was to have a fall-out.

"Everything's great." Jem certainly sounded chirpy. "We're busy doing all the food. Lucy and I are burning sausages and chopping onions . . ."

"And Rupert?" See? She couldn't help herself.

"Oh, he's a lazy bum. He's in the bath!"

What a surprise. But Jem was laughing, too happy to mind that Rupert was supercilious, selfish, and not one of life's workers. Impulsively,

Ginny said, "Have you invited Davy to the party?"

"Mum, I'm beginning to think you've got a bit of a thing about Davy." Jem giggled. "You're always going on about him."

That's because he's a nice boy, Ginny longed to say. Unlike some people I could mention.

Aloud she said, "Sorry."

"To be honest, Davy and Rupert don't like each other much. So it was easier not to. Anyway," Jem changed the subject, "I haven't asked how things are with you. What are you up to this weekend? Anything nice?"

"Very nice, thanks." Letting herself out of the house enabled Ginny to talk freely without being overheard by Laurel. "In fact I'm off to a party myself tonight. The Carson Hotel's reopening at last, having a bit of a flashy do to celebrate. Carla invited me along with a friend and we're hoping for better than burnt sausages and fried onions."

"Hey, Mum, brilliant. Who's the friend, one of Carla's boy toys?"

"Actually, he's someone I've been out with a couple of times. We get on well." Ginny said it casually, as if she'd been out with gazillions of men.

"Mum!" Jem, who knew she hadn't, was instantly agog. "Who *is* he?"

"Just someone nice. Don't get excited." It had been killing Ginny not to mention Perry before now but she still didn't dare give him a name. Never one for discretion, Jem had once loudly announced on a bus that Father Christmas wasn't real, reducing a dozen younger children to tears.

She'd only been ten at the time, but still.

"Don't tell me not to get excited. I *am* excited! Is he handsome? Has Carla met him yet? This is so cool!"

Ginny crossed the road as Carla came out of her house. "Yes, he's handsome. And Carla's about to meet him for the first time. In fact we're just off to the hotel now, so I'm going to say bye. Have a lovely time tonight, darling. Be good!"

Jem, sounding as if she was grinning, said, "You too."

"There he is." Pride welled up as Ginny pointed across the room to where Perry was standing, smartly dressed (hooray) and (double hooray) handsomer than ever. His red-gold hair gleamed in the brilliant light from the chandeliers, setting him apart from every other man in the room. He was wearing a dark blue suit and a blue and white striped shirt, and when he spotted Ginny with Carla he broke into a smile that sent tingles of lust zip-zapping up and down Ginny's spine.

He joined them and she performed the introductions.

"It's good to meet you at last." Perry shook Carla's hand.

"Hmm," Carla said coolly. "You may change your mind about that."

Perry turned to Ginny. "You said she was scary. You were right."

"Ginny's my friend. I'm looking out for her." Carla's tone was crisp.

"Well, guess what? You don't need to."

Her eyes flashed. "When I start seeing a new man, he's on the phone day and night. He can't keep away. We see each other all the time."

"As long as they've done their homework and their mothers say they're allowed out," Perry retorted.

"OK, stop it." Ginny stepped between them—God, this was turning into a soap opera. "No mud-slinging. I want you to be nice to each other."

Perry shrugged. "She started it."

"What are you, a complete *wimp?*"

"Don't," Ginny pleaded.

"Fine. I'm sorry. I'm sure he's wonderful." Briskly, Carla nodded and glanced around the room. "Well, I have to network. I'll leave you two to chat." And she left them.

Alarmed, Ginny said, "She isn't usually like that."

"Don't worry, I know the type. Some women can dish it out but they can't take it. Look at her hair." Perry's tone was disparaging. "The outfit, the makeup. Hard as nails, desperate to prove herself. That's why she goes for younger men, so she can boss them around, be the one who calls the tune. But deep down? She's insecure." He sounded so sure, so dismissive.

"Carla isn't insecure. She's—"

"Enough about Carla. You're here and that's all I care about." Perry gazed deep into her eyes. "We're going to have a good time tonight."

Despite the tricky start, Ginny was glad to see him again. Perry took two glasses of champagne from the tray of a hovering waitress and they clinked them together.

"Here's to you. Looking fabulous." He eyed her dress with appreciation. "Now tell me what you've been up to this week."

So she told him about working at Penhaligon's and taking Laurel to the singles club, and about Laurel sitting at home in her droopy dressing gown watching sad programs on TV. "She was planning to invite you over this evening," Ginny added. "I felt terrible."

"Don't. You're great with her."

"But she's still depressed about Kevin."

"Think how much more depressed she'd be if she didn't have you." Glancing past her left ear, Perry said, "We're being watched, by the way. Not one of your exes, is it?"

Ginny turned and saw Finn a distance away, talking to a luscious brunette but with his gaze flickering in their direction. "That's my boss."

Finn's attention was recaptured by the curvy

brunette but Ginny, delighted he'd noticed them, found herself becoming more animated and moving closer to Perry, touching his arm as they talked. If Finn had been expecting her to turn up with some ordinary unprepossessing man, well, ha, she hadn't! She hoped he was impressed. Later, when the situation arose, they would wander over and she would introduce him to Perry. Ooh, more drinks coming around, lovely.

Carla had spent the last hour circulating, greeting people she knew, and introducing herself to those she didn't. The Carson Hotel was the only five-star hotel in Portsilver and its glittering reopening was a major event. Everyone was impressed by the Victorian-style conservatory, immaculately finished and commanding uninterrupted views over the ocean. Already she had been asked by three guests to supply quotes for extensions to their own homes or businesses.

So far, then, a successful evening. With one awkward but manageable exception.

On her way to the ladies' loos, Carla bumped into him. Without missing a beat, as smoothly as a conjuror executing a nifty magic trick, Perry pushed open a door leading off the long corridor and drew her into the empty room.

"What?" Carla demanded fiercely.

"Has this ever happened to you before?"

Her eyes narrowed. "You mean being kidnapped?"

"You know what I'm talking about."

He was looking down at her, holding her by the shoulders against the wall. Carla swallowed and realized she was trembling. "Let me go."

"You haven't answered my question."

"I don't have to."

"I think you should."

"If you're trying to scare me . . ."

"No need," Perry said with a smile. "You're doing an excellent job of scaring yourself. So, ready to admit it now?"

Carla's mouth was bone dry. "Ready to admit *what?*"

By way of reply he released one of her shoulders and laid the flat of his right hand over her sternum between the vee of her shirt and the base of her throat. Immediately—as if she needed reminding—Carla felt her heart thumping away, pounding as if she'd just run a marathon.

"Now, I'm no doctor," Perry's tone was intimate, "but I'd guess a hundred and twenty beats per minute."

She was losing. He *knew.*

"That's what happens when you're trapped in a room with someone." Attempting to press herself backward into the wall, she said, "Especially when it's someone you don't trust."

"Except it was happening before, wasn't it? When Ginny first introduced us back there in the ballroom. I saw it happen." Perry smiled again as

185

he lightly brushed a forefinger over the frantically pulsating, all too visible vein in her neck.

This was terrible, a full-blown nightmare. Carla had always, *always* been able to hide her true feelings. It was a gift she prided herself on. Then again, had she ever experienced sensations as intense, as overwhelming as these before? The moment she'd clapped eyes on Perry Kennedy, her body had reacted independently of her mind. She didn't believe in love at first sight, but if she did . . . well, it would feel like this.

Except this man belonged to Ginny. And Ginny was her best friend. She *couldn't* allow herself to give in.

"It's the same for me," Perry whispered. "Exactly the same for me. You're the one; you're everything I ever wanted. Sorry, I know that sounds corny. But it's true."

"Let go of me. This isn't going to happen. I don't want to see you again." Lightheaded and gulping for air, Carla tried to push him away.

"You will; you have to. Look, I don't want to hurt Ginny either. And I know we can't do anything tonight, but I do need to see you again. Just give me your number, and I'll ring you. Can we meet up tomorrow?"

"No." This time Carla managed to free herself. Panting, she said, *"No,"* and stumbled out of the room.

Dear God, why had this had to happen to *her?*

The ladies' cloakroom was thankfully empty. Locking herself in one of the cool marble cubicles, Carla sat on the loo with her head in her hands, covering her flaming cheeks and willing the last ten minutes to empty themselves from her mind. Delete. Rewind. Think of Ginny, think of Ginny, *don't* think of—

Brrrppp. Carla's phone trilled and she almost fell off the loo seat. Her hands shaking violently, she saw an unfamiliar number flash up. Leave it to go to voice mail, just leave it.

No, she couldn't.

"H-hello?"

"It's me."

She'd known it would be him. "I said don't ring me."

"No you didn't." Perry's voice was conversational, amused. "You said you wouldn't give me your number."

"So how . . . ?"

"*Luckily* there's a table out in the conservatory with your company's brochures on it." He paused. "Not to mention a pile of your business cards."

"I don't want to speak to you. I'm hanging up."

"I live in the flat above my shop. Twenty-five B, Harbor Street. Eight o'clock tomorrow evening suit you?"

Carla closed her eyes, pressed her trembling

knees together. "You're out of your mind. Ginny's my *friend*."

"Eight o'clock it is then."

"I'm going to tell her about this. I'm going to go out there right now and tell her what you're doing behind her back."

"Eight o'clock," said Perry.

Click.

Carla gazed at the phone. He had hung up.

Chapter 21

"HERE HE IS." GINNY was standing with Finn. Proudly she introduced Perry.

"Hi. Good to meet you." Shaking Finn's hand, Perry said, "Sorry to be so long. I got chatting to someone I know."

Ginny said gaily, "That's nothing. I've been chatting to lots of people I *don't* know, telling them why they should come to Penhaligon's! One couple is going to book a table for next week; they're looking for somewhere to hold their daughter's wedding reception."

"Wedding receptions." Perry shuddered. "Sorry, my idea of hell. Kids running around screaming, babies crying . . . do you have children?"

"No." Finn's jaw was taut.

"Sensible man. Don't go there. Can't see the attraction myself. Everyone tells you kids change your life . . . well, I don't want to change mine, thanks very much. I'd rather keep it just the way it is. Who needs all that grief?"

"Probably not the best thing to say," murmured Ginny when Finn had excused himself and moved away to resume his conversation with the luscious brunette. "His girlfriend had a baby last year. Finn assumed it was his, but it wasn't. She ended up leaving him and going off with the baby's father."

"That's what I call a lucky escape. Oh, come on; don't look at me like that." Perry grinned and slid his arm round her. "Kids aren't my thing, that's all. And trust me, there's nothing worse than a broody woman. I mean, look at Laurel. Half the reason she's taking this whole Kevin thing so badly is because she thinks she won't find another man before it's too late. Her hormones are in panic mode, flying around like headless chickens." He gave her waist a squeeze. "That's what I like about you."

"What? That my hormones are flying around like headless chickens?"

"That they *aren't*." Perry's green eyes glinted with amusement. "You and Laurel are the same age, but you've already done your bit, got the whole breeding thing out of your system. Don't get me wrong; I think it's great that you have a daughter. I'm just not interested in having any myself."

"You sound exactly like Carla."

"God, don't tell me there's something we actually agree on. I'm not sure I'm happy about that."

"Carla's all right." Ginny so badly wanted the two of them to get along. "Wait till you get to know her better."

Perry pulled a face. "I'd rather not."

"Don't be mean. She's my best friend."

"She's a viper. Anyway, why are we wasting time talking about her? I haven't even kissed you yet."

With this audience? Alarmed, Ginny squeaked, "You can't do that in here!"

"I know, I'm not a complete heathen." Keeping his arm around her waist, Perry steered her through the crowded ballroom, acknowledging an unsmiling Carla with a friendly nod as they passed her in conversation with a potential client. "That's why I thought we might take a walk around the grounds."

"It's dark out there. I'll trip over something and land flat on my face."

"You won't, there's a full moon. And the gardens are floodlit." Opening the doors that led outside, Perry ushered her through. "Hang on to me. I won't let you fall."

Ginny loved the way he said it, like James Bond would. It made her feel safe.

Carla couldn't help herself. When she saw Finn Penhaligon at the bar, she went over and stood next to him. He raised an eyebrow in recognition.

"Can I ask you something?" God, her stomach was in knots. "What do you think of Ginny's bloke?"

"I only spoke to him for a minute. I don't like to make snap judgments about people." Pausing, Finn said, "Although in his case I'll make an exception."

"And?"

His tone was contemptuous. "The man's an arse."

This was what Carla wanted to hear. She picked up a cocktail stick and snapped it in half.

"And?" Finn mimicked lightly. Funny how such an outwardly attractive man could have zero effect on her, whereas . . . oh God, don't even go there, don't even *think* about Perry Kennedy.

Carla nodded and reached for another cocktail stick to snap. "I think so too."

The music was bouncing off the walls of the flat, making the floor vibrate. A rumbustious game involving seeing how long you could balance an open can of lager on your head before it fell off was in progress in the living room, with much shoving and spillage going on. The carpet was drenched and empty cans were strewn everywhere. Jem, watching as one of Rupert's friends tackled another to the ground—splat—felt sorry for the cleaners from the agency when they arrived tomorrow to clear up.

A hand on her bottom made her jump. His mouth brushing her ear, Rupert murmured, "What are you thinking?"

"That if this lot are planning to sleep on this floor tonight, they might drown."

"Their problem, not mine. Are you wearing any knickers?"

"Yes!" Jem wriggled as his warm fingers roamed over the back of her jeans.

"Shame. Hey, no one would notice if we slipped away for a few minutes. Fancy a quickie?"

"We can't do that." Jem turned and grinned at him. "It's not polite to abandon your guests."

"Bugger the guests. It's my party, and I'll shag if I—"

"Rupert, can you do something about Tilly and Marcus?"

This time Jem jumped because Lucy had appeared out of nowhere behind them. Gazing hard at Rupert, she went on, "They've locked themselves in the bathroom and there are people desperate for the loo."

"Great minds think alike," Rupert whispered in Jem's ear before levering himself away from the wall. "OK, I'll go and sort them out. Spoil their fun."

When he'd gone, Lucy said in an odd voice, "What was Rupert saying to you?"

Oh God, surely she couldn't have overheard. Awkwardly, Jem said, "Nothing. We were just talking about the carpet getting wet with all the beer being spilled. Like that." She nodded across the room as another can of lager went flying, spraying froth.

"It didn't look like that to me." Lucy's hands were thrust stiffly into the front pockets of her low-slung jeans. "The way you were whispering together."

Jem's mouth was dry. At least Lucy hadn't seen Rupert groping her; thank goodness he'd been discreet.

"And did he have his hand on your backside?"

"No . . . well, he was just mucking around," Jem stammered. "It didn't mean anything."

Lucy frowned. "Is there something going on between you and Rupert?"

See? It was clearly bothering her. This was exactly why she couldn't admit the truth.

"No." Jem looked astounded. "God, are you serious? No way! I can't believe you even thought that."

There, was that convincing enough? Exuding innocent outrage, she held her ground and prayed Lucy wasn't about to whip out a lie detector.

"OK," Lucy said levelly. "But you'd tell me if there was, wouldn't you?" Her words were brittle, like dry sticks. "I mean, I'd want to know."

Of course she would. And if she did find out? Then the easy, happy atmosphere in the flat would be spoiled, Lucy would feel like a third wheel, and the next thing you know, she'd be moving out.

Jem didn't want that to happen. Lucy was her closest friend here in Bristol and a perfect flatmate.

"I'd tell you if there was anything going on," said Jem, "but there isn't, I promise. Crikey, I'm not nearly posh enough for Rupert!"

A faint smile tugged at the corners of Lucy's mouth. "You could be his bit of rough."

"Charming!" Relieved that the interrogation was over, Jem pretended to tug at one of her friend's gaudy earrings. "Speak for yourself."

Lucy grinned back, equally relieved. "Can you smell sausages burning?"

Jem could. It was a wonder the smoke alarm hadn't gone off. Thankful that the crisis had been averted and eager to please, she said, "You've done loads of cooking; I'll take over in the kitchen now."

"And we need more onions chopping up."

"Fine, I'll do it."

Lucy tilted her head to one side and said lightly, "Guilty conscience?"

"No!" Jem made an attempt to grab her other earring. "As if! I just want first pick of the sausages so I get the ones that aren't burned to a crisp."

"I took them out of the oven," said Davy when Jem burst into the kitchen. The trays of sausages were smoldering on top of the hob and Davy, shirt sleeves rolled up, was busy peeling and chopping a mound of onions.

"My hero! I didn't even know you'd arrived!" Jem hugged him, delighted that Davy had been able to make it; following the phone call to her mother earlier, guilt had prompted her to send him a text inviting him to the party. Now she was extra glad she had. "And just in the nick of time too. You saved our sausages!"

"Not all of them. Some are pretty cremated."

"Trust me, this crowd won't notice. The state half of them are in, they'd eat lumps of coal if we served them up in bread rolls with a squish of ketchup. Here, try one of the unburned ones." Choosing the best sausage and breaking it in two, she popped half into Davy's mouth and the other half into her own.

Damn, it was hot.

"Aaarrgh." Jem let out a shriek of pain.

"Yeeesh." Davy, his hands otherwise occupied with half an onion and a chopping knife, held the sausage clamped between his teeth and waggled it at her like Groucho Marx.

"Hot-hot-hot," Jem gasped, flapping her arms and hopping from one foot to the other.

"You'll never get off the ground," drawled Rupert behind her.

"Mmpph." With her mouth full of sausage, Jem swung round.

Rupert said, "What's he doing here?"

Jem chewed and swallowed, fanning her mouth. "I invited him. And he's helping with the food."

"Not to mention eating it."

"I'll write you a check," Davy said evenly.

"Don't bother, it'd probably bounce. Anyway, I like to do my bit to feed the poor."

"Rupert! God, you can be such a pig sometimes." Jem turned to Davy. "He doesn't mean it."

Drily, Davy said, "Of course he doesn't. Don't worry; I'll leave you to it."

Jem was alarmed. "You're not going."

"No." Having rinsed and dried his hands, Davy smiled at her. "I'm not."

When he'd left the kitchen, Jem said, "I hate it when you do that."

Rupert grinned, moved toward her. "But it's fun."

"It isn't. And you mustn't do that either." Darting out of reach as he made a playful grab for her, Jem said, "Lucy saw us just now. She's getting suspicious."

"What did you tell her?"

"That nothing was going on, of course. I said you weren't my type. Which you *aren't,*" Jem added pointedly, "when you're being mean to Davy. If you can't say anything nice about a person, don't say anything at all."

"Bloody hell, where's the superglue? May as well seal my mouth shut now. God knows how I'll be able to drink."

Rupert sauntered out and Jem dealt with the rest of the onions. When she rejoined the party twenty minutes later, a limbo contest was in noisy progress in the middle of the room. Rupert was laughing as Lucy collapsed in a heap on the floor. Hauling her to her feet, he had a go himself and somehow—miraculously—managed it. His boisterous friends clapped and roared their approval, finding it something of a challenge to stay on their feet even without the distraction of a limbo pole. Then they roared again, having spotted Jem and her tray of hot dogs. Within seconds they'd descended on her like a pack of wolves.

But friendly wolves, thank goodness. Slapping away a few hands—not all of them after the hot dogs—Jem managed to save three and crossed the room to where Davy was chatting to a plump but pretty brunette.

The girl's name was Suze, Jem discovered, and she was Patty Carson's sister. Patty, on their English course, was currently smooching with one of the rugby boys. Suze, a nurse down from Birmingham for the weekend, seemed glad of Davy's company. Jem gave them each a hot dog and was pleased Davy had found someone nice to talk to.

"Door," bellowed several people as the bell shrilled, indicating yet more late arrivals. Realizing that no one else was planning to let them in, Jem rolled her eyes and excused herself from Davy and Suze. Task completed, she was about to head back to the party when an ear-splitting crash came from the kitchen.

"Oh, Jem, I'm really sorry." A red-faced Patty Carson clutched her arm. "Ben came over all masterful and got carried away. We knocked the big glass salad bowl off the kitchen table."

Patty and Ben, both of them many sheets to the wind, were more of a hazard than a help. After they'd each cut themselves three times, Jem banished them from the kitchen and embarked on clearing up the shards of broken glass herself. It was safer this way for all concerned, plus between them Patty and Ben had used up the last of the plasters.

"Don't come in," yelled Jem as the door handle turned.

"Only me." Davy let himself in anyway. "Need a hand?"

A sober hand, what a luxury. Jem nodded gratefully and said, "What about Suze?"

"She's giving Patty a good talking-to. There's a lettuce leaf in your hair, by the way."

"There's glass and lettuce everywhere. And oil. Mind the floor; it's all slippy with dressing. Patty and Ben looked as if they were having their first skating lesson." Jem pushed her bangs off her forehead with one elbow. "I had to get them out of here before one of them severed an artery."

Together they cleared up the mess. When they finally rejoined the party, Rupert was talking to Suze Carson. Picking a bottle of lager out of the tub of melting ice cubes, Davy said, "That's me out of the picture, then."

"It doesn't mean anything. He's just being friendly."

"Hmm. Very friendly." Davy raised an eyebrow and when Jem glanced over again she saw with a jolt that they were kissing. Suze's head was tipped back and her arms were wrapped ecstatically round Rupert's neck.

Jem hurriedly looked away and took a gulp of wine. The next moment, Lucy shimmied over and grabbed her hand. "Let's dance," she shouted happily above the blaring music. "Come on, Davy, you too."

By four o'clock the party was on its last legs. People were crashed out on sofas and chairs; those not fast enough to bag them had to make do with the soggy floor.

"Bed," Lucy yawned, switching off the CD player and almost tripping over a snoring body behind the door. "Night, Davy. Night, Jem. Night, all you drunken bums."

Acting normally was almost killing her but Jem had spent the last few hours doing it and she wasn't about to give up now. Rupert had spent the evening flirting with and enthusiastically kissing Suze Carson. At two o'clock, Patty and her bowl-smashing rugby player had left the party. Shortly after that, Rupert and Suze had disappeared into Rupert's bedroom and she probably wasn't teaching him first aid. Jem had given her best impression of a single girl without a care in the world while her stomach had been busy tying itself up in one giant knot.

Now, utterly miserable, she looked over at Davy and said, "Want me to phone for a cab?"

Davy sounded hesitant. "Well, you did say I could crash out here if I ever needed to. And it is pretty late."

It was. She had. It was just so hard to concentrate when all you wanted to do was run down the hallway and hammer on Rupert's locked bedroom door yelling, "Stop it, stop whatever you're doing, STOP IT!"

Jem nodded. "Of course you can. Sorry, I just thought you'd be going home."

"I told my mum I'd be staying here. She was OK about it, considering. One small step for man." Davy's smile was self-deprecating. "One giant step for me."

"That's great, Davy." Jem wished she could summon up more enthusiasm for his triumph, because it was a big deal. "Good for you."

"Don't worry about where to put me." He gestured to a space on the carpet in front of the sofa. "I'll be fine here."

The carpet was squelching beneath his feet and

Tommy Beresford-Smith was snoring like a walrus on the sofa; if he tried to turn over in his sleep, he'd roll off and squash Davy flat.

"You can't sleep there." Rubbing her tired, smoke-reddened eyes, Jem said, "Better stay in my room. The carpet's dry and I don't snore."

Chapter 22

IT FELT LIKE FIVE minutes later when Jem woke up but a glance at the alarm clock revealed that it was eleven thirty. Davy's impromptu bed of cushions and blankets on the floor was empty and the sound of male voices drifted through from the kitchen.

Jem crawled slowly out of bed, dehydrated and dry-mouthed with apprehension, just as the door opened and Davy walked in carrying two mugs of tea.

"Hi. I made these."

"Thanks." She took the steaming mug he handed her. "Is everyone else up?"

"Only Rupert."

"I need a glass of water. Back in a minute." Running her fingers through her slept-in hair, Jem made her way past Davy.

Rupert was in the kitchen looking disgustingly healthy and unaffected by the amount of drink he'd put away last night. He was wearing jeans and a wicked grin, and piling sugar into two cups of coffee.

"Morning, gorgeous." He winked at her. "Sleep well?"

Sick with jealousy, Jem closed the kitchen door so they couldn't be overheard and said, "Did you have sex with her?"

"With who?"

"Scarlet Johansson." Jem shook her head vehemently. "Who d'you think? That girl!"

"Oh, you mean Suze. *That* girl." Amused, Rupert said, "Of course I didn't."

Jem seized a pint mug, swilled out the dregs of last night's lager, and shoved it under the tap, managing to spray ice-cold water all over the front of her nightie. "I don't believe you."

He shrugged. "Well, I can't help that. But it's the truth. We just crashed out."

"You were kissing her." God, it was horrible sounding like a neurotic nagging shrew, but what else was she supposed to do? He'd been *kissing* her.

"I thought you'd be pleased," said Rupert.

"Pleased!"

"Lucy was suspicious about us. By taking Suze back to my room, I've put a stop to that. Stroke of genius."

Jem swallowed. "Is that why you did it?"

"Yep. Well, that was one of the reasons." Breaking into a grin, Rupert drawled, "The other

one being to get her away from your pal
Davy."

"Why?"

"Why d'you think? To piss him off."

"I still think you slept with her."

"Well, I didn't. But fine, think what you like.
Anyway," said Rupert, "you can talk. What
happened between you and Davy?"

"Nothing!"

He tilted his head. "So you say. But let's face it;
he spent last night in your room, which has to be
the first time he's ever stayed out overnight. What
better way to celebrate?" There was a glint in his
eye as he went on, "Bloody hell, what's his
mother going to be doing now? She's probably
spent the last six hours dialing 999. There'll be
helicopters circling overhead, police divers
searching the river."

"He told her he was staying here. And he slept
on the floor. You *know* we didn't do anything,"
said Jem. "I *wouldn't*."

"You mean I just have to trust you? Well, snap."
Dropping a lazy kiss on her bare shoulder, Rupert
carried the mugs past her. "But remember, it's
thanks to me that you've got Lucy off your
back."

She weakened. Even a passing shoulder kiss had
the power to make her go weak at the knees.
Watching him leave, Jem experienced a violent
rush of longing. You knew you were a lost cause

203

when you found yourself embroiled with someone who actually was sexier than Johnny Depp.

Back in the bedroom she drank her cooling tea and listened to Davy's brief telephone conversation with his mother.

"Yes, Mum, I'm still alive. No, I didn't take any drugs. No, the police weren't called. Mum, everything's fine. I'll see you later, OK? Yes, me too."

Jem sat down on the bed. How awful to have such a clingy, neurotic mother. She watched as Davy ended the call then keyed in another number.

"Hi, it's me. Where are we and what time do we start?" He listened, nodding, then reached for a purple felt-tip pen on Jem's dresser and began scribbling down an address.

He didn't get very far.

"Right," Davy said evenly. "I'll see you there."

When he'd switched off his phone, Jem said, "Going somewhere nice?"

He shrugged and held out the scrap of paper upon which he'd written down the first line of the address. Jem frowned. "But . . . that's *here*."

"Just my luck."

"I don't understand. Who are you meeting up with?"

Davy puffed out his cheeks and rubbed the back of his hair. Finally, he said, "The rest of the team from Spit and Polish."

Spit and Polish. The contract cleaning company hired by Rupert to come and restore the flat to some semblance of normality. More than a semblance, actually, given the prices they charged.

"I didn't know you worked for them," said Jem.

"I only started a couple of weeks ago. A few hours on a Saturday, and again on Sunday. The money's not bad and it seemed like a good idea at the time." Heaving a sigh, Davy said, "Rupert's going to have a field day when he finds out."

Jem had done her best to chivvy everyone awake and get them out of the flat but it was like trying to shovel mud in a swamp. At twelve o'clock on the dot a bright orange van with Spit and Polish emblazoned in turquoise along each side pulled up outside the flat. Out jumped five ready-to-go cleaners in neon orange and turquoise boilersuits.

"Here they are then." Turning away from the bedroom window, Davy said, "And brace yourself. The one in the headscarf is Rhonda."

"Hello, my love, Spit and Polish at your service." When Rupert opened the door he was almost knocked sideways by a mini whirlwind in a fluorescent orange headscarf. "Ooh, my Lord, cracking party by the looks of things, what a state, these walls are going to need some elbow grease." Barreling past him and beadily surveying the scene of post-party chaos with her head on one side, Rhonda patted Rupert's hand and said, "Never mind, love, we're here now to do all your dirty work for you, we'll have this mucky old flat spick and span again in no time. My word, you're a handsome lad, aren't you? Now what we really need is for everyone to clear out of here and leave us to get on, then when you come back at three o'clock you won't recognize the place, that's a promise!"

"We'll go and grab some lunch." Rupert counted the boiler-suited individuals piling into the flat armed with buckets and cleaning paraphernalia. "I thought there were meant to be six of you."

"There are, love. The last one hasn't arrived quite yet but don't you worry, he'll be here in two shakes of a lamb's—oh my word, speak of the devil. Davy, love, you beat us to it after all! Janice, give the lad his overalls and we can get cracking."

Rupert struggled to keep a straight face as Janice threw the orange jumpsuit at Davy, standing in the doorway. Davy climbed into it and zipped it up to his neck.

"You work for this company?" said Rupert.

"Yes, I do."

"So you'll be cleaning my flat."

"Looks like it."

"Nice one. Don't forget to scrub the toilet, will you?"

"It'll be done," Davy said evenly.

"But I'd really like you to be the one who does it. That'd make my day."

From the kitchen, Rhonda yelled, "Goodness me, what a state! Davy, love, come and help me make a start in here."

Rupert smirked. "Better get a move on, Davy, love. The kitchen, eh? In that case let's hope for less of the spit and more of the polish."

Still on a high from last night, Ginny couldn't wait to ring Jem and find out how the party had gone. At one o'clock—surely it was safe to do it now; they couldn't still be asleep—she made the phone call.

It was picked up on the fourth ring. "Hello?"

Not Rupert. *Good.* Ginny said brightly, "Hi, is Jem there?"

"Sorry, no. Everyone's out."

"Oh. Right." Did the male voice sound faintly familiar? "But you're there."

"Yes." There was a moment's hesitation. "Is that Jem's mum?"

"It is." Caught off guard, Ginny said, "And who are you?"

"Davy Stokes. You probably won't remember, but you gave me a lift home to—"

"Davy! Of course I remember! How lovely to speak to you again. How *are* you?"

"Fine thanks."

"So you must have gone to the party last night.

I was just calling to find out how it went." A thought popped into Ginny's head. "Oh my goodness, Jem isn't there but you are. Does this mean you and Lucy are an item?"

He sounded amused. "Wouldn't that have been good? Sorry to disappoint you. I reckon I'd have more chance with Claudia Schiffer."

"So what are you . . . ?"

"Doing here? Rupert hired a cleaning team. I'm one of the team." Drily Davy added, "Which, it goes without saying, made Rupert's day."

"I can imagine." Ginny paused because she and Davy shared the same low opinion of Rupert; it was their guilty secret. On impulse, she said, "Can I ask you something?"

"Fire away. Something about Jem?"

"And Rupert." She chose her words with care. "Is there anything . . . well, going on between them?"

Davy sounded surprised. "You mean are they a couple? I don't think so. She hasn't said anything to me."

"No?" Ginny wished she felt more reassured. "But would she tell you?"

"Look, I'm sure there's nothing going on. I slept on her bedroom floor last night. Rupert was with someone else."

"Oh. Right." This was more like it; this was far more encouraging.

"Have you asked her?"

"I haven't dared, in case she says yes. Anyway, you must be right if Rupert hooked up with another girl." Ginny breathed a sigh of relief. "Well, I'd better let you get back to work. Tell Jem I'll give her a ring later. And good luck with Claudia Schiffer!"

They said their good-byes—*such* a nice boy—and Ginny tried next to ring Carla, to see if she wanted to meet up for a spot of lunch. But Carla's mobile was switched off, which probably meant she was working, following up on all the leads she'd so assiduously collected last night.

Oh, well, never mind. Maybe head into town and go shopping for a new dress instead.

Or sit listening to Laurel relate the latest installment in the ongoing Saga of Kevin.

Ginny reached for her bag. Definitely go shopping instead.

Chapter 23

RUPERT HAD BROUGHT THEM to Pink, the latest trendy restaurant to open on Whiteladies Road, and the weather was warm and sunny enough to sit outside. There were ten of them altogether, and the champagne was flowing, easing the pain of last night's hangovers. Jem was feeling more relaxed now although she'd feel better still if Suze would give up, accept defeat, and go back to her sister's flat, leaving the rest of them to carry on without her. It was painfully obvious that she was crazy about Rupert, sitting next to him with a besotted smile on her face, clearly fancying her chances with him later if she just hung around long enough.

But it was just as apparent that Rupert wasn't remotely interested in her. The banter being batted back and forth across the table excluded Suze. Rupert and his smart friends down from London were on top form and Jem and Lucy were joining in, part of the team.

"Uh-oh, here comes the big boss." Rupert grinned as the manager threaded his way between tables toward them. "Maybe he's going to kick us out."

Jem hoped not. "Are we being too noisy?"

Rupert, his eyes glittering, said, "I can be loads noisier than this."

"Me too." Suze smirked and wriggled her chair closer to his. Jem rolled her eyes at Lucy. Inwardly, she felt like pushing Suze off her chair.

But the manager hadn't come over to ask them to leave. He explained to Rupert that a photographer from a glossy lifestyle magazine was here to take pictures to accompany a feature on upmarket restaurants in the southwest.

"Your table epitomizes our target clientele," said the manager. "OK with you if we have some photos taken?"

"Oh wow!" Suze looked excited and began fluffing up her hair. "Cool!"

Which just went to show how completely uncool she was.

"Fine by me." Rupert shrugged, glancing around the table. "Everyone else all right with that?"

The photographer joined them and Suze trilled, "Wait until my friends hear about this. I've never been in a magazine before! Ooh, I'd better go and re-do my makeup!"

How completely pathetic. Jem couldn't bear the possessive way Suze was clutching at Rupert's arm, emphasizing their togetherness. Everybody was probably a little bit excited about being featured in a glossy magazine but only Suze was making a show of herself by admitting it.

"Actually, could we move things around a bit?" The photographer swung into action, studying angles and indicating that a couple of chairs should be moved out of shot. Addressing Rupert, he said, "You stay there, I want you in the center of the shot. Now, I need a girl either side of you . . ."

"I fit that job description." Simpering, Suze stayed put.

"You and you, could you two move closer together?" The photographer indicated Lucy and one of Rupert's raffishly handsome London friends, then looked from Jem to Suze. "And could you two girls swap places?"

Yes, yes, yes! Jem could have kissed him. The smile slid off Suze's face like an iced bun melting in the rain. And now the photographer was getting himself into position, concentrating his camera on Rupert's side of the table. As Jem slid into the seat sulkily vacated by Suze, Rupert draped an arm casually over her shoulder and murmured in her ear, "Welcome to the world of the beautiful people."

"Could we just move the ashtrays out of shot?" The photographer made vigorous clearing gestures with his hands. "And cover up that wine stain on the tablecloth?"

"Where's Davy when you need him?" Rupert mockingly clicked his fingers. "Dammit, you can't get the staff these days. Still, just as well he isn't here—who'd want to bother taking our photos when they could take Davy's?"

"Don't be mean." Jem said it automatically.

"I'm not mean. I'm just being honest. The guy's a loser." Rupert lifted a bottle from the ice bucket and refilled their glasses. "I mean, be fair. Life is for living. Which would you rather do? Sit out here in the sun, drinking champagne, eating amazing food, and having your photo taken for a feature in a glossy magazine, or dress up in an orange nylon jumpsuit that frankly doesn't suit you and scrub out someone else's toilet?"

Lucy said easily, "You're such an obnoxious git, Rupert."

He winked at her. "I know, but I'm a bloody good-looking obnoxious git. And I know how to have fun."

The photographer was busily snapping away now. Everyone else outside the restaurant was watching them. Feeling special and glamorous and reveling in the attention, Jem shook back her hair—snap snap—and took a sip of ice-cold champagne.

There was no getting away from it, Rupert had a point.

Penhaligon's had been taken over for the evening by a work party celebrating their boss's fortieth birthday. Before they arrived, Finn and Ginny put the finishing touches to the dining room, as specified, including tying a bobbing silver helium balloon to the back of each chair.

Ginny tied the last one and stepped back to survey the effect. "It looks like a children's party."

"This is what they wanted." Finn shrugged. "And they're paying for it. Apparently it's a work tradition—they all unfasten the ends of the balloons after the meal, suck in lungfuls of helium, and sing 'Happy Birthday' in Mickey Mouse voices."

"Some companies have strange traditions."

"And this is a firm of chartered accountants. There, all done." Finn straightened a couple of chairs. "Let's hope they charged the balloons to expenses."

From where she was standing, Ginny had a clear view of the courtyard. A small van had just rolled up and a man now emerged carrying a vast cellophane-wrapped bouquet.

"Did the accountants say they'd arranged for flowers to be delivered?"

"No." Finn looked out of the window. "Could be for you, from that chap of yours."

There was something ever so slightly offhand about the way he said it. Niggled, Ginny replied, "His name's Perry. And if he were sending me flowers he'd have them delivered to my house." She managed to make it sound as though Perry sent her flowers at least three times a week, if not on a daily basis. Ooh, though, what if these were from him and he just didn't want to risk Laurel reading the accompanying slushy card?

"Hello, love." The delivery man addressed Ginny cheerily when she pulled open the door. "Sorry, we've been rushed off our feet today, but better late than never, eh? Could you sign for these?"

She scribbled her signature and took the flowers, an excitingly exotic arrangement of striking blues and oranges. Then turned over the accompanying envelope and saw the name on the front. Bum.

"They're for you." Ginny held them out to Finn, who raised an eyebrow.

"Why, thank you so much, how kind of you and how unexpected. Is this to thank me for being such a great boss?"

"Absolutely. Best ever. And these cost me a fortune, so a pay rise wouldn't go amiss." Ginny watched him open the envelope, skim the card. "Who's it really from?"

"Catherine."

"Zeta Jones? Now I'm impressed."

Finn's mouth twitched.

"So? Catherine *who?*"

"Nosy."

"Not nosy. Interested," said Ginny. "You can't say her name then not tell me who she is."

"You saw her. She was at the Carson last night. I just gave her a lift home, that's all."

The curvy, sexy-looking brunette. Picturing her, Ginny said, "Dark hair, white dress?"

"That's the one."

"And now she's sent you flowers? Must have been a hell of a lift."

"We aim to please."

Ginny knew she was being juvenile—he was single and presumably Catherine was too—but the faintly derogatory way he had referred to Perry had brought out her competitive side. "I'd say you succeeded. Will you be seeing her again?"

"Might do, might not. I haven't really thought about it. Actually, probably not." Pulling a face, Finn said, "It feels a bit odd, being sent flowers by a woman. That's never happened to me before. You can have them if you like." He was holding out the bouquet, offering it to her. It must have cost at least fifty pounds.

"No thanks. I don't want your cast-off flowers. Poor Catherine," said Ginny. "She must really like you. You'll have to phone and thank her."

He gave her a look. "Nosy *and* bossy."

"I'm serious. Honestly, single men can be horrible sometimes."

"Not speaking from experience, I hope." Finn's tone was light but she was almost sure he was having another dig.

"Not personal experience, no. And I'm very happy with Perry. We had a great time last night."

"Glad to hear it. Good for you. Well, looks like our party's arriving." As Finn spoke, a convoy of taxis streamed into the yard. "I don't know which one's the birthday girl."

Out of the second cab jumped a lively-looking blond in a bright red dress, wearing big plastic Mickey Mouse ears and a battery-operated flashing necklace proclaiming 40 TODAY!

"Call it female intuition," said Ginny, "but possibly that one."

"And she's their chief accountant," Finn marveled.

Ginny tut-tutted. "Making snap judgments again. You think accountants don't know how to have fun. That's such a job-ist attitude."

"You're right. I'll make it up to her." Finn went to greet the party at the door, kissing the chief accountant on both cheeks before presenting her with the bouquet.

"Oh, that's so kind of you. Really, these are beautiful." Delightedly the blond buried her nose in the exotic blue and orange blooms and came back up dusted with pollen. "So thoughtful! And you'll never guess what; my sister rang this morning and told me she'd met you last night! You gave her a lift home from the Carson, isn't that a coincidence?" Beaming, she went on, "Catherine said you were one of the nicest men she'd ever met!"

Chapter 24

IT WAS TEN PAST eight on Saturday evening. Ginny was out at work. Carla was standing in her kitchen determinedly not looking at her switched-off phone.

If she owned a pair of handcuffs she'd chain herself to the stove and swallow the key.

Oh God, this was unbearable. She was wavering badly. Last night she'd barely slept at all, her mind frenziedly replaying every second of the brief and fateful encounter with Perry Kennedy. And every minute of today had been filled with more of the same, because she couldn't stop thinking about him. If there was a switch to turn off, she would.

But there wasn't.

Twelve minutes past eight. She was winning so far. Meeting Perry mustn't happen, it just *mustn't*. He wasn't single; he was taken. More to the point, taken by Ginny. And Ginny was besotted with him, which made him so completely off limits it just didn't bear thinking about.

Dry-mouthed, Carla looked again at her watch. Twelve and a half minutes past now. He was there, waiting for her. And she was here. Which was the *right* place to be. And OK, maybe it was killing her but she only had another fifteen or twenty minutes to endure because surely if she hadn't turned up to meet him by eight thirty he would realize she wasn't coming and would go out.

Thirty minutes passed.

Forty minutes, then fifty. She was still here; she hadn't gone to Perry's flat. So why wasn't she feeling more relaxed?

At nine fifteen the doorbell shrilled and every nerve in Carla's body went into overdrive. This was why she hadn't felt more relaxed.

She opened the front door an inch, keeping the chain on, and hissed, "Go away. I'm not going to do this."

"At least let me in." Perry was wearing a hat as an attempt at a disguise and spoke in an anguished whisper. "I can't believe you made me come here.

Laurel's just across the road; she could look out of the window at any moment and see me."

Oh God, oh God. "I can't let you in. I just can't."

"Carla, I'm not leaving." He clearly meant business. "This is too important. We need to talk, you know we do."

Carla trembled; she knew it too. But not here in her house, across the road from Ginny's.

"I'll come to your flat. You leave now. I'll follow in ten minutes." Would she? Wouldn't she? She didn't even know herself.

"Promise," Perry whispered.

"I promise." Was that another lie? Maybe, maybe not.

"Ten minutes," said Perry. "I'll be waiting."

"OK. Bye." Carla closed the door and saw his shadow recede through the hall window as he slipped away down the path to wherever he'd left his car.

She mustn't go, *she mustn't*.

She parked her car haphazardly at nine forty, too agitated and filled with self-loathing to even check her reflection in the rearview mirror because that would mean having to look into her guilt-riddled eyes.

The car park was two hundred yards from his flat. Hurrying along the narrow, darkened street, Carla reminded herself that she knew barely anything about Perry Kennedy. When you met someone for the first time, you could be wildly attracted by their outward appearance, but that didn't tell you what they were like beneath the surface—they could have any number of wildly unattractive character traits that you had yet to discover.

OK, here it was, Perry's shop with its window full of printed T-shirts, and next to it the door leading up to his flat. Just an ordinary dark blue door with the 25B picked out in brass lettering that could do with a polish. See? She really didn't know him at all. Maybe a quick glance around Perry's flat would be enough to magically decimate any feelings she might have had for him, in less time than it took to squash a cockroach. He might live in utter squalor, for instance. That would be enough to turn her stomach. Or cat food bowls left soaking in the sink along with the rest of the washing-up—perfect. Or he might harbor a secret passion for train-spotting complete with model railway occupying pride of place in his living room. Or he could have the walls plastered with posters of topless girls reclining on motorbikes. Or maybe he liked to save all his toenail clippings and keep them in a glass jar in the kitchen.

Or better still, *other people's* toenail clippings.

Sick with excitement and shame, lust and fear, and hoping against hope that there would be *something* up there to put her off him, Carla rang the bell and prepared herself for Perry to answer the door.

She took a deep breath and waited. And waited. Rang the bell again.

Waited some more.

Nothing, oh God, he wasn't even here. Carla's heart began to clamor as panic rose; how could he not be here now?

Still no sign of life. She couldn't ring the bell again—he wasn't in the flat and that was that. Or he was there and was determined not to come to the door. Or he was there but he'd slipped in the shower, knocked himself unconscious, and was at this moment bleeding tragically to death on the bathroom floor . . .

OK, so he'd deliberately gone out.

Carla turned to leave. That was that then, over before it had begun. Well, she should be glad that at least one of them had come to their senses and—

"Carla."

She spun round, saw him standing there in the doorway and let out a strangled cry of relief. The next moment Perry, now minus his absurd hat, was wrapping her in his arms, frenziedly kissing her face and squeezing the air from her lungs.

"I thought you'd changed your mind," Carla babbled helplessly.

"Never."

"You didn't answer the door!"

"I was up there." He pointed to the curtained first-floor window. "I wanted to see how long you'd keep trying."

"Sadist."

"I needed to know if this means as much to you as it means to me." He paused, gazing deep into her eyes. "Does it?"

"You know it does. Otherwise I wouldn't be here, would I? Ginny's my best friend, I *hate myself* . . ."

"Shhh, come on, let's get you inside." He bundled her through the doorway and led her upstairs, and Carla knew that nothing about his flat, not even toenail clippings in the kitchen sink, could put her off him now.

But it was still a relief to see that there weren't any. Perry, watching her swiftly explore his domain, said, "What are you doing?"

"Checking you out. Don't interrupt. This wallpaper is hideous, by the way."

"I know. I don't care. It's only a rented flat."

"Your pillowcases don't match the duvet cover."

"I'm anti-coordination."

Carla swept past him out of the only bedroom and into the living room. "How charming, a surfboard propped against the wall."

"Glad you like it."

"And a banana skin in the wastepaper basket. Banana skins should go straight into the *kitchen* bin," said Carla. "I *hate* the smell of bananas."

"Ginny did mention you were freakishly tidy."

"I am." She was investigating the bathroom now. "And proud of it. The blade in your razor is blunt, by the way."

"When it's time to slash my wrists I'll buy a new one. Shampoo meet with your approval?"

"It's all right I suppose." Carla smelled the contents of the shampoo bottle. "I'm not wild about hair smelling of coconut."

"Fine. I'll shave it all off."

"And blue loo roll is just tacky."

Perry had his hands on his hips, his head tilted to one side. "You're criticizing everything."

"This lot needs to be criticized."

"Why are you doing this?"

"You kept me waiting," said Carla, "standing outside like an idiot." She gestured briskly. "Well, this is me, getting my own back."

Perry half smiled. "That's the other thing Ginny told me about you. She said you gave your men a hard time."

"Could we please not talk about Ginny? I feel bad enough as it is."

"OK. In fact I've got a better idea. Why don't we not talk at all?"

Adrenaline whooshed through Carla's body as she moved toward him. In her whole life she'd never felt like this before. And she was here now; they'd kept each other waiting long enough.

Clasping Perry's face between her hands and

gazing hungrily at his thin, beautifully carved mouth, she said, "Fine by me."

Their lovemaking was frantic, frenzied, and heightened by guilt. Carla had never known sex like it—and in her time she'd known a lot of sex. But now, instead of a purely physical connection, her emotions were involved too. For the first time, Carla belatedly realized. The connection between Perry and herself was *there,* inescapable and so overwhelming she wanted to cry.

This was what she'd been waiting for all her life and she hadn't even known it.

It didn't matter that the pillowcases didn't match the duvet. Where were the pillows anyway? Carla leaned up on one elbow and peered over the side of the bed. There they were, scattered on the floor along with the clothes she and Perry had torn off each other. Her dress was linen and would look like a dishrag unless it was hung up.

Who cared?

She closed her eyes. They had more important things to worry about than a crumpled dress.

"What are we going to do?"

"Hmm?" Perry was kissing her shoulder, snaking his hand along her thigh. "I'll give you a clue . . . I may need a few minutes before we try it again."

"I mean about Ginny."

The hand stopped snaking. "I don't know."

"We have to tell her."

"We can't."

"We can. We have to. I'm an honest person," said Carla. "I don't lie to my friends."

"Did you tell her you were meeting me this evening?"

"No, because I haven't spoken to her all day. I've deliberately kept my phone switched off. But I won't deceive her. If you want to be with me, you have to tell Ginny it's over."

"Oh God." Perry rubbed his face in despair. "I *do* want to be with you. But . . . I just . . ."

More buts. Why was he hesitating? "OK," said Carla, "which of us do you prefer?"

"You!"

"Because we're alike. You know it and I know it. I don't even really *know* you." Her eyes filled with unexpected tears. "But I know we have to be together and I can't even believe I'm saying these things. Nothing like this has ever happened to me before, but it's happening now."

Perry nodded, clearly torn. "You're right. It is. Bloody hell, this is difficult." He turned his head to look at her. "Ginny's going to hate you."

"I know, and I hate myself. She'll be distraught," Carla said miserably. "And it's a double betrayal. Like being kicked in the teeth twice."

"Does she really like me?"

"*Yes.*"

"How much?"

Carla rolled her eyes. "A *lot*. Plus, she thinks you like her too."

"I do," said Perry. "She's beautiful and funny and great company. I *do* like her. Just . . . not in *that* way."

"Why not?"

"God, I don't know, do I? You can't help how you feel about people. Ginny's a lovely person. Maybe she's too nice for me. She's nicer than you," he added with a brief smile. "But that's irrelevant. You're my type; you're the one I want. And she's not."

They were going around in circles. Carla completely agreed with him that Ginny was a far nicer person than she was. She, Carla, was the focused successful saleswoman with the laser-sharp brain and body to match. Her wardrobe was super-chic, her life was just as she wanted it to be, and there was no aspect of it that she didn't like. Ginny, contrastingly, was warm and impulsive, disorganized and accident-prone. Clothes-wise, she was less than cutting edge. She was, as Perry had pointed out, beautiful and funny in a dizzy-blond kind of way, but she was also overwhelmingly maternal, cuddly, and nurturing, and with a capacity for forgiveness that Carla knew she could never hope to achieve.

Although she suspected even Ginny might find this a betrayal too far.

"We have to tell her," Carla repeated.

"We can't."

"But you said it yourself; Ginny's not your type! I don't know why you even *started*—"

"Look," Perry interrupted, "there's Laurel to consider. I'm not proud of this, but I was pretty desperate. I charmed Ginny into taking my sister off my hands and the only way I could persuade her to let Laurel stay was by . . . well, I suppose you could call it emotional blackmail. But it worked. If I finish with Ginny, she'll chuck Laurel out; it's as simple as that."

Carla recognized in a flash how alike she and Perry were; he had behaved ruthlessly toward Ginny and now she was equally prepared to be ruthless where Laurel was concerned.

"So? She's not five years old anymore. She's a *grown-up*."

Perry heaved a sigh. "She's fragile. I know she's my big sister but she's always been the one who needs looking after. And since Kevin bailed out, she's been worse. She's depressed and clingy, and I know I shouldn't have to feel responsible for her, but I can't help myself. Going to live with Ginny was perfect, but if Ginny won't keep her anymore . . . well, I don't know what I'll do. Laurel will want to move back in here with me. God knows, it's not what I want to happen, but she'll beg and plead and I'll end up not being able to say no." He turned his head and said bluntly, "Because she doesn't have anyone else or anywhere else to go."

Oh God, this was turning into a nightmare. Carla couldn't bear to think about the trouble this thing with Perry was going to cause. Life would have been so much simpler if they'd never met.

But they had, and now she wanted to make love to him again because one thing was for sure. Perry Kennedy had tipped her calm, ordered, super-efficient world off its axis and whatever else happened she knew she couldn't give him up.

Chapter 25

"I'M GOING TO BE in big trouble," said Finn as he poured red wine into three glasses. "And it's all your fault."

It was midnight and the noisy, happy accountants had finally hokey-pokeyed their way into the string of waiting taxis. Ginny, Evie, and Finn were gathered around one of the tables having a drink to celebrate the end of a successful evening.

"You can't blame me," Ginny protested.

"I can. You should have graciously accepted the flowers when I offered them to you."

"You shouldn't have offered them in the first place! Damn cheek! If you took someone out to dinner, you wouldn't like it if they walked out of the restaurant and handed their plate of food over to some stranger in the street."

"That's completely different. Catherine didn't

ask me if I'd like her to send me flowers." Finn paused. "Maybe she won't find out what happened to them."

Ginny and Evie caught each other's eye, because only a man could think that.

"Oh, she will," said Ginny.

"And Catherine's feelings will be very hurt," Evie added helpfully. "She'll be furious. In fact, from now on you might want to check under your car for incendiary devices before you start the engine."

Finn took a slug of wine. "You're a big help."

"I could have been a big help." Evie's eyes danced. "You see, I'm not as choosy as some people. I'll accept cast-off flowers from anyone. If you'd offered them to me I'd have taken them, then you wouldn't have been able to give them to Alex's sister."

"Alex?" Finn frowned. "Who's *Alex?*"

"Oh sorry, silly me, that's the name of the woman in *Fatal Attraction*. Glenn Close played her, remember? Got rejected by Michael Douglas and turned into a deranged stalker. Fancy me using that name," Evie said cheerfully. "Slip of the tongue! I meant Catherine."

"Thanks," Finn said drily. "And if you'd been around when the flowers arrived, I would have offered them to you. But you weren't here, were you? You were late."

Evie was unrepentant. "Ah, but for a very good

reason. My darling daughter rang me as I was about to leave the house. She's just moved into a new flat in Salisbury and they're throwing a house-warming party tomorrow. So I'm going to be driving up there tomorrow morning!"

Ginny tried to suppress a stab of envy. Lucky Evie, off to see her daughter Philippa. She'd give anything for Jem to ring her up and say, "Hey, Mum, we're having a party, you'll come along, won't you?"

God, she'd be there in a flash, like Superman fired out of a cannon. *And* she'd provide gorgeous food and do all the washing-up afterward.

But there didn't appear to be any danger of that happening. The happy weekends she'd envisaged Jem and herself sharing in Bristol hadn't materialized and the ones here in Portsilver were woefully few and far between.

Lucky, *lucky* Evie.

"What's the flat like?" said Finn.

"Second floor, renovated Edwardian, two bedrooms. I can't wait to see it for myself. Ooh, you don't have a road atlas, do you?" Evie touched his arm. "My neighbor borrowed mine and lost it."

"There's one lying around somewhere. No idea where." Finn frowned. "Salisbury, would that be the A36? I can look it up on the internet if you like."

"I know where it is." Ginny jumped up.

"What, Salisbury?"

"Your road atlas. I saw it the other day."

The atlas was in the second drawer down behind the bar, almost hidden beneath a pile of telephone directories. Feeling smug and efficient, Ginny produced it with a flourish, curtsied modestly, and said, "Thank you, thank you, it was nothing."

"I love it when people do that." Evie clapped her hands delightedly. "I'll have to bring you back to my house to find all my long-lost bits and pieces. There's a blue sandal somewhere that's been missing for years."

"What's that?" said Finn as something slipped out from between the pages and landed face down on the floor. Ginny bent to retrieve it.

"A photograph?" Evie guessed, because it was the right shape and size.

It was a photograph. Ginny only looked at it for a split second but the image remained imprinted on her mind. She glanced over at Finn and handed it to him without a word. Evie, her eyes widening with glee, exclaimed, "Finn, is it rude? Don't tell me it's a photo of you with some scantily clad girl!"

Ginny bit her lip and turned away, because in a manner of speaking it was. In the photograph Finn was sitting on a stone wall wearing jeans and a white T-shirt. It was a sunny, breezy day and the wind had blown a lock of dark hair across his forehead. In his arms he was holding a baby with equally dark hair and eyes. The baby, clad only in a tiny pink and white sundress, was beaming at Finn. And Finn was smiling back at her with a look of such love, joy, and utter devotion on his face that anyone who saw the photograph would get a lump in their throat even if they didn't know the full story behind it.

"What *is* it? Show me," Evie demanded, reaching for the photo in Finn's hand. Then she saw it and her expression abruptly changed. "Oh."

An awkward silence ensued before Finn took the photograph back from Evie and put it down on the table. Turning to Ginny, he said, "You must be wondering what this is about. The baby is the daughter of an ex-girlfriend of mine. Well, ex-fiancée."

Ginny wavered for a split second, then realized she couldn't tell him she already knew about Tamsin and Mae. Evie wasn't saying anything either; she had related the story in confidence and the chances were that Finn wouldn't take kindly to discovering he'd been gossiped about behind his back.

"Right." She braced herself; this was the kind of lying she found hardest to pull off. Assuming her I-know-nothing expression—a tricky balance between neither too wide-eyed nor too village-idiot—Ginny nodded and said innocently, "So you were . . . um, engaged."

232

Oh brilliant. *Mastermind* next. Then maybe a degree in astrophysics.

"I was." Finn paused. "I also thought Mae was my daughter. But it turned out she wasn't after all."

"Oh! How awful." Ginny put her hand to her mouth and shook her head in dismay. Act natural, *act natural*. "That must have been . . . so, um . . ."

He nodded. "It was. Tamsin got back together with Mae's father. They're living in London now. He's a very wealthy man."

"Is . . . is he?"

"But then you already knew that."

Whoosh went Ginny's face, faster than a Formula One car. Struggling to look as if she didn't have a clue what he was talking about, she raised her eyebrows and said, "H-how would I know that?"

"Let me hazard a guess." Finn glanced pointedly at Evie. "Someone told you. Because I have to say, you're the world's most hopeless liar."

"Yes, it was me." Evie came clean.

"Thanks a lot," said Finn.

"She wasn't gossiping about you," Ginny put in hastily. "She was just *explaining*. After that time I put my foot in it and said something awful about it being obvious you weren't a father. I felt terrible about that."

"OK." Picking up the photo once more, Finn said, "So what do I do with this now? Throw it away, I suppose."

"You can't." Ginny snatched it away before he

233

could crumple it in his fist. "Not to a photograph like that."

A flicker of something crossed his face. "But it's based on a lie."

"You're still not throwing it away." To lighten the mood, she said, "For one thing, it makes you look human."

Finn said drily, "Thank you again."

"But it's true. Promise me you won't," said Ginny.

He rolled his eyes but put the photograph in his shirt pocket.

"Right, I'm off." Evie drained her glass and scooped up the road atlas. "Can I take this and bring it back on Monday?"

Ginny said enviously, "Have fun tomorrow."

"Oh, I will. I can't wait to see my baby again!" Too late, Evie realized what she'd said. "Finn, me and my big mouth. I meant Philippa. I know she's grown up but she's still my baby to me."

In a flurry of good-byes, Evie left and Ginny finished her drink too before collecting her things together.

When Finn showed her to the door, Ginny said, "I really am sorry about tonight."

"Not your fault." The corners of his mouth twitched. "For once."

"And I'm sorry about what happened with Tamsin and Mae. I can't imagine how that must have felt. You must have gone through hell."

For a moment, Finn didn't reply. Then he nodded, his face turned away in enigmatic profile. "I'd say that pretty much covers it. Mae was the center of my world, the most important thing that had ever happened to me. One minute she was there and I would have died for her, literally. Then the next minute she's gone, and it turns out I was never even her father in the first place. She's alive but I don't suppose I'll ever see her again. And there's no reason why I should want to, but she's still the same child." He paused again. "Just not *my* child anymore."

It was the most unbearably sad story. The lump was back in Ginny's throat. If Finn had been anyone else she would have thrown her arms around him. Instead, clutching her car keys and handbag, she said awkwardly, "You'll meet someone else. The right person. And then you'll have a proper family of your own."

"I thought I had a proper family last time. And look how well that turned out." His dark eyes held hers for a second before he turned back to concentrate on the door handle. His tone dismissive, indicating that this conversation was now well and truly over, Finn said, "I'm not sure I'd want to try again."

Rolling over in bed, Carla reached for her mobile and peered at the screen. If it was Ginny, she definitely wasn't answering it.

"Make it stop," Perry groaned, burrowing under the pillows.

It was a number she didn't recognize, possibly a new client. Dredging up her efficient voice, Carla said, "Hello, Carla James."

"Woo, you make me want to buy a *huge* conservatory. Hi, Carla, it's Jem!"

Jem. For God's sake, it was months since she'd last heard from Jem. Instinctively turning onto her side, away from Perry, Carla said, "Well, this is a surprise. Everything OK, sweetie?"

"Everything's fine. I'm just bursting with curiosity about this new chap of Mum's and she's not giving me nearly enough information. I know he's nice and she really likes him but that's all I'm getting. She just keeps saying it's early days," Jem complained goodnaturedly. "But I can't help it; I want to hear more than that. And I know you met him on Friday night so I thought, ha, I'll ring Carla and find out what he's really like."

Carla's heart plummeted. It was Sunday morning and she was here in Perry's bed. How could she have sunk so low? What would Jem say if she told her the truth? How would Ginny, her best friend, react when she found out that—

"Get off," Carla hissed over her shoulder, covering the receiver and wriggling out of reach as Perry's hand trailed down her spine. Hot with shame, she said, "Jem, I only met him for a couple of minutes; I can't really tell you much. Like your

mum says, it's not been going on long enough to get serious. I think they're just seeing each other every now and again."

"*Noooo.*" Jem let out a wail of disappointment. "Not fair! You know what Mum's like, it's years since she's been keen on anyone," she protested, "so of course I'm interested. This could be my new stepdad, for heaven's sake. And now you're clamming up on me too! At least tell me if he's good-looking."

Perry overheard this. He tapped Carla on the shoulder and nodded.

"He's all right, I suppose." Carla winced as the taps turned into jabs. "OK, he's quite good-looking. For a redhead."

"And does he seem like a nice person?"

"I couldn't really tell. Nice enough."

"Hopeless," Jem scolded. "OK, if you met him at a party, would you fancy him?"

This was agonizing.

"I prefer my men younger." Carla slithered out of reach again as Perry, outraged, seized her arm in a pincer-like grip.

"Well, we all know that. You're not fooling me, by the way."

"What?"

"Not for a second," said Jem.

Carla almost stopped breathing. "Meaning?"

"I'm not completely stupid."

"Aren't you?"

"And I'm not five years old either. I know what's going on." She couldn't know. She just couldn't.

"What's going on?" Carla was dimly aware that she sounded like a parrot.

"You're pretending you're on your own." Jem's voice was playful. "But you aren't. You've got someone there with you."

Oh. "How could you tell?"

"You mean apart from me hearing you cover the receiver and tell him to get off?"

"Bit of a giveaway, I suppose," Carla admitted.

"And I bet there's something else I know about him too."

Carla's sigh of relief abruptly went into reverse. Sucking in air, she braced herself. "And what would that be?"

With an air of triumph, Jem said, "I bet he's a good ten years younger than mystery man Perry."

Chapter 26

LAST WEEK, GINNY HAD been envious of Evie. Now she no longer needed to be because it was— *tra-laaa!*—her turn. Jem was coming home at last for Easter week.

"I swapped my shifts at the pub," she told Ginny. "Rupert's off to the south of France and

Lucy's going back to Birmingham so I thought why stay here on my own when I can come and see you?"

So Rupert would be abroad; was that what had prompted Jem's visit? If so, hooray for Rupert. Joyfully, Ginny said, "That's *such* good news. I can't wait to see you again. And you'll be able to meet Laurel at last."

"Not to mention Perry." Jem sounded mischievous. "I definitely want to meet him."

Hmm, if he was able to spare the time. It had occurred to Ginny lately that Perry might not be quite as besotted with her as he claimed to be; being busy at work was one thing, but she was beginning to suspect that something else might be up.

Still, asking him if he'd like to meet Jem might give her a chance to find out what that something might be. "Yes, but you'll have to be discreet. Remember what I told you about Laurel."

"I remember. Although I think it's pretty ridiculous, the two of you having to skulk around keeping it a secret."

Ginny thought it was pretty ridiculous too, but at the same time she could see that Perry had a point. Not that they'd been doing much skulking around recently—he claimed to be so rushed off his feet at the moment they hadn't managed to meet up all week.

"I know, darling, but she's his sister and he's

trying to spare her feelings. She's just been a bit depressed, that's all."

"Well, tell her I'm great at cheering people up. I'll be down on Friday evening. Mum, you know how much I love you . . . ?"

"Shameless child." Ginny grinned, because this was a familiar grovel. "Of course I'll pick you up from the station."

"Yay. So you're free on Friday evening?"

"Absolutely."

"In that case," said Jem, "why don't we have dinner at Penhaligon's to celebrate me being back? My treat!"

"Jem, you can't afford it."

"Can't I? OK then, your treat! How about a table for three?"

"You, me, and Dad? That's a nice idea." Ginny made a mental note to ring Gavin; she wasn't sure if he was still seeing Cleo but he could surely bear to give her a miss for one—

"Actually, I've already rung Dad—we're meeting up on the Saturday. I was thinking more you, me, and Perry." Sounding pleased with herself Jem said gaily, "Clever eh? This way I'll get to meet all your lovely new friends in one go!"

Just the sight of the peeling blue front door had a magical effect on Carla, drawing her toward it like a drug she was unable to resist. She'd been coming here for twelve days now and the magic was more powerful than ever. She rang the bell and Perry answered it. From then on they were cocooned in their own little world with trespassers prohibited and it was a feeling like no other she had ever known before. Total love. Total security. Total happiness.

Until Ginny found out.

Carla hated what she was doing but she couldn't stop doing it. Raising her hand to the bell she rang it quickly, twice. Waited breathlessly for the sound of Perry running down the stairs. Felt her heart quicken as the door began to open.

He grinned at her, ushered her speedily inside. "Hello, you."

Here came the feeling again. Sheer bliss. How could anyone give up something so utterly perfect?

After they'd made love Carla sprang her surprise.

"Tomorrow night we'll be doing this in a four-poster bed."

"What?"

"I've booked us into Curnow Castle. Their best suite." At an eye-watering three hundred pounds a night, it had better be their best suite. Not that she regretted a penny of it—she'd wanted to make a splashy extravagant gesture, to celebrate how she felt about Perry. Stroking a damp tendril of red hair away from his forehead, Carla said, "You'll love it."

"I won't, because I can't go. You'll have to cancel."

"Why?"

He shrugged. "I'm seeing Ginny tomorrow night."

"What?" Carla sat upright in bed, ice forming in the pit of her stomach. "But *I* want to see you. Tell Ginny something's come up!"

Perry grinned at the choice of phrase, then regretfully shook his head.

"And I want to see you—of *course* I'd rather see you—but I can't. She wants me to meet her daughter."

"Jem?"

He clicked his fingers with relief. "That's the name. Jem. I keep thinking it's Jenny."

Carla listened with growing dismay as Perry patiently explained that Ginny had called him last night and invited him to join them at Penhaligon's. He had gently attempted to turn her down but Ginny had practically begged. Evidently Jem was keen to meet him and . . . well, it had been an awkward situation. In the end he hadn't had the heart to say no.

"It means a lot to her," Perry concluded reasonably. "I couldn't let her down."

"Because of Laurel." Carla saw beyond the altruism in an instant. "Because you need to keep the charade going. To keep Ginny happy."

He spread his hands. "Exactly. Not because I want to see her."

"This is all wrong." Vehemently Carla shook her head. "Laurel's ruling your life, keeping *us* from being together."

"Hey, hey," Perry protested, "we *are* together."

"Are we? Hiding here in your flat like fugitives when we haven't even done anything wrong? I want us to be a proper couple!" Carla gazed at him in desperation. "I love you. We can't carry on like this. It's not fair on any of us. And you're making a fool of Ginny. She's my *friend*," her voice rose, "and she doesn't *deserve* this."

"I know. But we don't have any choice, not now at least. When the time's right I'll sort it all out." Perry's tone was soothing, willing her to trust him. "But not yet."

"Sure she's not too heavy?" said Finn.

"Not too heavy." As Ginny had been leaving the restaurant after a busy Friday lunchtime shift, Finn had pulled into the courtyard in the van. Back from a country house auction on Bodmin Moor, he'd proudly shown off the Victorian marble statue he had acquired. Since Tom, his assistant in the shop, was currently busy with a customer, Ginny had offered to help him lift it out of the van and into the shop.

Actually, marble was heavier than it looked. But today was Friday and Jem was coming home. Ginny was on such a high she was pretty sure she could lift the statue and the van single-handed, if required.

Luckily it wasn't.

"Got her?" Finn double-checked.

"Stop fussing. I'm stronger than I look." Shaking her hair out of her eyes, she grinned at him and wrapped her arms securely around the ankles of the female statue. Finn, at the other end, had his arms round the woman's bare chest. Together they moved backward across the gravel, negotiated the doorway, maneuvered the statue into an upright position . . . and breathed out.

"Well done." Finn gazed at Ginny appraisingly. "I thought you were going to drop her. You *are* stronger than you look."

"Just give me a telephone directory," Ginny said modestly, "and watch me rip it in half." She ran her hand over the cool, silky-smooth marble of the statue's shoulder, thinking idly how nice it would look in her garden. "How much are you going to be selling her for?"

"Three grand."

Yikes, maybe not then. Perhaps the home store did a cheaper version in fiberglass.

"Good job you didn't tell me that before. I'd definitely have dropped her."

"She's one expensive lady." Finn gave the statue's bottom an appreciative pat. "And older than she looks."

Ginny couldn't help wondering how it felt,

having your bottom patted by Finn. Hastily she dismissed the thought, pulled herself together. "No cellulite though. She's taken good care of herself. Or else gone under the knife, had a bit of a nip and tuck. You could call her Cher." As Ginny said it, her phone began to ring and Carla's name flashed up on the screen. "Speaking of women without cellulite . . . hello, you! Where have you *been?*"

"Just . . . busy." Carla sounded more subdued than usual. "Hi. Listen, I'm at home and I'd really like to see you. What are you doing?"

"Just finished work." Intrigued, Ginny said, "You sound mysterious. What's this about?"

"Can you come over now?"

"I've got some stuff to pick up in town first, but I can be there in about an hour. Jem's coming home!"

There was a momentary pause before Carla said, "Is she?"

"I'm picking her up from the station at six thirty. I'm so excited I can't wait. And guess what? We're having dinner with Perry, the three of us together!"

"Great." Carla appeared to have other things on her mind. "Um, so you'll be here in an hour?"

Ginny checked her watch. "By four o'clock, I promise. I wish you'd tell me what this is about."

"When I see you."

She definitely wasn't sounding like herself.

Catching Finn's eye, Ginny said, "Carla, have you done something naughty?"

Another pause.

"Yes."

"Tell me!"

"I can't," said Carla.

Ginny put the phone back in her pocket. "Carla's being mysterious."

"You'd better get off then. We'll see you tonight."

"Eight o'clock." Ginny beamed. "I can't wait for you to meet Jem."

"And she'll be meeting Perry as well. What if she doesn't like him?"

Was that a dig? Honestly, just because Perry had made one innocent, off-the-cuff remark about children and fatherhood. Couldn't he just be happy for her?

"She'll love him," Ginny said firmly.

Finn shrugged. "She might not."

"Two things. One, I know my daughter. And two"—her eyes danced because today of all days nothing was going to dampen her mood—"don't be such a pessimist."

Chapter 27

"RIGHT, I'M HERE. TELL me what's going on." The moment Carla opened the front door, Ginny threw her arms round her. It wasn't until she'd been driving back from the shops that it had occurred to her that Carla might be ill. She had asked jokily if she'd done something naughty and Carla had soberly agreed that she had. But what if she was referring to the fact that last year a letter had arrived in the post reminding her that her next cervical smear test was due, and work had been so hectic that she hadn't got around to making the appointment?

The moment this possibility had lodged itself in Ginny's brain she hadn't been able to think of anything else. And now Carla wasn't hugging her back, she was standing woodenly with—Ginny now saw—tears swimming in her eyes.

"Oh my God." Ginny gazed at her in horror, a sensation like wet cement settling in the pit of her stomach. Barely able to speak, she clutched Carla's hands tightly and felt her throat tighten with fear. "Is it . . . is it cancer?"

Carla abruptly turned away, heading for the kitchen.

"It's not cancer."

Oh.

"Well, *that's* a relief." Following her, Ginny exhaled noisily and patted her heaving chest. Then, to be on the ultra-safe side, she said, "So it's not any kind of illness?"

"No."

Now she was truly relieved. "Because you can't imagine what's been going through my mind."

"Ginny, I'm not sick." Carla turned to face her, and there was that weird edge to her voice again.

"Has someone died?"

Carla's perfectly symmetrical bob swung from side to side as she shook her head, but her lips stayed pressed together.

"Then you have to help me out here," said Ginny, "because I just don't know what this is about. I have no idea."

"I know you don't," said Carla.

"What's *that* supposed to mean? Why are you saying it like that?"

"Ginny, you mean the world to me. You're my best friend and I never wanted to hurt you." Carla gripped the edge of the granite worktop behind her as the words came out in a rush. "Believe me, I *never* wanted to have to do this. But it's Perry. He's seeing someone else."

The kitchen was silent; it felt as if all the oxygen had been sucked out of the air. Carla couldn't bring herself to say the rest of it just yet. One bombshell at a time. Her fingernails ached from gripping the worktop. This was hell, but it had to be done. Ginny was gazing at her, clearly lost for words and as shell-shocked as she had every right to be. God knows, she—oh, that *bloody* phone.

But when Carla looked at the bloody phone and saw who was calling, she knew she had to answer it.

"Hi, it's me. Listen, I'll be back by midnight at the latest," said Perry. "Wait for me at the flat."

"Actually, I'm at home. Ginny's here."

"Really?" He sounded impressed. "I thought you'd been keeping out of her way."

"Not anymore." Carla paused, heard her own voice echoing weirdly in her ears. "I've just told her."

"*What?* You're not serious! About *us?*"

"Yes." Well, near as dammit. She was about to.

"Jesus Christ, what have you done?" shouted Perry. "I told you not to say anything!"

And where would that have got them? It was a job that needed to be done. Evenly, Carla said, "Well, I have."

She switched off the phone. Ginny was staring at her, her eyes huge.

"Who was that?"

"I'm sorry."

"Was it Perry? What's going on? OK, so you saw him with someone." Ginny shook her head in bewilderment. "But maybe you got it wrong, made a mistake."

"I'm not wrong."

"So he admitted it? You know he's definitely seeing someone else? What a *jerk*." Her hands trembling, Ginny reached for a glass and ran cold water into it from the tap. "When did you find out? Where did you see them? Damn, I really liked him too." The glass clunked audibly against her teeth as she gulped down half the water in one go. "Why can't anything ever go right for me? Do you know, I really thought we had something. And it turns out he's just another filthy rotten cheat after all. Oh no, poor *you*."

"What? Why?" It was Carla's turn to be confused.

"Having to be the one to tell me. I bet you've been dreading it." Ginny's lopsided smile failed to conceal her disappointment. "It's always horrible being the bearer of bad news. But I'm glad you told me, really I am. Don't worry, I won't shoot the messenger!"

Carla couldn't speak. The last few precious seconds of their friendship were ticking away. There was an unexploded bomb right here in the kitchen and any moment now she was going to press the detonator.

"So did you actually see her?" Needing information, Ginny said, "I suppose she's younger than me. What does she look like?" Only a couple of seconds left now. Carla's mouth was so dry she could hardly speak. "She looks . . . well, she looks like me."

"Complete opposite of me then. I might have guessed." Surveying her reflection in the window and running her fingers disparagingly through her tousled Goldie Hawn hair, Ginny said, "Nature's way of telling you it's time you went to the hairdresser." Then she patted her gently rounded stomach. "And possibly had a go at a few sit-ups."

"There's nothing wrong with you." Carla couldn't bear to see her running herself down. Fiercely, she said, "You're warm, funny, *beautiful*—"

"But not good enough for Perry, because he prefers someone who looks like *you*."

Carla's finger had been hovering over the detonator button for what felt like hours. She didn't have to do this; she could carry on seeing Perry in secret.

No, she couldn't. That would be deceitful.

She could stop seeing Perry. *No, she couldn't.* That would be impossible.

She could . . . she could . . .

No, she couldn't.

Carla pressed the detonator. "It's me."

"What's you?"

"Perry prefers me. I'm the one he's been seeing. And I'm so *sorry,*" Carla blurted out. "I hate myself; I can't believe this has happened. But it has. And you're my best friend," she pleaded. "I wouldn't hurt you for the world, but I've never felt like this about anyone before . . . I met Perry and it was just . . . well, like an earthquake or something. If I could have stopped it, I would. But I just *couldn't* . . ." She ground to a halt, nauseous and mortified, her fists clenched in anguish. Forcing herself to meet Ginny's gaze, she whispered helplessly, "And I'm so, so sorry."

Ginny felt as if she was watching a film, one with a twist she hadn't been expecting, the kind that takes your breath away and leaves you wondering what on earth will happen next. Carla's face was chalk-white, taut with strain. She had said what she'd clearly planned to say. She was like a stranger or a character in *Doctor Who* peeling off her face to reveal the robot beneath. Because one thing was for sure, this was no longer the Carla she'd known and loved and trusted for the last fifteen years.

"You wouldn't hurt me for the world?" Ginny was privately amazed she could still speak. "I'm your best *friend?*" Her voice rose. "Well, that's fascinating. If this is how you treat your best friend, I'd hate to see what you do to your enemies."

Carla flinched. "I'm sorry."

"Will you stop saying you're sorry? It doesn't mean anything! If you were really sorry, you'd never have started seeing Perry behind my back, would you? You would have said thanks but no thanks, like any normal friend, and walked away. It's called loyalty." Ginny shook her head in disgust.

"I know and I *wanted* to do that. Believe me, I did. But I couldn't. I love him," pleaded Carla. "And he loves me. Sometimes these things just happen." As she said it, they both heard the sound of a sports car screeching to a halt outside. A door slammed and footsteps raced up the path. The doorbell rang.

"Prince Charming, I presume. Riding to the rescue. How sweet." Ginny's heart was hammering against her rib cage. "How masterful. I suppose you've been sleeping with him."

"Of course I've been sleeping with him." Carla went to get the door. "It's what normal couples do."

The knife twisted in her stomach. With a jolt of pain, Ginny realized she was right. All that so-called gentlemanly stuff about wanting to take things slowly and get to know her properly first hadn't been romantic after all. It had just been . . . lies.

And here he was, the liar himself, bursting into the immaculate kitchen with a wild look in his eyes and his hair uncombed.

Suddenly he wasn't looking quite so irresistible anymore.

Which, under the circumstances, was handy.

"I'm sorry. Ginny, I'm so sorry."

Oh, for crying out loud, not that again.

"You're a wonderful person," Perry went on, "and I wouldn't hurt you for the world . . ."

And that.

"This is getting repetitive," said Ginny.

"But I wouldn't, I swear to God. I never expected anything like this to happen. Neither of us did. But . . . it has." Perry's hands fell to his sides, signaling defeat. "It was a . . . a *coup de foudre.*"

"Right." Ginny fantasized about seizing the heavy glass fruit bowl and hurling it at his head.

"It means love at first sight," Perry added.

He thought she was gullible *and* dim.

"Actually, it doesn't," said Ginny. "It means struck by lightning." Struck by lightning, struck by a heavy glass fruit bowl, she didn't mind which.

"Anyway. We love each other. You weren't supposed to find out like this but—"

"From the look of things you didn't want me to find out at all." Leaving Carla out of it for now, Ginny concentrated all her attention on Perry. "How long has it been going on?"

"Since that night at the Carson Hotel. We couldn't help ourselves. Took one look at each other and that was it. We just knew."

"How lovely. Very romantic. So did you shag her in the toilets or in the bushes outside?"

"I didn't." Perry frowned, offended. "I was with you."

"OK, the next night then. Carla isn't the type to hang about." From the expressions on their faces she'd guessed right. For good measure, Ginny said, "Although you're a damn sight older than the ones she usually goes for."

"I'm sorry," Perry said *again*. "And I know this has come as a shock to you, but I hope we can still be friends."

It was the pleading, let's-be-reasonable tone of voice he used that confirmed what Ginny had already suspected. Perry Kennedy had fooled her from the word go, manufacturing a relationship purely in order to offload his sister into her care. As if Laurel were a bin bag of old clothes and Ginny was his local branch of Oxfam.

And now, from the look of him, he was terrified she was going to give the bin bag back.

Interestingly, Ginny found she was able to separate out her emotions, like sorting knives, forks, and spoons into a cutlery drawer.

Humiliation because she'd thought he liked her and he didn't.

Anger because Jem was on her way home and today was supposed to be such a *happy* day.

Humiliation again because the three of them were booked into Penhaligon's and she had boasted so freely to Finn that Jem would love Perry to bits.

Anger because Perry had regarded her as a pushover. And yet more humiliation because Finn would be hard pushed to hide his amusement when he heard what had happened.

So that was the spoons and forks accounted for. But what of the knives? Her stomach churning,

Ginny realized that they were what Carla had been using to stab her in the back. Because anger didn't begin to describe how she felt about Carla, her supposed friend. Seething boiling fury was closer to the mark. And this was what hurt more than anything, because being betrayed by your best friend was a million times worse than being betrayed by a man.

With men, sooner or later you kind of deep down expected it.

Well, Carla and Perry were welcome to each other. More than welcome. And—how sweet—Carla was getting herself a ready-made family.

"So do you want to tell Laurel or shall I?"

Perry was looking nervous. "Tell her what?"

"Oh, I think you know. You tricked me into taking your sister off your hands in the first place," said Ginny. "Well, I don't want her anymore. You can have her back."

He blinked rapidly. "Ginny, you *can't*—"

"The three of you can live together. Won't that be fun?"

"But she's happy with you," Perry pleaded.

"Irrelevant. Not my problem. Believe me; I'll be happy when she's gone."

"You wouldn't throw her out."

"Wouldn't I? Watch me." Ginny marched across the kitchen, pausing only to glance back in disgust at Carla. "And I never want to speak to either of you again as long as I live."

Chapter 28

IN TWO HOURS SHE had to pick up Jem from the station. As Ginny slipped back into her own house she prayed Laurel was out or asleep or upstairs listening to a Leonard Cohen CD.

No such luck. The second the front door clicked shut Laurel emerged from the kitchen.

"There you are! Now, does Jem like chocolate? Only I've made a lemon drizzle cake but if she'd prefer chocolate I can easily—*oh.*" Laurel looked concerned. "What's happened?"

"Nothing. Nothing's happened. Lemon's fine. Or chocolate. Jem likes any kind of cake."

"Only you look as if you've seen a ghost. Something's wrong."

To tell her? Or not to tell her? Ginny was saved from having to make the decision by Laurel moving past her, opening the front door, and peering out in search of whatever it was that might have caused the upset.

"That's Perry's car." She pointed across the road. "What's going on? Where's Perry?"

"OK." Closing the door and leading her back into the kitchen, Ginny said, "Would you be upset if I told you I've been . . . kind of seeing Perry?"

Laurel looked astounded. "You? And Perry? Seriously? But that's great! Why would I be upset?"

Exactly. Why would she have been? Tempting though it was to open a bottle of wine, Ginny grabbed a can of Coke from the fridge and sat down.

"Sorry, Perry said you wouldn't like it. Anyway, I'm not seeing him anymore." She yanked the ring-pull and watched foam spill over the top of the can. "It's over now."

"Oh phew, thank goodness for *that*."

Ginny looked up. "Why?"

"Because he's a *nightmare*." Laurel rolled her eyes. "For your sake, I'm so relieved it's over. I mean, don't get me wrong, I love him to bits, but Perry's relationships always end in disaster. Where women are concerned he has the attention span of a gnat. One minute he's crazy about them, the next minute they're history. Oh God"—she covered her mouth in dismay—"is that what he's just done to you?"

"No . . . no . . ." Ginny didn't have the heart to admit the real reason Perry had pretended to be keen on her. "Well, kind of, I suppose. He's seeing someone else now."

"Par for the course. To be honest, you're well rid of him." Laurel leaned forward, her forehead pleated with concern. "Are you devastated?"

Devastated. Ginny tried and failed to summon up devastation. She could do humiliation and anger—oh yes, plenty of that, no problem—but devastation over Perry wasn't an issue. Losing her best friend—her *alleged* best friend—was far more upsetting than losing Perry Kennedy.

She shook her head. "No. We only went out a few times. It wasn't serious."

This clearly wasn't the answer Laurel wanted to hear. Or else she simply didn't believe her. "You must be upset though. He's let you down. These things are bound to hurt." Earnestly, she said, "But I'm a good listener. You can talk about it as much as you want. It doesn't matter that he's my brother, you just let it all out, get everything off your chest, because I know there's nothing worse than feeling miserable and not being able to talk to someone about—"

"Actually, I don't do it that way." Ginny had a brainwave. "I find endlessly thinking and talking about a failed affair makes things worse. I prefer out of sight, out of mind. In fact, you could really help me if you want to. Make sure I *never* talk about Perry."

"Of course I will! Don't you worry." Laurel shook her head eagerly. "I'll tell you the *moment* you mention his name."

"And . . . and it might help if you try not to mention Kevin's name as well," said Ginny. "Because if you do, it'll only remind me of Perry, and to be honest, the less I'm reminded of him the quicker I'll forget he ever existed." *Oh yes, brilliant.* Perry had his uses after all.

"Good point. OK, I'll do that. And don't worry;

you've had a lucky escape. Think how much worse it would have been if the two of you had been together for as long as me and Kev—*oops, sorry!*" Laurel pulled an apologetic face. "Nearly did it then!"

"But you stopped *yourself.* That's excellent." Nodding encouragingly, Ginny said, "And we'll both get better with practice."

"I'm sure we will." As if the concept had never occurred to her before, Laurel straightened her shoulders and said with pride, "Out of sight, out of mind!"

"Oh. Just one thing before we start it properly. The reason Perry's car's outside is because he's seeing Carla now."

"Carla? Your best friend?" Laurel's light green eyes widened in horror.

"Well, she *was* my best friend." Ginny watched her fingers tighten around the Coke can. "They just told me."

"I don't believe it! You mean she stole him? What a *witch!*"

"Thank you. I thought so too."

"At least you know it won't last." Laurel's tone was consoling.

"It might. This time it's different," said Ginny. "They're in love. Perry had a—"

"*Coup de foudre*?" Laurel gave an elegant snort of amusement. "God, not another one."

Ginny took another gulp of Coke, marveling at

this revelation. It *was* a consolation to know it wouldn't last.

"One other thing." Overcome with curiosity, she said, "Why did you never tell me this about Perry before?"

Laurel looked surprised. "You never asked."

Right. Fair enough.

"He's my brother," Laurel went on. "And he's always been great to me. I'm not going to go around bad-mouthing him, am I? And I didn't know there was anything going on between the two of you." Vigorously, she shook her head. "If you'd mentioned it, I could have warned you."

"But Perry said—"

"OK, *stop*." Laurel held up both hands like a traffic cop. "Stop it *now*. See what you're doing? You're leading the conversation around to Perry again, obsessing about what happened! And it's my job to make sure you don't. So just clear him out of your mind. Stop thinking about him. He isn't worth it."

Ginny struggled to keep a straight face. She'd never imagined Laurel could be so bossy and forceful. Obediently, she said, "Right."

"Trust me." Nodding wisely, Laurel broke four eggs into a bowl and began briskly beating them. "It's the only way."

The day may have been tainted but it hadn't been ruined. The moment Jem jumped down from the train, all thoughts of Perry and Carla flew out of Ginny's mind. For almost thirty seconds they just stood there wrapped around each other, hugging tightly. Jem, her baby, was home again, and that was all that mattered. Burying her face in Jem's blond, pink-tipped hair, Ginny inhaled deeply, delving beneath the trendy new perfume until she managed to locate the precious, infinitely subtle but familiar body smell that reassured her that this was her daughter.

Finally, grinning like idiots, they pulled away from each other.

"Oh, sweetheart, it's so good to see you again." Her heart aching with love, Ginny said, "You've had your hair cut."

Jem reached out and gave Ginny's overgrown blond hair a mischievous tug. "You haven't."

"And where are the sacks of washing? I thought it was in the student rules that you have to bring home at least a hundred-weight of dirty clothes."

"We've got a top of the range Bosch washer-dryer."

"In that case I'll bring my washing to you. How's Lucy?"

"Fine."

"Rupert?"

"He's fine too."

"And Davy?"

Jem shrugged. "He's OK. Busy cleaning other people's houses. Anyway, I'm here. Let's go. I can't wait to meet everyone." Tucking her arm through Ginny's as they made their way down the station platform, she added with a complicit squeeze, "Especially Perry."

"I still can't believe it. How could he prefer her to you?" Franz Ferdinand was blaring from the stereo and Jem had to shout to be heard over the noise. "And as for bloody Carla . . . I'm never going to speak to her again as long as I live. She's a complete *cow*."

Ginny was touched by her vehemence. It was seven thirty, they were on their way to Penhaligon's, and Jem was continuing to let off steam in the passenger seat. Since Laurel had banned them from discussing *that* subject in the house, Jem was now making up for lost time. Knowing how intensely proud Carla was of her perfectly geometric bob, the latest plan was to sneak into her house while she was asleep and hack off her hair with garden shears. And possibly perform a spot of reverse liposuction while she was there, by injecting a few liters of wibbly-wobbly fat into Carla's tanned, super-toned thighs.

"I bet that's who she was with when I phoned her," Jem said suddenly. "I've only just realized. God, talk about two-faced . . . they were probably in bed together. She's such a slapper. In fact, I could quite easily slap both her faces."

"You won't," Ginny said firmly. "If we see her, we ignore her."

"Spoilsport."

"She's going to have her conscience to live with. And from what Laurel says, it won't last long. Perry will dump her. I'll look forward to that."

"And after it's over?" Jem was looking at her. "What then? Don't tell me you'll be friends with Carla again."

Ginny shook her head; her mind was made up on that score. "That's not going to happen."

"Good." Jem sat back, satisfied.

"So what do you think of Laurel?" Reaching forward and turning down Franz Ferdinand, Ginny changed the subject.

"I like her! She's really nice. You said she was depressed but she seemed really cheerful to me."

Ginny smiled to herself. This was true; the change in Laurel had been staggering. Who would have guessed that all Laurel needed to snap her out of her misery was another depressed person in the house? She was now positively reveling in her newfound role as chief cheerer-upper, even if Ginny wasn't mourning the loss of Perry quite as much as Laurel seemed to want to believe.

"And her cakes are out of this world," Jem added cheerfully. "That has to be a bonus."

"It is." Ginny nodded with relief because she might have told Perry she no longer wanted Laurel in the house, but in her heart of hearts she'd known all along that she would never actually kick her out.

"So hang on a minute, let's just get this straight. You thought Carla was a great friend and it turns out she's a complete witch." Jem was now counting on her fingers. "You believed Perry was perfect, the man you'd been waiting for all these years. And as far as you were concerned, Laurel was depressed. You know, I think it's a good job I'm here," she told Ginny. "Because, basically, you're pretty hopeless. You've been wrong about everyone so far."

Chapter 29

FINN EMERGED FROM HIS flat as Ginny was parking in the courtyard.

"Is that your boss? And you didn't tell me he was that good-looking either. For an older man," said Jem.

"Shhh, keep your voice down." But as he came over to greet them, Ginny suspected Finn had overheard.

"You must be Jem." He smiled and shook her hand. "We've heard a lot about you."

"Ditto. You're the man who tried to have my mother arrested."

"I hardly ever do that anymore," said Finn.

Jem gazed past him. "I'm being hissed at."

Ginny saw Myrtle, her tail swishing, staring disdainfully down from the high, ivy-strewn courtyard wall. The cat blinked and bared her teeth again.

"Her name's Myrtle. Not the world's friendliest cat," said Finn. "We think she's pregnant but nobody's been able to get near enough to find out for sure."

"If she's this touchy, it's a miracle she ever managed to get pregnant in the first place. I suppose it's like some women," Jem went on pointedly. "They don't look sex mad on the outside, but deep down, they're nothing but tarts."

Finn threw a questioning glance at Ginny, who felt herself turning red. Oh brilliant, did he think Jem meant her?

"And if Myrtle's pregnant she shouldn't be climbing high walls. It's dangerous." Moving past Finn, Jem held her arms up and made kissing noises. "Come on, sweetie, it's all right, let's get you down from there, shall we?"

Myrtle looked at Jem as if she was deranged before haughtily turning her back on everyone and springing like Spider-Man from the top of the wall to the upper branches of the mulberry tree beyond it.

"Dr. Dolittle, I presume." Finn was amused by Jem's failure.

"I'm usually good with animals." Disappointed, Jem watched as Myrtle elegantly picked her way along the branch before leaping across to the next tree. "She doesn't look pregnant to me."

Inside the restaurant, Finn looked around and said, "No sign of Perry yet."

"Just as well," Jem retorted, "if he doesn't want to end up being stuffed into a food processor."

"He won't be joining us," Ginny put in hurriedly. Another raised eyebrow from Finn.

"Mum's been chucked. And guess who he's been seeing behind her back? Only her best friend," said Jem.

"Who, *Carla?*" Finn looked startled. "But she told me she didn't—"

"Like him? She lied. Could we change the subject now?" said Ginny. "My daughter's home and that's all I care about. We're here to celebrate."

"And get the teeniest bit drunk." Jem beamed at Finn, who was moving behind the bar. "So we'll have a couple of glasses of house white to start with. Bucket-sized, if you've got them."

"That's not celebrating." Taking a bottle of champagne from the fridge and removing the wire, Finn expertly uncorked it. "Here, on the house."

"Hey, I like this place!"

"Don't get used to it. Strictly a one-off."

Jem's smile broadened as he filled their glasses and scrunched the bottle into a bucket of ice. "You're nicer than I was expecting."

His mouth twitched. "You mean nicer *and* better looking?"

"Yes. Still single?"

"Jem!"

"Why?" said Finn.

Jem looked innocent. "No reason. Just asking."

After an hour, Ginny began to relax. Introducing Jem to Evie had been a joy, followed by Evie asking where Perry was and having to hear about what had happened, which wasn't. Then Evie had relayed the information to Martha who was even more outraged on Ginny's behalf. But after that it had got easier, helped along by the rest of the bottle of Moët—so much more delicious when you weren't paying for it yourself. And Dan the Van had come up trumps too, supplying the restaurant with sublime asparagus and artichokes, Jem's favorite vegetables in the world.

"That was so gorgeous. I want to lick my plate," Jem said longingly.

"Might be best not to. Finn'll turf you out."

"So he runs the antiques center by day and works here in the restaurant in the evenings. Isn't that an awful lot of hours?"

"They're his businesses. He wants them to do well. And the customers like having him around."

Jem watched Finn chatting to a table of eight. "But when does he get time off?"

"When he needs it." Suspicious of the direction her daughter's thoughts were traveling in, Ginny leaned forward and changed the subject. "Anyway, tell me what's been happening in Bristol. You haven't mentioned boyfriends for a while. Anyone exciting you want to tell me about?"

"Maybe the reason I haven't mentioned boy-friends is because I've been working too hard too." But Jem's blue eyes were sparkling, her tone playful. Relaxed by the champagne, she was clearly in the mood to spill some beans tonight.

"Don't believe you." Ginny waved her last spear of asparagus tantalizingly over Jem's empty plate.

"We-ell, maybe there is someone."

"And his name is . . . ?"

Jem said, "Do I get the asparagus?"

"Depends. Maybe. And his name is . . . ?" Wouldn't it be great if she were to say Davy?

"It's Rupert," said Jem. And blushed.

Right. Bugger. Well, it wasn't really a huge surprise.

"Rupert? Gosh, that's a surprise! You two, a couple." Ginny shook her head in amazement. "Wow!"

"He's great," Jem said eagerly, fencing the asparagus spear from Ginny's fork and snaffling it before she could change her mind. "Well, you've met him; you already know how good-looking he is. We've been seeing each other for the last few weeks." Energetically, she chewed and swallowed the asparagus. "The thing is, though, we haven't told Lucy. It's a bit awkward, you see, the three of

269

us sharing the flat. Because we all get on so well together, she might feel left out if she knew. So for now it's our secret."

Déjà vu. Déjà vu clanging away like a big old bell. Was it some kind of inherited condition? Ginny wondered. Were she and Jem destined only to meet men who didn't want their relationships made public?

Carefully, she said, "Was that your idea or Rupert's?"

Jem considered this. "Well, both really. I mean, Rupert said it. But it just makes sense. I'd hate Lucy to feel like a third wheel. *I'd* hate it if I was the third wheel."

This was a fair point—indeed, a familiar point—but Ginny couldn't help feeling a sense of unease. So all they were doing, presumably, was sleeping together behind Lucy's back. How romantic.

"But you're happy?"

Jem beamed and took a gulp of champagne. "Very happy." Then she paused. "I thought you'd be happy about it too."

"Oh, sweetheart, I am. If you like him, that's . . . great. I suppose I was just thinking about this keeping-it-secret business because it's what Perry said to me. I don't want you to get hurt."

"But that was completely different. Laurel is Perry's sister. To be honest, Mum, it was a dodgy excuse in the first place. You were a bit gullible.

270

But Rupert's not like Perry; he's only doing it to spare Lucy's feelings. He's a nice person. And he's fun. Loads of girls at uni have a crush on him," Jem concluded with pride. "He could have anyone he wants. But he's chosen me."

"That's because he has good taste." Ginny reached across the table and gave Jem's hand a rub. Forcing herself to sound suitably enthusiastic she said, "He's a lucky boy. And I can't wait to meet him again properly. The two of you could come down and stay for a weekend, how about that? Everyone enjoys a trip to the seaside, don't they?"

"Mum, Rupert isn't eight." Jem rolled her eyes in amusement. "What would we do, have picnics on the beach and build sand castles?"

What was so terrible about a picnic on the beach? "Well, no, but . . ."

"He's in the south of France now, staying in his dad's villa. I've seen photos of it," said Jem. "It's the most incredible place you've ever seen. Joan Collins is a neighbor!"

Lucky old Joan.

"Rupert's gone down there with an old friend from boarding school." Leaning forward, Jem whispered excitedly, "And *his* father's a billionaire!"

Was that the problem? Did Jem think her house wasn't glamorous enough to impress Rupert? Because they didn't have a vast swimming pool, hordes of servants, and a panoramic view over St. Tropez harbor?

"Oh well then, that'll just have to be my next move," Ginny said lightly. "Marry Rupert's friend's father."

Jem giggled. "Don't be daft; you're far too old for him. He married his fifth wife last year, and she's twenty-two."

Their main courses arrived and Ginny ordered a bottle of wine. The conversation turned away from Rupert and they chattered instead, far more pleasurably, about clothes, shoes, Jem's customers at the pub, and the rich American who had come to Penhaligon's last Wednesday and ended up offering Finn half a million dollars for his jukebox (*yes,* he'd been drunk).

Just after nine thirty the door opened and a family of six piled in. One of the girls immediately spotted Jem and rushed over to their table.

"Jem Holland! You're back!"

Jem jumped to her feet and hugged Kaz Finnegan, her old school friend. "Kaz, so are you!"

"This is brilliant. Hi, Ginny! Someone told me you were working here."

"I am." Ginny was very fond of Kaz. "But Jem came home today so I'm having a night off."

"Working for dishy Finn. Lucky you. Now listen, it's my birthday next Tuesday." Kaz looked at Jem. "Will you still be here then?"

Jem nodded. "I'm back for a week."

"Yay, so you can come to my birthday party. We've hired a huge tent for the garden, and there's a band and everything. Loads of people invited." Persuasively, Kaz said, "And fireworks!"

Jem hesitated then looked over at Ginny. "What d'you think, Mum? Would that be OK with you?"

"And Niall's going to be there," Kaz went on. "He'd love to see you again."

Ginny smiled, because Jem and Kaz's older brother had had a teenage romance a couple of years ago and although the relationship had foundered when Niall had moved away to study for a degree in history at Manchester, she knew Jem still had a soft spot for him.

Ginny had a soft spot for him too, basically because he wasn't Rupert. "Go," she told Jem. "You'll have a fantastic time. I'm working on Tuesday evening anyway."

"With Finn Penhaligon." Kaz's eyes sparkled. "My mum has such a crush on him it's embarrassing. Is he fun to work for?"

At that moment, Finn walked past their table. "He's a nightmare," said Ginny. "A complete slave driver."

Without slowing down Finn said, "Some slaves need to be driven."

By the time the dessert menus arrived, Jem was sharing the last of the wine between their glasses. Dabbing at the drops she'd spilled on the tablecloth, she sat back and tilted her head to one side.

"What?" protested Ginny. "Why are you looking at me like that? If you're trying to hypnotize me into saying I don't want a dessert, it's not going to work."

"I wouldn't do that. I might try to hypnotize you into giving me your dessert." Jem beamed. "But that's not what I was thinking about."

"OK." To tease her, Ginny returned her attention to the menu. "Now I'm either going to have the orange crème brûlée or the double chocolate tart. Ooh, or the mango and lime cheeseca—"

"You're supposed to ask me what I was thinking about!"

"Go on then." Ginny was feeling thoroughly relaxed now; the day might have been traumatic but she was enjoying herself. It was so wonderful to have Jem, her beloved daughter, back at last. That was all that mattered.

"We-ell, he's good-looking. And Kaz's mum fancies the pants off him." Jem signaled with her eyebrows to let Ginny know who she was talking about, just in case Ginny might think she meant the fat bloke on table six. "So what I'm wondering is, have you given it any thought at all?"

OK, Ginny amended; *sometimes* it was wonderful to have her back.

"No." She shook her head, hastily blanking out the mental image of that four-poster bed and those cream curtains billowing in the breeze while a semi-naked—"No, never, not at all, God *no*."

"That's a lot of nos."

It was. Too many. Ginny forced herself to stop shaking her head, which had acquired a momentum of its own. "I just don't think of him in that way! He's my *boss*."

"That's a rubbish excuse," Jem pointed out. "Lots of people fancy their bosses."

"Well, I don't." Feeling a bit hot, Ginny took another slug of wine. Whoops, chin.

"Why not?"

Why not? Off the top of her head Ginny could think of a hundred reasons, chief among them the fact that her confidence had just taken the kicking of its life. Because, let's face it, she'd made an almighty fool of herself falling for Perry's lies, and given half a chance she would have leaped into bed with him before you could say floozy. But that hadn't happened because Perry hadn't been even remotely interested in sleeping with her, to the extent that he had resorted to the feeblest of excuses.

How much of an ego boost was that?

And basically, if Perry found her that unattractive, why on earth would someone like Finn be tempted? He could have anyone, for heaven's sake. Even Kaz's mother.

A beady-eyed Jem, meanwhile, was still waiting for an answer.

"Look, we get on well together," Ginny improvised. "And that's enough of a miracle in itself, considering what happened the first time we met. But it's only been a few hours since I found out about Perry and Carla. I really don't think I'm cut out for this dating malarkey. I'd rather just . . . you know, live without the hassle."

Jem looked disappointed. "But I think he's nice. And I want you to be happy."

Her heart swelling up like a giant marshmallow, Ginny reached across and clasped the hands of the daughter who meant the world to her. "Oh, sweetheart, how can I not be happy? *You're back.*"

"But only for a week. What about when I leave? Then you'll be all on your own again." Jem's face lit up. "I know! Why don't I have a quiet word with Finn, see if he fancies you?"

Ginny's fingers tightened around Jem's hands, then tightened again until she flinched. "Darling, that's so sweet of you. But you can't do that."

"I could! I'd be really subtle and—*ow, Mum!*"

"Because if you did do that," Ginny continued, her smile angelic, "I'd have to break both your legs."

Chapter 30

"THE THING IS, I look at you and I just want to *yawn . . .*"

"Dad, that is so rude! Honestly," Jem complained, "you're turning into a juvenile delinquent. You're just asking for a slap around the face."

"Luckily for him, I'm not into violence," Laurel said placidly.

"I'm so sorry about my dad," said Jem. "He's always been like this. He's so embarrassing."

It was Saturday afternoon and Gavin, just arrived, was being his usual shy, retiring self.

"You didn't let me finish." Undeterred, Gavin stretched out an arm and helped himself to the last slice of lemon drizzle cake. "I was talking about Laurel's clothes, the impression she makes on people when they meet her. Everything droops," he complained, waving the cake as he gestured at Laurel. "OK, maybe not the boobs, but everything else. Droopy skirt, droopy top, droopy *hair*. I'm just offering some constructive criticism. What's wrong with that?" he demanded as Jem rolled her eyes. "First impressions count. You want people to look at you and go, wow."

"Is that what they say when they see you?"

Gavin, who was wearing a multicolored striped

shirt, black trousers, and a bright red waistcoat, said with pride, "Nobody looks at me and thinks I'm boring."

"No," said Laurel. "But nobody looks at me and thinks I'm fat."

There was a stunned silence. Then Gavin started to laugh. "That was funny."

Laurel looked bemused. "It isn't. Being fat is a serious health issue."

"You said something funny. I love it!"

"You should lose thirty pounds," Laurel retaliated. "Look at your stomach."

"You should stop offering me cakes then."

"I didn't offer you any cakes. You helped yourself."

Still grinning, Gavin eyed her with new respect. "Know what? You're getting better. Buy yourself a perky new outfit and you'll be unrecognizable."

"I don't want a perky outfit. I like my clothes the way they are."

Ginny, rejoining them in the living room, looked suspiciously at Gavin. "Are you giving Laurel a hard time?"

"Quite the opposite. I'm giving her an easy time, complimenting her on her sense of humor. She's making progress," Gavin declared. "Plus, I've been here ten minutes and she hasn't mentioned Kevin once, which has to be some kind of—"

"Shhh," Laurel said severely. "We're not mentioning that name. New rule."

"Excellent rule. Why didn't anyone think of that before? You're on a roll now. Hey, what are you doing on Wednesday night?"

Laurel's huge green eyes widened in horror. "Please don't ask me out on a date."

"Sweetheart, I said you were on a roll, not that you'd scooped the jackpot. I was just going to suggest you giving the singles club another go. I'll make sure Hamish turns up this time. You never know, you being more cheerful now could make all the diff—"

"Not in a million years," said Laurel.

"But I just know you two would hit it off. And," Gavin added persuasively, "we're having a quiz night. Any questions about droopy clothes and you'd clean up."

"Is that another joke?"

He grinned. "Yep. Well done for recognizing it."

"Thank you," said Laurel, "but I'm still not coming to your singles club. And you could still do with losing weight."

"So cruel." Gavin clasped his chest. "Like a dagger in my heart."

"You'd be better with one in your stomach." For the first time there was a glimmer of a smile around Laurel's mouth. "Then it might go down, like a popped balloon."

"I don't know how it got there." Mournfully, Gavin patted his stomach. "It crept up on me when

I wasn't looking. I used to have a fine figure, didn't I, Gin?"

"You used to have lots of fine figures," said Ginny. "Sadly they all belonged to bimbos in miniskirts."

"There she is!" Jem, who had been gazing idly out of the window while the grown-ups got on with their bickering, shouted, "She's back! Look at her, scuttling inside like a rodent. God, I'd love to go over there and tell that lying tart what I think of her."

"Well, you're not going to." Envisaging some hideous street brawl, Ginny said, "This isn't Jerry Springer. We're just going to ignore her, OK?"

"But that means she gets away with it!" Indignantly Jem said, "How can that be fair?"

"Hang on." Gavin was looking blank. "Is this Carla we're talking about? Gets away with what?"

Everyone congregated at the window to watch Carla hurry into her house, slamming the glossy black front door behind her.

"Gets away with *what?*" repeated Gavin, bewildered.

"I was about to tell you." There was a horrid tightening knot in Ginny's stomach as she filled him in on the situation. When she'd finished she put the question she knew she needed to ask. "Did anything like that ever happen with you?"

Gavin's face was a picture. "You mean did Carla ever make a play for me?"

"Or vice versa."

"Bloody hell, Gin, I can't believe you even think that!"

"I can't believe it either, but until yesterday I thought I could trust my best friend." Ginny shrugged. "And look how well that turned out."

"Well, nothing happened, and that's a promise. Carla never tried it on and I wouldn't sleep with her if you paid me." Straight-faced, Gavin said, "I'd rather sleep with droopy Laurel."

Droopy Laurel rolled her eyes. "You wish," she said.

Carla had evidently whizzed home to pick up a change of clothes. Within ten minutes the front door reopened and she emerged carrying a small suitcase, her gaze deliberately averted from Ginny's house as she hurried back to the car.

"I'm going to go over there and give her a piece of my mind," Gavin announced.

"Oh no you're not." Touched by his loyalty, Ginny nevertheless moved to the living room door to block his exit.

Which was a fairly pointless exercise, seeing as Gavin launched himself at the window instead, flung it wide open, and bellowed across the road, "Hey, Carla, has he told you he's got herpes?"

Carla didn't look up but a young postman, cycling past at the time, did an alarmed double-take and almost wobbled off his bike.

"Poor kid." Gavin watched with grim satisfaction. "Looks like she's had him too."

For once all the diners had left in good time. By half-past ten the restaurant was empty, leaving only Ginny and Finn to finish clearing up.

"Early night for you," Finn observed. "You'll be pleased."

"Jem's gone out for the night. It's Kaz Finnegan's birthday do. Anyway, I've got that chef program to watch," said Ginny. "The one about the French guy who bought the crumbling castle in Wales and turned it into a restaurant."

"Damn, I missed it. Everyone's been telling me about that."

"No problem, I recorded it." Ginny, collecting cutlery to lay a table for ten, said eagerly, "I can lend you the DVD."

Finn shook his head. "It's OK, don't worry about it."

"But it's supposed to be brilliant. You'll enjoy it!"

"Really, it doesn't matter." He turned his attention to counting the twenty-pound notes in the till.

Something about the way he said it aroused Ginny's curiosity.

"Don't you have a DVD player?"

Defensively, maybe even too quickly, Finn replied, "Yes, of course I do."

"So why don't you want to borrow the DVD?"

He paused in the middle of cashing up, looked over at her for a moment.

"Because the DVD machine's still in its box."

Mystified, Ginny frowned. "OK, I know this is a pretty radical suggestion, but how about . . . ooh, let's see, taking it out of the box and connecting it up to the TV?"

Another lengthy pause. Finally he gave in, exhaled slowly. "Because I tried that and I couldn't make it work."

Oh, brilliant. Ginny did her best to keep a straight face. "Right, so did you read the instruction manual?"

"Yes. But that just made everything worse; it kept going on about *scart* leads and . . . and *grinch* cables and stupid stuff that made *no* sense at all." Finn shot her a warning look. "And if you're laughing at me . . ."

"I'm not laughing." Heroically, Ginny bit her lip but she was only human. "OK, maybe smirking a bit."

"It's not funny," said Finn. "It's embarrassing. I'm a *man*."

"It's not as embarrassing as having to admit you're impotent." Ginny said it without thinking, then hastily added, "Not that I'm saying you *are* impotent, of course."

"I'm not," Finn said gravely.

"But you have to admit, it is *quite* funny."

"We're not talking about impotence now, are we?"

Equally seriously Ginny shook her head. "No, because impotence is never funny."

Good grief, was she really having this conversation?

"I can't set up DVD players." Finn admitted defeat. "Or video recorders. Or TVs, come to that. It's a recognized phobia," he went on, "of electrical leads and sockety things and manuals that deliberately set out to confuse you."

He was hating this; she was loving it. Ginny's mouth was twitching uncontrollably now. "So, um, how do you usually deal with this?"

He looked slightly shamefaced. "Get a man in."

A man. Of course. Giddy with power, Ginny said, "Would a woman do?"

This time she definitely detected a flicker of amusement. "Would a woman do what?"

"Would you like me to set up your DVD player for you?"

He shrugged offhandedly. "If you want."

"Sorry. That's not good enough. Not nearly enough enthusiasm."

Finn gave in gracefully, broke into a broad smile, and pushed the till shut.

"OK, you win. Yes please."

Chapter 31

THEY MADE IT ACROSS the darkened courtyard without, for once, being ambushed by Myrtle. Upstairs in the flat, Finn brought out the DVD recorder, crammed haphazardly into its original packaging as if someone—*ahem*—had previously had a go and ended up losing his temper with it. The expression on Finn's face as he handed it over made Ginny smile all over again.

It took her less than fifteen minutes to sort patiently through the spaghetti-like tangle of wires, plug them into the relevant sockets, set up the recorder, and tune in the relevant channels.

"I don't know how you can do that." Finn watched as she sat back on her heels and expertly keyed in instructions via the remote control.

"It's easy. Look, let me show you how to set it in advance."

"Don't even try. I'll just press record when it's time to record something. That's as technical as I get." Holding out a hand, he helped Ginny to her feet. "But thanks, I appreciate it. Now, do you have to rush off or can I ask you another favor?"

She breathed in the scent of his aftershave, experiencing a tremor as his warm hand clasped hers. "You want me to fix your kettle?"

"The kettle's fine. I'll prove it to you. What I really want is for you to give me your honest opinion of this room."

Ginny gazed around at the decor. "I thought you'd never ask."

It had, she learned, been Tamsin's idea to hire an outrageously trendy interior designer, lure him down from London, and have him transform the flat while Finn had been away on a buying trip. Upon Finn's return, he had been confronted with the mother of all make-overs involving aubergine-and-silver striped walls, a pistachio-green ceiling, and a sixties-style, pop-arty aubergine-and-pistachio carpet. The lighting was modern, verging on the futuristic. The sofas, sleek and uninviting, were upholstered in lime-green tweed flecked with silver.

Austin Powers would have thought it was shagtastic.

"You don't want to know how much it cost," Finn said with a shudder.

"Did you tell her you hated it?"

"Couldn't. It was my birthday present. And Tamsin was so thrilled, I didn't have the heart to hurt her feelings."

He must have loved Tamsin an awful lot. Whenever Gavin had bought her something horrific for her birthday Ginny had trained him to hand over the receipt at the same time. Then again, that was the beauty of coordinated outfits from Marks and Spencer. It wouldn't be quite so easy lugging an entire room back to the shop.

"So what happens now?"

"It has to go. The whole lot. I would have done it before but the restaurant had to take priority. It's been easier to just ignore it. But the other day I picked up some paint charts," Finn went on firmly. "And this time I won't be hiring a bloody designer."

He made coffee with the non-broken kettle. Ginny sat down on the sleek, slippery sofa and spread the paint charts over the brushed aluminum—brushed *aluminum!*—coffee table. For the next hour they debated wall colors, curtains, furniture, and accessories. Out with the new and achingly trendy, in with the unflashy and traditional. Ginny sketched out ideas and drew the room with cream curtains billowing gently at the open windows.

"Not blue curtains?" said Finn.

"No, too dark. Definitely cream." Her mind was made up on that score; it might not be the bedroom but Ginny was adamant there would be cream curtains. And billowy ones at that. Oh yes, they would billow if she had to smash all the windows herself.

"So how are you feeling about Perry now?"

Thanks for reminding me. "Like an idiot."

"Well, you shouldn't. He's the idiot."

Acutely aware of Finn's proximity to her on the

sofa—their shoulders were only millimeters apart—Ginny said, "I'm out of practice when it comes to dating. I should have realized what his game was, but I didn't. Maybe if I'd been out with more men I wouldn't have been so gullible."

"Don't blame yourself. You're better off without someone like that. Carla would probably be better off without him too, but now she's the one being gullible." Drily, he added, "And look how much practice she's had."

"You think I should feel sorry for her?" Ginny half smiled. "I can't see that happening."

"Maybe not. You just have to put it behind you and move on."

"Is that what you did?" She felt brave enough to ask him now. "After Tamsin left?"

Finn shrugged and this time his shoulder made contact with hers. "It's the only thing to do."

"But it's easier for some people than others. Like you with that girl Catherine," said Ginny. "The one who sent you flowers the other week. Why did she do that?"

He sounded amused. "Because I gave her a lift home?"

Ha, and the rest. Bluntly, Ginny said, "Did you sleep with her?"

There was a pause then Finn nodded. "OK, yes. I did."

"You see?" Vigorously Ginny shook her own head. "I'd love to be able to do that!"

Now he was definitely smiling. "You'd love to sleep with Catherine? Or with me?"

Oh Lord, what a thought.

"Neither! I *meant* I'd love to be the kind of person who could do that." Ginny felt the heat creeping into her cheeks. "I wish I could go out, see someone I like the look of, and . . . well, have a one-night stand, just for the hell of it. But I can't, because I'm not that kind of person and I never have been."

"Never?"

"Never. It's really annoying. Men do it all the time. And so do loads of women, I know that. But I've never been able to." Recklessly Ginny said, "If I told you how many men I'd slept with, you'd fall off the sofa laughing. Honestly, I'm pathetic."

Finn raised a playful eyebrow. "So you're saying you want to be like Carla?"

"God, no, nothing like that. Just . . . you know, once in a blue moon it'd be nice to think, oh sod it, why not?"

"Find someone you like the look of and just go for it?"

"Well, yes." Ginny knew her cheeks were on fire now; she still couldn't quite believe she was having this conversation, and with Finn Penhaligon of all people. But her pent-up feelings were spilling out uncontrollably like molten lava. "What are you doing?" she added, because he was now twisting round on the sofa, peering out of the window at something in the sky.

"Just checking if it's a blue moon."

Her breath caught in her throat. This, subconsciously or otherwise, was exactly what she'd wanted to hear him say. Maybe it was pathetic, but after having her confidence dented—more like *smashed*—by Perry, she was ridiculously flattered to know that Finn Penhaligon would be prepared to have sex with her.

Except, terrifyingly, he appeared to have made his offer and was now awaiting her response to it.

Except, aaarrgh, what if it hadn't been an offer at all? Maybe he was a keen astronomer genuinely interested in discovering whether the moon tonight might actually be blue?

"Well?" Finn prompted, his dark eyes questioning.

Hopelessly unsure and petrified of making a twit of herself, Ginny said, "Is it?"

"Take a look." He gently turned her round to face the window. "Tell me what you think."

There was an unromantic *thunk* as Ginny's ankle knocked against the edge of the coffee table, setting the coffee cups rattling against the metallic surface. Her heart hammering against her rib cage, she followed the line of Finn's pointing finger and saw the moon hanging low in the inky-black sky, partially obscured by the branches of a sycamore tree.

"So, does it look blue to you?" The words came out as a whisper, his warm breath circling her ear in such a way as to send Ginny's nervous system into a frenzy. But she still didn't know if this was all part of his seduction plan or simply an experienced astronomer asking a hopeless ignoramus an easy question.

"It looks . . . um, well . . . I think maybe it looks a *bit* blue."

"Really?" Now he sounded amused—oh God, was that the wrong answer?

"White with a hint of blue?" hazarded Ginny. "Sort of . . . very faintly . . . bluish?"

"Hmm." He nodded thoughtfully. "You know, I think you could be right."

"Yiawoooooow."

"What's *that?*" Startled by the unearthly noise, faint but clearly audible, Ginny's eyes widened.

"Sounds like Myrtle, somewhere outside."

"Yiiaaarrrrlll."

"She's not happy. Oh God, what if she's been cornered by a fox?"

"Poor fox, he doesn't know what he's let himself in for. She'll rip him to shreds."

"Mwwwwaaaaaoooowwwwww," Myrtle yowled, sounding more outraged than Ginny had ever heard her before.

"She's being attacked by something. I'll go and let her in." Leaping up and slipping past Finn, she headed downstairs and opened the front door.

"Myrtle? Come on, sweetheart, it's OK, come inside."

But although she heard another faint yowl, Myrtle didn't materialize out of the darkness and shoot past Ginny's ankles in a blur of indignant black fur. Finally, she closed the door and made her way back upstairs. If Finn had a torch, they could go in search of her.

But when she reached the landing, she saw Finn standing at the far end of it, his hand resting on the handle of a half-open door that, if she'd got her bearings right, had to lead into the master bedroom. His dark eyes locked with hers for a moment, his expression unreadable. Then he held out his other hand and slowly beckoned her forward. His voice low and with a husky edge to it, he murmured, "Come here."

Oo-er. Tingling all over, torn between finding a missing cat and being drawn into Finn Penhaligon's bedroom, Ginny hesitated. Then again, what had Myrtle ever done for her? Maybe the time had come to be selfish for once. If Finn had decided that the moon was blue, who was she to argue?

Wandering in a dreamlike state toward him, she imagined herself unbuttoning Finn's white shirt, removing the leather belt that held up his black trousers, undoing the zip in a sensual manner. Oh Lord, she was disastrously out of practice; she hoped she didn't show herself up. Socks, for instance. Would he take his own socks off before the trousers came down? Surely he wouldn't expect *her* to deal with them. Heavens, she couldn't remember how socks got disposed of; she was going to make a complete fool of herself and—

"Take a look at this." Finn noiselessly opened the bedroom door and drew her inside. As she held her breath, the first thing Ginny realized was that she wasn't going to have to wrestle with sock etiquette after all.

Not with Finn either, come to that.

Another realization was that as far as her long-cherished fantasy was concerned, she couldn't have got it more wrong if she'd tried. There was no four-poster, no cream hangings billowing gently in the breeze. The bed was king-sized and ultra-modern with a leather headboard and a heavy, expensive-looking dark blue suede bedspread.

Except it wasn't looking quite so expensive at the moment, what with all the gunk and slime smeared in the center of the bed over the supple, top-quality suede.

"Oh . . ." Ginny's hand flew to her mouth.

"Yiaaaaaawwwwww," Myrtle yowled, furry paws extending and rib cage heaving as the next contraction gripped her body. As they watched, a silvery parcel emerged, slithering out of Myrtle and onto the bedspread only inches from the first

blind mewling kitten. Twisting round, clearly relieved to have got a second one out, Myrtle used her sharp teeth to remove the covering membrane and bite her way—*eww*—through the umbilical cord.

"I didn't even realize she was here in the flat," Finn whispered. "She must have jumped across from the tree outside and climbed in through the window."

"Like a true cat burglar."

He grinned. "Give her a motorcycle and she'd out-leap Evel Knievel."

"Oh *looook*." Ginny tugged at his shirtsleeve as the first kitten, having staggered to its feet, promptly fell over the second. Struggling to get up again, it then slipped on a patch of dark green slime and landed on its back. It lay there mewing piteously until Myrtle took pity on it and unceremoniously hauled it by the scruff of the neck over to her stomach.

"How do they know how to do that?" said Finn as the kitten, without a moment's hesitation, latched on and frantically began to feed.

"How did Myrtle know she had to bite through the cord?" Ginny shook her head in wonderment. "I'm glad I didn't have to do that when Jem was born."

Myrtle turned and blinked majestically, topaz eyes surveying her audience. For once she didn't snarl or hiss at them. "Maybe now she's a mother she'll turn into a nicer cat." Finn didn't sound too hopeful.

"Maybe she just has more important things on her mind right now, like bracing herself for the next contraction. How much did your bedspread cost, by the way?"

"Hundreds." Finn paused. "And hundreds. Tamsin chose it." Another pause. "Almost a thousand, I think."

Consolingly, Ginny said, "It'll probably dry-clean."

Since seduction was no longer on the menu—if it ever had been—they left Myrtle to get on with the task in hand and headed back to the living room. Finn made more coffee and paced the kitchen while Ginny perched on a high stool at the counter and surfed the Internet on his laptop.

"Sit down," she complained. "You're making me jittery."

"I am jittery. I feel like a prospective father."

"Well, you aren't." Ginny winced the moment she'd said it. What a thing to come out with. Luckily, typing "cats giving birth" into Google diverted her attention.

Yikes, cats giving birth wasn't the straight-forward procedure she'd imagined.

"What?" Observing her look of alarm, Finn plonked a mug of coffee in front of her.

"Are you squeamish?"

"Why?"

"There's a whole list here of all the stuff you need when your cat goes into labor. A maternity bed."

"Well, she's already helped herself to that," Finn said drily. "What else? Gas and air?"

"A heating pad," Ginny read aloud. "Clean cloths or towels. A weighing scale."

"I've got bathroom scales." Finn frowned.

"Sharp scissors," said Ginny, pulling a face. "Disinfectant. A small syringe. And dental floss."

"Do I want to know why?"

"If the mother doesn't sever the umbilical cord, you have to do it yourself. You tie the dental floss round the cord before you cut it."

"Interesting use of the word 'you,'" Finn observed. "How about if we toss a coin?"

"I only fix DVD recorders." Ginny held up her hands "Besides, she's your cat."

He grimaced, then nodded at the computer screen. "So is that it, then?"

"Not quite. Petroleum jelly." Ginny read the accompanying instruction. "If the mother is having trouble giving birth, you need to put some petroleum jelly on her to help ease the kitten out."

"Fine. I'll put some on her ears."

"And we're going to need three tennis balls and a washed lettuce."

"What?"

"Joking." Ginny beamed.

"Yaaaaiiiiooooooooow!"

296

As they hurried back to the bedroom, Finn said, "I don't think Myrtle found that joke funny."

By three o'clock in the morning it was all over. Myrtle had given birth to a litter of four kittens and, thankfully, hadn't required the services of two incompetent human midwives. She had delivered her babies, chomped her way with relish through their afterbirths (*bleurgh*), and was now lying peacefully on the bed with all four babies curled up at her side.

Finn, busy making up the bed in the spare room seeing as Myrtle had nabbed his own, came out and saw Ginny yawning and collecting together her jacket, bag, and car keys.

"Are you off now? Drive carefully."

Not *the* most romantic of sentiments but understandable, considering the circumstances. It crossed Ginny's mind that he might even have given her a good-bye kiss if she hadn't been yawning offputtingly, like a hippo.

"I will. Sorry, bit tired." She waggled her fingers at him. "See you tomorrow."

Who knew how their evening might have turned out if Myrtle hadn't chosen to give birth in Finn's king-sized bed? Oh well, it had been an experience.

"See you," said Finn.

Was that a note of regret in his voice or was she imagining it?

Cattus interruptus, thought Ginny.

Damn.

Chapter 32

SAYING GOOD-BYE DIDN'T GET any easier. Jem was on her way back to Bristol and Ginny's throat was aching dreadfully with the effort of not making a public disgrace of herself. Having Jem at home again had been wonderful, but now their week together was up and she couldn't bear it.

To add insult to injury the train was on time. As it pulled into the station, there was a clap of thunder overhead and the first fat raindrops began to fall.

"Oh yuck." Having painstakingly straightened her hair and keen to avoid it going stupid, Jem threw her arms around Ginny and gave her a kiss. "Don't hang around out here, Mum, it's going to tip down."

"I don't mind. Text me when you reach the flat, just so I know you've got back safely." Ginny had to force herself not to stroke her daughter's face—"Mum, that's *embarrassing*"—as she had always done when Jem was young.

"Yes, Mum, and I promise to eat plenty of fruit and vegetables and always wear a coat when it snows."

"Don't make fun of me. It's my job to worry about you."

"Well, you don't need to because I'm a big girl

now." Hauling her vast rucksack onto her shoulders, Jem moved toward the waiting train. With a grin she added, "And you have to behave yourself too. No getting up to mischief while I'm not here to keep an eye on you."

Without meaning to, Ginny's thoughts turned to Finn. Chance would be a fine thing. Since the arrival of the kittens, there had been no more talk of blue moons. No flirtatious looks either, to the extent that she now wondered if she'd imagined them ever being there in the first place.

The heavens opened and with a squeal Jem leaped into her carriage. "Bye, Mum! See you soon!"

"Bye, sweetheart." Ginny blew a kiss as the train's doors slid shut and the ache in her throat gave way to tears. Thankfully the rain streaming down her cheeks disguised them and she kept a bright smile plastered to her face.

Jem blew extravagant kisses back, the train pulled out of the station, and moments later she was gone.

Back to Bristol, back to Pembroke Road in Clifton, back to Rupert whom Ginny just *knew* wasn't right for her.

But what could you do? Jem wasn't six years old anymore; Ginny couldn't simply forbid her to see him because, like skateboarding without a crash helmet, if she did, Jem'd only end up getting hurt. Jem had to be allowed to make her own mistakes now. And hopefully learn from them.

Like the rest of us, Ginny reminded herself, thinking of Carla and Perry and the sorry mess that was her own nonexistent love life.

Jem had texted Rupert on the train. He had flown back from Nice airport that morning. Letting herself into the flat, she called out joyfully, "Hi, honey, I'm home!"

"Hey." He appeared in the hallway, impossibly tanned and clutching a bottle of lager. "Honey, you shrunk your T-shirt."

Jem gazed down at her front; the storm had followed her all the way from Cornwall and rain was bucketing down outside.

Her cropped white T-shirt was now drenched and transparent, thanks to the long walk from the bus stop on Whiteladies Road.

"Don't try and cover yourself up. I like it." Grinning, he gave her a cool, beery kiss and trailed his hand down her chest.

"Is Lucy here?" Jem had to double-check.

"Not back yet. Which I have to say I'm quite happy about. So, good time?"

"Great." With an expert shoulder wiggle Jem released the straps of her wet rucksack and let it fall to the ground with a *thunk*. "I went to a party, met up with loads of old friends."

"Old friends, eh? Would that be old girlfriends or old boyfriends?"

"Both." Entranced by the idea that Rupert might be jealous, Jem said, "Actually, there was one old boyfriend there."

Rupert raised a playful eyebrow. "Should I be worried?"

"No. I don't fancy him anymore." It was the truth; bumping into Niall again had had zero effect on her. Compared with Rupert he'd just seemed so . . . ordinary.

"Good." And then Rupert was kissing her, and all thoughts of Niall Finnegan flew from her mind. It was too busy experiencing its own fireworks display instead.

"What about Lucy?" breathed Jem as he led her by her wet T-shirt in the direction of his bedroom.

"Relax. She won't be home for hours." As skillful as an ice dancer, he maneuvered her through the door, simultaneously unzipping her skirt and pulling the T-shirt off over her head. Jem didn't even care that he'd stretched it beyond repair.

"Anyway, what about you in the south of France?" Teasingly, Jem prodded his chest. "Surrounded by beautiful girls in bikinis? You must have been chatted up."

"The thing is, you call them beautiful girls in bikinis. I call them a bunch of old slappers. Of course I was chatted up," Rupert drawled. "But all they're interested in is bagging themselves a guy with money. The moment they spot your platinum credit card they're all over you like a swarm of wasps. Not my idea of fun." Gently he pushed Jem onto his double bed, gazed down at her, and said with a smile, "That's why I'm here now. Because you are definitely my idea of fun."

Afterward, Jem ran her fingers through her disastrous hair. "I must look like a wet hedgehog."

"You look gorgeous." Rupert kissed the tip of her nose. "Sexily disheveled."

"Sexily disheveled." She wrinkled her nose doubtfully. "Is that flattering?"

"Now you're fishing. OK." Gravely he surveyed her naked body. "You have a great figure." He ran an experimental hand up her shin. "No stubble, always a bonus."

Jem giggled. "Cheek."

"Ah yes, glad you reminded me." Skillfully flipping her onto her side, Rupert carefully inspected her bottom. "Excellent, no cellulite either."

"Of course I don't have cellulite!" Jem dug her fingernails into his shoulder by way of protest.

"But you never know; it could arrive any day now. Just take up residence whether you want it there or not. Does your mother have cellulite?"

"No she does not!"

"Hey, I only asked. It's just that these things can be hereditary. We saw a few prime examples ourselves last week, let me tell you." Laughing,

Rupert rolled out of reach before she could hit him. "Like mother, like daughter, wibble-wobbling along together across the sand. That's on the public beaches, of course. No gloopy cellulite allowed on the private ones."

"You're wicked," said Jem.

"But you love me." He flipped her back over, his hazel eyes glinting with intent.

Jem's stomach contracted with desire as one of his knees slid between hers. She wouldn't admit it for the world, but she was beginning to think she did actually love him. Let's face it, he was gorgeous. And they got on so well togeth—

The front door slammed.

Beneath Rupert, Jem froze. They heard the click-clack of high heels out in the hall, then Lucy called out, "Where are you?"

"Damn it," Rupert breathed. Eyes wide and brain racing, Jem glanced over at the wardrobe. Bulging with clothes, unread textbooks, tennis rackets, and in-line skates, there wasn't room for a hamster let alone a fully grown eighteen-year-old.

A *naked* eighteen-year-old.

A hysterical giggle rose up in Jem's throat. Oh well, maybe it was fate. Sooner or later Lucy was going to have to find out about them anyway.

"Shhh." Rupert, who wasn't laughing, lifted himself off her in one swift movement. "Hide under the bed."

Was he joking? Clearly not.

"Rupert?" Lucy was knocking on the door now.

"Get down there," hissed Rupert, rolling Jem to the edge of the mattress. Still grinning, she decided to humor him and dropped silently to the ground. Moments later, having hastily gathered up her discarded clothes, Rupert thrust them into her arms.

"Lucy? That you?" Yawning noisily, he called out, "What time is it? I've been asleep."

Under the bed and clutching her clothes, Jem came nose to nose with a semi-deflated blow-up sheep (a bachelor party prop rather than a perversion). The sheep had a dopey, crumpled look on its face.

"You lazy bum, it's four o'clock! Where's Jem?"

"No idea. I don't think she's back yet."

"She is. Her rucksack's on the floor." The bedroom door was flung open and Jem saw Lucy's emerald-green high heels. "You're not hiding her in here, are you?"

The bed creaked as Rupert sat up. "If she's not in her room she must have gone out. Hang on, I'll get up. Why don't you make us some coffee?"

There was a pause. Jem held her breath. Then Lucy said, "I've got a better idea. Why don't I wake you up properly?"

Jem frowned. What was that supposed to mean? She watched the shoes move toward the bed; Lucy was so close now that if she reached past the sheep she could touch her ankles. That'd give her a fright.

"Don't muck about, Luce. I've got a headache."

"Now that's something I never thought I'd hear you say." The bedsprings creaked again and one of Lucy's shoes disappeared from view; in disbelief, Jem realized that she was now sitting *on* the bed.

"Stop it," said Rupert.

"Sorry." Evidently unfazed, Lucy murmured, "But I just don't think I can. Come on, what's the matter with you? Haven't you missed me?"

What? WHAT?

"Luce, will you—"

"Because I've missed you. Loads. In fact," Lucy paused then said silkily, "I'd say I missed you *this* much."

Jem felt as if she'd been plunged into a vat of dry ice. Logically, she knew what was happening, but her brain was refusing to make sense of it. She was in such a state of shock she wasn't even sure she could move.

"OK, that's enough." Rupert's tone was brusque. "Game over."

"What's the *matter* with you?" protested Lucy.

"Oh, I don't know," Rupert drawled. "Why don't you take a look under the bed and see if you can work it out?"

Jem couldn't believe he'd said it. Then again,

Lucy hadn't given him much choice. She closed her eyes, bracing herself. Above her she heard Lucy say, "Don't tell me you've been playing about with that stupid blow-up sheep."

Chapter 33

WHEN JEM OPENED HER eyes again, she saw Lucy, crouching down, staring at her.

"No. No." Lucy shook her head. "Tell me this is a joke."

"I'll make the coffee myself," said Rupert.

"You've been shagging both of us?" shrieked Lucy.

"Be fair, you pretty much threw yourself at me. It was fun while it lasted." He sounded bored. "But now it's run its course."

"You arrogant jerk! Get out of here," Lucy screamed at him. "I need to talk to Jem."

"Fine by me." Dragging on a pair of jeans, Rupert sauntered out of the bedroom.

"I don't believe this," Lucy exploded. "I just do not bloody believe it. He's been playing us for a couple of fools."

Jem, emerging from beneath the bed, said, "Could you look away while I get dressed?"

"Oh, for God's sake." Impatiently, Lucy turned away. "So this is what's been going on behind my back. Rupert must have thought it was hilarious."

She was fuming, tapping her foot and shaking her head at the thought of it.

Hurriedly, Jem shook out her balled-up clothes and climbed into them, shuddering as the cold clamminess of the T-shirt hit her skin.

"Why didn't you say anything?" Lucy blurted out.

Stung by her tone, Jem shot back, "Why didn't you?"

"But you never asked me! I actually *asked* you. At the party when I saw him groping your backside." Lucy's dark eyes flashed with anger. "I asked if there was anything going on between the two of you and you said there wasn't."

"Rupert didn't want you to feel left out."

"Funny, that's what he said to me too."

Jem took a deep breath. "I can't believe this is happening."

"I can't believe you lied to me!" Lucy said vehemently, before holding up her hands. "OK, OK, I lied to you too. But Rupert lied to both of us. This is all down to him. Well, he's really blown it now. *Jerk.*"

"I heard that." Rupert, leaning against the door, took a swig from another bottle of lager.

"Good." Lucy swung around. "And you can find yourself a couple of new flatmates. Because we are *out* of here."

Jem looked at her in alarm.

"You're leaving? Fine. In fact, excellent."

Rupert shrugged, then in turn fixed his gaze on Jem. "But you don't want to leave, do you? Lucy never meant anything to me; it was only ever a casual fling. But you and me . . . well, it's different. Something special."

Jem's heart was racing; this was what she'd longed to hear for weeks.

"Forget it!" Incandescent with rage, Lucy yelled, "We're both going!"

"You know, bitter and twisted really doesn't suit you." Rupert raised an eyebrow. "A woman scorned is never a pretty sight."

"You make me sick," bellowed Lucy.

"Carry on like this and you'll give yourself wrinkles."

"Oh, bugger off."

"I think that's your job, sweetheart. You've already promised." Taking another swig of lager, Rupert smiled at Jem. "You know why Lucy's so mad, don't you? She's upset because I prefer you."

"You jerk!"

"Again? This is getting boring. Anyway, don't you have some packing to do?"

"Come on, Jem," Lucy ordered. "Let's go."

"She's not your pet dog," Rupert said coldly. "She doesn't have to do what you say." He turned to Jem. "It's up to you. I don't want you to leave."

"Oh shut up, you arrogant wanker."

"Jem?" Rupert tilted his head to one side.

"Jem!" snapped Lucy.

"I'm going to my room," said Jem, "to think."

She sat on her bed and buried her face in her hands. Everything had been going so well and now this. From next door came the crashings and bangings of drawers being yanked open and slammed shut as Lucy emptied them of her belongings. When her own door was pushed open she didn't look up.

"Don't go." As Rupert spoke, the mobile in his jeans pocket beeped, signaling the arrival of a text. "I want you to stay. It'll be just the two of us from now on. We can be a proper couple."

Jem's chest was aching so much she felt as if she was quite literally being torn in two. Her instinct in the past had always been to side with a girl-friend against a boy; it happened so automatically she'd never even questioned it. But this time was different; there was so much more at stake. Because, OK, Rupert had behaved badly but that was over now. And boys will be boys, after all. Especially boys with the kind of upbringing he'd had.

Far more important was how they felt about each other now that all the bad stuff was behind them. And she knew how she felt about Rupert. More to the point, she was realizing how he felt about her.

Jem trembled. Lucy, her friend, was exotic, sexy, and stunningly beautiful. Jem knew she herself was pretty enough in a ditsy, blond-hair-streaked-with-pink kind of way, but she couldn't begin to compete with Lucy in the glamour stakes. Yet when it had come down to it, Rupert preferred her. How flattering was that, for heaven's sake?

No wonder Lucy was spitting teeth.

CRASH went the wardrobe doors next door, followed by the furious jangle of coat hangers.

Rupert finished reading his text. "My mate Olly's invited us to a party next weekend. Up in Scotland. Fancy that?"

Olly, Olly. Oliver MacIntyre-Brown. "Is he the one with the castle?" said Jem.

"The one with the bloody enormous castle. Olly says we can hitch a lift up there in his uncle's helicopter if we want."

Helicopter.

Castle.

She'd never been to Scotland before, not even on a train.

"Sorry," Rupert continued. "Jumping the gun. You might be about to call me a jerk and start emptying your wardrobe too."

Jem looked up at him. Life without Lucy would be horrible.

But life without Rupert would be infinitely worse.

"I'm not."

He broke into a wide smile. "Really?"

"Really."

"I'm glad." Rupert's gaze softened as he put down his phone and the bottle of Pils. "Very, very glad. Hey, you. Come here."

He kissed her and Jem knew she'd made the right decision. They were a proper couple now. And the way she was feeling, she suspected it might be the real thing after all.

If this wasn't love, she didn't know what was.

There was a sharp knock at the bedroom door. Bracing herself, Jem peeled herself away from Rupert and went to answer it.

Lucy, her shoulders rigid, said, "Well?"

"I'm staying."

"With him?" Her mouth twisted into a pitying smile. "You sad cow."

He chose me over you, Jem wanted to retort, but stopped herself. Lucy already knew that.

"Do you think he loves you?" Lucy demanded. "Is that it? Because if you really think that, you're even more stupid than—"

"Everything packed?" Rupert broke in coolly. "Called the taxi yet? Tell you what, I'll even pay the fare. No hard feelings, sweetheart. It was a good contest but the best girl won."

"You arrogant git."

"Ah, but a generous arrogant git, you can't deny that." Having pulled out his wallet, Rupert began counting out twenty-pound notes. "Here you go; one month's deposit back and an extra twenty for the cab. Lucky I went to the cashpoint."

"Does it not bother you, living off your father's money?"

"Funnily enough, not in the least. I love it. You should give it a go yourself sometime—oh sorry, I forgot your family doesn't have any money. Bad luck, sweetheart, you don't know what you're missing."

Jem knew he didn't mean it nastily; Rupert was always making flippant, derogatory remarks about his own family's wealth or other people's lack of it.

"I feel sorry for the pair of you." Lucy's eyes flashed as she uttered the words. The next moment she'd stalked out of the room.

"Obviously keener on me than she was letting on." Rupert shrugged. "*And* a bad loser."

"Don't." Jem felt a pang of guilt. "She's my friend."

"Not anymore she isn't." Sliding his arms round her waist he winked and said, "You're all mine now."

Lucy hauled her bags out of the taxi and looked up at the unprepossessing terraced house with its blue front door and neat, pocket-sized front garden. The door opened and Davy came out to greet her.

It wasn't ideal, but leaving Rupert's flat in a rush during the Easter break hadn't given her a lot of choice. Most of her friends had gone home for the holidays. At least Davy was here.

And he understood.

"Davy, thanks so much for this. I couldn't stay there." Lucy hugged him. "She's lost her mind; she actually thinks he . . . he . . ."

"I know. Shhh, it's OK."

"Oh, Davy, I'm so *mad*. How can she be so stupid? It's not that I'm jealous." Dashing away angry tears, Lucy gibbered, "It's just . . . how could she find out what he's been doing and forgive him?"

"Come on, let's go in. Mum's waiting to meet you."

"Oh God. And here I am, pitching up and dumping myself on you. Is she angry?"

Davy grinned. "Are you joking? She's over the moon."

Rhona Stokes was making tea in the tiny kitchen. In her late forties, she was an older, female version of Davy with the same big dark eyes and shoulder-length dark brown hair. When she crossed the kitchen, Lucy saw that she walked with a slight limp.

"Hello, love, welcome. Crikey, Davy said you were a looker but he didn't tell me you were a supermodel." She beamed and kissed Lucy on both cheeks. "It's going to get the neighbors talking, having you here. They'll think our Davy's got himself a cracking girlfriend at last!"

Davy rolled his eyes. *"Mum."*

"Oh, I'm only joking. Sorry, love." Turning

back to Lucy, Rhona stage-whispered, "I know I'm an embarrassment."

"It's your house; you can be whatever you like. It's so kind of you to let me stay." Lucy gestured awkwardly at her pile of bags. "I'll be out of here as soon as possible, I promise, the moment I find another flat."

"No hurry at all. You're welcome to stay as long as you like. Here, drink your tea while it's hot and help yourself to biscuits. Then we'll get you settled in your room. It's only weeny, I'm afraid—smaller than you're used to."

Lucy was overcome with gratitude. "I don't care about that. I'm just glad to be here, away from Pembroke Road."

"I'll carry your stuff upstairs," said Davy.

"It's the first time I've met one of Davy's university friends," Rhona confided when he'd gone. "He said you've always been kind to him."

Kind. "Well . . . why wouldn't I be?"

"Can I ask? Does he have many friends there? It's just, you know what boys are like," Rhona went on. "They keep quiet about things like that."

"I think he's fine." Lucy was diplomatic. "He always seems quite happy to me."

Rhona's dark eyes searched hers for clues. "Only I wondered if he ever gets teased, you know? For still living at home with his mum."

Lucy burned her mouth on the steaming tea. How was she supposed to answer a question like that without offending Rhona? She put down her mug. "Well, one or two people might have said something, but they're idiots. The rest of us just ignore them."

Well, what could she say? That Davy was a laughingstock?

"Oh, that's good news then." Relieved, Rhona picked up a Maryland cookie. "Not that Davy's ever said anything, but I did wonder."

"He's a nice person." Lucy meant it. How many books had he lent her over the past months? Not that she'd actually wanted to read them, but still. It was the thought that counted, and you couldn't ask for a more thoughtful person than Davy.

"He's the light of my life," Rhona said simply. "I do feel bad sometimes, keeping him here, but it's not as if I don't have a reason." For a moment she grew misty-eyed, then visibly gathered herself and gave Lucy's arm a pat. "Anyway, bless you for putting my mind at rest, love. I honestly don't know what I'd do if Davy moved out."

Chapter 34

"SHOULD HAVE THOUGHT OF this years ago," said Finn. "Inviting women to come up and see my kittens. Beats etchings any day."

"That's because etchings are boring," Ginny told him, "and kittens are unbelievably cute. The only problem is, the women are going to be so bowled over by them, they won't take a blind bit of notice of you."

Finn nodded gravely. "Story of my life."

"As if. I bet you've spent your whole life fighting them off."

Finn uncorked a bottle of wine and poured out two glasses. As he put one down next to her, he raised a playful eyebrow. "So does that mean you think I'm moderately attractive to the opposite sex?"

Luckily, Ginny had the distraction of a kitten on her lap. The kitten promptly obliged by letting out a minuscule stream of wee that missed the hem of her skirt by an inch. By the time she'd mopped up the dinky puddle and returned the perpetrator to Myrtle, the need to reply had passed. Instead she raised her wine glass and said brightly, "Here's to toilet training. Cheers."

"To toilet training." Finn paused. "Not the most glamorous toast I've ever heard."

"Sorry. I'm not in a glamorous mood." Ginny, who had spent the evening putting on a determinedly brave face, shook her head.

"Is it about Perry?"

"God, *no*."

"Jem then," Finn guessed.

She nodded. "Yes."

"You're missing her."

"Missing her and worrying about her. She's got

herself involved with a boy I don't trust an inch." Ginny could recall this afternoon's breezy phone call from Jem practically word for word. Evidently, she and Rupert were a proper couple now; Lucy had moved out to give them some space, and everything was fantastic. When Ginny had said worriedly, "Lucy's gone? Won't you miss her?" Jem had laughed and said blithely, "Mum, why would I miss her when I've got Rupert? Everything's cool!"

Her laugh, Ginny hadn't been able to help noticing, had got a bit posher in the last fortnight.

"She's only eighteen. It probably won't last." Finn was doing his best to reassure her.

"Yes, but what if it does? They're living together." Ginny shuddered as she said it. "And he's not a nice person. Too much money, too little . . . heart. He thinks he's God's gift."

"Good-looking, then?"

"Very."

"Is that why you don't trust him?"

She nodded. "That and his personality."

"Then she'll see through him," said Finn. "Jem's not stupid. She's a bright girl."

"I didn't think I was stupid either," Ginny retorted, "and look at what happened to me."

"Well, that's over now. Ready for another one?"

For a split second she thought he meant another man. But no, he was only taking her empty glass.

Crikey, two whole units of wine and she didn't even remember drinking them.

"It's just so hard, having to sit back and do nothing. I know I have to let her make her own mistakes but I'm her mother." Taking the refilled glass, Ginny said, "It's like standing by while a surgeon operates on your daughter, knowing he's incompetent and doing it all wrong."

"Hey." Finn patted the empty space next to him on the sofa. "They're young. Give them a couple of weeks and it could all be over."

Ginny left the squirming kittens in the cat basket and joined him. The shirt he was wearing was her favorite, cobalt blue cotton and as soft as peach skin. Well, it looked as soft as peach skin; she hadn't actually touched it. Nor was she about to tell him it was her favorite.

"I hope you're right about that. She's smitten at the moment. He's whisking her up to a castle in Scotland this weekend. In a helicopter, for God's sake."

Drily, Finn said, "Sounds familiar."

"Oh bugger. Sorry." Too late, Ginny remembered how Tamsin had made her exit from Portsilver, whisked away by her wealthy Italian lover in a helicopter. She clutched Finn's arm. "I'm really sorry; I didn't mean to remind you."

Ha, the material of his shirt was as soft as peach skin.

He smiled slightly. "I hadn't actually forgotten."

"Wine's gone to my head. I was too wound up to eat earlier." Ginny patted her empty stomach by way of explanation. "Now I'll have to get a cab home."

"My fault for opening the bottle."

"Or mine for coming up to see your etchings. I mean kittens."

"Hey, you're here now. You've seen the kittens and the bottle's open. We may as well finish it."

It? Singular? Now that the alcohol was spreading nicely through her bloodstream, Ginny couldn't help feeling that one bottle between two people somehow wasn't quite . . . ooh, what was the word?

Oh yes. *Enough.*

Sensing her disappointment, Finn topped up her glass once more and said good-humoredly, "Don't worry, there's another one in the fridge."

Myrtle and the kittens fell asleep. For the next forty minutes they drank wine, ate crisps, and discussed the restaurant. Evie had been chatted up earlier by an estate agent who had done his best to persuade her to give him her phone number.

"I don't know why she wouldn't." Finn frowned. "He seemed like a nice enough chap."

"Too nice." Ginny did her best to explain why Evie hadn't been remotely tempted. "Verging on oily. That man was a super-smooth operator. Yuck."

"He was handsome though, wasn't he?"

"Way too handsome. You wouldn't want to get involved with someone like that, not in a million years." Ginny dabbed at the crisp crumbs speckling her top and licked her fingers, then washed down the saltiness with more wine.

"I don't want to get involved with him," said Finn.

She gave him a nudge. "I meant no woman with an ounce of brain would want to. Good-looking men are nothing but trouble."

"First Rupert, now the guy from table six. They're good-looking so you automatically don't trust them." Finn paused. "Isn't that a bit prejudiced?"

"Absolutely. But it's also common sense. OK-looking men are OK, but really handsome men are a nightmare. Number-one rule: don't touch them with a barge pole."

"I see." Raking his fingers through his hair, Finn said thoughtfully, "Can I ask you a question?"

Ginny was in a generous mood. "Anything you like."

"Would you say I was good-looking?"

Yeesh, not *that* question.

"What?" She sat back, as if he'd asked her to calculate a tricky algebraic equation. Actually, an algebraic equation would have been easier.

"I'm interested. When I look in a mirror I just see me, the same me I've always been," said Finn. "Dark hair, straight not curly. Gray eyes. Scar on

left temple from some kid at school hitting me with a discus. Nose got broken once playing rugby, but still in one piece. Jaw, generally in need of a shave. That's it, that's all I see." He gazed at Ginny. "But I have been told I'm a good-looking bloke. Quite a few times, to be honest. So I just wondered what your opinion was. Do you think I am?"

If he had the guts to ask, Ginny decided, then she had the guts to answer. Glad of the insulation provided by several glasses of wine she said, "OK, first things first, you really shouldn't have allowed your nose to go off and play rugby. And second, of course you're good-looking."

Finn tilted his head a fraction, still doubtful. "Really?"

Did he seriously have no idea? Ginny nodded and said, "Really." Then, because he clearly needed the reassurance, she added, "Very."

Finn studied his wine glass for a couple of seconds, but she began to suspect that he was struggling to keep a straight face. "So you're saying it doesn't matter how nice a person I might be or how much I might like you; you wouldn't be interested in me because of the way I look."

Oh, for heaven's sake, he'd been teasing all along. If she'd been sober, Ginny realized, she would be all of a fluster now. In fact, in a state of utter fluster.

But by a stroke of luck she wasn't, so she shrugged and said cheerfully, "Correct."

"That's discrimination."

"Don't feel too sorry for yourself. You don't do too badly. Plenty of women out there who wouldn't turn you down." Teasingly, Ginny added, "Flower girl for a start."

"But I'm not talking about other women. I'm talking about you. You're saying you wouldn't consider a relationship with someone like me, purely because of my external appearance."

Now Ginny was beginning to feel flustered but it was too late to back down. Anyway, he was only saying "someone like him." It wasn't as if he was actually referring to himself.

She didn't know whether to nod or shake her head. "Yes . . . I mean no . . . I mean, that's *right*."

"But that would be unfair. You'd be dismissing me without giving me a chance. So technically I could take you to court," Finn said idly. "I could sue you for unfair dismissal."

Decidedly hot now, Ginny took another glug of wine. "Fine. So sue me."

There was a glimmer of amusement in his eyes. "I'd rather try and persuade you to change your mind."

"That's bordering on smooth talk. If you carry on like that, you'll end up like Evie's estate agent."

"Sorry. Fate worse than death. So you're saying men like me are useless when it comes to long-term investments. We're only good for meaningless flings, have I got this right?"

"Pretty much." Ginny shrugged in agreement.

"And you were only saying last week how you wished you could have a meaningless fling."

OK, now there was no getting away from it. He was definitely suggesting what she thought he was suggesting. Her mouth drier than ever, Ginny said, "Was I?"

"Oh yes. You were." There was a note of playful challenge in his voice. "And I'm just saying, if you still feel the same way, I wouldn't object."

Yeek.

"That's very generous of you." Ginny paused. "But where would I find a good-looking man to have a meaningless fling with at this time of night?"

Finn laughed. Then he leaned toward her. "Close your eyes."

Yeeeeeek.

"Why?" As if she didn't know.

"Will you stop arguing and just do it?"

He wanted to. And he was gorgeous. What's more, she'd fantasized about this happening for months.

Casting all doubt aside, Ginny stopped arguing and just did it.

How could you regret an experience like that? God, how could anyone?

It was one o'clock in the morning when Ginny slid out of bed. The sex had been glorious, like losing her virginity all over again. Actually, that was a stupid comparison; tonight had been a million times better than her first time. But it was also, now, undeniably tinged with awkwardness because she had to keep reminding herself that she and Finn weren't in a relationship, that this *was* only a meaningless fling. So instead of the two of them lying in each other's arms, whispering and laughing together and, well, making plans to see each other again, she had to pretend to be a modern, no-strings kind of girl who'd had a great time but now needed to get home, put it behind her, and get on with her busy, single-girl life.

Like Carla.

Finn raised himself up on one elbow. "Going to the bathroom?"

In the darkness she could just make out the glitter of his eyes. If she could see him, did that mean he could see her? Hastily holding in her stomach and reaching for her shirt, Ginny said, "No. Home."

Just like Carla.

"Why?"

She was filled with sadness. "Because it's time to go."

"You don't have to," said Finn.

He was being polite, saying the gentlemanly thing. The last thing he wanted was for her to leap back into bed with a squeal of delight, crying, "OK then, I'll stay!" As far as men like Finn were concerned, girls who outstayed their welcome were the bane of their lives. Their worst nightmare was finding themselves trapped with someone clingy and overkeen.

"Thanks, but I'd rather get home." Dressing at the speed of light, Ginny shot him a casual, unclingy smile. "We've had a nice time, haven't we? But now it's over. Time to leave. No need to get up," she added as he made a move to push aside the bedclothes. "I'll see myself out. And don't worry, I won't be sending you any flowers!"

Finn sounded taken aback. "Are you all right to drive?"

"Absolutely fine." She'd downed four glasses of wine earlier but that had been two hours ago. Now she'd never felt more sober in her life. Stepping into her shoes and hastily smoothing down her hair, Ginny bent and gave him a quick careless kiss on the cheek. "Thank you, that was fun. Bye."

After a pause, Finn said, "Bye."

And that was it. Easy.

If Carla could see her now, she'd be so proud.

Chapter 35

DAN THE VAN RATTLED into the courtyard in his mud-spattered green van at midday. Ginny, poking her head through the kitchen door, called out, "It's all right; he's here. I'll go and fetch them."

Dan had blotted his copybook this morning, forgetting the raspberries when he'd arrived earlier with the rest of the fruit and veg. As Ginny made her way out of the restaurant, he leaped out of the van looking harassed and burbling apologies. "I'm so sorry, I can't think how it happened, I could swear I ticked everything on the list, this has *never* happened to me before . . ."

"Dan, it's fine." Ginny attempted to calm him down; normally shy and retiring, Dan was the world's most conscientious delivery man. "You're here now and it's only twelve o'clock. Really, it doesn't matter a bit."

"I feel terrible though. You trusted me and I let you down. Do you think I should apologize to Finn?"

"There's no need; he doesn't even know about it. Hello, beautiful," cooed Ginny as Dan's dog whimpered a greeting from the passenger seat of the van. As sweet-natured and shy as Dan, Stiller was a lanky, tousled, slightly unhygienic mongrel with eyes like Pete Doherty and a curly tail.

"OK, if you're sure." Unloading the tray of raspberries and evidently still racked with guilt, Dan thrust them into her arms. "But if he finds out, please tell him I swear on my life it won't happen again."

"Don't worry, we know that." As Ginny took the tray, they both heard a car coming up the driveway. "Sounds like our first customers arriving. I'll take these through to the kitchen."

"Don't forget to tell chef I'm sorry."

"Dan, stop apologizing, it really doesn't—"

"Hello? Excuse me? Where would I find Finn?"

Ginny turned to look at the owner of the voice, which sounded as if it had been dipped in golden syrup. Another of Finn's conquests or a business contact? Very pretty, certainly. In fact very pretty. The girl was tall and probably in her late twenties with glossy, almost waist-length brown hair and silver-gray eyes. She was wearing a black T-shirt and narrow white jeans with—

"Finn Penhaligon," the girl elaborated, clearly wondering if Ginny understood English. Pointing first to the antiques center then to the restaurant and enunciating slowly she said, "Is he here?"

Resisting the urge to enunciate back, Ginny said, "I think he's in the antiques center."

"Thank you." The girl opened the rear door of her black car and leaned into it, scooping out a baby in a scarlet sundress. She hoisted the baby onto her hip and began to make her way toward the honeysuckle-strewn entrance of the shop. Then, abruptly stopping, she thought for a moment before turning back to Ginny. "Actually, could you do me a favor? I'll wait out here and you take her in."

Ginny froze, because the baby had twisted around to look at her and there was no longer any question of who Finn's visitors were. "Sorry?"

"Take her in; tell Finn there's someone here to see him. Yes," Tamsin nodded, pleased with herself, "that's a much better plan."

"I can't do that."

"Of course you can. Don't worry, she won't cry. Just give the raspberries to him." Tamsin nodded at Dan the Van, who was so stunned he immediately took the raspberries from Ginny. "There, you see? Not too difficult! And now you take Mae. This is important; I want Finn to see her before he sees me. There you are."

Ginny wanted to shout, "I can't do this; I slept with Finn last night!" But it was too late; Tamsin had already plonked Mae into her arms.

"I'll take the raspberries in." Dan the Van scurried off.

"And I'll stay here." Tamsin, her silvery eyes sparkling with anticipation, gave Ginny a gentle push in the direction of the shop. "Don't worry; he's going to love it. Off you go!"

But I'm not going to love it, Ginny thought. I

slept with Finn last night. She shook her head and said, "I'm sorry, I really can't; it's not—"

"Oh, for heaven's sake, what is the big deal here? One little favor, that's all I'm asking!" Stepping away and raising her eyebrows in disbelief, Tamsin said, "What possible difference can it make to you?"

Inside the antiques center a dozen or so potential customers were browsing, the warm air was heavy with the scent of old, cared-for wood and beeswax polish, and "Unchained Melody" was playing on the jukebox. Ginny saw Finn standing with his back to her, chatting to a couple of Japanese tourists who had just bought a Georgian writing chest.

She waited for him to finish the conversation. Mae gazed around the Aladdin's cave with interest and spotted a life-size enameled parrot. Entranced by the bright colors she pointed and exclaimed, "Birdie!"

"I know," whispered Ginny, her heart hammering wildly. "Clever girl."

"BIRDIE!"

Finn smiled and turned to see who was making all the noise. When he spotted Ginny his smile broadened but at the same time she could tell he was wondering what she was doing here. Then his gaze shifted and the expression on his face changed as he recognized the baby in her arms.

The smile fell away, and in the split second that followed, Ginny glimpsed shock, anguish, and joy.

It was heartbreaking to imagine the pain he must have gone through.

"Birdiebirdie," babbled Mae, pointing at the ceiling and beaming over at Finn.

He excused himself from the Japanese couple and came over, his jaw taut. "What's going on?"

"Tamsin's outside. She asked me to do this. I didn't want to," said Ginny, "but she insisted. Here, I need to get back to the restaurant." Hastily, she handed Mae to him. Unperturbed by all the pass-the-parceling, Mae reached out with both hands and spread her fingers like tiny starfish against the sides of Finn's face. Maybe subconsciously she recognized him as having been a previous fixture in her life, because her smile was so dazzling, a lump rose in Ginny's throat.

"Bah!" cried Mae, her dark eyes luminous and her mouth opening wide to reveal pearly miniature teeth. "Kawawaaa," she babbled, happily kicking her legs against the front of Finn's white shirt. *"Birdie."*

For several seconds, oblivious to his surroundings, Finn stood there holding Mae in his arms. This was the baby he had witnessed being born and fallen in love with at first sight, the baby that had changed his world forever. For four months she had been his daughter and he would, without question, have died for her. Until the day in October last year when she had vanished from his life—had been summarily removed from it by Tamsin—and he had learned that she wasn't his daughter after all.

But love, as Finn had discovered to his cost, wasn't as fickle as a DNA test. His feelings for Mae hadn't dissipated. And although he had known, logically, that he'd probably never see the child who wasn't his daughter again, it hadn't meant he'd stopped thinking about her or wondering what she looked like now or grieving for the loss of the child who had made his life complete.

Making his way out into the sunshine, Finn saw Tamsin waiting for him.

"What's this about?"

"Hello, Finn." Tamsin smiled, though there was a note of tension in her voice. "I thought you might like to see Mae again."

"Boobooboo," burbled Mae, delightedly waving her arms.

"And?" Finn said steadily.

"Boo*boo*booboo . . . boo*boo*."

"And?" Tears welled in Tamsin's silvery eyes. "Oh, Finn, I suppose I was kind of wondering if you might like to see me again too."

"I can't believe she's turned up!" Evie was agog, peering through the restaurant window, torn between indignation and glee. "The nerve of that girl. What do you suppose she's doing here? Damn, *why* did I never take up lip-reading?"

"Come away from the window." Ginny didn't have any idea what was going on either, but she knew she felt sick.

"I can't; it's not physically possible. Oh God, look at Mae, she's so gorgeous. I can't believe how much she's *grown*."

"Evie, they'll see you."

"Ha, you're joking. They wouldn't notice if we ran out there naked and did the Macarena."

Ginny flushed. Last night Finn had seen her naked. She'd seen him naked too.

"Tamsin's crying," Evie announced with relish. "She's wiping her eyes. Have we got any binoculars?"

"No, but we've got a table of eight arriving any minute, so maybe we should—"

"Damn, they're going!"

"Tamsin and the baby?" Unable to help herself, Ginny rushed up and hovered behind Evie, keen to see them getting back into the car. No such luck. When she peered over Evie's shoulder, she saw all three of them disappearing through the front door that led up to Finn's flat.

"Some people are so thoughtless." Evie heaved a sigh of frustration. "No consideration for others. Wouldn't you just love to know what's going on? I'm telling you, I'd give my right arm for a listening device."

· · ·

"What's going on?" Finn looked at the girl he'd once loved, the beautiful girl he had planned on spending the rest of his life with. Unlike most people, Tamsin even managed to look beautiful when she was crying.

"Oh, Finn, you don't know how hard this has been for me. I made the biggest mistake of my life when I left you." Biting her lip, Tamsin said tremulously, "I've been such an idiot. Believe me, if I could turn back the clock, I would. I wish I'd never met Angelo."

"He's the father of your child. If you'd never met Angelo, you wouldn't have Mae."

"I know, I *know* that, but I'm trying to say I wish Mae was yours. I made one mistake." Tamsin held up a French-manicured index finger for emphasis. "One. You were away and along came Angelo. He made a fuss of me, flattered me, swept me off my feet. It was a moment of madness. I slept with him. He wanted me to dump you and become his girlfriend but I told him I couldn't because I loved you. And I thought that was the end of it. I said I couldn't see him again and I meant it, I truly meant it because you were the one I wanted to marry. So I *did* stop seeing him and yes, of course I felt guilty afterward, but it was just a one-off with Angelo and I learned a valuable lesson. I told myself that as long as you didn't know about it, we'd be OK."

"And then you found out you were pregnant." Finn spoke without emotion.

"Yes." Fresh tears were now rolling down Tamsin's tanned cheeks. "But I convinced myself you were the father. I refused to even consider the possibility that it could be Angelo's. Because I just so desperately *wanted* it to be you."

Finn looked over at Mae, who had fallen asleep on the sofa. He could remember every moment of the night she'd been born. When their eyes had met for the first time, he had experienced a rush of emotion so overwhelming that he'd known life would never be the same from now on.

Well, that had been the truth.

"But it wasn't me."

"I know, I know. And you loved her so much." Tamsin wiped her eyes with the back of her hand. "I thought I could handle not knowing for sure, but once she was here I just couldn't. It was the guilt, I suppose. I couldn't bear the thought that I might be deceiving you. I just had to know the truth." She paused, swallowed. "That's when I had the test done. And then the results came through. Oh God, that was the worst day of my life. I'd so wanted it to be you. But I knew I had to tell Angelo. He had a right to know. I'm sorry, this is so difficult . . ."

"So you told him," Finn supplied. That day hadn't been great for him either. When Tamsin and Mae had disappeared, she had left him a letter but this was the first time he'd heard the explanation from her own mouth.

"I did. And he decided he wanted us to be together. He convinced me that I'd be doing the right thing and I was in such a state by then that I couldn't say no. Angelo's a forceful character; he organized everything and I just went along with it." Tamsin shook her head. "I hardly knew what was happening. It was all a blur."

Finn looked at her. "And now?"

"Oh, Finn, I was wrong. So wrong. It's over between me and Angelo. The only person he cares about is himself." Shaking her head, Tamsin said wearily, "He liked the idea of having a daughter to show off, but you wouldn't catch him changing a nappy. Ask Angelo to look after Mae for an hour and you'd think I was telling him to chop off his own legs. We had a day nanny and a night nanny. Materially we had everything. But I knew I didn't love Angelo. And I don't think he really loves Mae."

"And now you've left him." Finn's tone was even. "You've brought Mae down here. But you still haven't told me why."

"You know why." By contrast Tamsin's voice was wobbling, her hand splayed across her chest as she struggled to breathe evenly. "Oh, Finn, you *know* why I'm here. I made the worst mistake in the world and I'm sorrier than I can ever say, but I never stopped loving you. And I know how much I must have hurt you, but we were happy together before, weren't we? You, me, and Mae were a proper family. So I suppose what I'm saying is, do you think there's any chance—for Mae's sake, if not mine—that you could ever forgive me and we could be happy again?"

Chapter 36

LUNCHTIME IN THE RESTAURANT had been an ordeal for Ginny, what with Evie's endless speculations and the nest of snakes squirming away in her stomach. Finally the last diners were dispatched, the dining room was in a state of readiness for this evening's influx, and Ginny was able to leave.

Finn emerged from his flat as she was about to unlock the car. At the sight of him heading toward her, the snakes went into frenzied wriggly overdrive. Ironically too, the shock of this new situation with Tamsin was far greater than when she'd found out about Carla and Perry, which just went to show how much less Perry had meant to her than she'd imagined at the time. Last night with Finn had been in a completely different league, Ginny realized. It wasn't helping either that she was still experiencing vivid flashbacks to last night when both of them had been naked and doing something considerably more intimate than the Macarena.

It was disconcerting to think Finn might be getting flashbacks too. Although to be fair he probably had more on his mind right now than yesterday's casual fling.

When he reached her, Ginny saw the signs of strain in his face. His hands were pushed into the pockets of his trousers and his shoulders were tense. Fixing a troubled gaze on her, he came straight to the point.

"Ginny, sorry about this but there's something we need to discuss. Obviously, Tamsin's turned up. Not what I was expecting, but there it is. And there are issues to sort out." Finn paused, clearly hating every second of having to explain to her. "Now, last night was great, really it was, and I don't want you to feel . . . well, pushed aside or ignored, but now that Tamsin's here it's a bit of an awkward—"

"Look, it's fine." Ginny blurted the words out, unable to bear his discomfort for another second. He was being a gentleman again, doing his best to let her down gently, making sure she understood the situation. "You don't have to say anything. I completely understand. Crikey, there isn't even anything to apologize for! It's not as if we're in a relationship," she went on. "We're two adults who just happened to fancy a bit of, you know, fun. It was one night, it was what we both wanted at the time, but it didn't *mean* anything."

Finn looked slightly taken aback at the vehemence of her tone, startled but at the same time visibly relieved. "Right. Well, um, absolutely. So long as you're sure you're OK about it."

There was definitely a note of disbelief in there too. Oh God, did he think she might secretly be harboring strong feelings for him, laced with bunny-boiler tendencies? Keen to emphasize just how completely OK she was, Ginny vigorously shook her head and exclaimed, "Please, last night wasn't a big deal. In fact it was a very *small* deal! If you're hungry, you grab something to eat. Same with sex. But sleeping with someone doesn't have to mean anything. It doesn't automatically follow that you want to keep on seeing that person. Like last week I had a really great Chinese meal," she added. "King prawns, mushroom chop suey, and a spring roll. But it didn't make me think I had to sell my house, jump on the next plane, and go live in China."

Finn looked at her, possibly a bit stunned by the chop suey analogy. But Ginny felt she'd convinced him at last. He nodded and said awkwardly, "Of course not. Well, that's sorted then. Good, thanks for that. So we'll just . . . carry on as normal."

"Completely as normal. As if it never happened." Ginny nodded firmly, because it was so clearly what he needed to hear. Then, unable to contain herself a moment longer, she said, "But are you all right? Am I allowed to ask what's going on? What are they doing here?"

Finn hesitated, finally shaking his head. "It's difficult to explain. I can't really—"

"Oh God, she's coming out," Ginny yelped. Her heart leaping with fresh guilt, she yanked open the car door. "I'll leave you to it."

But she was stopped by Tamsin hurrying over to them waving one arm to attract Ginny's attention. "Hello," she called out, making her way across the courtyard. "Don't rush off!"

But I *want* to rush off, thought Ginny, panicking that Tamsin might somehow have discovered it was her who had spent time last night in Finn's bed. Had she found a stray blond hair on the pillow perhaps and carried out a quick DNA test? Or spotted a stray pair of knickers and immediately deduced that there was only one woman around here frumpy enough to wear sensible, black size tens from a bulk pack? No, it couldn't be that; she'd definitely been wearing pants when she'd left the flat.

"Can I ask you something?" Tamsin, who was surely a size four La Perla thong girl herself, reached the car and touched Ginny's arm.

No!

"Yes." Cautiously, Ginny nodded, praying she wasn't about to be asked if she could just give that DNA sample now.

"It's just that you were so good with Mae earlier, and Finn and I *really* need some quality time together." Tamsin's smile was complicit, her tone confiding. "So I wondered if you'd be an angel and babysit for a few hours this evening."

"Um . . ." Caught off guard, Ginny faltered. It was a terrible idea.

"We'll pay you, of course. Whatever the going rate is." Tamsin gestured airily, signaling that she hadn't the least idea what the going rate might be. "Sorry, I'm used to live-in staff; I'm going to have to learn all this new stuff! But don't worry, Finn will sort you out."

Actually, he gave me a pretty good sorting out last night. Ginny wondered what would happen if she said this aloud. Instead she shook her head and said, "Sorry, I can't do it. I'm busy tonight."

"Really?" Tamsin looked shocked, as if Ginny had just turned down the offer of a week on Necker Island with George Clooney. "Are you sure? Isn't it something you could cancel?"

"No, it isn't." Ginny didn't have anything on this evening, but she was buggered if she was going to babysit.

"It doesn't matter," Finn cut in impatiently. "We don't need a babysitter. We're not going anywhere."

Tamsin said, "Oh, but—"

"Tamsin, just think about it. I haven't seen Mae for eight months." He shook his head firmly. "Why would I want to leave her here with someone else?"

Especially with *me,* thought Ginny.

Chapter 37

JEM DOODLED A SERIES of boxes in the margin of her legal pad to give the impression that she was working, although she hadn't taken a single note so far. It was Monday morning and the lecture theatre was stuffy and airless. The lecturer, droning on about Milton's *Paradise Lost,* could have been babbling in Swahili for all the difference it made. Right now nothing useful was permeating her brain.

Three rows in front of her, Davy and Lucy were sitting together, paying attention like model students, and industriously scribbling away. Passing her on the way into the hall, Lucy had flicked a dismissive glance in her direction before turning and whispering something in Davy's ear. Jem had pointedly ignored them; she might be here in Bristol, but she may as well be invisible. She told herself they were pathetic, acting like ten-year-olds, but the cold scrunched-up feeling in the pit of her stomach refused to go away. It wouldn't be so bad if Rupert could have been here with her, but he wasn't. Rupert was back at the flat, missing this morning's lecture in order to nurse his hangover and recover from what had, reportedly, been a truly epic weekend in Scotland.

Imagining the epic-ness of the weekend caused Jem's doodling pen to dig into the writing pad and tear the paper. In the end there hadn't been room in Olly's uncle's helicopter for two extra passengers. Rupert had gone on his own to Olly MacIntyre-Brown's party and Jem, who had spent practically the whole of last week casually mentioning to anyone who'd listen that they were flying up to Scotland to stay in a castle, was forced to invent a debilitating attack of food poisoning as the reason she hadn't been able to go. This in turn had meant she couldn't leave the flat all weekend. Basically, she'd never watched so much television in her life.

The lecture ended and the day dragged on tediously. At four o'clock Jem arrived back at the flat. Letting herself in, she quietly pushed open the door to the bedroom in case Rupert, who could sleep for England, was still out for the count.

The bed was empty.

So was the rest of the flat. A flutter of disquiet made its way up through Jem's chest, although there was no need to feel anxious. Of course there wasn't. She took out her phone and rang Rupert's mobile, which went straight to the answering service.

Where was he? She needed a hug, needed—after a day of near ostracization—the comfort of his arms around her and the knowledge that someone was on her side. And being hugged by Rupert would more than make up for all the crap she was being put through by Davy and Lucy. Or, as Rupert had taken to calling them, Booty and the Beast.

Except he couldn't hug her because he wasn't bloody well *here*. Grimly ignoring the feelings of unease—Rupert hated being nagged about his whereabouts—Jem emptied her rucksack of textbooks and sat down on the sofa to get some work done. She had essays overdue, studying to tackle, end-of-year exams looming like thunder-clouds. Right, think positive, use this time profitably. If Rupert didn't come home before six, it meant she had two hours in which to . . .

OK, she'd just make a coffee first. And have a toasted cheese sandwich because nobody could revise on an empty stomach.

In the kitchen, Jem tried Rupert's phone again. Still no joy.

She found a KitKat in the back of the fridge and ate it while the cheese sandwich toasted. Where was Rupert anyway?

Back in the living room, after flicking through a textbook, Jem pushed it to one side and switched on the TV. After this quiz, then *Richard and Judy*, she'd get down to some work.

Definitely.

• • •

"It's a beautiful DAAAAAY." Rupert was back and he was singing, the bellowed words accompanied by Bono-style strutting and air-punching. Having burst into the bedroom and thrown himself onto the bed like an upturned beetle he played a set of imaginary drums and roared, "DAAA, DAAA, DA-DAAAAH, it's a beautiful DAYYYYYY."

Except it wasn't. It was midnight. Jem, who hadn't been asleep, was torn between indignation that he had put her through hours of stomach-churning anxiety and relief that he was home at last. Even if his crash landing on the bed had scored a direct hit on her left ankle.

"Where have you been?" She sat up and pushed her bangs out of her eyes.

"Out."

"Where?"

"Ah, the dreaded inquisition." Rupert rolled over and surveyed her with a playful grin. "Sweetheart, it was all completely innocent. I got up at three o'clock and I was hungry. There was no Parma ham in the fridge. So I went down to Chandos Deli to buy some, that's all it was. Then on the way back I happened to bump into Maz and he dragged me against my will into this wine bar. I didn't have any choice, I promise you. He *plied* me with drink."

"For nine hours?"

344

"No, no, *no*." Rupert gravely studied his watch. "Eight hours and eleven minutes, your honor. Not a second more than that."

"I didn't have any idea where you were," said Jem. "And your phone was switched off. You could have called and let me know."

"I could." He nodded in agreement, considering this point. "But then I thought, I'm nineteen years old and you're not my nanny. I'm allowed out of the house on my own; I can even cross big roads if I'm careful and look both ways first. Plus, you said you had loads of studying, so I thought I'd be doing you a huge favor, keeping out of your way."

"You have loads of studying too," Jem pointed out.

"I know, I know. But it's so bloody boring. Now, have you stopped nagging me yet? Because I've got something to tell you."

He was winning her over, regarding her with amusement. Jem said, "What kind of something?"

"Two things actually. To make up for being a naughty boy and not phoning you, I'm going to take you to Byzantium tomorrow night. How about that?"

Byzantium was possibly the glitziest restaurant in Bristol, with magicians and belly dancers. Glowing and feeling loved—see? he was sorry—she hugged her knees. "What's the other thing?"

His eyes danced. "U2 are playing a concert in Rome this weekend. Maz has tickets."

Jem let out a squeal of delight. "You're joking!"

"I know, can you believe it? Talk about fate, bumping into him like that this afternoon. So we'll be flying out on Friday night."

Jem was beside herself, her mind in a whirl. "Oh my God, that is fantastic! I'm supposed to be working on Saturday, but I'll get someone to swap shifts; that won't be a—"

"Whoa, hang on, did I say it wrong?" Rupert held up his hands, forestalling her. "Maz has tickets for the concert. The two of us are flying out to Rome. The two of *us,*" he explained. "Me and Maz."

Oh. Disappointed wasn't the word. Crushed was more like it. Or stupid, possibly.

"Sorry, sweetie, didn't mean to get your hopes up there." He patted her knee. "It's just, I knew you were working in the pub this weekend, which is why I thought I might as well go. Maz was supposed to be taking his girlfriend, but they broke up last week. When he mentioned the spare ticket, I jumped at it. Chance of a lifetime. Hey, cheer up," said Rupert, playing imaginary drums on her thigh. "It's a beautiful daaaaayyyyy."

It wasn't; it had been a completely awful one. Jem felt her bottom lip begin to lose control. Now she wouldn't be seeing Rupert this weekend either.

"Oh, look at you. Don't get upset." He abandoned

the drumming and put his arms round her, patting her on the back like a baby. "I couldn't turn down an offer like that, could I?"

Jem shook her head; this was U2 they were talking about, after all. "No. I'm just going to miss you."

"But it's only for a couple of days." Pulling back the duvet, Rupert gave her hip a gentle prod. "See this?" Then he pointed to his own denim-clad hip. "And this? We're not joined. We don't have to spend every minute of every day in each other's company."

"I suppose not." Jem's voice was small. The thing was, when you loved someone, surely it was only normal to want to spend as much time together as possible? She couldn't help feeling that Rupert wasn't as emotionally involved in their relationship as she was.

"Hey, no need to get all girly about it. Don't cry," he warned as her eyes filled up. "We're off to Byzantium tomorrow, remember. Unless you don't want to go."

She forced back the tears.

"I do want to go."

"Good girl. Now give me a kiss." His mouth, warm and reeking of alcohol, came down on hers. Drunk or not, he still knew how to kiss. Finally, pulling back and flashing his naughtiest smile, he shifted on top of her. "Mmm, I'm starting to change my mind."

"About what?" Jem knew better than to hope that he might decide not to go to Rome after all.

Rupert began unfastening his jeans. "Sometimes there's nothing I like more than being joined at the hip."

Chapter 38

THE LAST TIME CARLA had seen Tess Whelan she had felt incredibly sorry for her. It had been four weeks ago and Tess, then nine months pregnant, was lumbering around her house like an exhausted elephant. As she'd made a pot of tea and flicked through the color brochures of conservatories, she had been massaging her aching back, complaining good-naturedly about not being able to paint her toenails, and giving Carla . . . well, far too much information, frankly, about practice contractions, piles, and the need to visit the loo roughly every twenty minutes because the baby's head was pressing down on her bladder.

What's more, Tess had been wearing a hideous T-shirt stretched over her grotesquely swollen belly and elastic-waisted trousers. She might have been pretty once but now she just looked knackered. Carla, feigning sympathy but inwardly repulsed, hadn't been able to get out of the house fast enough.

She hadn't been much looking forward to coming back again either. If Tess Whelan had been a wreck before giving birth, God only knew what she'd look like now with a wailing, puking baby in tow.

And if the house smelled of poo she was going to be in and out of there in ten minutes flat. Tops.

"Hi there! Lovely to see you again. Come on through."

Carla's jaw dropped open at the sight of Tess. Her blond hair was shining, her face glowed, and she was wearing size six jeans and a lacy pink cropped top.

"Good grief, what happened to your stomach?"

Tess grinned and patted her flat abdomen. "I know, isn't it great? Like a miracle. All thanks to breastfeeding, my health visitor tells me. And I'm eating like a horse but somehow everything just snapped back into place. Come on through and meet Alfie."

Carla was stunned. Tess's figure was fabulous, both front and back. The house didn't smell of poo either, which was a bonus. "So how's it going?" she asked as she followed Tess through to the living room.

"Fantastic. So much easier than I'd been expecting. You hear all these nightmare stories about having babies, don't you? But Alfie's so good, he's an absolute angel. I've never been happier." Tess paused then said, "To be honest, I was never the maternal type. Babies didn't interest me. But my husband was so keen I kind of felt obliged to go through with it. And now Alfie's here, I'd just die for him. I can't imagine life without him. He means the world to me, makes my life complete."

That's how I feel about Perry, Carla thought smugly.

"And here he is!" Tess's face lit up with love and pride as she presented her son for inspection.

Carla gazed down at the baby, awake but silent, lying on a squashy blue and white beanbag. Alfie was wearing a tiny white T-shirt and a nappy. His dark eyes were watchful, his hair grew tuftily on top of his head, giving it a pointed appearance, and his miniature fingers clenched and unclenched as he steadily returned Carla's stare.

Oh God.

Oh God . . .

"Are you all right?" said Tess anxiously.

"Fine," Carla croaked. "Fine." Then she said the four words she'd never said before in her life and had certainly never envisaged herself saying. "Um . . . can I hold him?"

It was extraordinary, an epiphany, beyond anything she'd ever experienced before. Tess bent down and picked up Alfie then tenderly kissed him before handing him over. Carla took him in her arms and felt as if . . . oh God, as if her life could at last become complete.

Not with Alfie obviously. He belonged to Tess. But with a baby of her own.

Hers and Perry's.

How could she ever have imagined she didn't want a child? Well, it clearly hadn't been the right time before now. And she hadn't met the right man.

Cradling Alfie, Carla bent her head and inhaled the blissful baby smell of him, an indescribable mixture of milk and warmth and newness. His skin was beyond soft, as soft and silky as the lining of a just-opened horse chestnut; she could happily have stroked it for hours. In truth Alfie wasn't the most beautiful baby in the world but when you looked at him and held him he made you think he was. When his tiny starfish hand closed around one of her own fingers, Carla wanted to explode with happiness.

This, *this* was what she wanted.

"Look at you." Tess nodded approvingly. "You're a natural."

"I've never held a baby before. Ever." There was a catch in Carla's voice. "Never wanted to."

"How old are you?"

"Thirty-six."

Tess smiled. "Tick tock."

"I didn't think I even had a biological clock," said Carla, blinking back tears of happiness. "I still can't believe this is happening to me. I feel as if I've just discovered the meaning of life."

And she didn't care if that sounded ridiculously sentimental. It was *true*.

"You what?" Perry started to laugh.

"I want a baby." It was like finding God, as pure and as simple as that. Carla had barely been able to concentrate earlier on closing the deal for the Whelans' new conservatory but somehow she'd managed it. Turning up at Perry's shop afterward, she had persuaded him to come for a walk with her along the beach.

"This is a joke, right?" He stopped and tilted his head to one side.

"It's not a joke."

"But you hate kids. You told me that. You said you'd never wanted children of your own."

"I know I did. But I was wrong." Carla couldn't contain her happiness, her certainty. "My body *told* me I didn't want them, because I hadn't met the right man. But now I have." She reached for Perry's hand, which had slipped out of hers. "And I want one more than anything, with you. Isn't it incredible? We'll be even *happier* . . . you won't have to miss out after all."

He looked genuinely flummoxed. "Miss out on what?"

"Having children! Oh, you were fantastic before, not saying anything." Carla shook her head, moved by his generosity. When she had explained—on that first momentous night, in fact—that she was anti-babies, Perry had accepted the news without an argument. It hadn't affected how he felt about her, thank God, although of course he must have been dismayed deep down. But that was a *coup de foudre* for you, Carla now realized. You took the rough with the smooth and it didn't make an iota of difference. If Perry had told her that if she wanted to be with him, she'd have to move to Iceland and live with him in an igloo, she would have accepted that too. Because so long as they were together, nothing else mattered, *nothing*—

"Hello? Earth to Carla? What makes you think I want children? Did I ever say I did?" Shaking his head in disbelief, Perry gazed at her as if . . . well, as if she'd just grown a pair of antlers. "I can't stand bloody kids. I was delighted when you told me you didn't want any yourself. As far as I was concerned, it was the icing on the cake."

"But that was before today. I've changed my mind," Carla said urgently, "and so will you. Perry, this is so *right*. We love each other. It'll be perfect."

"I promise you, it won't."

Adrenaline was racing through her body. It was a blow, but she was a star saleswoman; she could win him around. Men often panicked at the prospect of fatherhood, but they succumbed in the end.

"If you hated the idea that much, you'd have had

a vasectomy." Carla's tone was almost playful.

"Jesus. If there's one thing worse than babies, it's the thought of some quack advancing on my tackle with a scalpel." Grimly Perry shook his head. "I've heard enough horror stories to put me off that idea for life. Anyway, if you were so sure you didn't want kids, why didn't you get yourself sterilized years ago?"

Carla was triumphant. "Because *obviously* my brain was telling me that one day I might change my mind! And it was right!"

Perry's smile was long gone. He gazed past her, out to sea, his left hand rubbing his chin. Gazing hungrily at him, at the golden bristles on his jaw and the glossy red-gold of his hair, Carla envisaged the baby they would have. She would be able to change his mind; this was a deal she could definitely close. Men just needed a bit of gentle persuasion sometimes, that was all.

"When did this happen?" Perry spoke abruptly as seagulls wheeled overhead and waves slid up the beach.

"Today. This afternoon. I went to this house and saw—"

"So you've still got your IUD in."

Carla nodded, smiling slightly. Never one to hang around once her mind was made up, she'd already phoned her doctor and made an appointment for tomorrow morning to have it removed. She was thirty-six after all, with no time to lose. If she could have tugged it out herself this afternoon she would have done, but the thought had made her toes tie themselves in knots.

"Hear that?" said Perry.

She listened to the sound of a baby wailing, turned, and saw an overweight, exhausted woman pushing a buggy along the hard wet sand.

"Look at the state of her. Do you want to be like that?"

"I wouldn't be." Carla was adamant.

"And that *noise*." Perry registered pain, because the baby was puce in the face, howling and kicking out like a maddened cat.

"Babies cry." Incredibly the sound of this one wasn't making her want to yank it out of the stroller and throw it into the sea. She wanted to rush over, pick it up, *comfort* it . . .

Actually, better not try that either. The mother weighed about three hundred pounds and looked as if she might pack a bit of a punch.

"Bloody hell, that's an ugly kid," Perry snorted.

"We wouldn't have an ugly one."

He looked at her, long and hard. Then he broke into a smile. "What are you trying to do to me?"

"Nothing horrible, I promise. Just show you how much I love you." Carla wound her arms round his waist, held him tightly. "It's the right thing to do, I promise you. You won't regret it."

Then Perry kissed her and she melted, almost feverish with longing for him. If the beach had been empty, she would have pulled him down onto the sand and ravished him there and then. But there were tourists all around, dogs bouncing in and out of the surf, teenagers playing football, and toddlers picking up shells.

"Shameless hussy," Perry murmured into her ear as she pressed herself against him.

"I can't help it." Carla's body was on fire, her breathing rapid. Prospective motherhood was turning out to be quite an aphrodisiac.

"Doesn't look like you can. I don't know; what am I going to do with you?" Amused, he turned her toward the stone steps leading up off the beach. "If we don't want to be arrested, I think we'd better get back to the flat."

Chapter 39

"FINN, WHAT'S GOING ON?" Evie demanded when Finn appeared in the restaurant on Friday lunchtime.

"Me? I've spent the morning selling antiques."

"Don't give me that. You know what I'm talking about." Evie, who wasn't in awe of Finn, asked the questions no one else dared to ask. Ginny, polishing glasses behind the bar, watched the look of annoyance on his face.

"It's none of your business what's going on."

"But are you *crazy?* Tamsin messed up your life

last year and now she's back. Does that mean you're going to let her do it all over again?"

It was early; none of the diners had arrived yet. Finn, clearly not in the sunniest of moods, squared up to Evie. "I don't have to explain myself to you. I'm an adult capable of making my own decisions."

"And trust me, you're making a bad one," she shot back.

"OK, just listen to me. When you had Philippa, how would you have felt if someone had come along when she was four months old and taken her away from you? Announced that you'd never see her again? Would you have handed your daughter over and forgotten her? Stopped loving her? Simply put her out of your mind because that was it, she was no longer a part of your life?"

Evie's eyes flashed. "No, but Mae isn't your child."

"I thought she was." Finn's voice was even. "She could have been mine. Plenty of men bring up other people's children and love them as much as if they were their own."

"So that's what you're going to do, is it? Never mind that Tamsin cheated on you and brazenly passed Mae off as yours, *then* buggered off with Mr. I'm-a-Billionaire without even telling you she was going. You've just forgiven her for that, have you? You're letting her get away with it scot-free? Well, how very *handy* for her!"

Ginny felt sick, but she couldn't stop listening, couldn't even escape to the safety of the kitchen because Finn was blocking her exit route. He was really pissed off now, a muscle going in his jaw as he gripped the bar. In fact now might not be the time to be thinking it, but he was actually looking incredibly sexy . . .

"Don't tell me how to live my life."

"Why not?" Evie retorted. "Someone has to try and knock some sense into you. And God knows everyone else can see that what you're doing is wrong." Gesturing toward Ginny, she said, "Can't we?"

Oh, for heaven's sake. Hastily Ginny said, "I don't want to get involved."

"But you *should*." Evie was adamant, on a complete roll now. "We all work together! We're friends, aren't we? That's what friends are for. Bloody hell, if I said I was having an affair with a seventeen-year-old boy who'd asked me to marry him and wanted me to lend him a hundred grand to pay off his gambling debts, would you two stand back and let me do it?"

"Right now? Like a shot," said Finn.

"See? And now you're angry with me." Changing tack, Evie said, "But you shouldn't be, because we're only saying all this because we care about you."

Less of the *we,* Ginny thought in alarm.

"And I know you love Mae," Evie went on, "but

358

I don't believe you still love Tamsin. And that's no basis for a relationship. OK, Tamsin's a beautiful girl. She's sexy, I appreciate that. But fancying a glass of milk doesn't mean you have to buy the cow. If it's sex you're after, there are plenty of women around here who'd be only too happy to hop into your bed. I promise you, Finn, all you have to do is click your fingers and they'll be queuing up for a quick—*urk*."

"Oooh!" Appearing in the restaurant doorway with Mae in her arms, Tamsin surveyed them with amusement. "All of a sudden there's an awkward silence. Should my ears be burning?" Then, as her gaze settled on Ginny, her smile broadened. "Except if they were, they couldn't possibly be redder than your face."

Ginny wished she could sink down through the floor. It was the comment about not having to buy the cow that had done it. Finn, sensing her discomfort—or possibly feeling as if he were standing next to a furnace, on account of the heat emanating from her cheeks—said, "We were talking about work. Did you want something?"

"Just came to say good-bye."

This pronouncement caused Evie's eyebrows to shoot up into her hairline, and Ginny's hopes to rise in similar fashion. Tamsin, swaying over to Finn, said cheerfully, "We're off into Portsilver to buy Mae some new clothes and have a play on the beach. Back by three, OK?" She proffered Mae for a kiss. "Say bye-bye."

Beaming, Mae gave Finn a kiss on the cheek and said, "Ghaaaa."

Finn softened and stroked her silky dark hair. "Ghaaaa to you too. Have fun."

"Look at them." Clearly reveling in the sight of Finn and Mae together, Tamsin said with pride, "Look at her face. She's crazy about him!"

Ginny swallowed disappointment and thought, me too.

To make up for the hour she'd taken off to go to the doctor's office, Carla had been forced to work until eight. Now she click-clacked her way down Hudson Street and stopped outside Perry's front door. Ringing the doorbell, she experienced a thrill of anticipation. If last night had been a night to remember, this evening was going to be even better.

And there were his footsteps on the stairs . . .

She was taken aback when the door opened to reveal Ally the dim Goth who worked in the shop.

"Hi, Perry's expecting me."

Ally blinked at her through a curtain of dyed-black hair. "Yeah, he said you might drop round. Come on up then."

It wasn't until they reached the living room that Carla realized there was definitely something not quite right going on here. For a start, there were disgusting incense candles smoldering in holders on the window sill. And there was a small mountain of assorted shopping bags stuffed with God knows what piled up on the sofa.

More to the point, there was no sign of Perry.

"Where is he?"

"Hmm? Oh, gone away." Peering round the room, Ally said vaguely, "Hang on, it's around here somewhere."

"Gone *away?*" Carla's stomach did an incredulous swallow dive. "Where?"

"No idea, he didn't say. Just told me he needed a break and put me in charge of the shop. Bloody long hours, but he said I could move in here while he's gone, so that makes up for it. Living with my mum's been doing my head in, you know?" Ally pulled a face, inviting sympathy, her blue lipsticked mouth turning down at the corners. "So I was well up for moving in here instead. Ah, here it is." She found the envelope she'd been searching for amid a pile of clutter on the coffee table and handed it to Carla.

How could Perry have gone away? In the space of . . . what? Eleven hours? He'd been fine when she'd left here this morning. Carla ripped open the envelope, turning away from Ally and her curious magenta-lined eyes in order to read the note.

Carla,
    I loved you but you've scared me. I don't want kids now and I never will. I'm going

away for a while to think things through. Don't bother trying to phone me—I won't pick up. I thought you were my ideal woman but now it's all spoiled. Your spare clothes are in the bedroom—take them with you when you leave.

Sorry, not much good at this. In future I'd better stick to women who've had hysterectomies!

Best, Perry.

Carla crumpled the letter in her fist and squeezed until her knuckles clicked. Best, Perry. *Best, Perry.* Yesterday he'd loved her but now it was over, in the past, switched off like a tap.

"Everything all right?" Ally tipped the contents of one of the bags—a lurid tangle of socks and knickers—onto the floor.

"Fine. Couldn't be better." Carla shoved the scrunched-up note into her bag and wondered if there was an extra-sharp knife in the kitchen drawer. Half of her wanted to slash her wrists but the other half—actually by far the bigger half—wanted to slash Perry's.

And maybe slice off another treasured appendage while she was about it.

If only she knew where he was.

Fury was uppermost but tears were threatening—which only made Carla more furious. Swallowing hard, she headed through to the bedroom and snatched up the pathetic pile of belongings he'd left for her to collect. One shirt, a spare pair of shoes, makeup remover pads, and a toothbrush. She stuffed them into her shoulder bag before checking quickly through Perry's wardrobe and chest of drawers. He'd taken most of his clothes.

"Off now? See ya!" sang Ally when she returned to the living room.

"Right." Carla nodded, feeling like a city employee sacked without warning and ordered to vacate the building. Jerkily, she said, "See ya."

Midnight and the pain had well and truly kicked in. In both senses of the word. The removal of the IUD had left Carla with griping cramps, requiring extra-strong painkillers, a hot water bottle pressed to her stomach, and a stiff Scotch. But it was nothing compared with the awful, aching emptiness in her heart. She'd lost Perry Kennedy, the love of her life. She had no one to blame but herself. And she couldn't do anything about it, because unbearable though it was to imagine a future without him, she still wanted a baby. More than anything. It was like a compulsion, a force of nature that refused to be denied.

And come hell or high water, she would have one. Just not with the man she'd chosen to do it with.

Oh God, why did it have to hurt so much?

Carla's head jerked up at the sound of a car

pulling into the road and slowing to a halt. Her heart lolloping like a landed fish, she flung aside the hot water bottle and leaped—ooch—out of bed. Maybe it was Perry, come to his senses, turning up to smother her in kisses and beg her forgiveness.

Well, if this were a film it might have been Perry doing just that. Except it wasn't. Lurking like a spy behind the protection of the drawn curtains, Carla peeped through the gap and saw that it was Ginny, back from her shift at Penhaligon's. Dry-eyed, too hollow with misery even to cry, Carla watched as she climbed out of the car. Disappointment mingled with regret, because if anyone could comfort her now it would be Ginny. Her best friend. Ex-best friend. The best friend whose man she had stolen.

She shrank back from the curtains as her ex-best friend swung around and looked up, almost as if sensing her presence. For a split second Carla longed to throw open the window and call out to her, to shout out that she was sorry and beg her to come over. Ironically, no one would understand how she felt better than Ginny. And she would console her, know just what to say to make her feel less wretched.

Except she knew she couldn't and it was too late anyway, Ginny had already disappeared into her house. The front door slammed behind her and the kitchen light came on. As Carla watched, she saw

Ginny and Laurel chatting and laughing together in the kitchen. Who would have thought that Laurel could laugh? But she was doing it now.

I'm on my own, thought Carla, turning away and clutching her stomach as it was gripped by another spasm of pain. And it's all my own fault. Ginny's got a new best friend now.

Chapter 40

"SEVEN PINTS OF BLACKTHORN, four white wines, and five Bacardi Breezers." Having shoved his way through the crowd to the bar, Spider-Man added in a friendly fashion, "You all right?"

Jem looked up. Oh yes, she was just tickety-boo. The beer pumps were playing up tonight and best bitter was splattered across the front of her white shirt. It was also dripping from her elbows, a sensation she hated. But Spider-Man was the first member of the costume party crew to say anything remotely friendly to her tonight, so she forced herself to smile.

"Great, thanks. Dry white?"

Spider-Man, aka Darren, grinned and said triumphantly, "I'd prefer wet."

Hilarious. When it came to razor-sharp ripostes, Darren was no Jonathan Ross. Then again, at least he'd been invited to Alex and Karen's party tonight, which was more than she had been. Jem got on with the business in hand, flipping the tops off the Breezers. All week she'd been hearing people chatting excitedly between lectures and tutorials about Alex and Karen's costume party, deciding what they were going to wear. Everyone was going apart from her and Rupert, who had announced that he'd rather sieve his intestines through a colander.

Jem began pouring the Blackthorn into pint glasses, the familiar sense of abandonment nestling in her stomach. Earlier this evening Rupert had made love to her and she'd felt wonderful, special, the luckiest girl in Bristol. Then afterward, he had showered and changed and driven up to Cheltenham for the bachelor party of an old school friend's brother, absently kissing her good-bye and telling her he'd be back sometime tomorrow.

Déjà vu. First Scotland, then Rome, and now this.

Which left her, yet again, feeling like Macaulay Culkin in *Home Alone*. Except the way things were going, she'd welcome a couple of burglars into the flat with open arms. At least they'd be company.

There was a burst of laughter from the crowd a short distance from the bar. Involuntarily glancing up from the cider pump, Jem saw Davy and Lucy dressed as a pair of New York gangsters in sharp suits and fedoras. Once upon a time Davy had been the ignored one, the geeky outsider. Now, unbelievably, Lucy had moved in with him and was busy dragging him by the scruff of his neck out of his shell. They were living with Davy's mother—how sad was that?—yet, weirdly, appeared to be having a good time. Davy was beginning to be more generally accepted; somehow he was no longer regarded as the nerd on the sidelines. Lucy's friendship had imbued him with cool. Jem had to admit he looked good tonight; gangster-style suited him. And it went without saying that it suited Lucy, who looked spectacular whatever she wore.

Neither of them had so much as glanced in her direction. She might as well be invisible for all the attention anyone else was paying her. Ugh, and now cider was dripping onto her jeans.

"Last orders," bellowed the landlord, clanging the bell at ten to eleven.

Jem finished lining up the wines, the ciders, and the Breezers. She totaled the bill and took Spider-Man's credit card, ready to slot it into the machine.

"So you'll be finishing soon," Darren said bouncily, his mask pushed up to his forehead and his manner jovial.

"As soon as everyone's gone."

"Are you coming along to the party, then?"

Was it Jem's imagination or did the pub suddenly go a few decibels quieter? Either Clint

Eastwood had just walked in, or Spider-Man had said the Wrong Thing.

She shook her head. "Um, no."

Darren, not the brightest spark in the firework box, was oblivious to his faux pas. "Why not?"

Because nobody wants me there. Everyone hates me, haven't you noticed? Jem didn't say this out loud. She hurriedly pushed the credit card reader across the bar and said, "I'm fine. Just put your PIN in, please."

"But that's daft if you're not doing anything else! Hey, Alex." Darren turned and grabbed Alex by the shoulder. "I've just been telling Jem, she should come along to the party, yeah?"

Jem felt hot and sick. Alex was looking embarrassed now while the rest of them were nudging each other and smirking, loving every minute.

"Er . . . the thing is, it's a costume party," Alex mumbled.

"And I have to get home," Jem blurted out, hideously aware of Davy and Lucy watching from a safe distance as the scene was played out for their entertainment. "But . . . um, thanks anyway."

Thanks for not inviting me to your party, Alex, and thanks to you too, Darren, for so efficiently drawing this fact to the attention of everyone in this pub.

It'd probably be front page news in tomorrow's *Evening Post*.

Ceris Morgan, whom Jem had never much liked and who she knew for a fact fancied Rupert, was dressed as a French maid. Unable to resist joining in, she adjusted her saucily low-cut top and said in a singsong voice, "We wouldn't be rich enough. Jem isn't interested in parties thrown by boring old *ordinary* people anymore. She's got Rupert."

Witch. Jem was sorely tempted to retort that Ceris too might stand a chance with someone like Rupert if only she didn't have fat ankles and a silly, horsy face.

She'd have done it too if it wouldn't have meant being sacked on the spot.

"Six pints of Blackthorn, four glasses of white wine, three Bloody Marys, and two Bacardi Breezers," said Alex, flushed with triumph at having made it back to the pub. "Oh, and fifteen packets of cheese and onion crisps."

It was Sunday lunchtime, and the bedraggled survivors of last night's party, still in costume, were all set to carry on. By the sound of things it had been a resounding success. Jem, who hadn't heard from Rupert, silently bent down and began pulling packets of crisps from the box under the counter. At least Davy and Lucy weren't here, which would only have made things more stressful.

Sadly, Ceris was.

"Alex, I don't want cheese and onion! Get me

ready salted." Her voice was louder than anyone else's and ear-splittingly shrill.

"Did you hear that?" said Alex, peering over the bar. Jem murmured, "I think the whole of Clifton heard it."

"And I don't want white wine on its own. God, my brain, I'm just soooo dehydrated." Clutching her head for dramatic effect Ceris shrieked, "Make mine a spritzer."

Jem straightened back up.

"Ooh, what a night. You missed out big-time." Ceris lit a Silk Cut and blew smoke through her horsy nostrils across the bar. "You really should have come along to the . . . oops, I forgot! You weren't invited!"

Flushing, Alex the peacemaker said hastily, "It's not that Jem wasn't invited. She just didn't have anything to wear."

"Oh, I don't know." Ceris smirked. "She could have come as a two-faced witch; that wouldn't have needed any dressing up."

Splooooooosh went the fountain of soda water as Jem's finger squeezed the trigger on the mixer gun. Heavens, how had that happened?

"Aaaarrrgh!" Ceris let out a screech as piercing as nails down a blackboard, her maid's uniform instantly drenched. Now that she'd started, Jem discovered she didn't want to stop. Ceris was a spiteful bully who reveled in belittling others and deserved to be taken down a peg or two. And how better to do it than with a drenching? Feeling empowered and better already, Jem carried on aiming the gun at Ceris until every inch of her was dripping with bubbly, ice-cold soda water. An unexpected but welcome bonus was realizing that other people were stifling laughter, acknowledging that this was no more than Ceris deserved.

Jem smiled because last night she had heroically resisted the urge to insult her and now she was glad she had. This was way more fun.

"Stop it, STOP IT," screamed Ceris, mascara sliding down her face as she struggled to dodge out of reach.

"No." Jem was enjoying herself; this was better than the water-shooting gallery at the fair.

"Will someone stop her? She's gone mad! It's *cold . . .*"

"And you have fat ankles." For good measure Jem added cheerily, "And a face like a horse."

Oh well, if a job was worth losing, it was worth losing well.

"Put the gun down." The pub landlord's big hands closed over Jem's, prying her away from her new favorite toy.

"You complete witch!" Spitting with rage and shaking soda water out of her hair, Ceris bellowed, "My dad's a lawyer; he's going to sue you!"

"No, he isn't." The landlord fixed Ceris with a look of weary distaste. "You're loud and you're drunk." Then he turned to Jem. "And you're fired."

At least she wasn't being ignored anymore; the whole pub was, by this time, agog.

"Great," said Jem, wiping her wet hands on a bar towel. "I've always wanted to go out with a splash."

Who cared anyway? There were a million other pubs in Bristol. Although she was beginning to wonder if she wanted to do bar work anymore, what with the way it messed up her social life. As Jem trudged back to the flat, it occurred to her that she could always take out another loan and just enjoy herself instead. Then she and Rupert would be able to see more of each other and he wouldn't go away so much. Wasn't that a better idea? Loads of people did it and didn't waste time worrying about being in debt. You just paid off what you owed at some stage in the distant future when it was more convenient. When you thought about it, a bigger loan made so much more sense.

Turning into Pembroke Road, Jem's heart leaped at the sight of Rupert's car parked outside the flat. Oh thank God, he was back. Her pace quickened. Rupert would roar with laughter when she told him what had happened and he'd tell her she'd done exactly the right thing. Best of all he would put his arms around her and make her feel loved, which after the last couple of days was exactly what she needed. To be cosseted and told she wasn't the worst person in the world.

She hadn't even told him yet about being called into her tutor's office on Friday afternoon, the shame had been too great. Except there was no need to be ashamed in front of Rupert—he'd find that funny too.

Jem ran up the steps, fitted her key into the lock, and pushed open the front door.

"Rupert!" Too bad if he was sleeping; she'd wake him up. Right now she needed him too badly to care.

But he wasn't asleep; she could hear the shower running in the bathroom. Just the thought of Rupert naked, lathering his tanned body with shower gel, produced a fizz of adrenaline and brought a smile to Jem's face. She kicked off one boot and stealthily tested the door handle in case Rupert had changed the habit of a lifetime and locked it. No, he hadn't. She levered off the second boot and peeled off her less than alluring purple socks. She'd never had sex in a shower before.

But Rupert had.

It seemed, in fact, he was doing it right now.

Jem froze on the threshold of the overheated bathroom as she saw too many arms and legs through the misted-up frosted glass of the shower cubicle.

Oh no. Please no. Don't let this be real.

Before anything more conclusive could happen—having to witness that would truly be the ultimate insult—Jem raced over to the sink and turned the hot tap on full blast.

It did the trick, like hurling a bucket of water over a couple of fighting dogs. Now she knew the true meaning of "cooling their ardor."

"Damn it," yelled Rupert as the water in the shower ran from steaming hot to stone cold in two seconds flat. "*Damn* plumbing."

"*Waaaah,*" screeched a female voice, frantically scrabbling to slide open the shower door. "Turn it off, turn it off!"

Jem grabbed the navy towels hung over the brass rail and bundled them into her arms. Moving back to the door she whipped out the key in the lock on the bathroom side and waited for Rupert and his companion to emerge from the cubicle.

"WAAAAAHHH." Having stumbled out and seen Jem standing there in the doorway, Caro let out an ear-splitting scream and stepped back, cannoning clumsily into Rupert.

Caro.

"Oh, for God's sake." Rupert looked over at Jem and exhaled. "You're supposed to be at work."

"Sorry to spoil your afternoon." The words were spilling out of Jem's mouth automatically. "I thought I'd come home early and surprise you. And guess what? I did." She turned to Caro. "Did Rupert tell you we're together now?"

"No." Exotic Caro smiled slightly. "He just said he'd been shagging you."

Caro had always had an intimidating, supercilious air about her. When you thought about it, so did Rupert.

"OK," said Jem.

"Look, I'm sorry." Moving toward her, Rupert held out a hand for the towels.

Jem took another step back. This was turning into quite some afternoon. "Actually, I don't think you are. But never mind." Her tone conversational, she added, "You will be."

Still clutching the collection of towels, she slammed the door shut and used the key to lock it.

From inside the bathroom, Rupert shouted, "Jem, don't be stupid."

"I'm not." Wiggling the key between her thumb and forefinger, Jem thought for a moment then said, "I've *been* stupid, but I'm over that now."

Was her plan too harsh? No, of course it wasn't.

Ten minutes later she banged on the bathroom door and sang out, "Right, I'm off. The key's in the kitchen bin. Don't you two catch cold now. Bye!"

Chapter 41

"JEM?" WHEN GINNY OPENED the front door at ten o'clock that night she thought she was hallucinating.

"Oh, Mum." Jem's face was white, stained with tears, a picture of grief as she stumbled into Ginny's arms.

"Sweetheart, what's going on? What's happened?" Over the top of her daughter's blond head Ginny saw a taxi at the gate and a barrel-chested taxi driver coming up the path.

"OK, love?" The taxi driver had a kind face. "There you go, you're safe home now." He looked apologetically at Ginny. "She was crying when I picked her up from the station. Hasn't got any money on her. It's fourteen pounds fifty."

Nodding, numb with fear, Ginny somehow managed to disentangle herself and fetch her purse from the kitchen. Twenty pounds later she closed the front door and held Jem again while she shuddered and wept.

Please don't let her be pregnant.

"Is it Rupert?" she said gently some time later when Jem had reached the messy, sniffing, over-the-worst-of-it phase.

"Y-yes." Jem nodded, then miserably shook her head. "W-well, no. He's only part of it."

"OK, sweetheart, you're here now. Don't you worry. Whatever it is, we'll sort it out."

Jem wiped her eyes on the sleeve of her sweatshirt. "No need. I've already sorted it out."

Had she murdered him? "What do you mean?"

"It's all over. I'm not going back. Not ever."

Something about the flat tone of Jem's voice caused the hairs on the back of Ginny's neck to prickle in alarm. Had she really murdered Rupert?

"Jem, you have to tell me what happened." Would she turn in her own daughter? Call the police? Or would she protect her, lie for her, whisk her off to Argentina for a life on the run from the authorities?

Yes, Ginny knew this was what she'd do. Nobody deserved to go to prison for murdering Rupert.

"Oh, Mum, it's all been so horrible. Rupert's been seeing someone else. I caught him with her today. It's Caro, his old girlfriend. You met her that time you called in."

"I remember." Ginny hadn't liked Caro either. "What did you do?"

Jem told her. When it became apparent that she hadn't left the two of them dead, Ginny hugged her harder than ever. "Oh, darling, you'll get over him in no time. Everything's going to be fine. How will he get out of the bathroom?"

"Through the window, I suppose. He'll have to climb down the drainpipe naked and ring someone else's doorbell to be let back in." She paused and wiped her nose. "Shame not to catch it on a camcorder."

Even the feeblest of jokes was surely a good sign. Ginny stroked Jem's hair and handed her a clean tissue. "You just wait; when you get back, everyone'll be on your side. All your friends will rally round and—oh Jem, don't cry; when they hear what you did, they'll love you for it."

"They won't, they won't." Sobbing again, Jem rocked with misery against her.

"They will!"

"They won't because I'm not going back. Because I don't have any f-friends, Mum. Everyone hates me . . . they *do* . . ."

"Oh, now that's not true! What about Lucy?"

"Hates me." The words were muffled by Ginny's mauve lambswool cardigan. "She was seeing Rupert as well. When he chose me, she moved out."

Oh Lord. So much she hadn't known, so much Jem had been keeping from her. Determined not to give up, Ginny said, "Well, there's Davy."

"Ha, he hates me too. And he's best friends with Lucy now. That's where she moved to when she left the flat." Pulling her messy face away from Ginny's shoulder, Jem said, "I don't have anywhere to live anymore. I lost my job in the pub today. And on Friday my course tutor called me into his office and gave me this big long lecture on how disappointed he is with me because I've been falling behind with my work. He thinks I'm going to fail my exams. And he's right, I am going to fail them, so what's the point of taking them? I was so worried about it yesterday," Jem raced on, "I didn't know what to do, but now that everything else has happened I don't have to worry anymore. Because I've made up my mind: I'm not going back. There's no point, because I hate it there. I just don't want to be in Bristol anymore."

"Sweetheart, you can't—"

"Mum, I *can*." Nodding vigorously, Jem clutched Ginny's arms. "I gave university a try and it didn't work out. So that's it. I've decided. I'm going to do what makes me happy instead."

Backpacking across Australia? Lap dancing in Thailand? Faintly Ginny said, "Which is?"

"I'm going to get a job." Jem's grip tightened around her elbows, her eyes shining as she managed a watery smile. "Right here in Portsilver. And I'm going to move back in with you."

"Excuse me? I don't want to be a nuisance." The elderly female customer on table four tentatively touched Ginny's arm as she passed. "But, um, do you think I could have my credit card back?"

Oh God.

"What are you looking for?" Finn found her two minutes later, rifling through a pile of menus and the sheaf of credit card slips.

"Mrs. Black's credit card." Feverishly, Ginny began rummaging through the contents of the wastepaper basket. "She gave it to me and now it's gone. I've lost it."

"First rule of stealing credit cards," Finn observed. "Try not to let the rightful owner see who stole it."

"What did I *do* with the damn thing?" In desperation Ginny peered into the bowl of white roses on the bar.

"Panic over." Having opened the till, Finn held up the missing Visa card. "In with the tenners."

Ginny fanned herself vigorously. "Sorry, brain's gone AWOL."

"I'd already noticed."

Damn, so he'd spotted her earlier, trying to serve dessert to the party at table eleven waiting for their starters.

"They didn't mind." Defensively, she said, "They laughed about it."

"I know they did. It's not a criticism. I'm just saying you're a bit distracted."

"A lot distracted."

"Anything you want to talk about?"

"Yes please." Ginny nodded, grateful for the offer. Her brain was in such a muddle she badly needed an impartial opinion from someone she could trust.

"Look, it's ten past two. Can you hang in there until three? What's so funny?" said Finn.

"Whenever anyone tells me to hang in there, I feel like an orangutan dangling from a branch."

He gestured around the busy restaurant. "Well, try not to dangle from any branches in here. When everyone's gone we'll have a proper chat, OK?"

"I don't know what to do," Ginny concluded an hour later. They were sitting at one of the tables by the window, drinking espressos. She had told Finn everything. "I'm torn. I was so devastated when Jem left home . . . in one way this is a dream come true. I can't think of anything nicer than having her home with me again. But I want what's best for Jem and I'm not sure that's it. Bloody Rupert Derris-Beck," she said angrily. "Up until this thing happened with him she was loving university. And I don't want to force her to go back, but I don't want her to feel like a failure either. What if she leaves and regrets it for the rest of her life?"

Finn, having paused for a moment, resumed stirring sugar into his coffee. "She can take a degree when she's eighty-five. There's no age limit."

"I know, I know there isn't. But she'd like to do it now, if only everything else hadn't gone wrong. She's always been so happy and popular. Losing her friends has knocked her for six and she just feels so alone. It breaks my heart, it really does."

Through the window Ginny saw Tamsin emerge from the flat with Mae on her hip.

"OK, this is only my opinion but Jem's almost finished her first year. Exams are coming up and it seems a shame not to take them," said Finn. "Then at least she's got the whole of the summer break to decide what to do."

Ginny experienced a rush of gratitude; he was being so kind. "That's what I think too."

"If she fails the exams, she can always resit them." Glancing across the courtyard as Tamsin and Mae disappeared inside the antiques center, Finn continued, "But you never know, she might still pass first time. And after that, it's up to her. She can find another flat to share, make new friends, carry on with the course. Or stay down here with you. Or she might decide to try something completely different, take some time out and go traveling. Like Dan did." He pointed through the window at the green-painted van trundling over the gravel. "He spent two years going round the world after finishing his PhD. Said it was an unforgettable experience. You could ask him to have a chat with Jem."

"Dan has a PhD? In what?"

"Astrophysics."

Blimey. Ginny watched as Dan, lugging crates of fruit and veg out of the back of the van, loped off in the direction of the kitchen. She'd never known that about him. And he'd ended up as a delivery driver, so what did that tell you about astrophysics?

"Did you go to university?"

Amused, Finn shook his head. "Too busy working for a firm of auctioneers, learning about antiques before setting up my own business."

Ginny sighed. And he'd ended up doing all right for himself. "I still don't know what to do about Jem."

"What does her dad say?"

Tuh, Ginny had phoned Gavin this morning and he'd been no use either. "That it's up to Jem."

"Cheer up. Everything'll sort itself out." Finn's gaze softened, distracting her for a couple of seconds with the kind of thoughts she didn't allow herself to think anymore. "Give her a few days to work things through."

"That's the other thing Gavin said. I just wish—"

"Aaaarrrrgh!" The ear-splitting scream jolted both of them; in a split second Finn was out of his seat. Through the window Ginny saw Tamsin racing across the gravel in her tiny skirt and spindly high heels, to where Mae was sitting behind Dan's van being cautiously investigated by Stiller.

"Get away from her, you BEAST," Tamsin yelled as Stiller interestedly sniffed Mae's face. Swooping down like a bony eagle, she scooped Mae up into her arms. Stiller, disappointed at having lost his new playmate, waggled his tail and licked hopefully at Mae's dangling feet.

"UGH! NO! *Filthy* animal! Are you out of your *mind?*" Tamsin roared at Dan as he rounded the corner of the restaurant. "Letting a dog run loose to attack an innocent *baby?*"

Poor Dan turned white with horror, searching for signs of blood.

Finn was out of the door now with Ginny inches behind him. "OK, calm down, nobody's been attacked."

"But they could have been," screeched Tamsin, long hair swinging as she inspected Mae for signs of injury. "That monster could have done anything!"

Gibbering with terror, Dan stammered, "I'm s-sorry, I didn't know, oh God I'm so sorry, I had no *idea* . . ."

"Dan, it's all right." Finn took control of the situation, gesturing with his palms down that Dan wasn't to get upset. "What I want to know is how Mae came to be on her own out here." He looked at Tamsin, who immediately tightened her grip on Mae and went on the defensive.

"Oh, so this is my fault, is it? I put my daughter down for two seconds because she didn't want to be carried. All I did was say hi to Tom and ask how things were going. The next moment I looked down and Mae had crawled out of the shop. In two *seconds,*" Tamsin declared vehemently, holding her thumb and forefinger half an inch apart for added emphasis. "You know how fast she can scoot along when she wants to."

"I do," Finn nodded. "But not fast enough to get away if a car had driven into the courtyard."

Tamsin's voice grew shriller still. "I was listening out for cars! My God, do you think I want my baby to be run over? If I'd heard an engine, I'd have been there. But to let a dog loose is just . . . irresponsible."

Poor Stiller, alarmed by all the shouting, had by this time backed away and pressed himself against Dan's corduroy trouser legs. Blissfully unaware of the kerfuffle she had caused, Mae clapped her hands together and burbled, "Dogga-dogga-bleuwwwww."

"OK, let's calm down." Finn was clearly keen to avoid a slanging match. "Mae's fine, nothing happened."

"Nothing *happened?* God, she reeks! Smell her," Tamsin ordered. "That bloody dog slobbered all over my baby—and it's not even a pedigree!"

Dan and Stiller were by now both quivering with shame. Rushing to their defense Ginny said, "Tamsin, Stiller's the sweetest, gentlest dog you could ever meet. I promise you, he wouldn't hurt anyone. Mae would never come to any harm with him." Her tone was placating, meant to make Tamsin feel better, but Tamsin was by this time beyond reassurance.

"No harm? Are you serious? A stinking filthy dog crawling with germs licks my daughter's face and you think that's *safe?*" Her eyes wide, she said hysterically, "My God, and I thought you were a competent mother! If that's how you feel I won't be asking you to babysit again."

Excellent, thought Ginny, because I wouldn't do it anyway.

And by the way, Finn deserves *so* much better than you.

Chapter 42

THE EXCITEMENT AMONG THE crowd was palpable, fans buzzing with growing anticipation as the hands of the clock moved toward seven thirty. It wasn't often that a genuine A-list Hollywood celebrity came to Bristol to sign copies of their autobiography, but Marcus McBride was on his way. Now forty, he had been a true star for almost twenty years, something of a hell-raiser early on in his career but talented and dedicated enough to get away with it. Not to mention in possession of buckets of sex appeal. With his dark, unconventional looks, undoubted intelligence, and quirky sense of humor, women all over the world had fallen for Marcus McBride's charms and many millions more had swooned over him from a distance. The opportunity to buy his just-published book, have it signed by Marcus himself, and actually get to shake his hand had been just too good to pass up.

"Look, I bet that's him!" Lucy pointed up at the gray sky and hundreds of pairs of eyes followed the direction of her arm as the faint winking lights of a helicopter appeared in the distance.

"And it's starting to rain." Davy pulled a face as a raindrop splashed into his left eye. "You know, we could always forge his signature, pretend we met him, and just go for a drink instead."

But he said it good-naturedly, knowing it wasn't an option. Lucy was looking forward to seeing Marcus McBride. And his mother would have his guts for garters.

"Poor Rhona, missing out on all this." Lucy was still watching as the helicopter grew larger. "She'd have loved it."

Davy smiled, because his mum had never made any secret of her crush on Marcus McBride. When she'd heard he was coming down to do a book-signing in Bristol, she had been beside herself with excitement.

It was just a shame she wasn't able to come down to the shopping center herself.

The helicopter landed somewhere behind the complex and everyone in the hundreds-long queue began mentally preparing themselves. Lucy checked her camera for the umpteenth time. "I'll take loads of photos," she had told Rhona, "of

Marcus and Davy together when he signs the book."

"Bless you." Rhona had smiled, touched by her thoughtfulness.

"Your collar's crooked," Lucy told Davy now, busily straightening it. "There, that's better."

"I'm sure it'll make all the difference. Along with this." Davy ruefully ruffled his new haircut, still unused to it. Lucy had dragged him along to a trendy salon in Cotham, standing behind him like a prison warden until she was completely satisfied with the short, spiky cut the stylist had teased out of his previously long, straggly, determinedly unstylish hair.

"Stop moaning, it looks great."

"It cost a fortune." Six whole hours of cleaning, to be precise, which was crazy when he had a perfectly good pair of scissors at home.

"Get a move on," the man behind them murmured impatiently. "The queue's moving."

It was, but with several hundred people ahead of them, Davy wasn't holding his breath. Marcus McBride hadn't even made his entrance into the bookshop yet.

"Look at him, that's the kind of man I could go for." Now they'd shuffled along a bit further, Lucy was able to drool over a huge promotional poster of Marcus in the shop window. "You can't call him handsome, can you? But he's better than that, more edgy and interesting than just handsome.

And those eyes. I wonder what he'd do if I kissed him?"

"Nothing," said Davy. "It's only a poster."

"You." Lucy dug him in the ribs. "I'm going to miss you when I leave." Tilting her head to one side she said, "Remember when you had that big crush on me? Whatever happened to that?"

"I don't know. Just kind of evaporated."

"And now you don't fancy me anymore. At *all*." She pulled a tragic face. "It's not very flattering, you know."

"Sorry." Davy grinned. "Don't take it personally."

"But you were besotted with me."

He shrugged, equally bemused. "I used to play my Darkness CD all the time too. I thought it was the best album ever. Then after a couple of months I didn't play it quite so often. And now I don't bother listening to it at all. The magic just . . . wore off."

"If you're saying I sound like Justin Hawkins, I'll give you a Chinese burn."

"You don't sound like him." Straight-faced, Davy said, "Mind you, looks-wise . . ."

They had a bit of a tussle outside the bookshop, won by Lucy as usual. Davy was glad his inconvenient crush on her had subsided of its own accord, to be replaced by an easy camaraderie. Because he was no longer hopelessly tongue-tied in her presence, they were able to banter together like . . . well, best friends.

He inhaled a blast of the peppermint chewing gum being noisily chewed by the man behind them. Lucy had picked up a sheaf of details from a flat-letting agency on the way home this afternoon. He would miss her too.

Aloud Davy said, "You don't have to go."

She slipped an arm through his, gave it a grateful squeeze. "I know I don't have to. But I should. Your mum's fantastic and I love her to bits, but I can't stay on forever. The whole point of leaving home and being a student is so you can live like a student and do studenty things."

"Making a mess, having all your friends round, getting drunk, sleeping with people your parents wouldn't approve of," said Davy.

"Arguing about who finished the milk and put the empty carton back in the fridge."

"Sorry, I forgot that one."

"Wondering where the terrible smell's coming from, then finally discovering an open tin of tuna under the living room sofa."

"That old classic." Davy shook his head sympathetically. "I can see why you miss it so much."

"There are good bits too. Like borrowing your flatmate's clothes," Lucy pointed out. "And sharing each other's makeup."

"That wouldn't really work if he was a rugby player."

They fell silent for a couple of seconds, both thinking.

"I wonder what's happened to Jem?" Lucy spoke at last. "No one's seen her all week."

Davy knew how hurt Lucy had been when the whole Jem and Rupert thing had come out, with Jem choosing to stay with Rupert rather than siding with her best friend. The two girls hadn't spoken since.

"Maybe she's ill." But they'd both heard about the mixer-gun incident and Jem's instant dismissal from the pub. "I could give her a quick ring," he suggested. "Check she's all right."

But Lucy was already shaking her head. "Don't bother. She's got Rupert to look after her." Pressing her lips together she said, "Anyway, let's not talk about them. Let's talk about whether this damn queue is ever going to move . . ."

At that moment, almost as if she had caused it to happen, a whoop of excitement went up inside the shop, indicating that Marcus McBride had made his entrance. Flashbulbs went off like fireworks, people were jumping up and down to get a better view and a round of applause broke out.

"Wow." Lucy was impressed. "I've never met a real film star before."

"You're not going to meet him now," Davy pointed out. "This isn't a cocktail party. You're not going to end up snogging in the stockroom. He's got hundreds of books to sign and one hour to do it in. While he's signing ours, you'll have about two seconds to take the photo."

"You really know how to squash a girl's fantasies," said Lucy.

Over the course of the next thirty minutes the queue edged forward, into the back of the store at last. Shop assistants demonstrated how to hold open their already-bought copies of Marcus McBride's autobiography at the title page, ready for his pen to make its illegible squiggle. As they neared the front of the queue and the desk at which he was sitting, they saw him for the first time. Flanked by burly minders and uniformed security staff with high-tech earpieces, Marcus was squiggling away and flashing his famous smile with production-line regularity. Anyone who'd hoped to stand and chat for a minute or two was firmly moved along. Nothing was allowed to interrupt the flow.

More minty fumes indicated the arrival of a fresh piece of chewing gum in the mouth of the man behind them, ensuring he had nice breath for his fleeting encounter with Hollywood royalty. When the queue advanced a couple of feet further and Davy was slow to catch up, the man prodded him in the back and said irritably, "Look, if you're not interested, don't bother."

Lucy raised an eyebrow and Davy flushed, trying to pretend he hadn't heard. This was when he felt his confidence deserting him, when strangers said something uncalled for and a braver person would stand up for themselves without giving it a second thought. Davy had always been embarrassed by the rudeness of others and had never known how to react; consequently he never did react, which was utterly pathetic. Had Lucy expected him to come out with some quick retort, some cutting comment that would have put the man behind them in his place?

Of course she had. Davy swallowed, ashamed of himself, and pretended to be engrossed in a shelf of Fiction for Teenagers. That was just the way he was, the way he'd always been, and there was nothing he could do to change it. Even if it did mean Lucy thought he was a complete wimp.

Almost there now. Marcus McBride was wearing a tight pink T-shirt, black jeans, and blue cowboy boots, because he'd reached the level of film stardom that meant you could throw on whatever you liked and not be laughed at. Which must be nice, Davy thought with feeling, as the overweight woman in front of him readied herself for her turn. Patting her permed hair and glancing over her shoulder at Lucy, she whispered longingly, "Ooh, isn't he gorgeous? If I was thirty years younger!"

"Got it open to the right page? Right, off you go," ordered the strict sergeant-major type in charge at the head of the queue. The woman tottered up to the desk, said breathlessly, "You're my favorite actor!" and held out her book.

Smile, squiggle, smile, all over.

"Next," barked the sergeant major as Lucy readied herself to take the all-important photo.

"Hurry *up,*" the man behind Davy hissed, blasting him with mint.

Davy moved forward, held out his book, and self-consciously half turned so that the camera wouldn't just get a shot of his back. He felt rather than saw the signature being scrawled on the title page of the book he was still holding and, glancing behind Lucy, noted that the man behind her was fidgeting in an agitated fashion with something in his trouser pocket. God, how embarrassing, he hoped the man wasn't doing what he appeared to be doing; then again, some people could get inappropriately carried away in the heat of the—

Flash went Lucy's camera, temporarily blinding Davy. He hoped he hadn't had a gormless expression on his face. The sergeant-major type made vigorous move-on gestures, indicating that their time was up. In the split second that followed, Davy glimpsed another flash, of metal this time. Blinking, he realized that Mint Man had pulled a knife from his pocket and was now gripping it tightly in his right hand, keeping it hidden from view beneath his jacket. Ever hopeful Lucy, flashing a dazzling smile at Marcus McBride, was making her way past the desk, and the sergeant major was making increasingly urgent sweeping movements with his arms. It was Mint Man's turn next.

"No!" yelled Davy, realizing that no one else had spotted the knife.

Mint Man shot him a look of wild-eyed fury and launched himself at the desk. Davy, who had always loathed rugby at school, flung himself at Mint Man and tackled him to the ground. God, it hurt. All the air was punched from his lungs, and Mint Man was now roaring like an enraged bull elephant. Dazedly realizing how right he'd been to hate rugby, Davy became aware that he was now being crushed beneath a scrum of bouncers and security guards. Next moment he felt himself being hauled to his feet and discovered that his legs had gone wobbly. He could hear screams of panic all around him, interspersed with barked orders from security and loud staccato cursing from Mint Man.

Someone yelled, "Oh God, he's been stabbed," and Davy stumbled toward Lucy, feeling sick at the thought that the knife had gone into the madman on the ground. Then he saw the look of terror in Lucy's eyes and heard her gasp, "Oh, Davy! Oh my God, *someone call an ambulance . . .*"

Chapter 43

"HE'S BEEN ARRESTED AND taken down to the police station. Long psychiatric history, it turns out." The sergeant-major type, who was actually Marcus McBride's PR manager, brought Davy and Lucy up to date in one of the offices behind the shop. "Apparently, Princess Margaret told him to do it."

"That woman, she's nothing but trouble. This was my best shirt." Davy stuck his finger through the slash in the heavily bloodstained blue-and-green-striped cotton and looked mournful.

"I'm sure we can come to some arrangement." Lucy's tone was despairing. "You got it from Oxfam."

"So? It's still my best shirt."

"There." The doctor finished applying the last of the skin sutures and peeled off his surgical gloves. "You'll live."

"I'll call it my dueling scar." Davy inspected the cleaned-up knife wound inflicted by Mint Man's panicky response to being brought down. At twenty centimeters long it had bled profusely and looked spectacular but was actually far less painful than it appeared, which he didn't mind at all. If it had been a stabbing injury rather than a shallow slice across his chest, on the other hand . . . well, the thought of it was enough to make him feel a bit queasy.

As if to emphasize this point, the sergeant major said, "That was a brave thing you did, son. Incredibly brave and unbelievably stupid."

Davy agreed with the unbelievably stupid bit. He didn't even feel as if he'd been brave back there on the shop floor, simply because he had acted without stopping to think first. If he had thought about it, he would certainly never have tackled a lunatic wielding a knife.

The door to the office opened then and Marcus McBride walked in, exuding charisma.

"Hey, kid. You did good." He shook Davy's hand and this time his smile was genuine. "You're a hero."

Embarrassed, Davy said, "I'm not really the heroic type."

Outside, they had to have their picture taken by a clamor of photographers. Davy, wearing his bloodstained shirt, stood awkwardly while Marcus McBride rested his arm across his shoulders. Still in a daze, Davy told the waiting journalists his name. They wanted to see the wound across his chest. When they asked him how he felt, he said, "Like a Page Three girl," and everyone laughed.

Five minutes later the press was dispatched. Marcus said, "Seriously, you did great. I don't know how to thank you. I'd offer you a signed copy of my book, but . . ."

"We've already got one." Lucy held up the shopping bag containing the copy Davy had flung aside before tackling Mint Man to the ground. Luckily it didn't have blood on it.

"We'll sort something out." The sergeant major consulted his watch. "Now, is your car here or do you need transport home?"

"We caught the bus," said Davy.

"No problem. I'll organize a car." Taking out his mobile phone, the sergeant major began rattling out orders. Marcus's helicopter was evidently waiting on standby to whisk him up to a TV appearance in Manchester. A car was summoned to take Davy and Lucy back to Henbury.

An idea had come into Davy's mind; he plucked up the courage to voice it. "Actually," Davy looked at Marcus, "you know you said you didn't know how to thank me?"

"Yes."

"Well, my mum would love to meet you. She couldn't be here tonight but she's only ten minutes away."

"Sorry, son." Having concluded his call, the sergeant major said firmly, "Can't do anything now, we're behind schedule as it is. Some other time, OK?"

Deflated, Davy said, "Oh. OK."

Rhona finished the washing up and took a cup of tea through to the living room. She switched on the TV and semi-watched a program about a woman so addicted to shopping for new clothes that she was on the verge of being declared bankrupt.

At least that was something that she was never going to suffer from. Even observing the woman on TV as she rushed through Marks and Spencer grabbing armfuls of dresses off the rails made Rhona feel jittery and nervous.

Oh well, never mind about that. It was a shame she hadn't been able to go down to the shopping center this evening but she couldn't help the way she was. Maybe in time the panicky sensations would subside of their own accord. And at least Davy and Lucy were down there getting a book signed for her, so she wasn't completely missing out . . .

When the doorbell rang some time later, Rhona padded out to the hall. She opened the front door and looked at Marcus McBride.

For several seconds she carried on looking at him, as if he were a crossword clue she couldn't quite work out. Because it couldn't *really* be Marcus McBride.

"Rhona?"

"Yes." How incredible, she could still speak. Well, just about.

"Hi, I'm Marcus." The visitor on the doorstep took her hand and gravely shook it.

"How . . . how, how . . . I mean, how . . . ?"

"Davy happened to mention that you'd like to meet me. And I said great, because I wanted to meet you too."

Rhona wondered if she had fallen asleep in front of the TV and was in fact having a dream. Then again, her dreams had never been as good as this. Unsticking her tongue from the roof of her mouth, she said, "Davy?"

"Your son?" Marcus broke into a smile. "That's why I'm here. I want to tell you, he did a very brave thing tonight. I'm very grateful to him."

"*My* son did a brave thing?" Rhona closed her eyes for a moment; when she opened them again Marcus McBride was still there, waiting on her doorstep and looking incredibly *real*. Forgetting that she wasn't wearing any shoes, she said, "Um . . . where is Davy?"

"Over there in the car. With Lucy. Look, I can't stay long; my PR guy's giving me a hard time. But when Davy said you'd like a visit, how could I refuse? He's fine, by the way."

"Fine? What d'you mean, fine? Why wouldn't he be fine?"

And, surreally, Marcus McBride explained what had happened at the book signing. Rhona's stomach clenched with horror and disbelief and she ran barefoot down the path to the waiting car. Wrenching open the rear door she shouted, "Davy, how *could* you? You might have been killed! Oh my God, look at your *shirt* . . ."

Lucy used up the rest of the film in her camera taking photos of Rhona and Marcus McBride. Finally Marcus gave Rhona a kiss on the cheek then laughed at the expression on Lucy's face and kissed her as well.

"Now I really have to go. Thanks again." He shook Davy's hand and said, "You take care of yourself."

"Bye," said Davy.

The car pulled away. Still barefoot, Rhona clapped her hand to her chest and said, "I don't know, I can't let you out of my sight for two minutes."

Davy rolled his eyes. "Mum, there's no need to fuss. *I'm OK.*"

Chapter 44

"OH!" EXPECTING THE POSTMAN and getting Finn instead came as something of a shock. Probably for Finn too, thought Ginny, clutching the front edges of her dressing gown together and praying her hair wasn't too scarily bed-heady.

Come to think of it, postmen had to be a hardy breed, trained not to flinch visibly at harrowing early-morning sights.

"Sorry. I was on my way into Portsilver and I wondered if you'd seen today's paper."

"It's eight o'clock. I haven't seen the kettle yet.

Why, what's in there?" Ginny reached out for the newspaper he was holding but Finn hesitated.

"Your daughter's friends in Bristol, Lucy and Davy. What's Davy's surname?"

Ginny searched her brain. "Um . . . Stokes."

Finn looked relieved. "It is the right one then. I thought it must be." He handed over the folded newspaper and added, "Bit of excitement up in Bristol. I thought it might give Jem the excuse she needs to ring her friends."

The doorbell had evidently woken Jem too. Appearing on the stairs behind Ginny, she said evenly, "I haven't got any friends in Bristol."

"No? Oh well then"—Finn retrieved the paper once more—"you won't be interested in seeing this."

Jem looked truculent. "What's my mum been telling you?"

"That you've given up on university."

She nodded at the newspaper. "What's Davy done?"

"If he's not your friend, why would you care?"

"Oh, for heaven's sake, give it to me!" Bursting with curiosity, Ginny snatched the folded paper. "I want to know!"

Finn said with amusement, "Don't show Jem."

Ginny's jaw dropped as she found the piece on page seven. "Oh, good grief."

"OK, OK," grumbled Jem, peering over her shoulder. "I want to know too."

Finn left them to it. Together Jem and Ginny devoured the article.

"Thank goodness he's all right," said Ginny. "He could have been killed."

"Mm." Jem carefully stirred sugar into her tea.

"Sweetheart, Finn's right. You should give Davy a ring."

"I can't." Clearly emotional, Jem failed to control her wobbling lower lip. "There's no point."

"There's every point. You can congratulate him!"

"I might not get the chance," Jem said miserably. "He'd probably just put the phone down."

It was no good; Ginny did her best to reassure her, but Jem was adamant, convinced that any attempt at contact with Davy or Lucy would be met with a snub.

"Can we change the subject, Mum? I don't want to talk about it anymore."

Her unhappiness was so apparent, Ginny thought her own heart would break.

Twenty-six hours later and Ginny's forehead was taut with concentration. Famous for her feeble sense of direction, she was now testing it to the limit. It had been seven months since she'd last made the journey up the M5 to Bristol and that time she hadn't needed to pay attention to the first bit of the return journey because Davy had been sitting next to her in the passenger seat instructing her when to turn left and right.

Now she was on her own, attempting to retrace the route through Henbury on memory alone and it wasn't an easy task. Had they turned right at the Old Crow pub or gone straight over the roundabout? When they'd reached the junction past the petrol station, had they turned left? Oh God, this was hopeless; at this rate, come midnight, she'd still be driving around in circles.

It took a while—OK, another forty minutes of being lost—but finally Ginny turned into a street she dimly recognized. This was it, she was sure. And the one thing she did remember was the tidy, pocket-sized front garden and the royal-blue front door. Trundling along in second gear like a curb crawler, she passed brown doors, red doors, white doors, green doors . . .

Ooh, there it was.

At last.

Would Davy even be in?

If he was, would he close the door in her face?

And would Jem ever speak to her again when she found out what she'd done?

Oh well, Finn had given her the day off work and she'd driven all the way up to Bristol for a reason. It would be silly to turn around and go home now.

The front door was opened by an anxious-looking woman who clearly didn't welcome the interruption. Glancing at her watch, then up at Ginny, she said distractedly, "Yes?"

"Hi. Is Davy here?"

"Sorry, he's out. Are you another journalist?"

Ginny took a deep breath. "No, I'm Jem Holland's mum."

"Oh, thank goodness! Come on in, Davy's about to be on the radio."

Not thank goodness she was Jem's mum, Ginny realized as Davy's mother bundled her into the house, but thank goodness she didn't have to miss hearing her son being interviewed.

And who would blame her? She'd have done exactly the same. Together they sat in the kitchen and listened in silence to the old-fashioned wireless on the kitchen table. After fifteen minutes it was all over.

"Phew, sorry about that. I'm Rhona," said Davy's mother. "Davy's never been on the radio before." Overcome with emotion she wiped the corners of her eyes with a tissue. "Was that presenter having a bit of a dig, d'you think?"

Ginny knew at once what she meant. To begin with, it had all been about what a hero Davy was, but toward the end of the interview the presenter had said slyly, "And I gather you still live at home with your mother, which seems extraordinary to me. Does that not set you apart from your fellow students?"

Davy, of course, had roundly denied it, but the interviewer had been unconvinced. "You have to admit, though, it's an unusual situation. Most young people starting university can't wait to grasp their independence. Did your mother not want you to move out, did she put pressure on you to stay, or was it your own decision? Are you a bit of a mummy's boy at heart?"

Now, with the radio turned off, Ginny wondered what she was supposed to say. She shrugged. "Honestly? Yes, I suppose he was having a dig. But who cares what he thinks? If Davy wants to stay at home, that's his choice."

Rhona nodded slowly, lost in thought. Then she looked over at her. "It was you who gave Davy a lift home once from Clifton, wasn't it? He told me you live in Cornwall. So you're up here visiting your daughter?"

"No. Jem's at home in Cornwall. She's broken up with her horrible boyfriend."

"Rupert." Rhona's lip curled. "I've heard all about him."

"Jem's eighteen. She made a big mistake. And now she's paying the price," said Ginny. "She wants to give up university, come back home, and live with me."

"How wonderful. But you don't seem that thrilled. Don't you want her back?"

Rhona clearly didn't understand. Ginny exhaled and twisted the bracelet on her wrist. "Of course I do, more than anything. But I want what's right for Jem, not what's right for me."

"Oh God," said Rhona. "You're so brave."

Ginny shrugged. "I don't feel it."

They sat together in silence for a while. Finally Rhona announced, "I had a brain hemorrhage you know, four years ago. In British Home Stores."

"You did?" Ginny was startled. "I didn't know that."

"No? Well, I don't suppose you would. Davy doesn't feel it's anyone else's business why he chooses to stay at home. But that's the reason, even though I was one of the lucky ones. Made a good recovery." Rhona tapped her left leg. "Apart from a bit of a limp. But it frightened the living daylights out of me, I can tell you. I've been terrified of it happening again and not having anyone around to help me. I get panicky in shops too, which isn't ideal. That's why Davy and Lucy were the ones queuing up to see Marcus McBride. Because I couldn't face it myself."

"I'm not surprised," exclaimed Ginny. "Oh, please," she added as Rhona's eyes filled with tears. "You mustn't blame yourself for what happened to Davy."

"I don't." Rhona fished up her sleeve for a tissue. "Well, I do, but it's not that. I love having Davy at home with me, but it's not fair on him, is it? I'm not an invalid, after all. And he's a young lad with his own life to live."

Ginny nodded in agreement. "He is."

"I can't do it yet." Rhona swallowed. "But I'll do it soon. I know it's nearly time to let him go."

"It doesn't mean he's going to stop loving you," said Ginny.

Rhona managed a watery smile. "He'd better not."

Davy arrived home fifteen minutes later. Rhona, greeting him at the door, hugged him hard and exclaimed, "You were brilliant on the radio. I was so proud! It sounded just like you!"

Then she murmured something Ginny couldn't make out and sent him ahead into the kitchen where she was waiting for him.

"Hello, Davy."

"Hello, Mrs. Holland."

Mrs. Holland. So polite. Ginny said, "You're looking . . . smart."

He rubbed a hand self-consciously over his head. "Lucy made me have my hair cut."

"It suits you."

"Thanks." He paused. "Is Jem all right?"

Would Jem ever forgive her for being an interfering mother?

"No." Ginny shook her head, a lump springing into her throat. "No, Davy, she's not."

"Any good?" said Davy.

"Disaster." Lucy flung down her pink jacket and a couple of shopping bags. Having replied to an advert in the *Evening Post* for a fun-loving fourth person to share a large flat in Redland, she was just back from visiting it. "In fact, nightmare. The flat was a health hazard, the room they're letting is the size of a dog kennel, and the whole place smelled of socks. Two hairy physics students and a beard-and-sandals geography teacher." She pulled a face. "Oh, and no music allowed in the flat because music distracts them from their studies."

Privately relieved, Davy said, "Are they sure they want someone fun-loving?"

"Are you kidding? They think they're hilarious! They have an imaginary pet cat. And they play tricks on each other by putting joke plastic cat poo in their bowls of All Bran. I tell you, my sides nearly split. Anyway, get that T-shirt off."

Davy's eyebrows went up. "Are you after my body?"

"I've bought you two new shirts." Lucy reached for the bags. "Come on, try them on."

"In a minute. We've got a visitor." Leading her into the kitchen, Davy pointed through the open window to where his mother and Ginny were sitting out in the sunny back garden.

"Who's that?" Lucy frowned, puzzled. "Is it . . . ?"

"Jem's mum." He took the shopping bags from her, wincing as he saw that one of the shirts was an eyeball-searing shade of lime green. "She wants to talk to you."

· · ·

It was five o'clock on Saturday afternoon and Jem was alone in the house, having spent the day with her father. Poor Dad, he'd done his best to cheer her up and probably thought he'd succeeded, but lovely though it was to see him again, she'd been glad to get back to the sanctuary of her old bedroom, released from the pressure of smiling and pretending to be fine.

Mum was still working at the restaurant, Laurel had gone shopping in Newquay, and it was a relief to be on her own, although watching *Moulin Rouge* on DVD probably hadn't been the best idea she'd ever had. Sprawled on the bed with a tin of Laurel's homemade biscuits, Jem's eyes brimmed at the thought of poor, gorgeous Ewan MacGregor and the heartbreak in store for him when Nicole Kidman finally died in his arms. Why couldn't she be adored by someone as wonderful as Ewan, who would never have had sex in the shower with an old girlfriend behind Nicole's back? How could she have been so stupid as to be taken in by Rupert's pseudo charms? Why, *why* hadn't she marched out of the flat with Lucy? She must have been out of her mind.

Tears slid down Jem's cheeks and dripped off her chin as she gazed blindly at the TV screen. Ewan and Nicole were singing "Come What May," promising to be together until their dying day. Not long to wait there, then. Miserably helping herself to another biscuit, Jem wondered how many people apart from her family would be upset if she died. Nobody from Bristol, that was for sure.

Nicole was looking stunning while elegantly coughing up blood when the doorbell rang a while later. Without enthusiasm Jem brushed cookie crumbs off her T-shirt, hauled herself off the bed, and padded downstairs.

Lucy was on the doorstep.

Dumbstruck, Jem gazed at her. Past Lucy, perched on the front wall, was Davy wearing an extremely green shirt.

Jem's heart was pounding; she was hideously aware of her swollen, froggy eyes. At last she said, "What are you doing here?"

"Oh, Jem, look at the state of you. Why do you think we're here?" For a second it seemed as if Lucy might burst into tears as well. Holding out her arms and shaking her head she said, "We've come to take you back with us."

"Really?" Jem's bottom lip began to tremble.

"Really."

"Oh, Luce, I'm sorry. So sorry for everything."

"I know. Come here."

They hugged and laughed and cried a bit on the doorstep. Then Davy, ambling up the path, said, "I'm not really a huggy person," and gave Jem's shoulder an awkward pat instead.

"I can't believe you came all the way to

Cornwall." Overwhelmed, Jem said, "How did you know this address? Did you catch the train?"

Lucy's dark eyes shone. "Your mum came to see us."

"My *mum?* When?" Did Ginny have a time machine she didn't know about?

"Today," said Davy.

"But she's working at the restaurant; they've got a wedding reception . . . oh . . ."

Lucy said gravely, "She lied."

"She's just gone to the shop to pick up some food. We're staying for the night. You can invite us in if you like." Davy rested his hand lightly on his chest. "It's not doing my terrible knife injury any good, you know, standing out here."

"Oh God, of course, come in!"

"He's having you on." Lucy rolled her eyes. "It's nothing more than a scratch. I could have done better with one of my fingernails."

"I want to hear all about it," said Jem as she ushered them inside.

"Ha, that's nothing. Wait till you hear what happened when your mum went to Pembroke Road to pick up the rest of your stuff."

Chapter 45

THE CHANGE IN JEM was unbelievable, heartwarming. For once in her life, Ginny discovered, she had acted on impulse and it had paid off. Jem, hugging her, had said, "Mum, I can't believe you did this. Everything's sorted out now. I'm so happy."

"She just couldn't bear the thought of having you back here with her," said Lucy. "She was desperate."

Ginny smiled at them, because every maternal fiber of her being longed to hold on to Jem for ever, keeping her safe from harm at home. They were young; they couldn't begin to understand that making it possible for her daughter to leave again was one of the most grown-up things she'd ever done.

But this time, she knew, Jem would be happy. Tomorrow evening she was driving them back up to Bristol. For the last few weeks of term all three would be staying with Rhona in Henbury. It was complicated but not impossible; Davy was moving into the tiny bedroom that had been Lucy's, and Lucy and Jem were taking over his old room. Together, they were going to put all their energy into revising for their exams and hopefully Jem would be able to put in enough work to pass. Then, after the summer break, Lucy and Jem would get a flat-share together, hopefully with someone less good-looking but with a far nicer personality than—

"Mum, you have to tell me what happened with Rupert!"

Oh yes, that had been fun. Just for a split second when he'd opened the front door, Rupert's face had been a picture.

"Hello, Rupert," Ginny said brightly. "So you managed to get out of the bathroom then. I've come to pick up the rest of Jem's things. And her deposit."

His lip curled. "You're welcome to take her junk away. I'm keeping the deposit in lieu of notice."

"Rupert, don't be like that. There's no need." Marching into the flat, Ginny gave him a pitying look. "Besides, I'm not leaving until you've paid me back the money. In cash."

Well, why not? Five hundred pounds was five hundred pounds. And she must have looked as if she meant business, because Rupert heaved a sigh and disappeared into his bedroom, returning a couple of minutes later with a roll of twenty-pound notes.

"You don't have to count them."

"Oh, but I will. Honesty hasn't always been your best policy, has it?" Having checked that all the money was there, Ginny went into Jem's room and collected the last of her belongings. When she reemerged, Rupert was standing in the living room, smoking a cigarette, looking out of the window at Davy in the car below.

"So you've got Stokes with you. Don't tell me he's given up the cleaning job to become your minder."

"Rupert, he's worth ten of you." Patiently, Ginny said, "I don't suppose you'll ever understand that, but at least everyone else does. And Davy's happy with himself."

Rupert smirked, exhaling a stream of smoke. "You think I'm not?"

"Oh, I'm sure you are now. You're living your own life, doing whatever you like and not caring who else gets hurt. But that's the kind of attitude that comes back to bite you. And when it does, you'll know how it feels to be the one on the receiving end."

He raised a laconic eyebrow. "Lecture over? Am I supposed to fall to my knees and beg forgiveness for my sins?"

"Not at all," said Ginny. "In fact I'm glad it happened. My daughter made a huge mistake, but she's learned her lesson. With a bit of luck she'll steer clear of boys like you in future."

"Boys like me." Amused, Rupert flicked his cigarette out of the window.

"Plenty of money, no morals. Not what most

people want from a relationship." Annoyed by the cigarette thing, Ginny made the comment she'd been debating whether to mention. "I think your mother came to much the same conclusion, didn't she?"

The arrogant half smile disappeared from Rupert's face; he stiffened, instantly on his guard. "Excuse me?"

"Your mother. You told me she was dead, remember?" Ginny shook her head. "I felt terrible at the time. But you weren't actually telling the truth, were you?"

She watched him turn pale; God bless the Internet, and Finn too for dimly recognizing Rupert's double-barreled surname.

"She's dead as far as I'm concerned," Rupert said flatly.

"Your father had lots of affairs while they were married. He made her desperately unhappy, but she stuck it out because of you. Then, when you were thirteen and away at boarding school, she fell in love with another man. And when your father found out about this, he kicked her out."

"OK, said what you wanted to say? You can go now." Stony-eyed, Rupert lit another cigarette.

"In a minute." Ginny had no intention of stopping. "So you've refused to have anything to do with your mum ever since. But she's still with the same man and they're very happy together. He sounds like a lovely person."

"I wouldn't know." Rupert's jaw was taut. "Well, you've done your homework."

"Your mum must miss you terribly." Her tone gentler now, Ginny said, "I wish you'd consider seeing her again."

"No chance." A muscle flickered in his cheek.

"You've got two little half sisters you've never met."

"Who live in government housing in a tower block in Hackney. With my mother and a tattooed window-fitter called Darren. There, I've said it. Happy now?"

Ginny almost—*almost*—felt sorry for him.

"I'm fine. How about you?"

"Best day of my life." Flick went the second cigarette, sailing through the window and landing on the pavement below. "Congratulations. I suppose you've told Jem."

He was both furious and mortified. Ginny shook her head. "I haven't. But I might if I hear you've said or done anything to upset her. From now on, I'd just like you to keep away from my daughter and her friends, OK?" She gathered up the bags containing Jem's things and indicated that Rupert could open the front door. As he did so, she added, "And it wouldn't kill you to use an ashtray."

Since she wasn't a saint, it had almost killed Ginny to keep the story of Rupert's mother to herself. But a small part of her had known that publicly humiliating Rupert was unlikely to spur him into making contact with his mother.

Less altruistically, a far greater part of her had whispered that if softhearted Jem were to hear of it, she would only feel sorry for Rupert and might find herself being drawn to his new-found vulnerability.

That was the last thing they needed.

So she had heroically withheld the information. As far as Jem, Davy, and Lucy were concerned, she had simply given Rupert a coruscating piece of her mind and successfully wiped the smirk off his face.

"Which I did," she told Finn now, in the restaurant on Monday lunchtime. "Thanks to you."

He grinned. "My pleasure. Lucky he had an unusual name."

"Lucky you remembered it," said Ginny.

By delicious coincidence, Finn had actually met Elizabeth Derris-Beck eighteen months ago when she had come into his shop in London to sell her old engagement ring. Well-spoken, charming, and accompanied by her young daughters, she had relayed the whole story of her miserable first marriage and told Finn how deliriously happy she was now with her new man and new life. The ring had been a serious square-cut emerald flanked by top quality diamonds.

When the necessary paperwork had been completed, Elizabeth had hugged her girls and said cheerfully, "That's us off to Lapland to see Father Christmas. And the rest goes toward a new car."

"She sent me a photo of the four of them in a sleigh outside Santa's house," Finn added. "And a note thanking me for buying the ring. She said they'd had the best holiday of their lives."

"Maybe next year you and Tamsin could take Mae." Ginny felt funny saying it; next year was a long time ahead.

"Maybe. So your weekend was a success."

"Wonderful. Davy and Lucy are fantastic. We had a picnic on the beach yesterday, and a sandcastle competition. Lucy and Jem went swimming. Davy's phone hasn't stopped with friends calling to talk to him about how he saved Marcus McBride's life. It's done wonders for his confidence. I feel as proud as if he were my own son. And then last night I drove them back to Bristol. Jem's going to be fine, I know it. They'll look after her."

"That's good news. You must be relieved," said Finn.

Ginny smiled and nodded, because he sounded as if he really cared. And he was right; it was a happy ending. But what she couldn't tell him was that arriving back in Portsilver at midnight had been a depressing experience; Laurel was upstairs asleep and the house had seemed unbearably quiet. She had gone to bed feeling empty, lonely, and bereft all over again, unable to stop herself thinking, *What about me?*

Chapter 46

"STOP OGLING THE BOSS."

Ginny jumped, unaware that Evie had emerged from the restaurant kitchen. "I wasn't!"

"Yes you were." Evie's eyes danced. "Mind you, I can't say I blame you. Gorgeous shoulders. Spectacular bum."

"Shhh." Did Evie have to be quite so loud? Finn was only twenty feet away, showing out the last diners of the afternoon. And now he was closing the door, turning to see what all the shushing was about.

"What's going on?"

"Nothing." Evie, who had no shame, said, "We were just admiring your body."

"*You* were," said Ginny, glasses clinking as she indignantly gathered them up.

"Fine, I was admiring. You were ogling."

"I wasn't. I was thinking about Jem." Keen to change the subject, Ginny said, "She phoned this morning to tell me her tutor's really pleased with all the work she's put in over the last couple of

420

weeks. He thinks she might scrape through her exams after all."

"That's great news." Evie knew how worried she'd been about Jem. "But I still know an ogle when I see one. I have an eye for these things."

Not to mention a mouth. What a shame it couldn't be zipped shut. "You want to get out more." Ginny, clanking past with her hands full of glasses, said, "Some of us have more important things to think about than men's bodies."

Finn raised his eyebrows. "Even mine?"

The kitchen was empty apart from Tom, the washer-upper, busy at the sink.

"You look hot." He surveyed Ginny's hectically pink cheeks.

She took extra care unloading the glasses, giving herself time to recover. "Just busy, Tom."

God, life would be so much easier if only she didn't have this overheating problem.

OK, life would be so much easier if only she could get over this hopeless, pointless, *ridiculous* crush.

As if to hammer the point home, just as she headed back to the dining room, the front door opened and Tamsin burst into the restaurant with Mae on her hip.

"I'm in love." Tamsin's eyes were shining.

Which was the kind of announcement that might have got Ginny's hopes up, except that in her free hand Tamsin was waving some kind of glossy brochure. Rushing over to Finn, she gave him a don't-smudge-my-lipstick kiss and said, "Darling, you have to see it. Six bedrooms, sea views, Clive Christian kitchen, and an en suite bathroom to die for. It's the house of our dreams, a proper family home. I told the agent we'd meet him there at five o'clock."

"Six bedrooms." Finn studied the brochure in alarm. "Jesus, have you seen how much they're asking for it?"

"That's only a guide price; we can make an offer." Eagerly pointing to the photos, Tamsin said, "Look at the billiard room. And that garden! And six bedrooms aren't so many when this is the rest of our lives we're talking about." She turned her bewitching smile on him. "After all, you know we don't want Mae to be an only child."

Ginny felt a bit sick, but there was no escaping their domestic bliss. Tamsin insisted on showing her and Evie the brochure, cooing delightedly over every detail of the house and explaining how unsuitable the flat was now that Mae was walking.

"We have to get it. It's just perfect." Swishing back her long hair, Tamsin gave Ginny a sympathetic look. "Yours is only semidetached, isn't it? I bet you'd love to live in a house like this?"

Ginny wondered what Tamsin would do if she said, "Yes, but only if I could live in it with Finn."

Obviously she didn't say it. Heavens, what was the matter with her today? Half an hour ago she'd been quietly ogling Finn from a distance. (Wouldn't Evie be delighted to know she'd been right?) And now here she was, fantasizing about making smart remarks to her rival.

Except Tamsin wasn't a rival, was she? Tamsin was having a proper grown-up relationship with Finn, rather than a sad, not-proper-at-all fantasy one.

Dutifully Ginny said, "It looks wonderful."

"Dadadablaaa," sang Mae, clapping her hands at Finn.

"You want to go to Daddy? Here, you take her. She weighs a ton." Having passed Mae over to him, Tamsin gazed raptly at the two of them, then back at the photograph of the house. "How could any child not be happy, growing up in a place like this?"

Driving home from the restaurant, Ginny resolved to get a grip, put the whole Finn thing behind her, and get on with her life. Let's face it, she wasn't the first woman ever to have a one-off fling with her very attractive boss and she certainly wouldn't be the last.

Anyway, think positive, now it was time to move on. Absolutely. Make the most of what she had, which was a lot. Healthy happy daughter. A job she enjoyed. A nice house, even if Tamsin probably felt sorry for her having to live in such a shoebox. And there were so many other things to take pleasure in too, like art, books, walking on the beach, listening to music . . .

Feeling more positive already, Ginny buzzed down the car windows and made a conscious decision to find joy in those small things in life that it was only too easy to overlook, like the sunshine warming her face and those delicious little white clouds dotting the sky. Cornwall was beautiful. She was wearing her favorite white angora sweater, which looked a tiny bit like a cloud and hadn't gone bobbly yet. David Gray was singing on the radio and she loved David Gray, especially the way he wobbled his head. Turning up the volume, Ginny was tempted to sing along, but that might spoil it; the last thing David needed was her caterwauling mucking up his beautiful, heartfelt vocals. She'd just listen instead and think of other miraculous things like the velvety smoothness of pebbles, the crumbly deliciousness of Laurel's lemon drizzle cake, the incomparable sight of dolphins frolicking in the sea off Portsilver Point, the smell of hot tarmac . . .

Oh yes, hot tarmac, one of the all-time greats. And what a good job she hadn't been bellowing along to the radio. Having rounded the bend, Ginny slowed to a halt and beamed at the middle-aged man holding the Stop/Go lollipop sign currently directing her to Stop. Little did he imagine what a lucky escape he'd just had, not having been forced to hear her singing voice.

Ahead of him, two more council workers busily got on with the business of tarmacking a rectangular patch on the left-hand side of the road. A bus and a couple of cars passed through on the other side.

"Lovely day," Ginny called over to the lollipop man, who was wrinkled and leathery from long years in the sun.

"Too nice to be working." He beamed back at her, evidently a cheery soul. Well, why wouldn't he be, able to enjoy the smell of fresh tarmac all day long? With a flourish he swiveled the lollipop sign round to Go and Ginny gave him a little wave as she set off, breathing in deeply in order not to miss a single lungful of the hot, tarry deliciousness.

All too soon the moment was past, the joy behind her. Sniffing the air, desperate for one last hit and not finding it, Ginny was bereft. Half a mile further down the road and unable to bear it a second longer, she pulled into a driveway and rapidly reversed the car. It was no good; you couldn't open a bag of Maltesers and only eat one, could you? Exactly. And if she wanted to go back and experience the smell of tar again . . . well, was there anything wrong with that? Crikey, it wasn't against the law. And, unlike Maltesers, it didn't have any calories. It was one of life's harmless pleasures, for heaven's sake. What's more, it was free.

The lollipop man looked momentarily surprised when he saw her. As luck would have it, Ginny again found herself up against the Stop sign.

"You again?" He winked at her. "Are you stalking me? Look, I'd love to meet up with you for a drink but my old lady would have my guts for garters."

Ginny grinned, because guts for garters always conjured up a wonderfully bizarre image in her mind. Then she got on with the serious business of inhaling the tar fumes which were, if such a thing was possible, even more irresistible this time. In fact, would it be possible to buy some tarmac from these men? Would they think she was weird if she asked them? And if they said no, maybe she could come back after they'd gone, like tonight under cover of darkness, and just dig up a little bit of tar before it set solid?

"Forget something, did you?" Lollipop man nodded genially. "Bad as my old lady. She'd forget her head if it wasn't screwed on."

Jolly banter over, he swiveled the lollipop and waved Ginny through for the second time. She breathed in the addictive scent of the tar as she passed it being spread like glossy, sticky jam on the other side of the road.

Moments later the elusive sense of familiarity finally clicked into place in her brain and Ginny realized when she had last been enthralled by the smell, so long ago now that it simply hadn't registered before. There had been major road repairs going on outside the offices she'd been working in at the time and everyone else had grumbled constantly about the disruption, the smells, and the noise. But she had loved it all so much that she'd taken to sitting outside on the wall during her lunch breaks, watching the goings-on and eating her sandwiches.

Actually, *guzzling* her sandwiches, because that was when she'd been . . .

When she'd been . . .

Oh no, no, surely not . . .

Somehow, on autopilot, Ginny managed to park the car at only a slightly wonky angle in the town's central car park. When she climbed out, her legs almost gave way. OK, collapsing in a heap would just waste time and be an embarrassment. Girding herself, she clutched her handbag and headed for the shops.

At the threshold of the pharmacy, she stopped. The assistants knew her here; she'd spent many a happy hour browsing in the aisles, trying eye shadows on the back of her hand, and choosing lipsticks. What would they think if they saw her come in and buy a . . . no, she'd have to go somewhere else.

There was another smaller pharmacy in St. Aldam's Square that didn't stock any makeup so she'd never visited it before. Having done the deed, Ginny emerged and hurried away, checking left and right as she went, making sure there was no one around who might recognize her and demand to know what was in her bag.

The public lavatories weren't ideal but getting home wasn't an option; that would take fifteen minutes and she had to know now. And they were at least very nice public lavatories, scrupulously clean and freshly painted, with bright hanging baskets of flowers outside.

Locking herself in the far cubicle, Ginny trembled as she unwrapped the packet and read the instructions. She peed on the stick and closed her eyes, waiting for the chemicals to do their thing. Outside the cubicle she could hear a mother struggling with a baby in a stroller and simultaneously trying to persuade her young daughter to wash her hands.

"Come on, Megan, be a good girl, don't splash."

"It's water!"

"I know, darling, but Thomas doesn't like it. Just keep the water away from him."

Time was up. Ginny opened her eyes and looked at the stick thing.

Oh God.

Oh *God*.

Outside, a scuffle ensued, accompanied by the sound of vigorous splashing and the outraged wails of a small baby. Ginny gazed blankly at the gray door of her cubicle and heard Megan giggling in triumph, her mission accomplished. The baby, evidently drenched, emitted ear-splitting howls of protest.

Megan's mother said with resignation, "Oh, you silly girl, look what you've done now. *That's* not very clever, is it?"

You're telling me, thought Ginny.

Chapter 47

GAVIN DIDN'T MIND HAVING his bottom pinched. In fact he positively welcomed it. He just hadn't been expecting it to happen as he threaded his way along a crowded street in Padstow.

"Hello, stranger!" He threw out his arms and gave Bev a kiss, delighted to see her. "I was hoping it'd be someone young, female, and dazzlingly gorgeous."

Bev, her smile lopsided, said, "Oh well, one out of three isn't bad."

"Don't give me that. You wouldn't want to be twenty-one again. And for an older woman you're looking great." Gavin admired her shiny dark hair, scarlet dress, and voluptuous figure.

"And you still haven't signed up for those How to be a Diplomat evening classes."

He beamed. "I'm set in my ways. There's no hope for me. Anyway, fancy bumping into you here. We've missed you at the club."

Bev shrugged. "I gave up waiting for George Clooney to join. He must have had problems getting his visa. Anyway, you're looking well." She admired Gavin's suit. "Who'd have thought you could look so smart? I almost didn't recognize you without one of your loud shirts on."

"Business. Long boring meeting with a short boring client. How about you?"

"Much more fun. A very unboring meeting with a rather exciting new friend." Bev's eyes sparkled as she moved back to the table she'd been sitting at when she'd jumped up to surprise him.

"Excellent. Can I meet her?"

"Very funny. It's a male friend." Indicating with pride the empty beer bottle on the table next to her almost finished glass of wine, Bev said, "But you're more than welcome to stay and say hello. We're having a couple of drinks here before going on to dinner at the Blue Moon. He's just gone inside to buy the next round."

"So you've found someone you like at last." It was pretty obvious from the way her whole face was lit up that she was smitten.

"I know! Can you believe it? I stopped going to the club and told myself that from now on, if it was going to happen, it'd happen." Bev clicked her fingers and beamed at him. "And bam, a few weeks down the line, it did happen. Which just goes to show: you don't have to schlep along to singles evenings or join a gym or buy a dog and take it for walks so you can get chatting to other people with dogs. Guess how we met!"

"You took a job as a stripper."

"Gavin, you philistine, how did I ever fancy you? I was weeding my front garden! On my hands and knees with my big bum in the air, pulling up dandelions."

Gavin the Philistine wisely kept his thoughts to himself. But it was undeniably an enticing mental image.

"When this guy who was walking past stopped at my gate."

Of course he did, thought Gavin the Philistine.

"He was lost," Bev went on. "He asked me for directions to Lancaster Road."

Oh yes, classic maneuver.

"Which was back the way he'd just come from, so we had a laugh about that."

Naturally.

"And then somehow we just clicked." Bev clicked her fingers to demonstrate. "It was incredible; we just carried on talking and didn't stop. There was this incredible . . . God, *chemistry*."

Total pro.

"After about an hour, he asked me if I'd like to meet him for a drink that evening. And that was it. I said yes, of course. We went out and had the most amazing time. It was as if we'd known each other for ever," Bev said dreamily. "At last, I'd found my perfect man. He's so kind and such a gentleman, so interested in *me*. It's almost too good to be true. This is only our third date—I can't believe it's only our third date!—but I've just got this *feeling* about Perry, I really think this could be—"

"Whoa," Gavin abruptly halted her. "What did you say?"

"It's only our third date. We met last Sunday."

"Never mind that. Is his name Perry Kennedy?"

"Oh my God, yes it *is!*" Bev clapped her hands in delight. "Do you know him?"

Up until that moment Gavin had simply recognized Bev's new chap as a fellow womanizer, a man after his own heart, and where was the harm in that? Now, like plunging into the sea in diving boots, it struck him that there *was* harm in it. He hoped he wasn't as bad as Perry Kennedy. He did it because he had the attention span of a gnat, but he'd never deliberately set out to deceive a woman. He'd never been cold and calculating in his life.

Bev, her smile wavering, said, "Why are you looking at me like that?"

"I know him. He's bad news. A fake." Since there was no kind way to say it, Gavin didn't waste time wondering how to soften the blow. "He went out with Ginny, duped her, played her for a fool. She found out he was shagging her best friend. And it turned out he's done it a thousand times before."

Poor old Bev, the smile had well and truly melted from her face. Shock radiated from her. And any minute now, Perry would emerge from the bar with their drinks.

"I hate him for what he did to Ginny," Gavin went on. "He broke her heart"—OK, bit of an exaggeration—"and he'll break yours too."

God, he hoped she wasn't about to burst into tears.

But Bev was made of sterner stuff. She exhaled slowly and sat back in her chair.

"Sorry, darling. I couldn't not tell you."

"Story of my life. I suppose I should be used to it by now. If something seems too good to be true, it probably is. And there was me, thinking my luck had changed." She exhaled. "Thinking I was irresistible."

"Sweetheart, you are." For an older woman anyway, Gavin allowed. "All the more reason not to get involved with a liar like that. Trust me; he's all pain and no gain. You need to cut and run."

Bev glanced down at her shoes. "Easier said than done in these heels."

She was wearing red strappy four-inch stilettos adorned with butterflies, the shoes of a woman out to impress the new man in her life. Quite sexy, actually.

Gavin said, "You could always take them off."

"Oh God, why does this have to happen to me?" Bev glanced over her shoulder to see if Perry was on his way out.

"It doesn't only happen to you. Men like him need teaching a lesson."

"Pot." Her tone was dry. "Kettle."

"Ouch. That's me put in my place." Gavin's eyes crinkled at the corners. "I'd better get off, leave you to it."

"Where are you going?"

"To get something to eat. Probably not at the Blue Moon." He paused, watching Bev make up her mind. "Why?"

She shrugged. "Could you do with some company?"

"Only if you promise not to keep nagging me about my terrible ways."

Bev slipped her feet out of her stilettos, stood up, and drained her glass of wine. "And you aren't allowed to keep saying you could quite fancy me if only I wasn't so old. Just for once, try and be nice to me, OK? I'm a woman in crisis."

Gavin winked and said, "My favorite kind."

The queue at the bar had been ridiculous. Having finally been served, Perry emerged with a drink in each hand. Bev was nowhere to be seen.

What was this, a clip from *You've Been Framed*? He paused, peering around. The table at which he and Bev had been sitting was now occupied by a family of four. Approaching them, Perry learned that it had been free when they'd got here.

He scanned the rest of the drinkers gathered outside. No one else was wearing a red dress. Had Bev gone inside to the loo and somehow managed to slip past him unnoticed?

Yet more waiting. She didn't return. Feeling increasingly foolish, Perry finally approached the group of office workers at the table behind the one now occupied by the family of four. "Um . . . excuse me, did any of you notice what happened to the lady who was sitting over there? Dark hair, red dress . . ."

"She pulled." A freckled, tufty-haired boy grinned at his friends.

"Warren." The girl next to him gave him a nudge. "You can't say that."

"Why not? It's true."

"What do you mean?" Perry's shoulders stiffened.

"She was sitting there on her own. Then this guy walked past. The next moment she jumped up and launched herself at him. Pinched his bum and everything. They were all over each other."

"They talked for a bit," the girl at his side elaborated, "then walked off together down the road."

"He was carrying her shoes," a second girl chimed in. "Kind of like Cinderella, only the other way round."

The freckled boy looked scornful. "So, not like Cinderella at all then. More like he's got some pervy fetish thing for shoes."

"She just went off with him?" Perry blinked in disbelief. "What did he look like?"

"Forties. A bit overweight. Losing his hair at the front. Not exactly Pierce Brosnan." The first girl shrugged then said thoughtfully, "He had a nice smile though. And sparkly eyes. He looked quite . . . fun."

The boy sniggered. "She obviously thought he was fun."

Perry was in a state of disbelief. Bev had abandoned him for another man who wasn't even that good-looking. Gone off with him just like that, without so much as a good-bye.

How could she?

He'd never been so humiliated in his life.

Bev was smiling to herself.

"What?" said Gavin.

"I've just realized something." She turned onto her side to face him. "I bet I'm the oldest person you've ever slept with."

"By a mile. But you know what? It wasn't as scary as I thought."

"Cheek!" Bev hooked one of her bare legs over his.

"It's a compliment. Seriously." In return Gavin pulled her against him. "You know a lot of tricks."

"Years of practice. Almost as many as you. And a man in his forties is past his sexual peak. Whereas *I*"—she trailed the tips of her fingernails in tantalizing circles along his inner thigh—"am a woman in my prime."

"Past my peak? Now that's a slur I'm going to have to disprove." He rolled her over, intent on making his point, but Bev wriggled away before he could pin her down.

"No time now. It's eight o'clock. I have to be at work by nine."

This was frustrating but true. Neither of them had expected last night to end the way it had. Following dinner in Padstow, Gavin had invited Bev back to his house in Portsilver for a nightcap. At first they had talked about Perry Kennedy. Then they'd stopped talking about him, because that was just depressing, and had moved on to other subjects instead. It was at this point that Gavin had realized how refreshing it was to be able to hold a flirtatious conversation with someone who had a brain, intellectual curiosity, and a quick wit. Bev was terrific company; she made him laugh and she didn't look blank when he mentioned Nixon and Watergate. She knew who Siouxie Sioux was. She remembered a world before mobile phones. When it came to singing Duran Duran, she was word perfect.

OK, not everything they'd discussed had been intellectual.

After that, the rest had just happened. He'd been making coffee in the kitchen and Bev had been spooning sugar into his cup. His hand had accidentally brushed against hers and she'd jumped, spilling sugar all over the work surface. Amused, Gavin had said, "Do I really have that effect on you?"

"Yes," said Bev. "You do."

"When we were outside that wine bar, you said you used to fancy me. Was that a joke?"

She shook her head. "No, it was the truth."

"You never said anything." Gavin was enchanted by her honesty.

"No point. I couldn't turn myself into a twenty-two-year-old."

The last twenty-two-year-old of Gavin's acquaintance had been talking about this summer's V Festival. When Gavin had proudly informed her that he'd been at the original Live Aid concert, she'd trilled excitedly, "Oh wicked, we learned all about that at school in history!"

The next thing he knew, he'd found himself kissing Bev. Sugar crystals had scrunched underfoot as they'd clung to each other. The coffee had been abandoned; the spilled sugar was still there. Last night had been a revelation, all the better for being so unexpected. Sex with Bev was a joy.

A repeat performance would have been nice but she was out of bed now, hurriedly dressing in order to shoot home and shower and change before heading off to work.

In no time at all she was ready to leave. Gavin realized he didn't want her to go. When she gave him a good-bye kiss, he said, "What are you doing tonight?"

"Me? Nothing. Watching *Last of the Summer Wine*. Polishing my walker. Looking through my Thora Hird scrapbook." Bev shrugged. "How about you?"

"Well, if you could bear to give *Last of the Summer Wine* a miss, I could demonstrate that I'm not past my sexual peak."

Her eyes searched his face. "Would that be to prove it to me, or to yourself?"

"Hey, I want to see you again. I wasn't expecting this to happen and neither were you. But it has." He surveyed the tiny lines at the corners of her eyes and realized they gave her face character. Reaching up to touch the side of her jaw—at least she wasn't jowly; he *really* couldn't handle that—Gavin said, "And I'm glad it's happened."

"You're not just saying that to be kind, to cheer me up?"

"I promise you, I'm not that unselfish. So, Moneypenny, are you coming over here at seven o'clock tonight or not?"

"Coming over here for what?"

Gavin did his best Sean Connery impression. "I

439

thought maybe rampant sex and toasted cheese sandwiches."

"Oh well, if you put it like that." Bev's dark eyes danced as she kissed him on the nose. "I suppose I could always record *Last of the Summer Wine.*"

Chapter 48

THE POSTMAN HAD DELIVERED a hat trick of envelopes together with a small recorded delivery parcel addressed to Laurel. Ginny carried them through to the kitchen and opened the first envelope.

Electricity bill, fabulous.

The second was water rates, great.

The third was a bank statement. As ever, Ginny fantasized that this would be the one containing an outrageously vast sum that had accidentally been credited to her account instead of somebody else's, but—and this was the best bit—the person who should have received the money was so rich that he never realized he hadn't. Like when Sting, eons ago, hadn't noticed several million pounds being fraudulently siphoned from his account. Imagine that. And who was to say that a completely innocent computer blip couldn't do the same for her?

Sadly a quick skim through the statement

revealed that yet another month had passed and it hadn't happened.

Even more sadly, her balance was less than it should have been. Checking through more carefully, Ginny saw what was missing.

"Laurel?"

Laurel appeared in the doorway. "Yes?"

"Your rent hasn't gone through yet. Could you have a word with Perry, see what's happened?"

"Oh." Laurel shifted awkwardly, not meeting her gaze. "Um . . . he can't afford to pay it anymore."

"Excuse me?"

"Sorry. I meant to tell you." Laurel's tone was defensive; she'd clearly known for a while.

"So who is going to be paying it?"

"I don't know."

Ginny shook her head in disbelief. As if she didn't have enough to worry about. The past couple of weeks had seen Laurel slipping back into her old neurotic ways as the date of Kevin's birthday had approached. Laurel had for some reason convinced herself that Kevin would choose this date to come back to her. When it didn't happen, her misery had been of epic proportions. That had been a week ago and Ginny had done her best to sympathize, but now her patience was running out.

"Look, I have bills to pay." The words came out clipped and irritated. "Jem isn't working anymore so I'm having to help her too. You can't expect me to say, 'Oh well, never mind, maybe we'll have a lucky night at the Bingo.' If Perry's not paying your rent anymore, you'll have to pay it yourself."

With her pale green eyes, Laurel had never looked more like Ophelia. "But I don't have any money."

The knicker elastic of Ginny's patience finally snapped. "Then you'll just have to do what normal people do and get yourself a job!"

Laurel flinched as if she'd been slapped. "I can't."

"You *can*," Ginny shot back, "you just don't *want* to. And I'm sorry, but if you don't pay your rent, you aren't staying here. Because you aren't the only one with problems, OK? Things are pretty crap for me as well right now, but somehow or other I have to get on with it, because that's life."

Laurel welled up. She glanced at the small parcel on the kitchen table.

"That's yours. It came just now." Ginny eyed it jealously; how come Laurel got sent a parcel while all she got was stinking rotten bills?

"Thanks."

"Open it, then."

"Later."

Oh, for heaven's sake, what was the great mystery? It wasn't big enough to be a vibrator.

Too het up by this stage to even care that she was being unreasonable, Ginny barked, "Open the damn parcel!"

Miserably Laurel did as she was told. Her chin began to wobble as the wrappings came off.

Ginny's eyes widened. "Somebody's sent you a Gucci watch!"

"No."

"You mean you bought it for yourself?" Bloody hell, how much did a Gucci watch cost?

"If you must know," Laurel blurted out defensively, "I bought it for Kevin. I thought it would make him love me again. He's always wanted a Gucci watch." She unfolded the accompanying note, scanned the few lines, and crumpled it in her hand. "But not from me. I can't believe he sent it back. Oh God, why can't I ever get *anything* right?"

Ginny's own hormones were jangling. "Look, I thought you'd stopped all this. It's crazy, Laurel. Kevin's never going to love you again. He's never going to come back. It's over and you have to accept that." Before Laurel could start sobbing, she added hastily, "And look on the bright side. You can take the watch back to the shop and get a refund."

And pay your rent with it hopefully.

"I can't." Laurel sniffed and gazed mournfully down at the watch.

"You can! Unless it's a fake one." Ginny peered

more closely; actually, if it was a fake she wouldn't mind one for herself.

Laurel was outraged. "Of course it's not a fake! What kind of person do you think I am?"

Was she serious? "Well, obviously the kind of person who spends hundreds of pounds she doesn't have on someone who doesn't want anything from her. For crying out loud, just take it back to the shop and get a refund!"

"I told you, I can't. I bought the watch three weeks ago." Laurel fiddled with the dangly, too-long sleeves of her sage-green cardigan. "They only give you your money back if you return it within fourteen days."

God. Exasperated, Ginny said, "Next time, go to a department store and buy him a pair of socks."

"I'm sorry. I love him." Tears were once more sliding down Laurel's colorless cheeks. "I just don't know what to do anymore."

"Don't you?" It was knicker-snapping time again. With an embryo in her stomach and bills strewn across the kitchen table, Ginny felt the elastic go *twaannggg.* Her voice spiraling, she yelped, "Seriously, don't you? Because I can tell you. You have to forget Kevin and stop feeling so sorry for yourself. You need to sort out your life and start acting like an adult. And if you want to carry on living in this house, you have to get out there and find yourself a job."

Ginny took a deep breath. Crikey, had she really

just said all that? From the way Laurel stifled a horrified sob, ricocheted off the doorway, and stumbled out of the kitchen, it rather seemed as if she had.

Upstairs in Jem's bedroom, Ginny sat in front of the computer scrolling through images of embryos in the womb. Her own, she discovered, had by now developed fingers and toes and a face of sorts—albeit with huge alien eyes and low-slung ears. It also had a sense of smell (how could they *tell?*), a pituitary gland in its brain, and a tiny heart pumping away in its chest.

Oh God, she really was having a baby. One reckless moment and this was the life-changing result, how could she have been so—

"Um, hello?" A cautious tap was followed by Laurel pushing open the bedroom door. Ginny pounced on the mouse and fired frantically at the page-closer like a demented person on a rifle range, finally managing to clear the screen a millisecond before Laurel came into the room.

Prickling with adrenaline, she said, *"What?"*

Laurel flinched. "Sorry. Um, I'm just going out to the pharmacy to pick up my prescription. I wondered if there was anything you wanted while I was there."

Well, let's see, how about some nipple cream and a tube of that stuff that stops you getting stretch marks on your stomach when it's the size of a beach ball? And how about a box of breast pads, a thousand packs of nappies, and some teething biscuits? Oh God, actually she quite fancied a couple of Farley's rusks . . .

"No thanks."

"Oh. OK." Pause. "I'm really sorry about . . . you know, the rent."

Ginny steeled herself; Laurel knew she was a soft touch. Well, not this time. Stiffly she replied, "So you keep saying."

Her ploy evidently thwarted, Laurel's face fell. "Anyway, I'll be back in half an hour." She twisted the doorknob this way and that. "And I'm going to sort everything out. I promise."

Talk about emotional blackmail. Ginny refused to give in. Turning back to the computer she said, "Good."

Three hours later there was still no sign of Laurel. Ginny unloaded the washing from the tumble dryer and carried the basket of dry clothes upstairs. It was unlike Laurel to be gone for so long, but it hadn't been an ordinary day; maybe she'd gone into town to visit the Job Center or to see Perry.

By the time she'd finished sorting out the clothes, Laurel still hadn't returned. Her conscience by now beginning to prick, Ginny let herself into Laurel's bedroom in search of a clue as to where she might have gone.

The sunshine-yellow room was incredibly neat, like something out of a show home. Apart from the handbag on the bed, nothing was out of place. Laurel's handbag. Ginny frowned at the sight of it; surely when you left the house to go to the shops you took your handbag with you? Unless Laurel had decided to swap handbags for coordination purposes (which was, frankly, unlikely) and had emptied the contents of this one into another that went better with her sludge-brown dress and green cardigan?

But no, picking up the handbag, she discovered it was full of Laurel's things. *All* her things, including her purse and credit cards.

That was a bit weird, wasn't it?

Her heart beating a little faster, Ginny pulled open the drawers of the chest next to Laurel's bed. The first drawer contained underwear, ironed and folded and in no way resembling the tangle of bras and knickers that comprised Ginny's own collection. The second held tights and petticoats, again arranged as pristinely as if they were part of a shop display.

The bottom drawer contained several framed photographs of Kevin (who was so not worth all this angst and grief); the box containing the Gucci watch; an old, navy, man-sized lamb's wool sweater with holes in both elbows; and a pale gray leather-bound diary.

Ginny swallowed. Should she? Shouldn't she?

She had sneaked a look at someone else's diary once before. It hadn't been a happy experience, learning that: "Mum thinks she's a good dancer but she's really embarrassing, all my friends were laughing at her at the school Christmas dance." Followed by: "I wish Mum would buy proper name tapes for my school uniform; I'm the only one with my name in marker pen. Mrs. Hegarty (I hate her) was all sneery and said doesn't your mother know how to sew?"

Ginny prickled with shame at the memory. By the time she'd finished sewing on thirty-two Cash's name tapes and ended up with fingers like pincushions she had hated Mrs. Hegarty too.

And after the way she'd lost her temper with Laurel this morning, she was unlikely to read anything complimentary about herself now. More like: "Ginny Holland is a cold, selfish, money-obsessed witch who never dusts her skirting boards or irons her knickers."

Either way, this was Laurel's private diary, and she really shouldn't read it. Moving over to the bedroom window, Ginny peered out; nothing would make her happier than to see Laurel making her way down the street, heading home. Then she could put the diary back where she'd found it and avoid having to read uncomplimentary remarks about herself.

But the road was empty; there was still no sign of Laurel in her long dress and droopy cardigan.

She'd been gone for more than three hours. Without her handbag.

Feeling increasingly uneasy, Ginny opened the diary, flicking through dozens of densely written pages until she reached the most recent entry.

There were splodgy teardrops on the paper. Laurel had written:

> Kevin sent back the watch with a letter telling me not to contact him again. Ginny found out about the rent not being paid and went mad. I know she doesn't want me here anymore. She said if I don't get a job I'll have to move out, but how can I get a job when I feel like this? She doesn't understand. No one does.
>
> It's pointless. I can't carry on like this. I hate the person I've become. I know what I have to do and now's the time to do it.
>
> Good-bye, Kevin, I loved you so much. Enjoy your life. And don't worry, I won't be bothering you again.

Chapter 49

GINNY COLLAPSED ON THE perfectly made bed, shaking. Her mouth was so dry she couldn't swallow and there was a loud drumming noise in her ears. Oh God, this was so much worse than she'd imagined. The tear stains on the page were dry; Laurel had written these words over three hours ago, before leaving the house empty-handed.

Her heart clattering against her rib cage, Ginny reread the words. There was no mistaking Laurel's intention. She could be dead already, floating in the sea or lying in a battered heap at the foot of the cliffs. Or she could have gone to the pharmacy to collect her prescription for antidepressants and be taking them right now, grimly swallowing every last tablet in the bottle . . .

God, how could she have shouted at someone who'd been prescribed antidepressants? Snatches of what had been said zip-zapped accusingly through her brain.

Stop feeling sorry for yourself. Sort out your life. Kevin's never going to come back. He doesn't *want* you. Next time go to a department store and buy a pair of socks.

And what had been Laurel's last words to her before miserably leaving the house?

"I'm going to sort everything out. I promise."

Shakily, Ginny realized that she might as well have handed over the loaded gun herself. Laurel had come to her expecting sympathy and understanding, and had got yelled at by an over-hormonal harpy instead.

Ginny stood up, hyperventilating and feeling sicker than ever.

She knew what she had to do now.

• • •

Ner-ner-ner-ner-ner-ner-ner.

Come on.

Ner-ner-ner-ner-ner.

Oh please, please don't do this now. Just start, damn you.

Ner-ner-ner, ner-ner, ner-ner, ner-ner.

Ginny wiped a slick of perspiration from her upper lip and frenziedly pumped the accelerator, her stomach clenching as the rate of the ner-ners decreased.

Ner . . . ner . . . ner . . . ner . . .

Click.

Panting, she leaped out onto the pavement and tried to figure out what to do next. But what else was there to do? She jumped back in and tried again, praying that her car would take pity on her and summon all its energy for one last go.

Click.

Damn car. Ginny thumped the steering wheel and closed her eyes in despair.

A knock on the driver's window made her jump. Her heart plummeted when she saw who was standing next to the car.

"I've got a charger if you want to borrow it."

"What?" The unexpectedness of the encounter had caused Ginny's brain to go temporarily blank.

"Your battery's flat," said Carla. "You left your headlights on last night."

"What?" Ginny stared at the switch on the dash

and realized it was true. "You mean you *saw* my headlights were on and you did *nothing?*"

Carla stiffened. "You said you never wanted to speak to me again. I only came over here now because you look a bit agitated."

A *bit* agitated? "Oh fine. So if you'd seen me being run over by a bus last night you'd have left me lying in the road? Thanks a lot. You knew I'd have a flat battery today but you just . . . just . . ." Ginny bashed the steering wheel again, unable to look at Carla with her swingy geometric bob, pink power suit, and flawless makeup.

"Look, I said I'd lend you my charger."

"That's no good, that'll take hours. I need the car"—another thump—"*now.*"

"OK, if it's that urgent, I'll give you a lift. Where are you going?"

"I DON'T KNOW." Ginny let out a bellow of panicky despair. "That's the thing: you can't give me a lift because I don't know where I'm going. I just know I've got to try and find her before . . . oh God, before it's too l-late . . ."

"Right, get out of the car." Carla snatched the keys from the ignition, hauled Ginny out onto the pavement, and said briskly, "We'll go in mine and it doesn't matter how long it takes. Is she in Bristol?"

"What?" Ginny found herself being propelled across the road and into Carla's car; half of her didn't want this to be happening, while the other half acknowledged she didn't have a lot of choice. "Why would she be in Bristol?"

Carla looked at her. "Is this not Jem we're talking about?"

"No, no. It's Laurel." Shaking her head, Ginny spilled out what had happened this morning.

Carla, having listened in silence, said, "Shouldn't you phone the police?"

"I did! But Laurel hadn't written 'I am going to kill myself' so they just said wait and see if she turns up. You can't report an adult as missing until they've been gone for twenty-four hours. It's all right for them," Ginny said with frustration, "but how do they think I feel? It's all my fault."

"Don't blame yourself. If it's any comfort," said Carla, "I'd have pushed her off a cliff months ago. So where to?"

She was all ready to begin the search. Helplessly Ginny said, "Anywhere. Everywhere. The pharmacy, I suppose. The doctor's office. The Job Center, maybe."

"Tuh." Carla snorted in disbelief as they set off down the road. "In your dreams."

"Don't say that." Oh God, what if Laurel was already dead? With a shudder Ginny went on, "We could drive up to the cliffs. Or try the beach, ask the lifeguards if they've seen her. She was wearing her brown dress when she left the house."

"Long thin female, long red hair, long brown dress."

"And I suppose we should check with Perry. She could be with him." Ginny felt sick at the thought of explaining to Perry what had happened if Laurel wasn't there. Carla could do that.

"He's not living in Portsilver anymore. And he's changed his number." Carla paused then said bluntly, "It's over between me and Perry. I haven't seen him for weeks."

"You're kidding." For a second Ginny forgot about Laurel. "Why, what happened?"

"It's just over, that's all. I'll tell you later." Keeping her gaze fixed on the road ahead, Carla said, "For now let's just concentrate on finding Laurel."

They didn't find her. The four hours she had been missing became five, and five stretched into six. No one had seen Laurel anywhere; she hadn't been to the pharmacy to collect her pills, and there had been no sightings of her either along the cliff top or on the beach.

"Well, that's good news," said Carla, attempting to cheer Ginny up. "At least they haven't pulled any bodies out of the sea."

But this was no consolation. Laurel was still missing and in a desperately vulnerable state. Having left a message on the kitchen table for Laurel to call her mobile the minute she got back, Ginny nevertheless punched in her home number for the hundredth time and listened to it ringing in an empty house. It was hideously selfish and she was ashamed of herself for even thinking about it, but if Laurel was dead and the police read what was written in her diary, would she be held partly to blame for the tragedy, possibly even charged with manslaughter?

"Do you need the loo?"

Ginny realized she had her hand resting on her stomach. Abruptly banishing the mental image of herself giving birth in prison—in handcuffs and without pain relief—she snatched it away. "No, I'm OK."

"Where next?"

"Sadler's Cove, we haven't tried there yet."

"Right," Carla announced an hour later, "that's enough. I could have carried on longer, but not in these shoes."

Her impeccable black leather high heels were dusty and scuffed from scrambling down the narrow stony path to Sadler's Cove. Clouds had obliterated the sun and everyone was now leaving the beach for the day. Hollow with fear, it occurred to Ginny that when they arrived back at the house, there could be somber-faced police officers on the doorstep waiting to break the worst possible news.

But when they finally reached home there was no police car outside. Instead, mystifyingly, Ginny gazed at the battered green van parked behind her own broken-down car and said, "That's Dan."

Carla raised an eyebrow. "New boyfriend?"

"Hardly. Dan the Van, he delivers to the restaurant. What's he doing here?" Even as she was scrambling out of the car, Ginny could see the van was empty. How bizarre. Was Dan here visiting one of her neighbors?

"Oooh, you gave me a fright!" Laurel clutched her bony chest as the kitchen door crashed open. "What's the matter? You look as if you've seen a ghost!"

Wild-eyed and panting, Ginny surveyed the scene. Laurel and Dan the Van were sitting cozily together at the kitchen table, drinking tea and making inroads into the orange drizzle cake Laurel had baked yesterday. Like a small boy, Dan guiltily brushed cake crumbs from his wispy beard and attempted to stand up.

"Sit *down*," Ginny barked, causing him to hurriedly resume his seat. "What are you doing here?" Turning back to Laurel she said, "For God's sake, where have you *been?*"

Laurel looked alarmed. "Out. Why?" Then her expression changed as she saw Carla in the doorway. "What's *she* doing here?"

"I'm sorry." Dan the Van was clearly terrified. "Maybe I should go—"

"No you will not," Ginny and Laurel chorused.

"I'll tell you what I'm doing here." Carla, her eyes flashing, advanced into the kitchen. "I've been helping Ginny to look for you. Or, more accurately, to help her look for your dead body. Oh yes," she went on as Laurel blanched, "we've spent most of the day trawling the cliff tops and beaches, wrecking my shoes while we searched for your corpse. We called the police and spoke to the lifeguards and I've had to cancel three important appointments with clients, so God knows how much money you've cost me. It's just a shame you never learned to *read*." Reaching across the table she snatched up the note Ginny had left and shook it in Laurel's horrified face. "Because Ginny's been frantic, going out of her mind with worry, and all you had to do was pick up the phone and tell her YOU WEREN'T DEAD."

Ginny raked her fingers through her hair. "OK, let's all calm down."

"Why would you think I was dead?" Laurel was perplexed.

Carla glared at her. "Because you wrote all that stuff in your diary about how you were going to end it all."

"*What?* You mean you went up to my room and actually read my diary?" Laurel's voice rose. "My *private* diary? Well, thanks a *lot!*"

"You selfish, ungrateful *dimwit,*" Carla shot back. "You should be thankful Ginny bothered, because I'm telling you now, if you lived in my house, I'd—"

"Stop this, stop it." Ginny held up her hands like a football referee because too much was happening at once and all this shouting wasn't getting them anywhere. To Laurel she said, "I'm sorry I looked in your diary, but you said you were only going out for half an hour. You were upset. You didn't even take your handbag with you. Once I saw what you'd written, I was worried sick. That's why I left the note asking you to call me as soon as you got home."

"We only got back twenty minutes ago. I did try to ring you, but your phone was busy. I would have called again, but we were talking about . . . things. And then you burst in through the door like a tornado."

Carla shook her head. "So you've been out all day."

Mortified, Dan said, "It's all my fault."

"No it isn't. I just jumped to the wrong conclusion." Desperate for a cup of tea, Ginny filled the kettle and gestured for Carla to sit down. "Anyway, panic over. You can tell us what you've been doing. How did you meet Dan?"

Laurel looked blank. "Who's Dan?"

This was surreal. Surely Dan didn't have an identical twin brother. Ginny said, "Dan, help me out here. Am I going mad?"

Perplexed, Laurel turned to stare at Dan. "What does she mean? What's going on?"

He shrugged, embarrassed. "Everyone calls me Dan the Van because of my job. But it's just a joke. My real name's Hamish."

Chapter 50

OVER CUPS OF TEA and crumbly slices of orange drizzle cake, Ginny and Carla heard the whole story. Having taken Ginny's outburst to heart and realized that the time had indeed come to get her act together, Laurel had left the house in order to pick up her repeat prescription, pondering her future en route. The queue at the pharmacy had been epic, practically trailing out of the shop, so she'd wandered down the road for a bit to give the pharmacist time to catch up—anything was preferable to being sandwiched between two competitive pensioners discussing the various qualities of their bowels and piles.

There was a bit of a queue in the bakery too, but this time Laurel waited in line. When it was her turn, she plucked up the courage to tentatively ask the baker if by any chance they had a vacancy for a part-time cake-maker.

The baker hadn't needed to be quite so blunt. Scornfully he informed Laurel that making bread and cakes involved getting up at three o'clock in the morning and finishing at six in the evening. It was hard physical work. Their particular specialty here was lardy cake, and no, they didn't have any vacancies anyway.

Humiliated by his rudeness, Laurel hurried out

of the shop. Behind her she heard a man protest mildly, "That was uncalled for."

She was on her way back to the pharmacy—irritable bowels and piles like blackcurrants were preferable to being sneered at—when someone tapped her on the shoulder. Turning, she saw the man who had been standing behind her in the queue.

"Don't let Bert upset you. His wife walked out on him last week."

"I'm not surprised." Her sympathizer was on the scruffy side, lanky and tall, but he had gentle eyes and a kind face.

"Look . . . um, I don't know if you'd be interested, but there's a woman in St. Austell who sells cakes at the farmers' market. I happen to know she's looking for help."

St. Austell was miles away, right down on the south coast of Cornwall. Tempted to say no outright, Laurel nevertheless found herself hesitating, reluctant to end the conversation. If anything, this man seemed almost shyer than she was.

"Would she bite my head off?"

He smiled and his whole face lit up. "Her name's Emily Sparrow. Can you imagine anyone called Emily Sparrow biting anyone's head off?"

"You lost your place in the queue." Laurel realized he'd left the bakery empty-handed.

"Hey, their pasties aren't that great. There's

another shop a bit farther down the road. Do you have a pen on you?"

Laurel indicated her bagless state; all she'd come out with was her house key and the doctor's prescription in her cardigan pocket.

"Me neither. Never mind, I've got one in the van."

He had a nice voice too, reassuringly gentle and well spoken. Laurel found herself walking with him to the next shop, where he bought three pasties. Then they made their way back to his parked van and he explained that he'd been out on his delivery rounds since seven o'clock. She jumped when he opened the van's passenger door and a big hairy dog scrambled out.

"Don't worry about Stiller; he's a softy. We always have a break around now. Are you hungry?"

"Actually, I am." Laurel hadn't realized until now how enticing the hot pasties smelled. "Did you buy that one for me?"

"I did. Although if you don't want it I'm sure it wouldn't go to waste. I'm Hamish, by the way."

Hamish? Hamish! Good grief, surely not the Hamish who wrote poetry and who'd failed to turn up at the singles club that night all those months ago. The one Ginny's ex-husband had insisted would be perfect for her.

The three of them entered the park where benches were dotted around, and Hamish shared the pasties out.

"Are you married?" The words came tumbling out; she had to know.

He smiled and shook his head. "No. Why?"

"Just . . . um, wondered." Laurel hastily bit into her pasty to stop herself asking if he was a poet. Since Gavin was unlikely to have said complimentary things about her, it was surely better if Hamish—if this *was* the same Hamish— didn't know who she was.

But her brain clearly had other ideas. As soon as the mouthful of pasty had been swallowed, she heard herself blurting out, "Do you know someone called Gavin Holland?"

Hamish looked astonished. Then he went red and nodded. "Yes. Why do you ask?"

All of a sudden Laurel felt extraordinarily brave. She looked directly at him and said, "You stood me up."

He stared at her. "I did? Oh God, you mean that time at the club? I lost my nerve at the last minute, chickened out. You mean . . . ?"

She smiled and nodded, no longer afraid. "My name's Laurel."

It had all become more extraordinary after that; it was as if several protective outer layers had fallen away, leaving them able to discuss anything and everything without embarrassment. There was a connection between them that Laurel had never experienced before, not even with . . . no, she wasn't even going to think about Kevin. Before she knew what was happening, they were back at the van and Hamish was writing down the name and address of the woman in St. Austell who ran a cake stall at the farmers' market. Then he looked at Laurel and said shyly, "I know this is awfully presumptuous, but if you're free, I'm on my way back there now."

And that had been that. Together the three of them had driven down to St. Austell and Hamish had introduced her to Emily Sparrow who, as promised, wasn't shouty at all. He offered to pick up the supply of cakes Laurel made each Tuesday while he was on his rounds, so they could be sold at the Wednesday market. It was all so simple and straightforward that tears of relief had sprung into her eyes. OK, it wasn't a full-time job, but it was a start.

To celebrate, they had taken Stiller for a long walk on the beach. The conversation didn't falter once. When Laurel asked Hamish if Gavin had described her as boring, Hamish was perfectly honest. "Yes he did, but have you seen his girlfriends? Giggly airheads in miniskirts." With a shudder he added, "Gavin's a nice enough fellow, and each to his own and all that, but his taste in women would be my idea of torture."

After three hours on the beach, they had driven back to Hamish's cottage and dropped off an exhausted Stiller. When Laurel had rubbed his ears and said good-bye, Stiller had gazed up at her with such a look of pleading in his liquid brown eyes that she'd found herself saying, "Don't worry, boy, I'll see you again soon." Then, realizing how presumptuous that sounded, had abruptly shut up and glanced at Hamish to see if he'd noticed.

"I hope so," said Hamish.

"Excuse me," Ginny interjected when she and Carla had been brought up to date. "You hate dogs."

Laurel looked genuinely hurt by this slur. "I don't."

"You do. You told me you hated *all* dogs, that they were messy and horrible." Pointing accusingly with the last slice of cake, Ginny said, "You said all dogs *smell*."

Laurel stared at her as if she'd gone mad. "I said some dogs smell. But Stiller doesn't."

This was so blatantly untrue that even Hamish said apologetically, "He does a bit."

"Well, I don't think he does *at all*. Stiller's perfect."

Which just went to prove, Ginny discovered, that love wasn't only blind: it had a peg-on-your-nose effect as well.

Chapter 51

"WAIT TILL GAVIN HEARS about this." Having watched from the window as Hamish gallantly helped Laurel into the van's passenger seat, Ginny rejoined Carla at the kitchen table. "He's going to be unbearable."

"No change there then." Carla's smile was tentative. "Just kidding. How is he?"

"Same as ever. Gavin's never going to change." Pausing, Ginny dabbed up cake crumbs with her finger and popped them into her mouth. "So, how about you?"

This was what they'd both been waiting for. Carla visibly braced herself.

"It was the biggest mistake of my life, the worst thing I ever did. And I'm sorry." Abruptly her eyes filled. "Oh, Gin, I'm so sorry. And I've missed you so much. Can you ever forgive me?"

Carla, who never cried, now had tears running down her cheeks. Quite suddenly, what would have been unthinkable twenty-four hours ago became the natural, the only thing to do. Plus, Ginny realized, if Lucy had been able to forgive Jem, then she could do the same with Carla.

Some men simply weren't worth losing a best friend over.

And Perry Kennedy was no loss to either of them.

"It's forgotten," said Ginny, and Carla threw her arms round her.

"Thank you, thank you . . . oh God, it's just been so *awful* without you. It's like when someone dies and you keep picking up the phone to ring them, then realizing you can't do it anymore. You wouldn't believe how many times I did that."

"Me too." There was a lump in Ginny's throat now; the last few weeks hadn't exactly been uneventful. "So tell me what happened with you and Perry. Did you chuck him or did he go off with someone else?" Despite having forgiven Carla, she still hoped it was the latter; saintliness was all well and good but there was something far more comforting about tit for tat.

"Neither. I told him I wanted a baby and that was it. He took off."

The word "baby" gave Ginny a bit of a jolt. Recovering herself, she said incredulously, "What on earth made you tell him that?"

"Because it was true."

"What?"

"I wanted a baby."

Ginny shook her head. "Is this a joke?"

"No! All my hormones exploded at once. It happened just like *that,*" Carla clicked her fingers, "and took me over. Like being abducted by aliens. I couldn't think of anything else. I couldn't even sleep, I was so busy thinking about it." She leaned across the table and confided, "It's like when you see the most perfect pair of shoes in the latest copy of *Vogue* and just know you have to have them, even if it means driving up to London at four o'clock in the morning so you can be there when the shop opens its doors."

Ginny had never been tempted to do this, although she had once seen an advert on TV for a new kind of Magnum ice cream and had driven to the nearest supermarket, only to discover that they'd sold out.

"Shoes don't wake you up in the night. They don't puke on your shoulder. When shoes get a bit boring, you can give them to a charity shop. The people who work in charity shops hate it when you try to give them your baby."

"I know, I know." Carla sighed and buried her face in her hands.

"So you told Perry you wanted a baby, and . . . ?"

"He panicked. I wasn't safe anymore. When I went round to his flat the next day, he was gone." Her smile crooked, Carla said, "You must be glad."

"For all our sakes. And how do you feel now?" The thought of unmaternal Carla wrestling with a colicky infant was as bizarre as Martha Stewart wrestling in the mud with a crocodile. "Do you still want a baby?"

"Kind of. I don't know. Sometimes I think I do

and other times I wonder if I'm mad. It comes and goes in waves," Carla admitted. "When I'm being sensible, I think it's a terrible idea."

"Just don't rush into anything until you've really made up your mind." The cake had long gone but Ginny could still smell the oranginess of the last few crumbs in the tin; would Carla think it odd if she finished them up?

"The nappy thing could be a problem." Ever fastidious Carla wrinkled her nose.

"Nappies are the pits."

"And then there's the vacation thing. I mean, what happens when you want to go out at night and enjoy yourself? Babies can be such a *tie*."

"They can." A glass of orange juice would be nice. "It's a shame you can't leave them at home, put them in the baby equivalent of kennels."

"Exactly! I was *thinking* that! Oh, you." Realizing she was being made fun of, Carla jumped up and gave Ginny another massive hug. "I'm so glad we're OK again. We should be celebrating! Is there wine in the fridge?"

"Sorry. We've got orange juice." Lovely fruity *orangey* orange juice . . .

"No wine at all? That's terrible! What's the matter with you?" Carla had by this time opened the fridge in disbelief, affording Ginny a tantalizing glimpse of the orange juice carton. The longing was now so fierce she was salivating.

"Never mind, I've got some." Closing the

fridge—it was like slamming the front door in Johnny Depp's face—Carla said, "I'll zip home, bring back a couple of bottles, and we'll have a lovely catching-up session. You can tell me what's been going on with you."

"You're kidding."

"No," said Ginny.

"Oh my *God*."

"I know."

Carla was so stunned she almost slopped red wine over her pink skirt. "What are you going to *do?*"

"Ah well. That I don't know." Ginny clutched her almost empty pint glass of orange juice. "It's all a bit of a mess. There I was, worried sick that Jem might get pregnant. And instead it's happened to me."

"Maybe subconsciously you did it on purpose," Carla offered. "You know, you missed Jem so much that you wanted another baby to replace her."

"I did not do it on purpose. And we weren't irresponsible either." Ginny shook her head in frustration; she'd been through that night in her mind a thousand times. "We used something, OK? The bloody thing just didn't bloody work."

"So. Are you keeping it?" Carla was ever practical.

Ginny, who wasn't, said, "I can't get rid of it."

"You'll have to tell Finn."

"I definitely can't do that!"

"Look, I know men are stupid," said Carla, "but sooner or later he's going to notice."

Was it the pint of orange juice or the thought of Finn finding out she was pregnant that was making her feel sick? Ginny took deep breaths. "Not if I leave the restaurant."

"But he should know!"

"As far as Finn's concerned, it was a one-night stand that meant nothing. God"—Ginny's face reddened at the memory—"he was practically doing me a favor. He's got Mae and Tamsin now. This is the last thing he needs." Realizing that Carla was gazing at her with an odd look on her face, she said defensively, "What are you thinking?"

"You've got a baby in there!" Dreamily Carla pointed at her stomach. "An actual real baby! When it's born, I'll be able to hold it as much as I want. And play with it and talk to it and . . . and *everything*."

"Ye . . . es."

"But don't you see how fantastic that is?" Triumphantly Carla said, "Now I don't have to worry anymore about having one of my own!"

Maybe it was just as well. As she watched Carla knocking back her fourth glass of wine, Ginny said drily, "So glad I could help."

Chapter 52

IT WAS A FLIMSY excuse but the best he'd been able to come up with at short notice. Finn felt like a teenager as he drove to Ginny's house, and it wasn't a sensation he was comfortable with.

Well, it hadn't featured in his life until recently. Having to work alongside her in the restaurant wasn't helping; his feelings for Ginny were flatly refusing to go away. It was killing him, not knowing if she felt anything for him in return. And now he'd made up his mind; he *needed* to know if there was any chance at all of some kind of future for them.

He pulled up outside Ginny's house, aware that it was a risky thing to do. The situation he now found himself in with Tamsin was impossible; he knew he didn't love her. Except there was Mae, whom he *did* love, to consider as well.

What a nightmare. But he was here now and he was going to tell Ginny the truth. Just like spotting a rare antique in an auction, you could maintain a poker face and apparent indifference for so long, but once the bidding started, sooner or later it became necessary to declare an interest. After that it was up to her; she could laugh in his face and tell him to get lost. Or she could say yes.

Either way, at least the agony of not knowing would be over.

Right, here goes. Finn switched off the car's engine and reached for the cardigan on the passenger seat. His stomach was clenched, his mouth dry, and he was about to make the riskiest bid of his life.

He rang the bell and watched through the distorted glass as a blur of pink approached the door. Recognizing Ginny's dressing gown, he pictured her naked beneath it before hastily banishing the image from his mind.

Talk about tempting fate.

Then the door opened and—*Jesus*.

"Hey, Finn. Good to see you!"

Completely wrong-footed, Finn found himself succumbing to Gavin Holland's enthusiastic handshake. As if mistaking Gavin for Ginny wasn't terrifying enough, he was now forced to make conversation with a man wearing a lace-trimmed pink dressing gown that failed to conceal his hairy chest.

"Excuse the outfit. I've just had a shower." Gavin, evidently unconcerned, said cheerfully, "So what brings you here?"

Thank God he had his flimsy excuse. Finn held up the pale green angora cardigan and tried not to look at Gavin's bare feet. "Er . . . Ginny left this behind this afternoon. I was just passing and thought she might need it. Is she, um, around?"

"Upstairs, having a bath. We're going out to dinner tonight."

We? Hoping he'd misunderstood, Finn said casually, "With that girl you brought to the restaurant that time? What was her name? Cleo?"

"No, no. Long gone, that one. My bimbo days are over now. I've seen the error of my ways."

"Oh." Ginny was upstairs in the bath and the ex-husband with whom she'd always remained friendly was wearing her pink dressing gown and announcing that he'd seen the error of his ways. And they were on their way out to dinner together. What was there to misunderstand? Swallowing that kicked-in-the-teeth feeling and marveling that he could sound so normal, Finn said, "Ginny didn't mention any of this."

"Typical woman, she's not sure it'll last. I've blotted my copybook too many times before for her liking. But I'm working on proving her wrong. It's taken me a while to come to my senses but this time it's for good, I just know it is." Gavin paused, his eyes sparkling. "This is my chance to do the decent thing at last and I'm not going to waste it. Those pretty young creatures are all very well, but sometimes the more mature woman just has . . . you know, that edge." He broke into a grin. "And if she heard me calling her a more mature woman she'd rip my head off."

"Right." Finn was out of here. "That's great," he lied. "I'm pleased for . . . both of you."

And then he left before he ripped Gavin's undeserving head off himself.

Ginny emerged shivering from the bathroom wrapped in a towel.

"When I said you could use my shower, I didn't mean you could use all the hot water. That bath was *lukewarm*."

"Sorry." Gavin, whose boiler had broken down, appeared at the foot of the stairs. "Anyway, how do I look?"

She softened, because the change in Gavin in the last couple of weeks had been a revelation. Whether it would last was anybody's guess— personally, Ginny was giving it two months, max—but he was certainly making an effort for Bev. "Very handsome. In an overweight, thinning-on-top kind of way."

"Charming. Sometimes I wonder why I divorced you. Then I remember."

"I divorced you," Ginny retorted. "Hot-water hogger. But I like your shirt."

Pleased, Gavin adjusted the cuffs of the smart, dark blue shirt he'd bought specially for tonight. It was the most ungarish one he'd ever owned.

"Bev said blue was my color."

"Bev said this, Bev said that," Ginny teased, because he was at that besotted stage where he liked to include her name in every conversation. "Who was that at the door earlier?"

Gavin was now busy admiring his smartened-up appearance in the hall mirror. "Hmm? Oh, just Finn. He dropped off the cardigan you left at work. Hadn't you better get ready? Bev's going to be here soon."

Following a business meeting in Exeter, Bev was coming straight to the house before the three of them went out to dinner together. Ginny said, "Are you sure I won't feel like a third wheel?"

"Of course you won't. We'll have a great time."

"No lovey-doveyness then. You have to promise."

"My hands shall remain above the table at all times." Gavin waggled them to illustrate. "Mind you, can't make any promises about other body parts."

Ginny headed for her bedroom, combing her fingers through her wet hair, but not before flicking a playful rude hand gesture at Gavin in the hall below. He was in love—again—and it wasn't his fault she was jealous. She *would* enjoy the evening once she got her happy head on; it was just the mention of Finn that had knocked her off kilter. Sitting at a table for three was fine in its own way, but if her life could have been different, how much lovelier it would be to have someone of her own and be part of a table for four.

Chapter 53

GINNY DIDN'T KNOW WHAT she was missing. Carla, sipping ice-cold Moët, watched as Lawrence deftly worked his magic on her hair. Still desperate to make up for her previous transgressions, she had done her utmost to persuade Ginny to come along to Lawrence's for the cut of a lifetime, her treat.

But Ginny, blinking her bangs out of her eyes and too impatient—as ever—to wait for an appointment, had taken the kitchen scissors up to the bathroom and performed her usual snip-and-hack job. Annoyingly, her hair had looked fine afterward.

"See?" Ginny had executed a happy twirl, showing off her habitual no-style style. "Look how much money I've just saved you!"

Frustrated didn't begin to describe how Carla felt. "But think how much more fantastic it would have been if Lawrence had done it."

Ginny had been unrepentant and Carla had given up. What Ginny didn't know—couldn't begin to understand—was that coming here to Lawrence's was about so much more than just perfect hair. His tiny one-man salon was possibly her favorite place in the world, rose-pink and womb-like, and Lawrence himself was a psychiatrist, therapist, and counselor rolled into one. You could tell him anything and he wouldn't be shocked. He loved to talk but never gossiped. Once upon a time he'd been married with children; now, in his early fifties, he was gay and happily ensconced with a policeman called Bob. Lawrence was funny and wise, adored by everyone, and a magical stylist; what more could you want from any man than that?

And he served champagne. Oh yes, Ginny definitely didn't know what she was missing.

"You're better off without him, darling," he said now. "Men like that? Professional heartbreakers, take it from me. And if you'd had a baby, what kind of a father would he have been?"

"I know that now. I was just so overwhelmed with the idea of it." Carla took another sip of champagne. "I wanted a baby; it didn't occur to me that he wouldn't feel the same way."

"Lots of men don't. After our first two, Linda wanted a third and I wasn't so keen." Wagging his scissors at Carla in the mirror, Lawrence shook his head and said ruefully, "I tell you, never argue with a woman whose hormones are raging, because you'll never win."

Carla knew he had three children, all grown up now, to whom he was extremely close. "So how did she get you to change your mind?"

"Fait accompli. She came off the pill without telling me. Oh darling, bless you for looking

477

shocked!" Lawrence chuckled. "You're new to this game. It's what women do."

"But how did she know you wouldn't leave her?" Until the Perry debacle, Carla had always prided herself on her honesty; it hadn't occurred to her not to tell him her plans.

"I loved my kids. Linda knew that once I was used to the idea I'd be fine. And of course she was right. Anyone ready for a top-up?" Lawrence added another inch to Carla's glass and refilled the one in front of the girl having her lowlights baked under the heat lamp.

Entertained, the girl said, "So it all worked out in the end?"

"Ask me what I'm doing tonight," said Lawrence.

She glanced over at Carla in amusement. "What are you doing tonight?"

"Babysitting two of my grandchildren. The ones that belong to my youngest daughter." His face suffused with pride, Lawrence said, "I have the best family in the world and I couldn't imagine life without them."

"Oh God," Carla wailed, "now you're making me want to have a baby again."

"But pick a better bloke next time." Lawrence shook a finger at her. "Find one who doesn't hate kids for a start."

"Then what? Just go for it?"

"Darling, exactly. But in a subtle way."

Pleasantly relaxed by the champagne, Carla grinned across at Lawrence's other client. "So announcing that I'd made an appointment to have my IUD whipped out probably wasn't my cleverest move."

The other girl and Lawrence looked at each other in horror and gasped, then burst out laughing.

"But I thought he'd be pleased!" said Carla.

"Such a novice." Lawrence patted her shoulder fondly. "Next time, subterfuge. Remember, you're the woman. You call the shots."

"Unless it's condoms." Carla pulled a face. "Not much you can do about them."

"Yes there is." The other girl winked. "That's easy. You just have to be discreet."

Carla snorted into her glass; this was why she *loved* coming here. "Come on! You mean slip it off halfway through and hope he won't notice?"

"When I wanted another baby, my fiancé said it was too soon. Same as you did." The girl pointed at Lawrence. "But my hormones were all over the place, and I *knew* I wanted another one. So I took this really fine needle and stuck it through every condom in the box." She grinned. "All twenty-four of them."

Carla clapped her hands in delight; she'd never have thought of that. "And he couldn't tell?"

"I didn't use a knitting needle. Just a teeny weeny one from a hotel sewing kit. And then you smooth over the hole in the wrapper with your finger so it's hardly visible." Warming to her theme, the girl said, "Trust me: by the time you've got a man reaching for a condom, he's not going to be stopping to examine it under a microscope."

"Did it work?" Carla was enthralled.

The girl waved her free hand and said airily, "Well, things changed. You know how it is. But hey, it could have worked."

It could. Carla marveled at such subterfuge; it was reassuring to know she wasn't the only one seized by that desperate, primeval urge to procreate. And this girl had a child but hadn't let herself go, which she also definitely approved of. Her figure was fantastic and she was wearing casual but definitely expensive clothes.

"Right, that's you done." Lawrence finished cutting and laid down his scissors with a flourish. "Now just give me ten minutes to deal with these lowlights and I'll be back to do the blow dry. There's a piece in here you'll love," he went on, handing Carla a glossy magazine. "Irish woman gives up her baby for adoption, twenty years later the daughter traces her but the mother's only got days left to live—it'll break your heart."

Carla took the tissues he was offering her. Unlike most hairdressers who just dumped a mountain of magazines in your lap, Lawrence scoured them himself and singled out all the best articles for his clientele. He loved—and knew that they all loved—a good old tearjerker.

Lawrence led his other client over to the sink and began removing the dozens of foil wrappings from her head while Carla buried herself in the story. It was a tearjerker, so much so that she barely noticed the ringing of the girl's mobile phone. God, imagine realizing you were dying of cancer and not knowing if you'd get the chance to meet your long-lost daughter again before you kicked the bucket, then hearing the doorbell go one day and looking up from your sickbed to see—

"Oh, *hi,* so you got my text! How have *you* been?" The girl's tone was flirtatious; she wasn't speaking to her maiden aunt. Carla attempted to shut out the sound of her voice in order to concentrate on the magazine article. She was just getting to the really good bit.

"Of course I'm fine; why wouldn't I be? Everything's great. I just thought we could meet up, seeing as I'll be in London for the weekend anyway."

This was someone she was definitely keen on. Carla carried on reading, tissues at the ready.

"Absolutely. It's a date." The girl was triumphant. "I knew you'd want to. Now, shall I bring Mae? Ha, thought not! No, no problem, I'll leave her here. God knows I deserve a couple of days off. What would you like me to wear?" She paused then gurgled with laughter at his reply. "Why am I not surprised to hear you say that?"

Carla frowned. She'd been doing her damnedest to concentrate on the magazine article but a part of her brain hadn't been able to help semi-listening to the one-sided phone conversation going on behind her.

Had the girl just said Mae? And if she had, why did the name ring a faint but somehow significant bell?

Mae, Mae . . .

Carla froze, placing it at last. Bloody hell. *Mae.*

Chapter 54

IT HAD BEEN AN eventful morning so far, what with saying good-bye to Laurel and now this. Ginny drummed her fingers on the steering wheel and inhaled the smell of fresh-cut grass while the drivers of the two cars yelled at each other and pointed increasingly dramatically at their dented fenders. Nobody had been hurt; it was only a minor accident, but they were blocking the road, and now she was going to be late for work.

Who'd have thought it? Laurel had actually gone, moved in with Dan the . . . no, not Dan the Van; she had to get used to calling him Hamish now. It just went to show, though, didn't it? As Gavin's granny had always said, there was a lid for every pot. And Hamish was Laurel's lid. They were perfect together, besotted with each other and so well suited that it didn't even seem strange that after so short a time they were going to be living together in Dan the—*Hamish's* tiny farm cottage. With Stiller, for crying out loud, to whose smelliness Laurel remained magically impervious.

Hamish had rattled up in his van this morning and lovingly loaded Laurel's possessions into it. Ginny, half guilty and half relieved, had hugged Laurel good-bye and waved them off, delighted that Laurel was happy once more and envying them for having found each other. She might not particularly miss Laurel, but she'd definitely miss her cakes.

A car horn hooted behind Ginny as another driver grew impatient. A door slammed and a woman shouted, "Oi! Shift those cars out of the way!"

The two men ignored her and carried on arguing. Ginny heard the tap-tap of irritated high heels. Next moment a woman peered into her car and said, "I'm not waiting here for the next hour, watching these two slug it out. If you give me a hand, we can bounce that Renault out of the way."

Ginny had seen cars being bounced before; it was a strenuous business. For a split second it crossed her mind that such energetic activity could precipitate a miscarriage, and that maybe it wouldn't be the worst thing in the world if it did. This could be her chance to make all the complications go away.

Except it wasn't an option. She looked at the woman and said, "Sorry, I can't. I'm pregnant."

Gosh, it felt funny saying the words aloud to a stranger. Almost as if it was really happening.

Bloody hell, I'm having a *baby*.

"Oh." The woman looked disappointed.

"Hang on." Ginny opened her door, clambered out, and approached the arguing men. "Hi, we need to get past. If you won't move your cars, we'll have to shift them ourselves. But I'm a little bit pregnant so I'd rather you did it."

The younger of the two men, with a shaved head and a body awash with tattoos, turned and looked her up and down. Finally, he heaved a sigh of resignation. "You sound just like my missus when she's trying to get out of the washing up."

Ginny was just pulling into Penhaligon's courtyard when her phone rang. Having squeezed between a Datsun and a Range Rover, she parked and flipped open her mobile. Carla.

"Hi there, I've only got time for a quickie."

"That's what got you into trouble in the first place."

"I'm late for work!"

"Never mind that." Carla sounded gleeful. "I've just found out a couple of things you might like to hear."

"What kind of things?" Hurriedly Ginny leaped out of the car; the restaurant was fully booked this lunchtime.

"OK, number one. I think I know how you got pregnant."

"Carla, I did biology at school. I *know* how it happened."

"Will you listen to me? Tamsin was desperate for another kid straight after she'd had Mae. I'm guessing it was because she wasn't sure Mae was Finn's and wanted one that definitely was."

"What? *What?*" Flummoxed, Ginny stopped racing across the gravel.

"But Finn *didn't* want another one, which was a bit of a pain," Carla machine-gunned on. "So Tamsin sabotaged his condom supply, punctured every last one of them. Except then the whole Italian-billionaire thing started up again and she left for London. But she forgot to tell Finn what she'd done."

Ginny frowned as the door of the restaurant opened. "Carla, is this what happened *in a dream?*"

"No! It's real! And she's gone shopping this afternoon so the coast's clear if you want to check it out. She has an IUD now so any condoms should still be wherever he keeps them."

485

Finn was standing in the doorway with Mae in one arm and a handful of folders in the other. "Ginny, you're late."

I know where he keeps them.

"Sorry, sorry, two cars crashed in front of me and the road was blocked."

"But, Gin, that's not all; you'll never guess what else I—"

"Come on, there are customers waiting in the shop, *and* I'm supposed to be phone-bidding at Sotheby's."

"Brrraaa brrraaaaa!" Mae waved her hands in the air like a demented bidder.

"I have to go," Ginny muttered into the phone.

"No! You can't! Wait until you—"

"Get the sack?" Aware of Finn's pointed gaze, Ginny said hastily, "I'll call you later," and cut Carla off in midsquawk.

"Are you OK?" Finn touched her arm as she rushed past him.

Oh God, why did he have to touch her? "Of course! Why wouldn't I be?"

"You look a bit pale."

"I'm fine." At least it made a change from being traffic-light red.

Bloody hell, was that how it had happened? Really?

Mae kicked her bare feet against Finn's jeans-clad hip and babbled triumphantly, "Brrraa-waaabrrra."

• • •

It was no good; she knew where he kept them and she had to find out if Carla was right. Lunch in the restaurant had gone on for what felt like weeks. At three thirty, Ginny lurked outside the entrance to the antiques center peering—without appearing to peer—through the crack in the door until she saw that Finn was occupied with a couple of potential customers.

He paused and looked up when she rushed in.

"Sorry, I brought something over for Myrtle and the kittens. I didn't realize you were busy . . . doesn't matter . . ."

"You could just leave it by the front door," said Finn. "I'll take it up later."

Nooooooo. Ginny clutched the foil-wrapped parcel of smoked salmon trimmings she had cadged from the kitchen. On the jukebox the Eurythmics were belting out "Would I Lie to You?"

"Or," Finn added as an afterthought, "you can take it up yourself if you wanted to see them."

Yesssssss. Beaming with relief, Ginny said, "Thanks, I'll do that. Just for five minutes."

But first things first. Once up the stairs she turned left along the landing and made directly for the master bedroom.

Oh God, this was mad. The outcome was the same, whether or not Tamsin had sabotaged the condoms. But the compulsion to know the truth

487

had her in its grip. Panting, Ginny headed for the chest of drawers on Finn's side of the bed and slid open the uppermost drawer. There was the box, right at the back, lying on its side with some of the packets spilling out amid a jumble of old belts, books of matches, pens, penknives, swimming goggles, and sunglasses. Scooping up a handful of packets, she realized it was too dark here in the bedroom to examine them properly and too risky to turn on the light. Closing the drawer she hurried through to the living room, ignoring the excited squeaks of the kittens. OK, over by the big window would be best. Ginny held the first one up to the light, her hands trembling as she ran the tips of her fingers over the plastic-coated foil. God, her heart was racing so hard it was impossible to—

"OW!" She let out a shriek as without warning something heavy landed on her shoulder. The condom packet flew out of her grasp and Ginny spun round in alarm. Bloody Myrtle, what a fright. Disentangling Myrtle's claws from her white Lycra top, she plonked the cat down and bent to retrieve the dropped condom.

Bugger, what were the odds? Ginny gazed in dismay at the packet, clearly visible but unreachable, in a deep gap between polished oak floorboards. You could fling five hundred condoms up in the air and not one of them would fall into one of the gaps between floorboards. And she couldn't leave it there; that would be just too bizarre.

OK, think, think. Stuffing the rest of the condoms into her bra, Ginny raced into the kitchen and yanked open the cutlery drawer. A knife? A fork? Grabbing one of each, she returned to the living room and fell to her knees in front of the window. The floorboards smelled gorgeous, of honey and beeswax, but that wasn't what she was here for now. The knife was useless, the fork no better. Damn, why did these packets have to be so slippy? It was like trying to hook out a strand of overcooked spaghetti, and the more often it slid back down into the gap, the more her hands shook and the sweatier her palms became. OK, deep calming breaths and try again, and this time—

"Ginny, what are you *doing?*"

Chapter 55

GINNY FROZE, KNIFE AND fork in hand. Slowly, very slowly, she looked over her shoulder. Finn had a point; what *was* she doing?

"Eating woodlice for lunch?" Finn suggested.

"Um . . . um . . ." It was no good; he was crossing the room now.

Finn paused with his hands on his hips, gazing down. Reaching out and taking the fork from

Ginny's grasp, he bent and deftly hooked out the condom packet in one go.

Typical.

"Right. Thanks." Ginny snatched it up and said, "Sorry about that! It just . . . well, Myrtle ambushed me and I jumped a mile . . . it just flew out of my pocket, and of course I couldn't *leave* it there . . ."

Finn frowned. "It flew out of your pocket?"

"Yes!"

"Your jeans pocket?"

Bugger, nothing else she was wearing *had* pockets. As she cast about in desperation, Finn raised a hand signaling that he'd be back in a moment. Returning from the master bedroom an uncomfortable thirty seconds later, he said, "How strange, I could have sworn I had a box of condoms in my bedside drawer. But the box is empty. They've all gone."

Ginny's mouth was as dry as sand. OK, here was her chance to come clean, to explain everything, to tell Finn that she was pregnant . . .

"What's that noise?" Finn was listening intently.

Superaware of the rapid rise and fall of her rib cage, Ginny said, "My breathing."

"That crackly sound."

"I can't hear it." She tried to stop breathing completely.

"Kind of plasticky and crackly." Finn's gaze

was now fixed on her chest. "One side of you has gone a funny shape."

Ginny looked down. Her right breast was smooth and normal. The left one resembled a Christmas stocking. It looked as if . . . well, almost as if she'd stuffed a handful of wrapped condoms into her bra. Slowly she reached into the V-neck of the thin Lycra top, scooped out the offending packets, and handed them over. "I'm sorry."

Finn gave her an odd look; frankly she couldn't blame him. "I don't get it. Can't you just go to a shop and buy your own? Or ask Gavin to do it?"

Definitely, definitely time to tell him now. Flustered and searching for a way to begin, Ginny said, "Look, I can explain, there's a reason for . . . for . . ."

"Carry on," Finn prompted when her voice trailed away.

But it was no good; from where she was standing by the window, Ginny had seen the car pull into the courtyard. She shook her head. "Tamsin's back."

He heaved a sigh, glanced down at the condoms in his hand.

"I'd better put these back in the drawer."

Ginny braced herself; she'd endured this much humiliation, what harm could a bit more do? Clearing her throat as Finn turned away, she said, "Could I have one?"

He stopped. "Excuse me?"

You heard. "Could you just . . . lend me a condom? OK, not *lend,*" Ginny hurriedly amended as his eyebrows shot up. "But I'll pay you back."

"Sure one's enough?" There was a definite sarcastic edge to his voice.

What the hell. "Better make it two." Oh God, what kind of a conversation was this to be having with the father of your unborn child?

Without another word Finn dropped two condoms into her outstretched hand before heading through to the bedroom. He reemerged as Tamsin ran up the stairs. Having jammed the two condoms into her jeans pocket—so snug that nothing short of a nuclear explosion would dislodge them—Ginny said hastily, "Hi, you've had your hair done! It looks great!"

"I know." Tamsin smugly shook back her glossy-as-a-mirror, chestnut-brown locks. "What are you doing here?"

Well, I *was* about to tell Finn that I'm having his baby.

Which would probably have captured Tamsin's attention, but Ginny couldn't quite bring herself to say it. "I brought some salmon trimmings up for Myrtle."

Not that grumpy, lethal-clawed Myrtle deserved them.

"What, *those?*" Tamsin eyed the still unopened, foil-wrapped parcel on the window ledge.

"And I needed to discuss next week's shifts with Finn."

"Thrilling." Losing interest, Tamsin waved her armful of glossy shopping bags at Finn. "Darling, wait until you see what I've bought. I've had such a lovely time! Where's Mae?"

"Martha's taken her out in the stroller for a couple of hours. We've been pretty busy today."

If Finn meant to make Tamsin feel guilty, it whizzed over her head.

"Great, maybe she'd like to babysit this weekend. My friend Zoe's invited me up to stay for a couple of days." Her hair swinging some more, Tamsin dumped the bags on the floor and began rummaging through them. "And I got you a fab shirt . . . hang on, it's in here somewhere."

Ginny made her excuses and left before Tamsin could find the fab shirt and make Finn try it on.

"About bloody time too." Carla was out of her house a nanosecond after Ginny arrived home.

In the sunny kitchen each of them held a wrapped condom up to the window.

"Three holes," Carla pronounced.

"Four in this one." The needle marks were practically invisible to the naked eye, but you could just feel them if you ran your fingertips over the plasticized foil. And concentrated hard. No wonder Finn hadn't noticed.

"So that's it. Now you know."

"Tamsin got me pregnant." Ginny pulled a face. "Sounds like the kind of headline you'd read in the *News of the World*, all about turkey basters and lesbians."

"*Anyway,*" said Carla, like a saleswoman going in for the kill, "you haven't heard the other thing yet. She's going up to London this weekend."

"I know. To see her friend Zoe. I was there when she told Finn."

"Hmm. I was there when she arranged it." A knowing smile played around Carla's perfectly lipsticked mouth. "And I'm telling you now. If that was a girl she was speaking to on the phone, I'm a banana."

It was another hectic night in the restaurant. Ginny hadn't meant to say it this evening, but she was being sorely provoked. Finn had spent the last two hours being decidedly offhand and shooting her filthy looks from a distance. It was both disconcerting and hurtful. When her pen ran out and she went through to the office to pick up another, he stopped her in the corridor on her way back.

"Sorry, we don't keep extra supplies of condoms in this office." If his mood had been better, it could have sounded lighthearted, even playful. But it wasn't, so it didn't.

"My pen ran out." Ginny held up the new one. "The old one's in the bin if you want to check. And I've already said sorry about earlier." Deep breath. "Look, I still need to talk to you about the . . . um, condoms."

Finn's jaw was set. "No need. But as far as I'm concerned, you're making a massive mistake."

"Am I?" Whatever he meant, it was clearly unflattering. Fury bubbled up and Ginny blurted out, "Well, maybe I'm not the only one. Because I'd double-check who Tamsin's seeing this weekend if I were you."

Yeek, she'd said it. Well, Finn *should* know.

He stood there, motionless. "What?"

"You heard." Ginny instantly wished she'd kept her mouth shut. What was that expression, shoot the messenger? Finn was certainly looking as if he'd like to shoot her.

"What makes you say that?"

"Don't ask me. Ask Tamsin."

Without another word Finn turned and left. God, what a mess; what an absolute balls-up. Shaking, Ginny realized that now he would accuse Tamsin of seeing someone else. Tamsin, in turn, would deny it and heatedly demand to know who was spreading these lies. And then what? Without any concrete evidence, it was Tamsin's word against hers . . .

It was too horrible a prospect to even contemplate. There was only one thing to do.

Ginny braced herself, clutched her new pen, and went back to work.

Waitressing was showbiz; you had to smile smile smile.

Chapter 56

TAMSIN HAD JUST HAD a bath and was wrapped in a turquoise robe, painting her toenails shell pink. When Finn entered the living room she looked up and smiled. "Hi, darling. Mae's asleep. What are you doing back so early?"

She was beautiful. Any man would lust after Tamsin. If what Ginny had said was true, it would be the best news he'd heard in months.

"I've been working too hard. Time for a break," said Finn. "We're going up to London together this weekend. I've booked us into a suite at the Soho."

For a second there was silence.

"Oh, Finn, I'd have loved that." Tamsin was filled with regret. "But I can't. I promised Zoe I'd stay with her. The thing is—and this is top secret—she's just had a facelift and looks a complete fright. I'm just going along to cheer her up and take her mind off the fact that she looks like Frankenstein's ugly sister."

"Right." Finn held her gaze, the confident unwavering gaze of a woman who could lie about the paternity of her child and not let it trouble her.

"But some other time," Tamsin beamed up at him. "Definitely. In fact, how about next weekend? Then we can—what are you *doing?*"

"Borrowing your phone. That's all right, isn't it?" Finn scooped up the tiny mobile that Tamsin never let out of her sight and began deftly scrolling through the list of names. "Ah, here we go . . ."

"That's *my* phone!" Tamsin leaped up in a panic as he held it to his ear. "Look, you can't just—"

"Zoe? Hi, this is Finn Penhaligon. How are you? Now listen, this is just a preliminary call, but I'm ringing Tamsin's friends to see who might be able to make it along to a surprise party for her at the Connaught this Saturday evening." He paused, listened, then said, "Well, that's great news," before handing the mobile over to Tamsin. "Here, you can speak to her now. Zoe's thrilled. She says she'd love to come."

Ginny jumped a mile and almost dropped the sticky toffee desserts she was carrying through from the kitchen when Tamsin burst into the restaurant. She was wearing jeans and a white T-shirt and had a face like thunder as she stood in the center of the noisy, crowded room beadily eyeing each table in turn. Evie, raising her eyebrows at Ginny, approached Tamsin and said, "Are you looking for someone?"

"I'm seeing who's here." The words came rattling out like marbles. "Finn wouldn't tell me, but it has to be someone in this restaurant." Tamsin continued to scan the diners before turning to blurt out, "You won't *believe* what they've just done to me, some petty, spiteful . . . jealous . . ." Her voice trailed away as her gaze came to rest on Ginny. Slowly, incredulously, Tamsin drawled, "Or maybe you would believe it. Look at your face! What is going on here? You know exactly what I'm talking about, don't you? Who told Finn?"

Ginny stared back. OK, this was now officially a nightmare. Licking dry lips, she said, "I did."

"You! *How?* My God, I might have guessed. You interfering witch." Tamsin's voice rose and her features narrowed. "Let me guess, you were jealous because I had Finn and you don't have a man of your own. You can't bear to see other people happy so you have to stir up trouble by poisoning their minds!"

Close, thought Ginny. I'm jealous because you have Finn and you don't deserve him. You're cheating on him, which is something I'd never do. God, look at everyone *watching* us.

Levelly she said, "I didn't lie."

"You've probably got a crush on him." Tamsin's upper lip curled, revealing catlike incisors. "Is that what this is about? Is that why you were upstairs in the flat this afternoon, hoping he'd take some notice of you?"

"Right, that's enough." Evie ushered Tamsin toward the door. "You're upset; let me take you back to—"

"No!" bellowed Tamsin, wrenching free. She grabbed a carafe of white wine from the nearest table, spun around, and hurled the contents straight at Ginny. "You witch, you've ruined my life!"

Everyone in the restaurant gasped. For the second time in three minutes Ginny almost dropped the sticky toffee desserts. Then, blinking wine out of her eyes, she saw that they'd been caught in the onslaught too, which meant they couldn't be served to paying customers. Oh well, waste not, want not . . .

"Aaarrrgh!" Tamsin, who clearly hadn't been expecting a mere waitress to retaliate, let out a shriek and leaped back. She gazed in disbelief at the brown sludgy gunk sliding down the front of her white T-shirt and jeans.

"It's not your day, is it?" said Ginny. "First your life is ruined, now your outfit."

Incandescent but unable to escape Evie's iron grip, Tamsin stamped her feet and let out another ear-splitting howl of rage. At various tables people began to whisper and giggle.

The husband of the couple who had ordered the sticky toffee desserts looked at Ginny and said tentatively, "Were those ours?"

Ginny's knees were trembling, but she managed to keep her voice steady. "I'm so sorry. And there aren't any more left. But I can really recommend the chocolate torte."

By some miracle she managed to drive home without ending up in a ditch. It was only nine o'clock, which had Carla running across the road shouting, "Oh my God, what happened?"

Ginny was incapable of sitting down. Revved up and hyperventilating, she paced around the kitchen. Finally she finished relaying the showdown in the restaurant and shook her head. "That's it, I've lost my job. I'm going to move to Scarborough."

"Sit down. Calm down. So he still doesn't know you're pregnant." Banging kitchen cupboard doors open and shut, Carla said, "Bloody hell, I'm trying to get you something to drink here and all I can find is hot chocolate." She took down the tin and gave it a shake. "Have you even been to Scarborough?"

"We went there on holiday once when Jem was a baby. It has a nice spa thingy. And it's a long way from here." Ginny's stomach lurched as the phone burst into life. Oh God, this couldn't be good for the baby.

"Don't answer it if you don't want to," said Carla.

But caller ID showed that it was Jem.

"Yay, Mum, you're there! You'll never guess what!"

Even when she was having a crisis, hearing Jem's voice cheered her up. Glad of the distraction, Ginny said, "What won't I guess?"

"Marcus McBride's got a beach house in Miami. He's just emailed Davy and said if we want a vacation in July, we're welcome to use it. And it's, like, the coolest house on the planet!"

"Gosh." Ginny wondered how much the plane tickets would cost.

"*And* he's taking care of the flights," Jem went on excitedly. "Isn't that amazing? We won't get to see him—he's going to be away filming in Australia while we're there—but when Davy said there'd be three of us, he was fine. He even said the more the merrier and why didn't Davy's mum go along too?"

"And is she?"

"No! Rhona said it was our trip and she'd stay at home. Which is serious progress, because she and Davy have never been apart before. That's OK with you then, is it? If I go to Miami in July?"

"Of course it is, sweetheart." Ginny's throat swelled; she and Jem had both had flings with unsuitable men. And to think she'd worried about Jem being the one ending up pregnant.

"I'd better get off now. Everyone's going to be

so jealous when they hear about it! So, everything all right with you, Mum?"

"Yes, yes, fine. Carla's here. She's just pouring me a drink."

"Let me guess, a huge glass of ice-cold Frascati!"

Ginny looked over at Carla, frustratedly trying to stir lumps of cocoa powder into microwaved hot milk, and said, "How did you guess?"

"That's someone else you're going to have to tell before the baby actually pops out." Carla was nothing if not full of useful advice.

"I know. Don't nag." Ginny put down the mug of hot chocolate which was vile and lumpy.

"It feels like we're waiting for the world to end. You'd think somebody would have phoned by now, even if it's just to tell you you're sacked."

"If Tamsin phones, it'll be to tell me I'm dead." A kind of hysteria struck Ginny. "She could call the police, have me done for assault with a deadly dessert. Oh God, what if she hasn't been cheating on Finn? What if I made a—"

Drrrrrrrinnnggg. The sound of the doorbell caused both of them to jump off their chairs.

"This really isn't good for me." Ginny pressed a hand to her breastbone.

"I'll go and see who it is."

"No." Shaking her head, Ginny said, "This is my mess. It's up to me to sort it out."

Her heart went into overdrive when she saw Finn,

who clearly wasn't in the mood to waste time.

"Can I come in?" Already over the threshold before Ginny could reply, he stopped dead when he saw Carla. Brusquely, he said, "Could you leave us?"

"No I couldn't."

"Carla." Ginny tilted her head helpfully toward the door. "Please."

"Please what?"

"Go home."

"But he might chop you up into tiny pieces and feed you to that she-devil cat of his."

"Out," said Finn.

"Spoilsport," Carla muttered as she left.

Chapter 57

"I'M NOT SORRY ABOUT the sticky toffee dessert, so don't expect me to apologize for that. And I'm leaving the restaurant, which saves you having to sack me." The words came tumbling out; until that moment Ginny hadn't even known she was going to say them.

"I wasn't planning to sack you," said Finn. "You don't have to leave."

Ha, he didn't know the half of it.

"I'm still going to." Her fingernails dug into her clenched palms. She was; it was the only way. Far better that he didn't discover the truth.

"It's all over, by the way. They've left." Finn's expression betrayed the way he felt. "Tamsin and Mae."

Oh God, how awful for him.

"I'm sorry." This time Ginny meant it. He must be devastated.

"It had to happen." Finn shrugged. "Getting back together with Tamsin was never going to work. I wanted it to, because of Mae. But it's no way to live. Tamsin wasn't the one who left Angelo, by the way, before she arrived back down here. He chucked her. It all came out tonight. She's been angling to get back with him for weeks. And was just about to, if she had her way." Surveying Ginny, he added, "She still doesn't know how you found out."

There was no reason not to tell him now. "Carla was at the hairdressers. She overheard Tamsin arranging it on the phone this morning."

"Carla again. I might have guessed. Anyway, it's over. They've gone. I don't imagine I'll be seeing them again."

How he must be feeling beneath the calm exterior didn't bear thinking about. Feeling horribly responsible, Ginny said, "But you could if you wanted to."

Finn shook his head. "It's over, dead and buried. As far as I'm concerned it was over between Tamsin and me long ago." He paused. "And Mae isn't mine. I know that now. Saying good-bye hurt like hell, but it's not like last year. This time it's been kind of inevitable."

"Really?" Well, that was a relief.

"Really. If I'm honest, I was looking for a way out. And for Mae's sake it's better that it happens sooner rather than later. So that's it. All over." Finn shoved his hands into his pockets. "Life doesn't always turn out the way you expect, does it? You think you're in control, but you're not. It's like getting on a plane to Venice, then getting off and finding yourself in Helsinki."

Ginny's stomach was in knots.

Tell him you're pregnant.

I can't, I can't do it.

Just *tell* him.

I really can't. God, news like that, tonight of all nights, could finish him off for good.

Aloud, she said, "Gavin and I went to Venice for our honeymoon. Maybe I should have gone to Helsinki instead."

It was meant as a flippant remark to make him smile, but clearly Finn wasn't in the mood. Almost angrily he said, "And did you think that at the time?"

Ginny was taken aback by his vehemence. "No, of course not. I knew what Gavin was like, but I was young and stupid. I thought I could change him."

"And now?"

She shrugged. "Now I'm old and stupid. But this time he tells me he's changed."

"Do you believe him?"

Did a leopard ever really change his spots? Who knew? But when you saw Gavin and Bev together, they certainly seemed happy. "I'm a romantic," said Ginny. "I want to believe it."

Finn looked at her as if there was plenty more he wanted to say. Ginny pictured his face if she blurted out the truth.

Tell him.

No.

"Right." Abruptly Finn said, "Well, good luck."

"Thanks." That was it, then. Resignation accepted. She wasn't going back to work.

"Bye." He turned and left the house, closing the front door without so much as a backward glance.

God, what a night. Ginny rubbed her face, then her hair. Too traumatized for tears, she picked up the phone to dial Carla's number even though Carla was doubtless, at this very moment, watching Finn get into his car.

The next moment the doorbell rang again. Speak of the devil. Padding barefoot down the hall, Ginny pulled open the door and—

"You're mad. I can't believe you're being so gullible."

"What?"

"Gavin." The look Finn gave her was fierce. "He's going to break your heart."

Mystified—yet at the same time ridiculously pleased to see him again—Ginny said, "Not my heart. What are you talking about?"

Finn was visibly taken aback. "So you're not seeing Gavin?"

"Bloody hell, *no!* We've been divorced for nine years. I went out to dinner last night with him and his new girlfriend. Her name's Bev and she's lovely." Ginny realized she was babbling. "And get this; she's as old as me!"

"I thought you and Gavin were back together." Frowning, Finn said, "When I dropped your cardigan off, Gavin was wearing your dressing gown."

"His boiler broke down." Gavin would think it was hilarious, Ginny realized, to answer the door in a girly dressing gown. "I said he could use my shower, that's all. God, if I ever thought of getting back with Gavin I'd have myself certified."

"Sorry. I can't believe I got it wrong." Finn shook his head, his expression unreadable. "So . . . um, will it work out, d'you think, with this Bev?"

"Truly? I shouldn't think so for a minute. Bev's great, like I said. But Gavin's never going to change. This is a novelty for him. Personally I give it a couple more weeks." It was a pretty irrelevant conversation but Ginny pressed on anyway. "And deep down, I think Bev does too. She said something last night about if it doesn't work out, at least she'll have got Gavin out of her system."

There was a long pause. Finally Finn said, "Not necessarily."

"Why not?"

He shrugged. "Doesn't always work that way."

"Well, they're adults." Ginny felt herself getting hot, unnerved by the intensity of Finn's gaze. "Why are you looking at me like that?"

Because if he knew, she would just *die*.

"Probably because I slept with you and didn't get you out of my system."

Ginny's knees almost buckled. "Wh-what?"

"Sorry. Being honest. You did ask." Finn raked his fingers through his hair. "And I know you only wanted a one-night thing, but I haven't been able to forget it. At all. Obviously, I couldn't say anything before, and maybe I shouldn't be saying it now." He swallowed and Ginny heard the emotion in his voice. "But it's been a hell of a day and I needed you to know how I feel about you. If I'm honest, it's how I've felt the whole time Tamsin's been back."

Seconds passed. Ginny was speechless. Finally, she stammered, "M-me too."

It was Finn's turn to look stunned. "Really?"

"Oh yes. *God,* yes. Really."

He kissed her and she'd never felt so alive nor so terrified. Pulling away, Ginny blinked and said, "There's something else I have to tell you."

Finn wasn't in the mood to take her seriously. "Don't tell me you were born a man."

Hardly. Ginny braced herself. "I didn't mean it to happen."

"Didn't mean what?"

Her courage failed. "I can't tell you."

Yes you can.

No I can't, can't, *can't.*

But you *must.*

"OK," said Finn. "Is it good or bad?"

"I don't know."

"I love you. Does that help at all?"

Tears sprang into Ginny's eyes. "I'm pregnant."

Finn was motionless. "You are?"

"Yes." She saw the look on his face, realized what he was wondering, and burst out, "It's yours, I swear. I haven't slept with anyone else—not for years. I'm sorry!"

To her relief Finn relaxed visibly, half smiling. "No need to apologize. I'm glad you haven't slept with anyone else." Glancing at her stomach he added, "Is everything OK?"

"With the baby? Oh yes. I've had a scan."

"Were you ever going to tell me?"

"No. I thought I'd move to Scarborough." Ginny was still in a daze of happiness. "Until this afternoon, you had a family."

Finn pulled her into his arms. "I had a child who wasn't mine and a girlfriend I didn't love." His gaze softened. "Even worse, I was *in* love with

509

someone who worked for me, but couldn't tell her because she was back with her ex-husband . . . hang on, so what was all that with the condoms?"

At last, a question she could answer. The two she and Carla had examined earlier were still in the fruit bowl on the kitchen table. Reaching over and fishing them out, Ginny said, "Tamsin wanted another baby last year, but you weren't so keen. So she stuck a needle through every packet in the box."

"Good job the vicar didn't call round this evening." Finn raised an eyebrow at the fruit bowl, then ran his fingers over the packet in his hand. "Just as well it didn't work."

"Except it did. Right result," said Ginny, "wrong womb."

"Are you kidding? Tamsin finally did something that turned out well." Pushing her wayward hair back from her face, Finn said, "This could be the happiest day of my life. In fact, I think we should celebrate."

Ginny trembled with pleasure as he kissed her again, then regretfully pulled away. "I should phone Carla. She'll be wondering what's going on."

"Carla's a grown-up." Finn surveyed her with amusement. "I'm sure she can hazard a guess."

"But she hates not knowing things. It drives her insane. Plus," said Ginny, "she'll come over and start hammering on the front door."

Her mobile was still lying on the kitchen table. Picking it up and locating Carla's number, Finn rang it.

Carla, evidently waiting on tenterhooks, snatched it up on the first ring. "I saw him leave and then go back in. This is killing me! You're either shagging him or having the most almighty row."

"Well done," said Finn. "Your first guess was correct."

"Waaaah!" Carla squealed.

"Thanks. We think so too. So we'd appreciate it if you didn't come rushing over here because Ginny and I are going upstairs now."

Ginny, seizing the phone, added happily, "And we may be gone for some time."

The next morning it was necessary to make another phone call, this time to Jem.

"Hi, darling, how are you?"

"Great, Mum. Did you get the photos I emailed you?"

"I did." Ginny smiled, because Jem's happiness was infectious and the photos of her with Davy and Lucy attempting to roller-skate had been hilarious. "Listen, there's something I have to tell you. It might come as a bit of a shock."

Jem's tone changed at once. "Oh God, are you ill?" Fearfully, she said, "Is it serious?"

"Heavens no, I'm not ill!" Looking over at

Finn, squeezing his hand for moral support and feeling him squeeze hers in return, Ginny said, "Sweetheart, I'm pregnant."

Silence. Finally Jem said soberly, "Oh, Mum. I don't know what to say. I suppose it's Perry Kennedy's."

"Good grief no, it's not his!"

"Mother!" Stunned, Jem let out a shriek of outrage. "Excuse me, but do you even remember that big lecture you gave me before I left home to start university? And now you're telling me you've gone and got yourself pregnant? How many men have you been sleeping with? And do you have the *faintest* idea who's the father?"

Jem was screeching like a parrot. Aware that Finn was able to hear everything, and that he was finding her daughter's reaction hugely amusing, Ginny offered him the phone.

"Oh no." Finn grinned and held up his hands. "This time I'm leaving it all up to you."

Chapter 58

SUMMER WAS OVER, AUTUMN had arrived, and red-gold leaves bowled along the station platform, threatening to get on the line and cause untold havoc with the train schedule. Ginny's mind flew back to this time last year, when she would have given anything for that to happen. Then she blinked hard, because although mentally she might be more able to accept it this time around, hormonally, any excuse for a well-up and she was off.

Luckily, distraction was at hand.

"Stop it," said Jem.

"Stop what?" Gavin looked innocent, which was never a good sign.

"Ogling that girl over there."

"I wasn't."

"Dad, you were. And the one who works in the ticket office." Jem looked at Ginny. "You were chatting her up. We both saw you."

"It's called being friendly," Gavin protested. "Can't you lot *ever* give me the benefit of the doubt?"

After twenty years? Frankly, no. Ginny rolled her eyes and felt sorry for Bev. Their relationship had lasted four months, which was longer than anyone in their right mind would have predicted. But now, like a *Big Brother* contestant clinging on by her fingernails, narrowly managing to avoid being evicted each week, Bev's time was pretty much up. She knew it, but just hadn't the courage to make the break and walk away.

Gavin was never going to change.

"The train's due in five minutes." Jem was gabbling into her phone, excited to be on her way back to Bristol. "I've got three bottles of wine in my case, and two of Laurel's cakes. Are we having pasta tonight?"

Ginny watched her, suffused with love and pride. Still deeply tanned after the three-week holiday in Miami, Jem was every inch the confident, vivacious nineteen-year-old looking forward to her second year of university. And she had plenty to look forward to, not least sharing a three-bed flat in Kingsdown with her two best friends. Poor Rhona. It hadn't been easy, but she'd finally accepted that the time had come for Davy to leave home and—

"Ginny, is that you?"

Swinging round, Ginny came face to face with a large, florid woman in a too-tight tweed coat who clearly knew her from somewhere.

"My goodness it is!" The woman let out a cry of delight. "How amazing! How *are* you?"

Always a nightmare. Ginny hated it when this happened. Pretend you recognize them and attempt to bluff it out, or admit defeat and hurt their feelings?

"I'm *fine!* Gosh, fancy bumping into you here!" Since it was already too late to come clean, Ginny submitted to being enveloped in scratchy tweed and kissed on both cheeks.

"I'm just catching the train home! I've been visiting my aunt in Tintagel. It's so good to see you again . . . you haven't changed a bit!"

You have, thought Ginny, frantically attempting to peel back the years and picture the woman as she might have looked. To make matters worse,

Jem had now finished her phone call and was making her way over.

"My daughter's catching the train too."

"Your daughter? Well I never!" Beaming at Jem, the woman said, "And what's your name?"

"I'm Jem." Jem turned expectantly to Ginny. "Mum? Who's this?"

Bugger, *bugger*. Ginny said, "Darling, this is . . . ooh, excuse me . . ." Pressing her hand to her mouth she failed to stifle a tickly cough, then another one, then another . . .

"Lovely to meet you, Jem. And I'm Theresa Trott. Your mum and I were at school together, ooh, *many* moons ago!"

Jem said brightly, "Oh! Friends Reunited."

"Well." Theresa looked bemused. "I suppose we are."

Ginny cringed, wishing her daughter didn't have the memory of an elephant when it came to names.

"No, I mean the website. You're the one who contacted Mum last year." Jem was delighted to have made the connection. "She drove up to Bath to meet you."

"That was someone else," Ginny said hurriedly.

"No it wasn't! It was Theresa Trott!"

By this time thoroughly bewildered, Theresa said, "But I don't live in Bath; I live in Ealing."

"What's going on?" Gavin joined in.

"Dad, do something with Mum. She's lost her marbles."

"OK, I'm sorry." Ginny held up her hands. "I lied."

Startled but determined to carry on as if nothing had happened, Theresa shook Gavin's hand and said, "So you're Ginny's husband, how nice to meet—oh, I say!" Her eyes widened as Ginny's voluminous white jacket parted to reveal the unmistakable bump beneath.

"Bloody hell!" Gavin stared at it too. Indignantly, he said, "Where did that come from? It sure as hell isn't mine."

He thought he was so funny. At that moment something snuffly brushed against Ginny's left ankle. Relieved, she turned and scooped the little dog up into her arms and said, "Rescue me."

Finn rose to the occasion like a pro. Back from taking Rocky for a discreet pee on a patch of grass outside the station, he fixed Theresa Trott with a winning smile. "Shall I explain? Gavin is Ginny's ex-husband. I'm her future husband and the baby's mine. The dog is ours as well. His name is Rocky. The baby's due in January, and Ginny's marrying me soon after that."

"He's going to be my stepfather." Jem grinned, sliding her arm through Finn's.

"How lovely." Dumbfounded but clearly entranced by Finn, Theresa said brightly, "Well, congratulations. And there's me, never been married at all!"

Ginny shot Gavin a warning look, daring him to

announce that this could be because she was fat, frizzy-haired, and wearing a coat that made her look seventy.

"Ah," said Finn, "but you never know when the right one's going to come along. It could happen at any time."

See? Ginny glowed with love and pride; that was the difference between Gavin and Finn. She'd definitely made the right choice this time.

Theresa, her chins quivering with gratitude, beamed up at Finn. "That's what Mummy and Daddy keep telling me." She blinked eagerly. "So how did you and Ginny meet?"

As the baby kicked inside her, Ginny heard the train approaching in the distance.

"Actually, I caught her shoplifting," said Finn.

About the Author

With over 5 million copies sold, *New York Times* and *USA Today* bestselling author Jill Mansell is also one of the hottest selling authors of women's fiction in the UK. She lives with her partner and children in Bristol and writes full time. Actually, that's not true; she watches TV, eats gum drops, admires the rugby players training in the sports field behind her house, and spends hours on the Internet marveling at how many other writers have blogs. Only when she's *completely* run out of ways to procrastinate does she write.

Center Point Large Print
600 Brooks Road / PO Box 1
Thorndike ME 04986-0001 USA

(207) 568-3717

US & Canada:
1 800 929-9108
www.centerpointlargeprint.com